A SILENT AND POWERFUL CONNECTION
SPRANG UP BETWEEN THEM.

So when Mike dipped his head and pressed his mouth to hers, Charlene was waiting for his kiss. What was it about him? He seemed to be able to chase the bad things out of her head and replace them with something fine and good. She let herself fall into the kiss, her body catching fire in ways that it hadn't in so long.

He suddenly groaned and then backed up three spaces.

They stood there staring at each other, eyes wide, breathing hard.

"I can't do this," he said.

All her self-doubts came crashing down on her once again. "But—"

"Look, Charlene, I want you to think about buying Timmy at the upcoming auction. You guys would be perfect together. I want the best for you and Rainbow, and the best means for you and Timmy to hook up and adopt Rainbow as your own. I'm going back to Vegas, and that's no place for a kid. I love Rainbow, and I'm smart enough to know that I'm not the guy she needs as a father."

And with that statement, Mike turned away from her...

Praise for Hope Ramsay's Heartwarming Series

Inn at Last Chance

"[Explores] dark themes about the past interfering with the present while making a delightful tribute to *Jane Eyre*...an upbeat, empowering, and still sweet novel about balancing community pressure with personal needs."　　　　　*—Publishers Weekly*

"5 stars! I really enjoyed this book. I love a little mystery with my romance, and that is exactly what I got with *Inn at Last Chance*."　　　　　*—HarlequinJunkie.com*

"5 stars! The suspense and mystery behind it all kept me on the edge of my seat. I just could not put this book down."　　　　　*—LongandShortReviews.com*

"Ramsay nods to Stephen King and Charlotte Bronte... The introduction of a ghost, a haunted house, and a tormented author keep this story from becoming just another small-town romance."　　　　　*—RT Book Reviews*

"Every time I read one of the Last Chance books, it's like coming back to my old family and friends...Each novel can stand alone but it is better to have read the earlier stories...[In] no time, you will be caught up in the characters' lives and flipping the pages madly until you finish."　　　　　*—FreshFiction.com*

Last Chance Book Club

"4½ stars! [A] first-class romance, with compelling characters and a real sense of location—the town is practically a character on its own. This entry is sure to keep Ramsay's fan base growing."　　　　　*—RT Book Reviews*

"Amazing...These lovely folks filled with Southern charm [and] gossip were such fun to get to know... This story spoke to me on so many levels about faith, strength, courage, and choices...If you're looking for a good Christmas story with a few angels, then *Last Chance Christmas* is a must-read. For fans of Susan Wiggs."

—TheSeasonforRomance.com

"Visiting Last Chance is always a joy, but Hope Ramsay has outdone herself this time. She took a difficult hero, a wounded heroine, familiar characters, added a little Christmas magic, and—voila!—gave us a story sure to touch the Scroogiest of hearts...It draws us back to a painful time when tensions—and prejudices—ran deep, compels us to remember and forgive, and reminds us that healing, redemption, and love are the true gifts of Christmas."

—RubySlipperedSisterhood.com

Last Chance Beauty Queen

"4½ stars! Get ready for a story to remember when Ramsay spins this spirited contemporary tale. If the y'alls don't enchant you, the fast-paced, easy read will. The third installment in the Last Chance series is filled with characters that define eccentric, off the wall, and bonkers, but most of all they're enchantingly funny and heart-warmingly charming."

—*RT Book Reviews*

Welcome to Last Chance

"Ramsay's delicious contemporary debut introduces the town of Last Chance, SC, and its warmhearted inhabitants...[she] strikes an excellent balance between tension and humor as she spins a fine yarn."

—*Publishers Weekly* (starred review)

"[A] charming series, featuring quirky characters you won't soon forget."

—Barbara Freethy, *New York Times* bestselling author of *At Hidden Falls*

"A sweet confection...This first of a projected series about the Rhodes brothers offers up Southern hospitality with a bit of grit. Romance readers will be delighted."

—*Library Journal*

"Ramsay has created a great new series...Not only are the two main characters compelling and fun, but as you read, the entire town of kooky but very real people become part of your life...I can hardly wait until I visit Last Chance again."   —FreshFiction.com

"Captivating...great characterization, amusing dialogue...I am glad that the universe sent *Welcome to Last Chance* my way, and I am going to make sure that it does the same with Hope Ramsay's future books."

—LikesBooks.com

LAST
CHANCE
FAMILY

Also by Hope Ramsay

Welcome to Last Chance
Home at Last Chance
Small Town Christmas (anthology)
Last Chance Beauty Queen
Last Chance Bride (short story)
Last Chance Christmas
Last Chance Book Club
Last Chance Summer (short story)
Last Chance Knit & Stitch
Inn at Last Chance

LAST
CHANCE
FAMILY

HOPE RAMSAY

FOREVER

NEW YORK   BOSTON

For my brothers Steve, Randy, and Scott.

Acknowledgments

Writing sometimes seems like a solitary profession, but every writer requires help and support. I would like to give a shout-out to authors Elise Hayes and J. Keely Thrall for reminding me that brotherly love can be a powerful thing. Without their sage advice, the character of Reverend Lake would never have fully developed and this book would not have turned out nearly so well. I'd also like to give a literary head scratch to Simba, my twelve-year-old cat. She has given me many years of love and lots of cat stories to tell. My talented editor Alex Logan always keeps me on track. She has a keen sense of what needs to be taken out and is not afraid to use her red pencil. She always makes every book better. I would not be where I am in my writing career were it not for the efforts of my wonderful agent, Elaine English. And finally, my husband, Bryan, holds it all together and keeps me sane. I am the luckiest wife in the world.

CHAPTER 1

The kid should have been named Stormy, not Rainbow.

She didn't wear pink or have girlie cartoon characters on her shirt. She didn't have cute pigtails or a precious smile. No. Rainbow wore faded Goodwill clothing that didn't fit her. Her hair stuck out in all directions in a big, nappy mess that thwarted all efforts to brush it. The five-year-old sat in the rented Hyundai's backseat with silent tears running down her cheeks. She had an equally bedraggled tiger-striped cat clutched in her arms. The cat was also weeping but only out of its left eye. Occasionally it would sneeze.

Mike Taggart, Rainbow's reluctant uncle, figured the kid had plenty of reasons for crying. Ten days ago her mother had been killed in another case of senseless gun violence on the streets of Chicago. A few hours ago, Rainbow had lost her grubby stuffed elephant, probably in the men's room at the Atlanta-Hartsfield Airport, where they'd made a pit stop before boarding their connecting flight to Columbia, South Carolina. And then the final blow fell at the baggage claim, when the cat arrived sneezing.

Mike swallowed down the acid churning in his stomach. He should have done more to rescue Angie, his half-sister, from the life she'd been living. But Angie hadn't wanted to be rescued. And her five-year-old daughter had paid the price.

He needed to make amends for his failure. Which explained why he'd brought his niece here to the middle of nowhere, determined to find her the kind of family that he'd always dreamed of as a little boy. Reverend Timothy Lake, Mike's half-brother and Rainbow's other uncle, was exactly the kind of upstanding citizen Mike wanted for Rainbow's new father.

The cat sneezed again, and the kid clutched it to her chest in a death grip that the animal tolerated with amazing patience. Clearly the cat played favorites, because it had pretty much shredded Mike's right hand when he'd battled it into the cat carrier in Chicago this morning. But it seemed to love the kid, and vice versa.

He didn't understand cats. Or little girls.

"Don't worry," he found himself saying. "We're going to find a vet right now."

This announcement did nothing to stop the silent flow of Rainbow's tears.

It would have been so much better if the kid had wailed or made even the smallest of sounds. But no. Rainbow had been silent from the moment she'd witnessed her mother's murder ten days ago.

He hoped he hadn't promised something he couldn't deliver. They had to have vets out here in the boonies of South Carolina, didn't they? They needed them to look after the cows. Not that Mike had seen a lot of cows during his drive south to Allenberg County. But he'd sure seen a lot of fields planted in various crops. There had to be cows someplace around here.

He touched the screen of his smartphone and keyed in a search for veterinarians. Lady Luck smiled on him. He had a bar and a half of service and managed to activate his GPS and set a course for Creature Comforts Animal Hospital, only ten miles away, just south of the little town of Last Chance.

It didn't take him more than two minutes to motor through the town, which was still swagged out in yards of red-white-and-blue bunting from yesterday's Memorial Day celebration. They probably had a parade or something down Main Street, which, in Mike's estimation, made Last Chance perfect in every way.

The vet's, a building of tan-colored cinder blocks with a green roof, stood about half a mile past the retail district. It could have been a medical building in any small town or suburban location, except for the collection of animal statues in its front yard.

A life-sized cement German shepherd, collie, and boxer guarded the front door. Half a dozen cats in a variety of colors frolicked on either side of the walkway. A squirrel and a raccoon peeked out from the bushes planted along the front of the building, and a collection of plastic birds hung on strings tied to the eaves. The tacky menagerie didn't inspire confidence.

Mike helped the little girl out of her booster seat, enduring the cat's hisses and dodging its claws. The cat refused to go back into its carrier, which was a moot point because Rainbow refused to let the animal go. She carried the cat right below its front shoulders, with the bulk of its body dangling over her little arms. Why the cat tolerated this was one of life's greatest mysteries.

In any case, Rainbow had control of the cat, which was more than Mike could say about himself. They made their way to the air-conditioned waiting room, where his luck ran out.

A fifty-something woman with obviously dyed red hair sat at the reception area guarding the inner sanctum like a bulldog. "We're about ready to close. Y'all will have to make an appointment for tomorrow. We don't have late hours on Tuesdays," she said in a drawl so thick Mike could practically slice it.

"This is an emergency. We just got into town. The cat is wheezing."

The woman arched her eyebrows and gave the cat a quick look. The cat fixed the woman with its strange, green-amber eyes and sneezed. "Hmm, upper respiratory infection," she said. "You know, if you didn't let your cat outside he wouldn't get sick."

Mike put on his poker face and gave the infuriating woman a smile. "We'll try to do better in the future, but for now, the cat is sick."

"It's a kind of herpes virus that causes this, you know. Once your cat gets it he'll have it for life."

Great. Rainbow's cat had herpes. It figured. It had lived in one of the poorest and meanest neighborhoods in Chicago. Mike remained calm and continued to give the receptionist the blank, emotionless stare that he used in poker games. "I'm happy to pay for emergency services. Are you the vet?"

The cat sneezed again, and the woman peered over

the side of the reception desk at Rainbow, who seemed to know exactly what was required of her. She stood there looking pitiful with tears running down her cheeks.

"Oh, you poor thing," the woman said. "I'll just buzz Dr. Polk and see if she can see y'all. She's got a meeting she needs to get to, but I know she'll make time. In the meantime, fill in this paperwork." The receptionist handed Mike a clipboard with a patient form.

It didn't take Mike more than a few seconds to realize that he couldn't fill in most of the blanks on the form. He only knew the animal's name because the cat had a collar with a name tag and rabies vaccination date. On the opposite side of the name tag was a phone number that didn't belong to anyone. He had no idea about Tigger's age or whether the cat had been fixed. And since Rainbow refused to talk, Mike was in the dark.

He couldn't even fill out an address because he didn't know where the cat would ultimately end up. The cat should have been sent to the animal shelter. But Rainbow had pitched a fit, and Rachel Sanger, her caseworker in the Chicago Department of Social Services, was a cat lover. Ms. Sanger had broken all the rules and found a way for Rainbow to take the cat with her to the foster home where she'd stayed for a week before they were able to locate Mike.

And really, now that she'd lost her stuffed elephant, the cat represented an important link to Rainbow's former life. Not that living in the slums with Angie had been all that idyllic.

Hopefully, Timmy could take both the kid and her cat. The management of the hotel where Mike hung his hat didn't allow cats. And besides, a man who made his living as a professional poker player and part-time day trader didn't need a cat.

Or, for that matter, an unhappy little girl named Rainbow.

Cindy, the receptionist, had said something about a sick cat. But when Dr. Charlene Polk walked into examination room two, all she found was a tall, redheaded, blue-eyed man with a square jaw, cleft chin, and oh-so-carefully groomed stubble.

He looked like a fashion plate standing there with his Ralph Lauren polo shirt open at the neck and his hands jammed into his AX jean pockets. He didn't look like your typical cat owner.

But then the missing animal spoke, giving forth an anxious *meeeooowwww*.

Charlene blinked and turned to find a little girl standing at the opposite side of the room. She bore no resemblance to the man with her. The child was maybe five and had brown skin and dark, frizzy hair. Unlike the logo-wrapped guy, the child wore a grubby-looking blue T-shirt and a pair of jeans with holes in both knees. The only clue to the child's gender was her long, delicate hands.

Her mixed-race looks grabbed Charlene right where she lived. This could have been Derrick's child. Except that she was about ten years too young.

Tears trickled down the girl's cheeks. She hugged her tiger-striped cat as if the animal were a toy. People who carried their cats into the office were one of Charlene's pet peeves. A cat should always be transported in a carrier. But in this case, Charlene decided to forgo her usual lecture.

She squatted down to be on the same level. "What's the matter?"

The child said nothing. But the cat let out another slightly squeaky meow.

"She doesn't talk," the man said.

Charlene looked up. "Oh, I don't know. By the shape of her face and pointy ears, I think she has a bit of Siamese in her, or maybe Abyssinian. They are notoriously talkative."

"No." The man shook his head, his blue eyes looking oddly animated in his otherwise expressionless face. "I mean Rainbow. She doesn't talk."

"Rainbow? That's a nice name for a cat."

"No." The man gestured toward the little girl. "Tigger is the cat's name. Rainbow is Tigger's owner. And Rainbow doesn't speak. I mean, she hasn't spoken for about ten days."

Charlene's disquiet grew. Something wasn't right. "Ten days?"

"Yeah, ten days. Since her mother died."

"Oh." Just a four-word sentence but it sure packed a wallop. The little girl had lost her mother. Charlene's heart turned in her chest. Rainbow's tears seemed endless. They left long tracks across her brown skin.

Charlene held her hands out toward the girl. "May I take Tigger?" she asked.

The girl sniffled once and then reluctantly allowed Charlene to take the cat, who promptly sneezed. Charlene stood and put the animal on the examination table and turned her attention back to the man. "I'm Charlene Polk, the assistant vet here. And you are?"

"Mike Taggart. We just arrived in town. I'm Timothy Lake's brother. Do you know him?"

She didn't see a resemblance, except that both men were tall. Pastor Tim had blond hair and a classically handsome face. This guy looked way more rugged, like he spent a lot of time out in the sun surfing or mountain climbing. "I'm acquainted with Pastor Tim," Charlene said. "But I don't know him well. I'm not a Methodist."

Mr. Taggart's face remained utterly impassive. The lack of emotion creeped Charlene out.

She began a routine examination of the cat while Mr. Taggart folded his arms and observed in an intense and unsettling manner. Rainbow watched, too. She stood on tiptoes, looking up at Charlene out of a pair of amber-green eyes that were almost the same shade as Tigger's.

"Uh, Mr. Taggart, Tigger is not a male cat," Charlene said as she checked the paperwork where the cat's sex was marked as male. Besides the cat's name and incorrect sex, the patient information sheet was entirely blank. What was going on here?

"Uh, its name is Tigger. Who names a girl cat Tigger?" he asked.

Who indeed? "Has Tigger been eating?"

"The cat was eating just fine before we put it on the airplane. *She* wasn't sneezing until we picked her up at the baggage claim," Mr. Taggart said.

"The cat was transported recently?" Charlene asked.

"Yeah, today, from Chicago to Columbia by way of Atlanta. We were transported the same way."

The poor cat. She'd obviously been stressed. Her placid demeanor might also be a warning of more serious conditions.

"How old is Tigger?"

The child remained silent. The man let go of a long breath. "I have no idea. Up until a few days ago, I wasn't even acquainted with the cat."

Charlene gave him a stare. He stared back, giving nothing away. Alarms went off. Maybe she should stall this guy and give Sheriff Rhodes a call. Things were not adding up. The man seemed not to care very much about the cat or the child.

Their gazes remained locked for a long moment before he eventually looked away. "Look," he said stabbing his hand through his fiery hair. "I know what you're thinking, but here's the situation. Rainbow's mother died about ten days ago. I'm her uncle, and Timmy is my half-brother. I am not parent material. But Timmy's a minister. So I'm here to leave Rainbow with her uncle. The cat got sick along the way, so you can call this an emergency fly-by-night visit. If you can fix it up, that would be great. But don't ask me any questions about it. I don't know anything, except that it has sharp claws." He ran his finger along a nasty scratch on the back of his hand.

"You should put some antiseptic ointment on that," she said.

"I will when I get to a stopping place. The animal didn't want to go into the cat carrier this morning." Mr. Taggart had the temerity to glare at the cat. The cat glared right back at him, obviously unimpressed and unperturbed.

Wow. The gossip mill in Last Chance would be running overtime once the members of the Methodist Altar Guild got wind of this. Those busybodies had been trying to find a wife for their minister since he arrived last winter. Even Charlene's aunt Millie, who wasn't a Methodist, had broadly suggested that a single woman of any faith would be crazy not to set her cap for the young, handsome pastor. If Pastor Tim agreed to adopt a child, the Altar Guild would have to go into hyperdrive or something.

"Does Reverend Lake know you're coming?" she asked.

"No."

"No?"

"No. I doubt that he remembers me at all. The last time I saw him I was five and he was three. But he turned out okay. And that's why we're here."

Charlene shifted her gaze to the child. Rainbow stood with slumped shoulders, her body language tragic. In that moment, she looked like the personification of every unwanted child who had ever lived.

Mike Taggart was a jerk. He seemed to have no idea how his words hurt Rainbow. And even worse, he didn't seem to care.

Familiar guilt tugged at her. She wanted to fold the little girl up in her arms and tell her that everything would work out fine. But she couldn't do that because Charlene knew that things might not work out for Rainbow.

Charlene quickly finished the exam and handed Tigger back to Rainbow. "She's going to be fine. I'm going to give your uncle Mike some medicine for her."

The child took the cat, hugging the animal as if she were a stuffed toy. Tigger allowed this indignity as if the cat knew how much Rainbow needed her.

"Now, I need you and Tigger to go sit quietly in the room outside. There are some yummy oatmeal cookies out there and a few cat treats. I'll be right here with Uncle Mike. I need to tell him what he needs to do for Tigger."

She ushered Rainbow into the outer office and handed

her one of the cookies the receptionist baked for staff and pet owners. She also gave Rainbow a treat for Tigger. When they were settled, Charlene returned to the examination room and shut the door behind her.

"Tigger's lungs are clear, so this is not an upper respiratory infection. It's probably a herpes virus outbreak brought on by stress. My guess is that the sneezing is probably a reaction to the lack of humidity in the airplane. The cat may be dehydrated, so make sure she has plenty of water. If the sneezing continues, you'll need to bring her back for a follow-up.

"In the meantime you'll need to put some drops in Tigger's eyes twice a day, and I've got some antiviral meds for her to take by mouth. The meds are disguised as cat treats so you probably won't get scratched trying to dose her."

She paused for a moment, wondering if she should go on. Every instinct told her that she should. But who was she to give parenting advice? She didn't know the first thing about kids.

Still, she couldn't let her concerns go unvoiced. She already had enough guilt to haul around. So she squared her shoulders and looked him right in the eye. "I'm equally concerned about Rainbow, who is probably one of the sources of the cat's stress. Have you any idea how frightening it is for a child to hear that you're planning to drop her off with someone she doesn't know and who doesn't even know that you're coming?"

That got a reaction. The mask he'd been wearing slipped, and anger flared in his eyes. "Look, lady, I came in here for vet services. I know precisely how sad Rainbow feels. And I'll bet you a thousand dollars that you have no clue. I'm sure you had a nice, middle-class upbringing and never once worried about whether you'd go hungry. I'm sure you didn't have a parent with a drug problem. I'm sure you got your clothes new, instead of from the Salvation Army. But Rainbow and I have both known that kind of thing. And I'm here precisely because I want her to have a better life. So butt out, okay? Just give us what we need for the damn cat and we'll be out of here."

CHAPTER 2

Once Tigger and her unsettling owners had departed, Charlene hung up her lab coat, snatched her purse from the hook behind her office door, and headed toward the reception area and the exit. She needed to hustle her bustle or she'd be late for the executive board meeting of the Allenberg Animal Rescue Coalition. They would be discussing the fund-raiser scheduled for June fourteenth—a bachelor auction at the VFW hall in Allenberg.

Even running late, Charlene took a moment to poke her head into Dr. David Underhill's office. He sat at his desk reading the most recent issue of the *Journal of the American Veterinary Medical Association*, his head propped up on his fist, his dark hair falling ever so perfectly across his high forehead. If you looked up "tall, dark, and handsome" on Wikipedia, there would be a photo of Dr. Dave. He had a square jaw, a set of amazing dimples, white, perfect teeth, bright blue eyes, and a body to die for, which he honed to perfection at the Allenberg YMCA gym.

Charlene knew this because she also belonged to the Y.

In her case, however, there was no honing involved. Charlene needed to drop about fifteen pounds so she would fit into the maid of honor dress for her best friend's wedding, scheduled for August sixteenth. Of course, her gym membership also afforded her the opportunity to watch Dr. Dave pump iron while she strolled on the treadmill.

To say that she had a crush on Dr. Dave was to understate the point. Her feelings verged on a deep, dark obsession. He was as handsome as Prince Charming. He was kind to small animals and children. He was smart. And he was...her boss. Which made him untouchable.

A year ago, he'd arrived in town from Charlotte, North Carolina, and bought the practice from old Doc Matthews. Doc had given Charlene the job as assistant vet a few years ago, right after she'd graduated from vet school. She loved old Doc, but he had never quite trusted her with the large-animal practice. Dave's arrival changed everything. Dave had no desire to go tramping through barns and stables. He felt way more comfortable in the surgical suite.

And Charlene loved horses. And cows, and sheep, and alpacas. If they had hooves, Charlene had a weakness for them. So when it came to caring for Allenberg's animals, Charlene and Dave were a great team. But Dave still signed her paychecks.

So throwing herself at him, or sneaking off with him to a no-tell motel, or otherwise indulging her fantasies by ripping off her clothes in his glorious presence was so not going to happen.

Besides, it always got messy where her hormones and heart were concerned. She had been in and out of so many relationships that she'd lost count. All in all, making a play for the boss would be stupid. But that didn't mean she had to keep her distance. After all, Dr. Dave was like poetry in motion. So she found reasons to talk to him, just so she could bask in the light of his male beauty, not to mention his adorableness.

"Hey, I'm off to the AARC meeting," she said. She couldn't help herself; she batted her eyes at him and leaned into the doorway. Maybe he'd notice how all that gym time had reduced her waistline by an inch.

He looked up. He gave her his dreamy smile. His blue eyes lit up, and Charlene knew a moment of hope. "Say hey to Angel and Wilma and the rest of the crowd." He looked back down at the medical journal. He had not noticed the slightly revealing neckline of her sweater. He had not noticed that her upper arms were beginning to shrink. He had not, in fact, noticed her at all, except in the most professional and vaguely friendly way.

"Will do," she said, trying hard not to show her disappointment in her voice.

On some level, Charlene knew Dave couldn't be Mr. Right. But she had reached the desperate spinster phase in her life. She was older than thirty, lived in a tiny town, and Mr. Right had passed her by. She wanted a family and kids. And she had to admit that Dr. Dave would make beautiful babies. The kind of babies Mother and Daddy would cherish and appreciate.

Charlene reluctantly left Dave's doorway and headed down the hall and into the reception area where Cindy was finishing up her paperwork for the day. "What did you think about the last appointment—the walk-in?" Charlene asked.

Cindy had a talent for reading people, even if she had

an appalling weakness for concrete yard art. Dave pretended to love the sculptures Cindy brought back from every trip she and her husband, Earl, took in their camper. Dave's tolerance for the statues made Charlene adore him even more.

"The little girl was pitiful," Cindy said, bringing Charlene back to the worry at hand. "I hope the cat's okay. Because I never saw a child cry like that without making a sound."

"The cat's going to be fine. But I felt the same way about the girl."

"You don't think that guy with her was..."

"I don't know. He told me Reverend Lake is his brother. And he said the girl's momma was killed ten days ago. He's brought that little girl here with the intention of leaving her with Pastor Tim. But the preacher doesn't even know he's coming. You're a Methodist, Cindy. Have you heard anything about the preacher having a half-brother or a long-lost niece?"

"No. I thought he was alone in the world. I heard his mother died of breast cancer, and his daddy died of a stroke or something. Not too long ago. I clearly remember him saying that he was an only child. He and I had a whole conversation about how lonely it was not to have a brother or sister. Did that guy really say he was the preacher's brother?"

"He did."

"Oh, my. I need to call Elsie right away." Cindy picked up the phone and started punching numbers.

Before tomorrow morning, every blessed member of the Methodist Altar Guild would know all about the stranger in town who claimed to be Pastor Tim's brother.

Charlene prayed that the town's busybodies would use that information to make sure little Rainbow got what she needed.

Charlene had great faith in the church ladies of Last Chance. They were, for the most part, angels of mercy.

With its soaring steeple, red brick facade, and Doric columns, the First Methodist Church looked as if it came from right out of a Norman Rockwell painting. It was as far away from the streets of Chicago as a person could get. And that made it perfect.

Mike helped Rainbow and Tigger out of the car. He decided against telling Rainbow that there were probably rules against taking a cat into a church. Mike didn't want any tantrums from either of them. So he held his tongue when Rainbow draped Tigger over her shoulders as if the cat were an old-fashioned fox fur.

Once the cat settled, Mike took Rainbow's hand, and they walked up to the big oak doors, which were open even at six o'clock on a Tuesday evening.

The churchy smell of the place—one part brass polish and one part old hymnal books—overwhelmed him the moment he entered the vestibule. He didn't like churches or the hypocrites who visited them on a regular basis. Good Christians tended to look down their noses at sinners like him. And that probably explained why he could count the number of minutes he'd spent inside a church on one hand.

But just because he hated churchy people didn't mean they didn't have something to give Rainbow. Maybe the church folks could save Rainbow from making the bad choices everyone in her family had made, except maybe Timmy and his father.

The foyer opened onto the sanctuary on the left. He peeked in. It could have been any Protestant church in any American town, with its whitewashed walls, oak pews, and brass cross. Rainbow would thrive here.

He turned away from the sanctuary. On the right, a long hallway with doors on either side extended to the back of the building. These had to be Sunday school classrooms, but even on a Tuesday, the sound of children's voices carried from the opposite end of the hallway.

He gave Rainbow's hand a reassuring squeeze and followed the sounds to an active and noisy day-care center that occupied several rooms at the back of the hall. Parents streamed through a back door that led to the church's parking lot, and it appeared to be pickup time. A lot of hugging and kissing was happening.

Rainbow tugged on Mike's hand. He looked down at her and wished she could talk. Watching parents pick up their kids must be breaking her heart. Did Rainbow even understand that Angie was never coming back? Maybe not. She was just barely five years old.

Tigger seemed excited by all the noise and activity, and she expressed her opinion with a couple of loud meows. A brown-haired young woman with a baby on her hip turned around and glowered at Rainbow and Tigger. "You can't bring a cat into the day care. We have children here who are allergic."

Rainbow said nothing. Tigger meowed again, as if she were telling the woman off. Mike found himself stammering. "Uh, I wasn't—"

"And who *are* you?" The woman shifted her gaze from Rainbow to Mike and then back again. He'd been getting that reaction a lot in the three days he'd been caring for

Rainbow. Maybe he should be worried. Last Chance was a sleepy southern town. For all its apparent wholesomeness, it might still be a place where Rainbow would never fit in.

His stomach churned, and he slapped on his poker face. "I'm looking for Reverend Lake."

"Does he know you're coming?"

"Uh, no, but we're family."

That shut the woman up. Her questioning gaze shifted a couple more times. Rainbow probably bore about as much resemblance to Timmy as she did to Mike himself. Too bad. Everyone in this one-horse town would just have to get over it.

"Do you know where I can find him?" he asked.

"I'm not sure. It's late. He could be in his office or he might have left for the day."

"And his office is...?"

She pointed down an adjoining hallway with yet more doors opening on either side. "His office is at the end of the hall."

Mike gave her his poker smile, but for some reason, this woman wasn't buying it. She kept staring, and he got the feeling she wanted to stick her nose into his business the way Dr. Polk had.

He turned away before the woman could give him the third degree and found Tim's office with ease. The pastor's name appeared on a plaque by the side of an open door.

Mike crossed the threshold, his heart suddenly racing. He hadn't seen his little brother in more than twenty-five years.

Timmy's office was medium sized with a window

overlooking the parking lot. A cluttered desk the size of an aircraft carrier sat in the middle of the room with a pair of grubby kid sneakers doing paperweight duty at one corner. A couple of cluttered shelving units jammed the space beside the desk. Two chairs and a couch sat in front of it.

A man wearing a Roman collar sat at the desk furiously typing on a laptop computer.

Timmy.

Timmy didn't look up from his computer, but he paused in his typing and pointed to the shoes. "Maryanne, if you're looking for Jesse's shoes, they're over there. He left them when the kids came down here for story hour."

"Uh, it's not Maryanne."

Timmy startled and turned a pair of piercing blue eyes on Mike. Mike's heart rate spiked again. Timmy was a dead ringer for his father—the only dad Mike had ever known. Not that Colin Lake was really Mike's father, but try explaining DNA to a five-year-old kid who never knew his own dad.

Timmy's blue gaze bored into Mike for a few seconds before it shifted to Rainbow and widened a bit, no doubt because of Rainbow's appearance and the presence of Tigger, who greeted Timmy with a sociable meow.

"We don't allow animals in the church," Timmy said.

"I know. But—"

Timmy stood up. "I'm Reverend Lake. What can I do for you?" He held out his hand over the cluttered desk.

Mike shook it. Timmy didn't have one of those weaselly handshakes. Relief loosened Mike's shoulders. Timmy would be a terrific father. He had been a great little brother.

Mike gulped down a big breath. "I'm Michael Taggart, and this is Rainbow. And..." He ran out of words the minute he read the lack of recognition on Timmy's face. Disappointment washed through Mike, even though he knew it was stupid to have expected his younger brother to remember.

Timmy waited patiently for Mike to get over his sudden emotions. No doubt men of God practiced patience.

Mike's sour stomach intensified. "Ah, look," he said, "I have a feeling you're not going to believe this, but the fact is I'm your half-brother. And Rainbow, here, is your niece. We've come here today because we need your help."

The minister should avoid playing poker. His eyes got a little bigger, and the corners of his mouth turned down. "I have no siblings," he said. He folded his arms across his chest, his body language telegraphing his emotions and thoughts.

"You do. You just don't remember. Your father was briefly married to my mother, Alice Taggart. She's your birth mom, although I bet you don't know that. I think she's still alive, but I don't know where she is. She's not worth much, so don't worry that you've missed anything special by not remembering her. When your dad found God and got sober, you were about three and I was five. I remember that day like it was yesterday. He walked out and took you with him. And as far as I know, he never did one thing to help Mom or me. Mom went on to have another kid, our sister, Angie. And Angie was killed ten days ago. Rainbow, here, is Angie's daughter, and she doesn't have a home, and the last thing she needs is a guy like me who lives in Vegas and makes his daily bread playing poker. So that's why we're here. Rainbow needs a home. Her grandmother is a drunk. And I'm a gambler. So that leaves you."

Tigger punctuated this speech with a loud, whiny meow. As usual, Rainbow said nothing, but she was clutching his hand like a vise, which reminded Mike of the argument he'd had with the vet. Maybe he shouldn't have spoken so bluntly in front of the kid. But it wasn't as if Rainbow didn't know the situation. She'd spent the last week in foster care.

Timmy stared down at the kid and the cat. Then he came around his big desk and hunkered down so he could be face-to-face with Rainbow. "Hi, Rainbow," he said. "What's your kitty's name?" He petted the cat.

The cat didn't hiss or claw or play any of its demonic tricks. Mike took this as a sign that Timmy, Rainbow, and Tigger were a match made in heaven.

His optimism evaporated quickly. Half a minute after touching the feline, the minister started sneezing. And not merely one sneeze. The poor guy sneezed five times in a row. He stood up and snagged a tissue from the box on the corner of his desk and blew his nose. But it didn't help much. His eyes were streaming and turning an angry shade of red.

"I'm sorry, Rainbow," Timmy said as he backed away. "I'm allergic to cats. But I'm more allergic to some cats than others. So what's your kitty's name?"

Rainbow said nothing, of course, so Mike filled in the blanks. "The cat's name is Tigger. And Rainbow has stopped talking ever since she witnessed her mother's death."

The minister's eyebrows lowered. "Good Lord." He

reached for the bottle of sanitizer next to the tissues and pumped a generous amount into his hands. Mike wondered if the guy always sanitized himself after every encounter with a kid. But maybe he was being unkind. The guy was clearly allergic. Which was a big problem.

Rainbow continued to grip his hand. He'd lost the feeling in his index finger.

"Look, I know this is a shock," Mike said. "But you and I are the only sober family Rainbow has, and unless one of us takes her, she's going into foster care."

The minister stared at Rainbow for a long moment before he raised his gaze. "Michael?"

"Mike."

He nodded. "Where did you say you and your mother were living when my father left you?"

"In Chicago."

"I grew up in Atlanta."

"You were born in Chicago."

"I know that. But I grew up in Atlanta."

"You didn't live there until you were three."

A charged silence filled the room before Timmy let out a big breath and held his hands out to Rainbow. "Honey, how would you like to spend a few minutes with Miss Maryanne in the day-care center while your uncle and I have a little chat? You can even bring your cat."

Rainbow squeezed Mike's finger even harder. She didn't want to leave him. But Mike handed the kid off to Timmy anyway.

Shaking off her grasp gave him no joy or relief. That surprised him. He'd been so sure that finding her a father was the right thing to do.

He stood there watching through the doorway as

Timmy and Rainbow headed down the hall and back to the day-care center. Just before they got there, Rainbow glanced over her shoulder. She reminded Mike of Angie, the day he had walked out on her. Angie had been seven. Mike had been almost eighteen.

And like Angie on that long-ago day, Rainbow looked scared, hopeless, and lost.

Tim left the little girl with Maryanne, who wanted to ask him a bunch of questions. He didn't elaborate. The entire congregation would find out every gory detail before the night ended. The Altar Guild had one heck of a grapevine that connected every single busybody and gossip in his congregation.

And there were legions of them.

His hands trembled by the time he returned to his office. All his life he'd wanted a sibling. He'd watched his parents' heartbreak every time Mom had a miscarriage. To learn that he'd always had a brother—a brother his father had never mentioned—left him shaken.

Assuming, of course, that Mike Taggart had told the truth. And if that were so, then Dad had lied to him.

Mike still stood in the middle of the office, hands jammed into his pockets. Tim had no idea what a con man looked like, but he supposed that Mike might be one. But why would anyone try to con him into taking a little girl? It didn't make sense.

"Have a seat." Tim gestured to the chair. Mike sat, and Tim crossed the room and collapsed into his office chair. The big desk gave him separation as his emotions battled with his rational mind.

It would be wise to be suspicious. "I have no recollection of ever having lived anywhere other than Atlanta with my mother and father."

"I'm not surprised. You were barely three when Daddy left."

"Daddy?"

"That's what I called him," Mike said, meeting Tim's gaze in a way that suggested he wasn't lying. "I didn't understand that he wasn't my biological father until I turned ten. I always expected him to come back for me."

The words hit Tim right in the solar plexus. But they didn't seem to affect Mike. He showed no emotion as he spoke. And that sent up a bunch of alarms. He didn't trust this man.

"Well," Tim said, "I empathize with your situation. But I need to be clear. I'm not going to allow you to abandon a child on my doorstep. It would be wrong. And it would be illegal."

"But—"

He held up his hand, and Mike stopped speaking. "Do you have legal custody of Rainbow?"

"I do. But, Timmy, you don't understand. She needs help. She hasn't said a word since she saw her mother murdered. And I'm not the right guy to help her."

Timmy? No one had ever called him that, had they? "I'm going to have to check out your story. In the meantime, we'll need to handle this sensitively and legally."

"Look, I need to get back to Vegas. There's a big poker

tournament coming up. And before you judge what I do, I want you to know that I make a good living playing cards. So I have no intention of skipping out on Rainbow financially. I promise I'll put a part of my winnings in trust for her."

Anger flared. "I don't care about your time or your money, Mr. Taggart. I care about the child you just hauled in here. I care that you stood there and told her that you didn't want her. I care that you're ready to abandon her right here without even consulting any legal authorities or without determining if I would make an acceptable guardian."

"You owe me one. And of course you're acceptable. You're a frigging priest."

Tim ignored Mike's colorful language. "I owe you nothing."

"Yeah, you do. You got the nice life. I got left behind. And Angie got dead."

"Angie?"

"Our half-sister. Rainbow's mom." Mike's voice rose, and his shoulders tensed. It was somewhat reassuring to see his emotional control slip. The man's pain seemed genuine. And if his story was true, then Tim could understand that pain.

If his story was true. Tim could not imagine his father abandoning a child. But if Dad had abandoned Mike, then maybe Tim *did* owe him something.

Not payback, precisely. But something much better. He owed him love. The love that had been denied both of them. Brotherly love. The moment this thought crossed his mind Tim knew it was right. It was almost as if the Lord had asked him if he were willing to be his brother's keeper. And he knew his answer needed to be better than Cain's.

Tim leaned over his desk. "Mike, I believe the Lord brought you and Rainbow here for a purpose."

"I'm happy you feel that way, but I'm not a believer."

"I'm not surprised."

"So where does that leave us?"

Tim made a quick decision and prayed that the Lord would bless it. "You'll need to stay here in Allenberg County for a little while until I can verify your story. During this time, Rainbow will have to stay in your care, since you are currently her legal guardian. But I'll help you. I know a good child psychiatrist over in Allenberg, and we'll set up an appointment for Rainbow and get the therapist's advice on what should be done. How old is Rainbow? Five? Six?"

"Five."

"If you can't afford to pay for counseling—"

"I can cover her expenses. That's not the problem." Mike paused for a moment and looked down at his hands. "It's my lifestyle that's the problem. She doesn't belong in Vegas with a professional gambler."

"You're probably right about that. But you can't just leave her on the church's doorstep like a foundling child."

Mike leveled his gaze on Tim, his face once again expressionless. "I'm not here to abandon her. I want her to have a good life."

"Then you'll stay with her for a little while until your story can be verified. And if your story checks out, and if Rainbow and I are okay with it, then we'll make the proper legal arrangements."

Mike's gaze shifted to the floor at his feet. "Okay," he said after a long silence, "I guess that makes sense. Maybe we can reconnect. There was a time when you used to follow me around wherever I went."

The notion that he'd had a big brother left Tim hollow inside, as if some essential piece of himself had been torn away.

"So, you got room for us in the parish house?" Mike asked.

A frisson of doubt slammed into Tim. Was he willing to let this stranger into his house? No. The Bible was pretty explicit about how strangers should be welcomed, but he wasn't that brave. Or that stupid.

This man might not be telling the truth.

Tim must have telegraphed his confusion in some way because, before he could respond, Mike spoke again. "Uh, look, I was only kidding. I don't expect you to take us in until you can verify my story. I can see where you might think I was trying to pull something over on you. So if I'm going to stay for a little while, I'll need to find a hotel room. Got any suggestions?"

Relief washed through Tim.

"No, we don't really have any hotels, since the Peach Blossom Motor Court burned down last winter," Tim said. "But I think I can arrange something better. Martha Spalding, one of my parishioners, has just moved to Tampa on a temporary basis to look after her sister, who's battling cancer. She's been looking to sublease her condo over at the Edisto Pines Apartments. It's fully furnished, and I know she's cat-friendly because she took her cat, Felix, with her down to Florida. You'll need the kitchen if you're taking care of a cat and a child."

"I guess today's my lucky day," Mike said, but the words had the bite of sarcasm.

"Mike, I ought to tell you right up front that, while I'm empathetic to your situation and will do all I can to help, I'm not entirely sure I would make a good parent. I'm not married and I have little experience with children."

Mike gazed at the pair of sneakers on his desk. "With all due respect, padre, you have more experience than I do. I live in Vegas. In a hotel. I play poker for a living. My world is not kid-friendly. And you have a day-care center right down the hall from your office."

Angel Menendez slammed the door of his Jeep and tried to keep his emotions in check. He had just had an unpleasant telephone conversation with Dennis Hayden, the Allenberg County executive.

Despite a letter-writing campaign and personal visits, AARC had failed to convince County Executive Hayden to give up his plan to outsource Allenberg's animal shelter to an adjacent county. The proposal would be brought up at the County Council's June meeting, and Angel feared that Hayden had the votes to approve the plan.

Animal lovers understood exactly what that would mean. One shelter serving two counties would result in more innocent animals being euthanized.

Hayden's refusal to back down meant that the AARC fund-raiser scheduled for the middle of next month—just a week before the council vote—had become more important than ever. AARC needed to raise a lot more money if it hoped to run the county shelter as a private entity.

Angel hurried into the Kountry Kitchen café where AARC's executive board, consisting of vice chair Wilma Riley, recording secretary Charlene Polk, and treasurer Matt Jasper, had gathered for their weekly planning meeting.

"Ah, our esteemed chair has arrived," Wilma said as Angel slipped into the booth seat. "I guess the Purly Girls' meeting went late this week."

Angel was Simon Wolfe's personal assistant, and that meant, among other things, chauffeuring Simon's mother, Charlotte, to her various activities. On Tuesday, the charity knitters known as the Purly Girls met at the Knit & Stitch, the local yarn shop. Since Angel loved knitting, taking Charlotte to her meetings didn't bother him.

"No," he said. "I was detained by a phone call from Dennis Hayden. I am sorry to say that he is not backing down from the outsourcing proposal."

Angel's committee registered their disappointment just as Flo came by. "Y'all ordering the blue-plate tonight?" she asked.

Everyone nodded. Angel wondered why Flo felt it necessary to actually take orders on Fried Chicken Tuesday. No one ever ordered anything else.

Once the waitress departed, Angel spoke again. "All right, let us get to work. I think you all know that we have a big problem with the fund-raiser."

"I could have predicted that," Matt said, rolling his eyes. Matt had been the only dissenting vote when the committee formally agreed to host an auction two months ago. Matt had not objected to the silent auction, but he had complained about the main event of the night—a bachelor auction.

"I wonder if this is perhaps a self-fulfilling prophecy," Angel said. "I have heard that Ross Gardiner has been discouraging members of the volunteer fire department from participating. Matt, we were counting on you to convince Chief Gardiner of the importance of this event." Matt was a deputy sheriff with Allenberg County, in charge of the tiny K-9 department, which consisted of him and his dog Rex, who never left Matt's side. Right now the big German shepherd relaxed in the corner by the booth, dozing lightly with his muzzle between his front paws. Matt also volunteered with the fire department.

Matt's face colored. "Angel, I'm sorry, but you don't get it. You should have heard what Ross said when he found out that the bachelors had to dress up in tuxedos and prance around onstage."

"What did he say?"

"It's not fit to repeat with ladies present."

"We could make the party less formal," Wilma said. "How about bathing suits?"

Matt groaned.

"I don't think you can judge Ross too harshly," Charlene said. "I mean he's practically engaged to Lucy. So if he participated, Lucy would be forced to buy him. I think that's one of the problems with this plan, Angel. There aren't that many truly single, unattached men in this town."

"Look, y'all," Wilma said in her take-charge voice. "We need to quit pussyfooting around here. We need guys like Ross Gardiner to participate. And what about the Canaday boys? And your cousin Drew, Charlene. If we can't get our friends and relatives to do this, we're just pitiful."

"It's not that easy," Matt said. "What man is going to allow himself to be put up for auction? I wouldn't if I were single."

"Really? All those women offering money for your time," Wilma said.

"Yeah. All those women offering money for my time." Matt scowled.

"Listen to me, people," Angel said. "I have spoken with four or five groups who have hosted very successful bachelor auctions. We need to work harder. And with County Executive Hayden refusing to back down, I think people will respond. I have made a list of bachelors that we need to sign up." Angel passed around a paper with a list of names.

"Dr. Dave isn't on this list," Charlene said.

Angel's face burned. How had he forgotten to put Dave's name on the list? Probably because he had limited his thinking to heterosexual men. Dave was trying hard to fly under the gaydar, and with some success, probably because he was a member of Calvary Baptist Church— one of the evangelical congregations in Allenberg County. The members of Calvary Baptist had strong views about homosexuality.

Which begged the question: Why would a guy like Dave belong to a church with such fundamentalist views? Maybe it would be better if Dave *did* participate. Although Angel hated the idea of helping him stay in the closet.

"Oh, uh, I have no idea why he slipped my mind," Angel said, not wanting to out a man who had yet to accept the truth about himself.

"I'm sure he would participate. I mean, he's the vet in town, right?" Charlene looked around the table. "Has anyone even asked him?"

The rest of Angel's committee looked uncomfortable but no one said anything.

"Ah, look," Angel said, "at the last meeting, I volunteered

to do a lot of outreach to the potential bachelors, but I think perhaps I was the wrong man for the job."

Wilma snorted. "Yeah, probably. Okay, Charlene, let's divvy up this list. You take Ross Gardiner, the Canaday boys, and your cousin Drew. I'll take the rest. This is what we get for leaving the heavy lifting to the men. We'll let you boys deal with the caterers."

"Uh, you want me to ask Dr. Dave?" Charlene asked.

"Sure," Angel said, and regretted his words the moment they left his mouth. As the main vet in town, Dave's absence would be noticed. But his participation would be awkward.

Angel looked down at the blue-plate special that Flo had just delivered. His appetite had suddenly fled. In truth, Angel wanted to buy Dave himself. But he could never do that, even though he had been out of the closet for years.

Mierda! He did not think he could stand to watch Dave being bought by some woman.

CHAPTER 4

Mike stuffed the microwave pizza box and paper plates into the flimsy plastic grocery bag, but he had no place to toss the garbage. The owner of this condo apparently didn't believe in trash cans. Although she certainly did have a thing for the color red. Or was it burgundy?

Either way, dark red café curtains swathed every window in the living room and kitchen, which made the place feel kind of dark. The chunky, oversized furniture in dark woods and burgundy velour upholstery didn't help. Neither did the tasseled throw rugs placed under the coffee table and at the feet of the big, ugly chair. All in all the apartment looked like the home of a seventy-something spinster.

Mike found it maddening that the owner had left her kitchen gizmos—not to mention the curio cabinet filled with porcelain dolls—but had taken her trash can. Some guys might have viewed this as permission to leave the trash sitting on the floor. But that went against Mike's grain, probably because he'd grown up in a filthy apartment where the trash mounted up whenever Mom went on a bender. Sometimes if the bender lasted for days on end, the trash would start to stink.

So by the time Mike reached the age of thirteen, he'd given himself the job of taking out the trash, just one of many small things he'd done for Angie's sake. He never really learned to cook, but he could make macaroni out of a box and he knew his way around a microwave. Angie had not gone hungry when Mike lived at home.

But he'd failed her in every other way, especially when Mom took up with Richard.

Mike squeezed his eyes closed. He should never have walked out on his little sister.

He blew out a breath. There had to be a Dumpster somewhere. He picked up the bag and headed for the front door.

But before he could reach his destination, the doorbell rang. It was after nine o'clock. Didn't the yokels in this town go to sleep at this hour? Apparently not.

He opened the door to find a roundish, fifty-something woman with dark skin and graying hair standing on the landing that led to his apartment and the one next door. She blinked up at him from behind her glasses in the wan glow cast by the exterior lighting.

"Good Lord," she said, "you're a redhead."

"Can I help you with something?" he asked, putting on his poker face.

The woman gave him a serious inspection, stopping momentarily to read the logo on the bag of trash in his hand. "Oh, honey, you don't want to do your shopping at the Piggly Wiggly over in Bamberg when there's a BI-LO right in Last Chance."

"Uh, thanks."

"Oh, I apologize. I would have brought you one of my coconut cakes, but I didn't really have enough warning. I promise I'll get one over to y'all tomorrow as a welcome. I live in the apartment over there." She jacked her thumb over her shoulder, pointing vaguely in the direction of the building on the other side of the parking lot. The Edisto Pines were walk-up garden apartments that looked as if they'd been built in the late 1990s. They were wrapped in white vinyl siding and every six-over-six window had black shutters. The landscaper had gone heavy on azaleas and dogwoods, and the whole place conveyed an "Old South" vibe.

The woman continued to inspect him from head to toe. "I just came over to get a look at you, is all. I guess the little girl's in bed, huh?"

Mike finally reached his limit. "Um, I don't mean to be rude, but I have trash to take out and I don't even know you."

"Oh, Lord have mercy, I'm so sorry. I'm Elsie Campbell. I'm the chair of the First Methodist Altar Guild. You can imagine how interested we all are in you and the little girl."

"Oh. Uh. No, not really."

"Of course we are, especially if the little girl is our pastor's niece. And you know—"

Just then, a car arrived in the parking lot and pulled into the spot reserved for the apartment next door. Elsie turned around. "Well, look who's here. It's your next-door neighbor." Elsie waved. "Hey, Charlene, how did the AARC meeting go?"

The pretty, dark-haired vet who had mouthed off at

him this afternoon climbed out of her Ford F-150 truck. Wow! He didn't remember her having a rack like *that*. She'd been hiding a killer figure behind her white lab coat and cool hostility. And the truck was pretty nice, too.

"Oh, it went as well as can be expected. Did you hear that we're having trouble—" The vet stopped midsentence and glared at Mike. "What are *you* doing here?" He hadn't noticed before, but she was kind of hot.

He gave her one of his careful smiles. "I live here. For the moment."

"You do not. That's Martha Spalding's apartment. She's in Tampa. How did you get—"

"Timmy acted as a rental agent for me. I'm subleasing for a while."

Dr. Polk came up the stairs to the landing where the stairway divided. His sublease stood to the left, and evidently her apartment to the right. So they were neighbors.

"Subleasing?" she said.

"That means I'm making Martha's payments and living here for a while. Hopefully just a short while, because I want to participate in the World Series of Poker coming up in mid-June. But Timmy has convinced me that I should stay until Rainbow gets to know him. And we'll probably have to find a new home for Tigger, because Timmy is really allergic. Maybe you can help with that."

"Tigger?" Elsie asked.

"That would be Rainbow's cat," Mike said.

Elsie squinted at him for a moment. "You know, you kind of look a little bit like Pastor Tim. Around the eyes. Even if you have redder hair and more freckles."

"Yes, well, dear old Mom was a strawberry blonde."

Exhaustion weighed Mike down. He wanted to escape. Talking about Mom had always been a complete downer.

"Where's the little girl?" Dr. Polk asked.

"She's asleep. It's been a long day. And I've dosed the cat and fed them both."

The vet's gaze landed on the flimsy trash bag in his hands. "On microwave pizza?" Her tone was accusatory.

Anger sparked, and he snapped a reply. "Back off. The kid won't eat anything but pizza. I looked up every pizza place within sixty miles, and I would have had to drive all the way to Barnwell to find a Pizza Hut. I figured getting her and the cat settled was more important than going out to eat. So the microwave stuff had to do for tonight."

"A child can't live on pizza alone." The vet crossed her arms over her boobs, blocking the spectacular view. She wasn't intimidated by him in the least, was she?

"You think I don't know that? But it's what she'll eat. Now, if you ladies will excuse me, I have trash to take out." He edged his way past the two busybodies and headed toward the Dumpster.

Apparently Last Chance, South Carolina, was the place everyone meant when they talked about that mythological village that raised children. Every darn female he'd met today had given him child-rearing advice.

This ought to have pleased him. But it didn't.

"He's not very friendly, is he?" Elsie said as she watched Mike Taggart stride toward the Dumpster. "But at least he's good about taking out the trash. It means he's almost civilized. I still have trouble getting Buck to take out the trash."

Elsie turned and looked up at Charlene. "So how'd the AARC meeting go?"

"I don't know, Elsie. This idea to have a bachelor auction doesn't seem to be working very well. We're having trouble signing up bachelors."

"Who's signed up so far?"

"I think we've got a couple of guys from the nursing home. And Roy Burdett, now that he's separated from his wife."

"Oooh. Not good."

"I've been deputized to twist some arms."

"If you want my opinion," Elsie said, "you should try to get Pastor Tim to participate. Every single female in town thinks he's a dreamboat."

"I'm going to work on Cousin Drew and the Canaday twins first. And Dr. Dave."

"Dr. Dave?" Elsie seemed surprised.

"He's the main vet in town, and he's not married. Of course I'm going to sign him up."

"If you say so," Elsie said in a skeptical tone of voice. "Well, I better get going. I've done my reconnaissance mission on Mike Taggart. All the gals are waiting for my report. We're scheduled for a Skype session at ten o'clock." Elsie watched Mike as he tossed his garbage. "Y'all might think about asking Mr. Taggart to be one of your bachelors. He's nice looking, isn't he? Maybe not as handsome as Pastor Tim, but still he's kind of rugged and boyish, isn't he?"

Yeah. *Bad* boyish. Charlene could imagine him wearing a pair of black leather riding pants sitting astride a Harley. He would be gorgeous. But she knew better than to get all hot and bothered by that fantasy. Been there, done that.

Mike had "jerk" written all over his beautiful body. He couldn't have been less like the caring and kind Dr. Dave. She needed to remember that.

"No one in town is going to be interested in buying that guy. He's from out of town and he's..." Charlene ran out of words.

"I think the word you're looking for is hot, honey. That man is hot, and dangerous like a dog on the prowl. I have no doubt that someone would want to buy him. But maybe not for dinner."

"He's probably not going to be here all that long, anyway. So it's idle speculation."

"Probably, but if you're looking for bachelors, I suggest you add him to your list. He'd probably get you top dollar. You take care, hon. I have a Skype call to make. The gals are going to be talking about this for weeks." Elsie headed down the stairs, and Charlene turned toward her apartment door.

She had just slipped the key into the lock when Mike's footsteps sounded on the stairs behind her. For some reason, her heart kicked into overdrive. And in her haste to get through the door, she managed to jam the lock, which had been malfunctioning for about a month. She was simultaneously wiggling the key and pulling on the door when Mike Taggart spoke to her back, making her jump a little.

"I'm not a criminal, you know." His voice sounded as deep as the ocean, his accent definitely from somewhere else.

She turned, her hands suddenly sweaty. He stood on the landing. The exterior spotlight lit up his hair like a flame and cast shadows across the sharp hollows and planes of his face.

She straightened her shoulders. "I never said you were a criminal."

"No, I guess not. You judged me from the beginning, didn't you?"

Her whole body flushed. She *had* judged him. And she'd been worried about the little girl.

"I didn't think it was appropriate for Rainbow to hear how you plan to abandon her." Why did Charlene's voice wobble like that? The idea of the child being abandoned ripped her heart apart. "And with a person who doesn't even know her."

The corners of Mike's mouth tipped with a self-assured grin that folded two sets of laugh lines along his cheeks. His deep-set eyes crinkled at the corners. "She doesn't know me all that well, either," he said. "I've seen her twice in her life, and she's been in my custody for only a few days. So it's not exactly like she's formed any kind of attachment to me. And besides, I'm not here to abandon her. I'm here to find her a family." He leaned back against the banister and shoved his hands into his pockets. He had an attitude a mile wide and a big, fat chip on his shoulder. He also had a sharp blue stare that unsettled Charlene.

Unlike Dr. Dave, he definitely noticed her new sweater, and he seemed to be appreciating her narrower waistline, too.

"Good night, Mr. Taggart," she said, turning back to the stubborn lock that refused to budge.

Mr. Taggart bounded up the stairs behind her. He cast a dark shadow over the door and radiated heat up her backside. "Here, let me," he said, his breath feathering against her ear. Her insides went all squishy.

He batted her hands away from the lock and with a forceful twist he had it opened in a matter of seconds. "It's all in the wrist," he said, backing up, taking his heat with him.

"Thank you," she said in a near whisper and hurried through her door, oddly annoyed that she'd let a person like Mike Taggart get under her skin.

CHAPTER 5

Wednesday didn't get off to a stellar start.

Mike awakened Rainbow at eight-thirty a.m. and fed her a slice of cold pizza. Then he dressed her in a threadbare pair of blue jeans and a faded Chicago White Sox T-shirt that had the name "Nathan" printed in indelible marker on the inside neck. A quick check of Rainbow's wardrobe revealed numerous and varied boys' names on the necks and waistbands of her jeans and shirts. The kid didn't own a dress or anything in pink.

Had Angie intentionally dressed Rainbow like a boy? The thought disquieted him. He knew all about the dangers of living in subsidized housing. Predators preyed on women and girls in those places. It broke his heart to think about what Rainbow had already been through.

But things were different now. They weren't in Chicago anymore. They were in a podunk town that looked like something from the cover of *Southern Living*. Rainbow needed to be a whole lot cuter. And that called for new clothes.

During breakfast, he made it clear at least five times that they were going shopping and that the cat had to stay home. But the moment breakfast ended, Rainbow disappeared. Mike spent a frantic few minutes searching for her until he found her curled up in a bedroom closet with a death grip on the cat.

The cat looked up at him with one of those big-eyed adorable looks. Tigger sure knew how to be cute when she wanted to. Why didn't the kid?

"We're going, now."

Apparently not. It took him a good five minutes to separate the girl from the cat. And by the time they hit the front door, Mike had hoisted Rainbow over his shoulder like a sack of potatoes. She kicked and cried, and for the first time in days, she made some noise. A lot of it, actually.

And, wouldn't you know it, the moment he opened the door, there stood his busybody neighbor looking lovely and judgmental in a tight red sweater, a pair of pants that showed off every one of her bodacious curves, and a frown on her beautiful face.

"It's not what it looks like," he said defensively. He paused to let Dr. Polk precede him down the stairs.

Rainbow let out a high-pitched wail that echoed around the apartment complex and probably wakened all the rest of his busybody neighbors.

"And what exactly is it?" Dr. Polk asked over the kid's screams. They had reached the sidewalk.

"We're going shopping."

The vet blinked. Obviously the idea of a little girl pitching a temper tantrum over a shopping trip threw her for a loop. It was a new one for Mike, too. Which probably explained why Dr. Polk wrinkled her brow and said, "You don't really expect me to believe that, do you?"

"Yes, I do. She's a different kind of kid. And she's mostly annoyed because I made her leave the cat behind."

"Oh?" The skepticism practically dripped from her voice.

The woman seriously ticked him off. He steadied the howling child on his shoulder. "Butt out, Dr. Polk. You don't understand what's going on here. I stupidly lost Rainbow's cuddle toy in the airport, and she has transferred her dependence to the cat. But, obviously, she can't drag a cat around with her like a stuffed animal, can she?"

Dr. Polk's dark eyes warmed, and he could almost feel her attitude unfreezing. "Poor child."

That did it. He didn't want Dr. Polk's pity, either. So he let her have it. "Yeah. It sucks to lose a parent." He turned away and strode off to his car, annoyed at himself for letting anger get the best of him. He shouldn't give a flying fart what she thought about him. But for some reason he did.

He fought Rainbow into the booster seat he'd bought before embarking on this odyssey. But did the good doctor even notice that he was buckling the kid into an age-appropriate safety seat?

No. Dr. Polk continued to level a judgmental stare at him that practically burned a hole into his backside. She stood there, arms folded, watching his every move until he got behind the wheel and peeled out of the parking lot. He hated the fact that his neighbor had made him feel so guilty for doing something that he knew was right.

Rainbow needed new clothes.

He expected Rainbow to give up her stubbornness

once they got to the mall in Orangeburg, but the kid proved him wrong. She certainly had staying power, he'd give her that.

He had to fight her out of the booster seat, and then she loudly refused to try on clothes, especially the cute pink ones he picked out. She didn't like dresses; she didn't want new shoes. He couldn't even talk her into a replacement stuffed elephant or a McDonald's Happy Meal with a Hello Kitty toy inside.

He failed on every level.

By the time he got back to the apartment, he wanted a good stiff drink. But it was only two o'clock in the afternoon. He collapsed in front of the television and watched CNBC, while Rainbow retreated into her room with the cat.

He sucked at this. The sooner Timmy took over, the better all the way around.

His frustration mounted an hour later when his cell phone rang. He checked the number—Paul Kozlowski, his agent. He punched the talk button.

"Hey, Paul, what's up?"

"When are you getting back?"

"I don't know. There's been a little snag."

"A snag?"

"Yeah, but I'm working on it. What's happening?"

"Look, Mike, you need to get your ass back here. I've got interest from Jimmy Huang of Dragon Casinos, and I think, if you could play a few preliminary rounds in the World Series of Poker next week, we could score a sponsorship for the main event, with maybe something longer term."

Mike squeezed his eyes shut. He'd been waiting for a

call like this for at least three years, ever since the U.S. government shut down online poker. Murphy's Law had struck again. "I don't know if I can get back by next week."

"What?" Paul sounded ticked off.

"Look, I'm sorry. You know damn well that my sister was murdered. I have to deal with her kid, Paul. I can't just walk away from this, even if you want to nail down a deal."

Silence beat at him from the other end of the line. "You could bring her back with you," Paul finally said.

"No. Vegas is no place for a kid."

"Are you serious about your career?"

"Paul, don't give me that BS. You know I am. I need a couple of weeks. I promise you I'll be back for the main event. And if I don't get a sponsor before that, I've already got my stake all saved up."

"You're a fool if you turn this deal down, Mike."

Of course Paul wanted him to grab that sponsorship. Paul would make 15 percent of any signing bonus. And in Paul's world, money was everything.

"I'm no fool. I'll be back in a week or two."

Paul grumbled at him for a few more minutes before Mike finally got him off the phone. The idea of a drink sounded better and better.

He had just about decided that a beer would be okay when his doorbell rang.

"What now?" he muttered as he opened his door to find Elsie Campbell with a Tupperware cake container in her hands. "Hey there, handsome, I told you I'd bring you a cake."

"Thanks, Elsie."

He started to reach for the cake container, but Elsie had other ideas. She marched right into his apartment and headed for the kitchen. "You look like you need a pick-me-up," she said. "I'll just get some coffee going."

He opened his mouth, intent on telling her that he didn't want coffee, but then he changed his mind. She was a busybody all right, but that meant she also knew a thing or three about Timmy's life.

His half-brother had been stingy with information when they'd worked out their little arrangement. And Mike didn't really blame him. After all, Timmy didn't remember anything about him. But Mike remembered Timmy. He remembered showing him how to kick a soccer ball. He remembered playing Matchbox cars with him. He remembered the way Timmy climbed into his bed whenever Mom and Daddy started arguing.

He remembered a lot.

So Mike sat himself down at the little kitchen table and let Elsie have the run of his kitchen. Which was sort of difficult for her because Tigger decided she liked Elsie. She came in from the living room where she liked to sleep and proceeded to rub herself up against Elsie's leg, while simultaneously letting forth a bunch of loud meows.

"You are a friendly one, aren't you?" Elsie asked in one of those silly, high baby-talk voices. She bent over and scratched the cat's ears. The cat closed its eyes and looked like it had entered some altered state.

"Nice cat, Mike."

"Yeah, whatever."

Elsie gave him the evil eye. "You don't like cats?"

"I never had a cat before. But that particular cat is possessed."

Elsie laughed. "Why do you say that?"

"Up until this moment, I truly thought she was a one-person cat. She's okay when I feed her, but otherwise she has her claws out whenever I'm around."

Elsie put a huge slice of coconut cake in front of him and then sat herself down. The demon cat hopped right up onto her lap and made herself comfy. Clearly the cat liked women better than men.

He took a bite of cake. Wow! Elsie sure hadn't spared the sugar. "Elsie, this is terrific," he said, hoping that the frosting wouldn't make his teeth hurt.

Her face lit up. He'd obviously made her day. Which kind of lifted his spirits, too.

"Thanks, hon. I reckon a single man like you doesn't get much in the way of scratch-made cake very often."

"No, I don't."

"So you live in Vegas?" she asked.

He proceeded to give her the Cliff Notes version of his life, starting at the moment when Colin Lake walked out with Timmy on his hip.

"Bless your heart, y'all have been separated for all these years?"

"Yes we have. And I don't know much about him. I mean, once I got older I looked him up and learned that he was in seminary so I knew that much. But you probably know more about him than I do."

"Oh, well, I don't know about that. He's pretty new in town."

"Elsie, I'll be honest with you, what I really want to know is whether Timmy has any girlfriends. I mean, I want Rainbow to have the best possible mother."

The cat meowed loudly and poked her head up. She

gave Mike a demonic stare out of her half-closed eyes. He really didn't like that cat.

Elsie didn't seem at all perturbed by the cat's behavior. She continued to give it lots of pets and scratches. "I understand completely," she said. "As it happens, Pastor Tim doesn't have any girlfriends. And the Altar Guild is a little concerned about that. We all thought that he might marry Jenny Carpenter, but that didn't work out. And recently he's been so busy with various church issues that he doesn't have much time for a social life."

"I see."

She and Tigger leaned in, conspiratorially. "I think we should work on matching him up with Sabina Grey."

"Sabina? Who's she?"

"She and her sister, Lucy, own the antiques mall in town. Sabina is cute as a button. And she's a regular member of the Altar Guild."

"I guess I'll have to stop by the mall and check her out."

"You do that. And, honey, the Altar Guild has discussed this situation at length, and we are all in agreement that you are telling the truth. We don't see any reason why you'd be trying to pull the wool over Pastor Tim's eyes. This has got to be a real shock for him, discovering he's got a brother and sister and a niece."

"I guess it is. But he's the lucky one, Elsie. He's the one who got out of a bad situation and into a good family."

Elsie nodded. "I understand entirely." She stopped scratching Tigger long enough to reach out and pat his hand. Maybe it was his imagination, but he got the distinct impression that the cat was not pleased by this.

"And I just want to let you know," Elsie said, "that we're all here to help you in any way we can. We'd like to see Pastor Tim adopt Rainbow. And we all believe this situation might be just what we need to get him into a matrimonial frame of mind, if you know what I mean."

That's the moment when the cat decided she'd had enough of Elsie. She jumped off the woman's lap, but not before she sank her sharp little claws into her thigh.

"Ouch!" Elsie gave the cat a black look.

"I told you. She's possessed."

"Yeah, with really sharp claws."

The cat turned and walked out of the room in a truly regal fashion, her tail held high.

"Sorry about that," Mike said.

"Oh, honey, it's okay. You warned me. And besides, cats can be funny sometimes," she said.

Elsie's cell phone rang. "Hang on a minute, Mike." She pushed the talk button and listened to the voice on the other end. It didn't take a poker player to read her face. Her complexion paled, and the corners of her mouth turned down. Within thirty seconds, Mike knew that the caller had conveyed bad news.

Elsie said a few words, then ended the call. "Mike, I gotta go. That was Ruthie Clatcher on the phone. I'm afraid her daddy, Ralph, died this morning. It's not entirely unexpected, since he was about ninety years old, but I need to get going on another cake and probably a casserole."

"Uh, Elsie, I love your cake, but if you need to take some of it over to Ralph's family, that would be fine by me. It's delicious. The best coconut cake I've ever tasted. But it's just me and Rainbow here, and the kid doesn't eat anything but pizza."

"Really? Not even sweets?"

He nodded. "I can't get anything but pizza down her throat. She's very picky."

"Oh, bless her heart."

"There's no way I could eat all this cake."

"You're a good man, Mike. Thanks. I'm sure Ruthie won't mind a bit that there's a slice missing."

Tim wanted to remember his childhood. But his earliest memory of his dad had to be when he was five or six, out on Lake Lanier fishing from the back of a pontoon boat. Try as hard as he might, Tim couldn't go back any further in time.

Unfortunately, he couldn't ask his father for the truth. Dad had died a year ago. So last night, Tim had pulled down the box of stuff he'd kept after Dad's death. He'd gone through everything in that box looking for answers. But he found none—only more questions.

The family photo albums contained no photos of him before the age of three. And none of him with Mother until he looked to be about four or five.

Why was that? And why hadn't he ever been curious about the fact that all his baby photos seemed to be missing? Those missing photos suggested that Mike's story was true.

If Mike had told the truth, then Dad had lied. And that rocked Tim's world. Dad had been one of the most honest people Tim had ever known. Colin Lake had been a man of great faith. A deacon in his church. An exemplary neighbor, husband, and father. How could he have kept such a monumental thing from Tim?

Tim wanted the truth. And yet he feared it. Perhaps that explained why he hadn't called Eugene Hanks to ask his advice about a private investigator. He had also procrastinated when it came to calling Mike, even though he needed to have a face-to-face conversation with him about arrangements for the little girl.

His cell phone rang as he brooded over these conflicting desires. He checked the caller ID: Elsie Campbell.

He didn't want to deal with the chair of the Altar Guild right at this moment. He could never predict what Elsie wanted when she called. It could be important or it could be nonsense. But he'd learned the hard way that he ignored her calls at his peril.

He pressed the talk button. "What's up, Elsie?"

"Ralph Clatcher has died. Ruthie needs you as quickly as possible."

It came as no surprise that Elsie knew about the old man's demise before Tim. Elsie was almost always the first to know anything.

This death, tragic as it was, gave him a reason to put off making any hard decisions. He needed to get over to Ralph's daughter's house and spend a little time with Ruthie, who had been taking care of her aged father for quite a long time. Which meant he'd have to cut short that face-to-face meeting with Mike he'd been dreading.

He finished his conversation with Elsie and then called Ruthie Clatcher to express his condolences and let her know that he would be there soon. Ruthie told him that the casserole brigade had already started to convene at her house, so that gave him a little wiggle room. Ruthie wasn't alone, and Martha Spalding's apartment at Edisto Pines was on the way to Ruthie's house.

Fifteen minutes later, Tim knocked on the condo's door. Mike answered a moment later, looking frazzled.

He hadn't shaved, his eyes were bloodshot, and he conveyed a sense of utter exhaustion. Concern tugged at Tim.

"So how's it going?" he asked.

"Okay, I guess." Mike didn't sound entirely sure of himself. "So, did you check out my story?"

"No, not yet. You've only been here twenty-four hours, and I've been very busy. How's the child?"

"Too busy?" Mike's forehead wrinkled. "A person who claims to be your long-lost brother shows up and you're too busy to check out his story?"

Tim's ears burned. He deserved Mike's frustration. He should have called Eugene first thing this morning.

He took a deep, calming breath and walked past Mike into the living room of Martha Spalding's condo with its lace doilies and café curtains. Mike Taggart belonged in this space like a gigolo at a ladies' sewing circle.

"I'm sorry about the decor of this place. Martha Spalding is about seventy years old."

"I figured."

"So where's Rainbow?"

"In the bedroom. With her cat."

"I guess I probably should keep my distance then." Tim sat down on the old-lady sofa and immediately sneezed. He pulled a handkerchief from his pocket and sneezed three more times.

"Wait a sec. I forgot," Mike said. "You had asthma as a kid. Really bad asthma. I remember one time when Daddy and I had to take you to the hospital. I think the asthma had something to do with Daddy leaving."

Mike's words touched something dim and distant, like the echo of a memory. Tim remembered being taken to a hospital. He'd been very young and scared to death. Dad had been there with him, steady and calm as always. Was there someone else in the car that night? Maybe.

"You're right about the asthma," Tim said. "And if it turns out that what you've said is true, then we're going to have to find another home for the cat. I can't have a cat in my house."

Mike sank down onto the ottoman, a picture of exhaustion. "Tim, I don't think you understand. Rainbow pitched a full-on tantrum this morning when I told her she couldn't take Tigger shopping with her. Separating her from the cat is going to be traumatic."

"It's got to be done."

"Right now?"

"I'm going to check out your story, but right now I've decided to give you the benefit of the doubt. Which means that Rainbow will eventually come to live with me. She can't bring her cat. And the sooner we begin to wean her from this dependency the better."

"It ain't gonna be easy. Get ready for some very bad behavior."

"Then I think this is an issue we need to take up with Andrea Newsome. She's the child therapist I told you about yesterday. She has an office in Allenberg. Not too far away. I made an appointment for Rainbow for tomorrow at three p.m. I thought I could drive her there."

Mike pressed his lips together as if this news annoyed him.

"Unless you want to drive her," Tim said. "I just thought that driving her to her appointment would be a good way for us to spend time together, without the cat."

Mike nodded his head. "All right, Timmy. I can see the logic in that."

Timmy again? How odd to be called that name. He scrutinized Mike for a long moment. Mike's shoulders slumped, and that emotionless mask he'd worn yesterday seemed a little worse for wear. He didn't look like a trustworthy person right at the moment.

Tim looked down at his hands, torn by conflicting emotions and fears. What if this guy was playing him for a fool?

There was only one way to determine that. He needed to call an investigator. And he needed to get a grip. "Look, Mike, I'm going to hire a private investigator to have your story checked out. But in the meantime, I want the little girl to be cared for. And I thought it might help if you enrolled her in the church's Bible camp. It starts on Monday. And with her at church, I could spend time with her, and you wouldn't be here babysitting her all the time. You could get some work done. And she could spend some time away from the cat." Tim looked up as he finished his speech. His eyes burned, and he could hardly breathe. But maybe the tightness in his chest had nothing to do with cat dander. Maybe it had everything to do with the fact that he might finally have a brother.

Mike leaned forward with his elbows braced on his knees and studied Tim's face. "Thanks for setting up the counseling for Rainbow. I'll help pay the cost. She needs some help, that's for sure."

"All right, I'm glad we agree," Tim said. "I'll be by tomorrow around three o'clock to pick her up." He blew his nose and wiped his eyes as he stood up. "I wish I could stay a little longer, but I'm having a crazy day today. Ruthie Clatcher just lost her father, and I have to run down to her house to meet with the family."

"I've already heard about Mr. Clatcher."

"You did? Really?"

Mike nodded. "Yeah, Elsie Campbell came by with a coconut cake, and she got the phone call while she was here. You'll be pleased to know I sent the uneaten portion of my cake off to the bereaved."

"Elsie was *here?*" Uh-oh, that had big trouble written all over it.

"Timmy," Mike said, the corner of his mouth sliding upward in a half smile, "the members of your altar guild are trying to find you the perfect wife. I gather someone named Sabina Grey is at the top of their list. I hope you understand why I'm planning to check her out. If there's a woman in your life, I need to know about it. I mean, whoever she is will become Rainbow's mom. And I hope you can understand why I want Rainbow to have the best mom in the world."

Tim squeezed his eyes shut. They were burning like nobody's business. He needed to get going, but not before he discouraged Mike from joining forces with the Altar Guild. "Ah, look, Mike, you don't really understand how things work in this town. Those women can stir up trouble. Big trouble. I've seen them do it on several occasions. So it's best to stay clear of them, okay? Before you get all caught up in their machinations."

"So you're saying you like being a bachelor?"

"Well, no, actually. I would like to settle down someday with the right woman. But I am not about to let the Altar Guild find her for me."

CHAPTER 6

Charlene usually spent Thursday in her car, traveling from one farm to another, checking up on the large animals in her practice. She loved these days. Caring for dogs and cats (and the occasional ferret) was fine, but she had landed her job with Creature Comforts because she'd specialized in large-animal care—a choice that Mother and Daddy never quite understood, seeing as she hadn't been raised on a farm.

But she had gone a little horse-mad when she'd been a teen and spent a lot of time in stables learning about the care and feeding of horses. In those days, she had to travel thirty miles to find a good stable with riding horses. But Dash Randall had changed all that when he'd started breeding American Paints right in Last Chance.

So she loved Thursdays, when she made her field rounds. She made a point of stopping by Painted Corner Stables every week to check up on the horses in Dash's care. She would check in with Walter Taylor, Dash's trainer, and nip any medical problems in the bud. She always made Dash's place the last stop. And sometimes, if she got there early enough, Walter would saddle up one of Dash's horses, and she'd take a little ride.

But not today. She had a million things to do today, and first on her list was stopping by the Last Chance Around antiques mall to pick up Daddy's birthday present—a 1927 hard rubber Waterman fountain pen that Sabina Grey had scored at an auction. Daddy would love it. He collected pens.

She pulled her pickup into a parking spot right in front of the mall, which had at one time been a Woolworth five-and-dime. About a year ago, Sabina and her sister, Lucy, managed to find an old F.W. Woolworth sign dating back to the 1950s. They had restored it and affixed it above the awning where the original sign had been. But instead of cheap, plastic merchandise in the front windows, the girls displayed antiques and vintage finds. Inside, the store had been gutted and partitioned into stalls for about thirty independent merchants. The place was crammed full of stuff, running the gamut from art deco jewelry to mid-century modern lamps and tables. You could also find some pretty weird stuff at Last Chance Around Antiques, like the collection of Dating Game lunchboxes that Sally McCrea sold in her stall.

She didn't expect to run into Mike Taggart at the antiques mall. But there he stood leaning a hip into the front cash counter talking with Sabina Grey, flaunting his oh-so-sexy laugh lines. His eyes seemed to have an unusual spark in them today. And by the look in Sabina's eyes, she was enjoying every minute of the conversation.

And who wouldn't? Mike Taggart looked like a candidate for *People* magazine's sexiest man alive issue. He had just the right amount of fiery stubble. Just the right amount of swagger. Just the right bad boy gleam in his eyes.

Yup. He was the kind of guy who would never, in a million years, meet with Mother and Daddy's approval. Which immediately made him irresistible.

Thank God, Charlene had moved past her rebellious stage. She'd learned her lesson about guys like Mike Taggart. And she needed to intercede right now before Sabina got herself in too deep.

"Hey," Charlene said in a big voice as she strode toward them. "I'm here to get Daddy's pen."

Mike straightened and turned toward Charlene in slow motion. The glint in his eyes cooled. Good. She wanted nothing to do with him.

"Oh, hey, Charlene, have you met Mike Taggart?" Sabina said.

"Yes. We've met. In fact, we're neighbors," Mike said. He managed to twist the word. Obviously he didn't like the fact that she was keeping an eye on him.

"Where's Rainbow?" she asked.

"You know, Doc," he said in his Yankee way, "you need to quit assuming that I'm some kind of ax murderer. I'm really a very nice guy who would never leave a five-year-old on her own. Rainbow is with Timmy."

"Timmy?" Charlene and Sabina echoed the name in unison.

"Yeah, Timmy," Mike said. "I know everyone around here calls him Tim. But he's my little brother, and I always called him Timmy."

"I'll bet he was a beautiful baby," Sabina said.

"Yes, he was. Blond hair, blue eyes, big smile. Big

heart." Mike stopped speaking and something changed in his expression. As if his mask has slipped. "I missed Timmy a lot when his father took him away."

"So that's what happened?" Sabina asked. Sabina was a member of the Methodist Altar Guild, so it was only natural that she had a lot of questions.

"Yeah. His father left when I was five and Timmy was three."

"You must have been heartbroken," Sabina said.

"I guess." Neither his face nor his voice betrayed any emotions, which was odd, given the topic of discussion.

He didn't elaborate. He just stood there for a moment, glancing at Charlene and then Sabina, as if he were trying to find some way to change the subject or trying to suppress emotions.

"Well, ladies," he finally said, "I'd love to stay here gossiping, but I need to get going. Timmy is bringing Rainbow back at four-thirty, and I have a few errands to run. It was nice meeting you, Sabina."

He turned and brushed passed Charlene. He got three paces away and then turned. "By the way, Doc, I like the boots and the *eau de cow* you're wearing." He had the gall to wink at her before he turned and strolled from the shop.

Charlene looked down at her feet. She hadn't taken off her heavy-duty rubber boots, the ones she always wore when she went tramping through barns and fields. Her boots were dirty up to the ankles with dried muck. They definitely smelled like barn, but that particular odor never bothered Charlene. She liked *eau de cow*.

Even so, her whole body went hot, right down to the ends of her hair. Damn. How could she allow a stupid comment from an idiot man to embarrass her? Her boots were a necessary part of her job. She often wore them around town on Thursdays. And no one had ever said a word to her about it before.

She turned toward Sabina, trying not to grind her teeth. "I came for the pen," she said.

Sabina snagged an oblong box from the shelf behind the counter. The box was teal-colored with the words "Waterman Fountain Pen" printed along the top. She placed it on the counter and opened the top to reveal a black pen with a brass clip and ink lever. It was in immaculate condition. The box even contained the original paper instructions that came with the pen.

"Daddy is going to love this."

"I'm sure he is. So what do you think of Mike Taggart?"

"Not much," Charlene said, reaching into her purse for her wallet. "Why was he here? He doesn't strike me as the kind of guy who loves antiques."

"I think Elsie Campbell sent him," Sabina said with a laugh as she took Charlene's Visa card.

"What? Why would Elsie send him here?"

"Honey, you don't know the political maneuvering that goes on inside the Methodist Altar Guild. The girls have all decided that it's past time for the preacher to get married. And since I'm the only single woman of marriageable age who's a member of the guild, naturally they think I should make a play for Pastor Tim." She rolled her eyes. "But, you know, I really don't feel any sparks in that department. The guy is really handsome but kind of a dork at times." She sighed mightily as she swiped the Visa card.

"But I still don't get it. What does Mike have to do with the Altar Guild?"

"We've adopted him, sort of. The prevailing view is that Mike's story is true and that his only motive for being here is to find a family for the little girl. Which is why Elsie told him that I would make the perfect wife for Pastor Tim."

"Oh, no."

"Oh, yes. So Mike came in here pretending to shop, but really he was checking me out. And then he engaged me in a conversation that felt a whole lot like a job interview."

"Really?"

She nodded and handed Charlene her credit card and the sales receipt to sign. "It's kind of cute, you know?"

"Cute? You think it's cute? It's annoying and...I don't know, wrong or something." She handed Sabina the signed receipt.

"I don't know. The idea that he would come here and try to find the perfect family for his niece is sweet, actually. He could have chosen to turn his back on the little girl."

"But that's exactly what he's doing. He's turning his back on her. He's come here to leave Rainbow on the church's doorstep."

"No, I don't think so. Why would he still be here? Besides, how can he abandon Rainbow if she's only been in his custody for less than a week? It's not like he fathered this child. He didn't even have to take custody of her. He could have left her to the foster care system. That would have been wrong. But taking custody, bringing her here, and trying to find a family for her—that's not abandonment in my book. And he seemed hell bent to get my entire life history."

"Really?"

Sabina nodded. "Yeah. He's completely misguided, of course. But his heart's in the right place."

Tim sat in the middle of a white leather couch in Dr. Andrea Newsome's office. The therapist sat facing him from behind a big desk with brass fittings. To the left, in a corner of the room, stood a low table where Rainbow sat quietly coloring a picture.

She'd just spent the last forty-five minutes with the doctor. Now it was Tim's turn, and he wondered how much of his own inner confusion he should admit.

He *wanted* to reveal himself to the woman in front of him. She had an open, kind face with widely spaced brown eyes.

"So," she said, folding her hands in front of her. She had good, capable hands devoid of fancy polish. "How do *you* feel about this turn of events?"

How did he feel? "Confused," he admitted.

She nodded. "That's understandable. So are you going to check out Mike Taggart's story?"

He looked down at his hands. "Can I be honest?"

"Honesty is what I'm looking for, Reverend Lake."

He looked up at her. "Please, call me Tim."

"All right."

"I don't want to check out Mike Taggart's story. I'm afraid to."

"Why?"

He shrugged. "If what he says is true then my parents lied to me."

"All parents lie. You know that, don't you?"

He looked up, frowning. "That's a cynical view."

"No, it's not. Parents lie about all kinds of things. Mostly to protect their kids. They don't tell children the truth about death. Sickness. Poverty. They make up stories about Santa Claus."

"Yes, but this is a bigger lie than that."

"Is it? Or did your father merely want to protect you from the fact that your birth mother was an alcoholic? That he once had a problem with addiction?"

He looked over at Rainbow. "Mike said I owed him something. He seems to be very angry with me. Or maybe it's Dad he's so angry with."

"That makes perfect sense. Your father abandoned him. That's tough on a kid. He's probably jealous of the life you got to lead."

Tim snapped his gaze back to the doctor. "Are you trying to make me feel guilty?"

She laughed. The sound seemed to find its way inside. What a remarkably joyful sound. "No. I don't try to make people feel guilty. That's not what my profession is all about. But I suppose that doesn't exactly hold true for yours, does it?"

"So you're saying that I've built my career on guilt, huh?"

Something mischievous danced in her eyes. Tim already knew Andrea didn't regularly attend church. "Well, I certainly sat through any number of sermons as a child in a Catholic household where the priest intended to make me feel guilty. And I rebelled against that. I believe guilt is a waste of time. So you shouldn't feel guilty about what your father did. The question is what are you going to do now to positively affect Rainbow's future?"

He let go of a big sigh. "I don't know. I can see where I might be in a position to give her a more stable upbringing. But I don't have the first idea of how to care for a child. I'm not even sure I'd make a good parent. And then there's the matter of the cat. Mike seems to think that separating the child from her cat would be traumatic."

Andrea nodded. "First of all, Tim, everyone who has ever become a parent enters into that role with trepidation. And as for the cat, I think we need to give that issue a few days. For now I think stability is what she needs."

Dr. Newsome unfolded her hands. "Let's talk about Rainbow for a moment. First, I can tell you unequivocally that she is not faking it. She has definitely suffered some kind of traumatic experience. I don't know if it's merely related to the violent death of her mother or if she's been abused. She's showing signs of regression. And I would imagine that she's probably having bad dreams. So, do you think Mike has harmed the child in any way?"

Tim looked down at the carpet. It was a calming shade of green. He closed his eyes and prayed for a moment before he looked up. "I don't believe Mike Taggart is the kind of person who hurts little children. I think he genuinely wants her to have a good home." He paused for a moment before he went on. "Of course I sometimes think Mike is a con man. And then I don't know what to think. This situation is ripping me apart."

Dr. Newsome gave him an empathetic look that was almost like a balm. "We need to make *sure* that he's not hurting Rainbow. So you will need to run a background check on him. And if you won't do that, then I will do it myself. I would also like to meet Mike. In these cases, it's important to start by ensuring the child is safe. We can't make any progress with psychotherapy if she's not."

"I agree."

"And, Tim, while I fully understand your conflicted feelings, I can't allow you to drag your feet on this one thing. If you won't take the steps to verify Mike Taggart's story, then I will. Because the girl has been traumatized. And it's my job to make sure that the authorities know if she's currently being abused."

"I understand. But, please, don't call them yet. I promise. I'll check him out as soon as possible."

On Saturday, Charlene met her best friend, Amanda Wright, at the Garden of Eatin', a new café that had just opened up in the old Coca Cola bottling plant. The café provided food for those visiting the art galleries and studios that now occupied the building. The eatery was trendy for Last Chance. The decor looked like something straight from Columbia or Atlanta, with light wood floors, white linens, and Ball jars filled with wildflowers on every table. Unlike other restaurants in town, the Garden of Eatin' didn't serve barbecue or fried chicken. It did, however, serve a nice selection of wines and fabulous low-cal salads.

An important factor, because Amanda's wedding was slated for mid-August, and both Charlene and her best friend still needed to shed a few pounds to fit into their dresses.

"Do you think orchids or roses?" Amanda asked as she sipped her glass of Chardonnay.

"I like roses," Charlene said.

"Orchids are classier."

"But more expensive. Honey, you don't have to impress Grant with orchids. He loves you, and he's totally down to earth. I wish there were more guys like him around." Charlene took a big sip of her wine. It tasted cold and tangy on her tongue.

"Don't be glum. You're going to catch someone someday. And it will happen when you least expect it. Just look at what happened with Grant and me."

"Actually, there is one guy who fits the bill. But he's my boss."

"You need to give up on Dr. Dave." Amanda's face sobered. It wouldn't be the first time that best friends had a difference of opinion about a man.

"Why?" Charlene asked.

"Because if it hasn't happened yet between you and Dave, it's never going to."

"You're probably right," Charlene said. "The truth is I no longer believe Prince Charming is ever going to waltz into my life when I least expect him. The clock is ticking, and pretty soon what's left of me won't be worth much. According to my master plan, I was supposed to find Mr. Right and have a few babies *before* I turned thirty."

Of course, she had made those plans as a nineteen-year-old, on that horrible day when she'd done what her parents wanted. She had told herself that there would be other babies for her. She had told herself that Derrick could never be Mr. Right—not if Daddy was able to buy him off so easily.

She'd been patient all these years. Looking for the love of her life. But he'd eluded her. And she'd finally come to realize that she had a weakness for guys who either couldn't commit or, like Dave, were beyond her reach.

"Honey, life has some wild twists and turns in it sometimes. I didn't expect to lose Tom or be a single mom for such a long time. And I sure didn't expect to find Grant the way I did. You just have to keep on being patient."

"Yeah." Charlene took another sip of the wine she shouldn't have ordered because it wasn't on her diet. She stared through the big windows at Palmetto Avenue. Her life had not gone the way she'd expected it.

Amanda leaned in and spoke forcefully. "I can see exactly where your mind is wandering off to. Stop it right now. We're not going to dwell on the past. So I'm changing the subject. What's the scoop on your new neighbor? The Methodists are in an uproar."

Great. She didn't want to discuss Mike Taggart. Sabina's comments about him last Thursday had wormed into her brain, making her second-guess herself. And every time she saw Rainbow, all her deep-down maternal urges came roaring through. She'd seen the little girl a couple of times, going and coming from the apartment next door.

There had been no further tantrums. Aside from Rainbow's crazy, wild hairdo and the fact that the child rarely smiled and never laughed, she seemed to be well cared for.

"I don't know the scoop on Mike Taggart. And I really don't want to talk about him."

"Whoa! What's the deal?"

"I'm not a busybody like Aunt Millie."

"Don't BS me."

Charlene put her wine glass down and stared at the

daisies in the center of the table. "The little girl—his niece, Rainbow—she's...so sad. And Mike Taggart is..." She didn't exactly know how to explain Mike. He gave off serious bad-boy vibes.° She'd been convinced he didn't care about the child. But Sabina had helped her see a different side of him. He had certainly managed to charm the Methodist church ladies.

"What?" Amanda asked in a whisper, pulling Charlene back into the conversation.

"I don't know. The other morning I saw him carrying the little girl over his shoulder while she threw a temper tantrum. It was an ugly scene."

Amanda gave her one of those best-friend stares before she said, "Obviously you're not a parent. Just remember you can't always judge a parent by the behavior of their child. Sometimes hauling a kid over your shoulder is the only damn way to get them into their car seat." Amanda had a five-year-old son named Ethan who had been born a few months after his daddy had been killed in Afghanistan, so Amanda knew the ins and outs of parenthood.

"It certainly looked like he was abusing her," Charlene said. "But then I heard the Altar Guild is completely down with his plan to hand the little girl off to Pastor Tim. In fact, they have gone into a matchmaking tizzy, and they've even enlisted Mike's help. Sabina told me that he went down to the antiques mall and practically interviewed her for the job of mother."

Amanda giggled. "He sounds kind of sweet."

"Believe me, there is nothing sweet about Mike Taggart."

"How old is Rainbow?"

"Five maybe. She's of mixed race," Charlene added as an afterthought and immediately regretted her words.

Amanda leaned forward, an avid look on her face. "Ah, I see. She's gotten to you, hasn't she?"

Charlene shrugged. "I guess."

"There's no guessing about it."

"Okay, I'll accept that. But it doesn't change the fact that I feel like the little girl is in trouble. I want to do something to help her. But I have no clue. And thinking about helping her has me kind of scared."

"Scared?"

"I don't know a thing about kids. What makes me think I could help this little girl? And besides, we both know the reason I want to help is all screwed up to begin with." Charlene looked out the window and clamped her back teeth together. She'd already said too much.

Amanda had the good sense not to say a single word. Instead she reached out and patted Charlene's hand. Amanda knew all of her secrets. They had been friends since grade school.

"I need to do something," Charlene said. "But what? I mean, I'm not the kind of person who brings over a cake or a pie. And I wouldn't want him to think I was flirting with him, because I heard that he's a professional gambler, and I'm sure money is the only thing he worships. I've sworn off guys like that."

"Guys like Derrick?"

Charlene gave her best friend a sober stare. "Yes. And Phillip the stockbroker from Charleston, and John the real estate lawyer from Atlanta, and Erik the plastic surgeon from Columbia."

"Good girl. It's important to learn from your failures."

"And there are so many."

"So this has nothing to do with the guy. It's all about the kid, right?" Amanda asked.

"I guess. I feel this compulsion to get involved. It's probably some deep-seated guilt."

"Probably."

"So I should stay away?"

"You won't, Charlene."

"But what should I do?"

"Take her a present. It sounds like she's had a pretty rough time of it. She deserves a little present."

"Like what? I have no idea what a little girl might want."

"Pete the Cat."

"What?"

"It's a book. Just go to Flights of Fancy Bookstore in Allenberg and ask them about it. Get them to teach you the song that goes with it. It's a book about a cat that doesn't let anything bother him. He's cool and adaptable. The book has a wonderful message about going with the flow. Maybe it will help the little girl. And it will probably get you through the door and give you an opportunity to read to her. You can tell a lot about what's going on with a kid if you read to them. And I think you need to do it for yourself, as much as for her."

"But it's not my place."

"Of course it is. It takes a village to raise a child," Amanda said, flashing her dimples.

"I want to."

"Of course you do. And you should. She needs a friend, and you need to channel your guilt into something worthwhile."

"I do?"

Amanda laughed and waved her hand at the waitress. "Yeah, you do. Trust me. So let's get the check, and I'll take you to the bookstore myself. You'll love this book the minute you read it."

And with that, Amanda took charge of Charlene's life.

CHAPTER 7

Mike discovered the playground at the elementary school on his way back from the BI-LO. It had a spiral slide, a crawl tube, a bunch of climbing structures, and a big sandbox. Rainbow didn't like the crawl tube, but she took to the sandbox. They spent several hours there on Friday. On Saturday he purchased a bunch of inexpensive sand toys at Dollar General, and Rainbow spent most of the afternoon making a sand castle with a little help from Timmy, who joined them in the afternoon.

The playground was deserted, which suited everyone. Mike didn't want to end up chatting with a bunch of young mothers. Timmy seemed a little stiff and uncomfortable playing with the sand toys. And Rainbow didn't talk, so she was probably better off without a bunch of kids around her.

"I've hired a private investigator," Timmy said as he dusted sand from his pants. He left Rainbow and sat with Mike on a bench. "You should know that Andrea insisted upon it. She wants to make sure that Rainbow is in a safe situation."

"Andrea?"

"Dr. Newsome."

"Does she think I'm abusing Rainbow?"

Tim pressed his hands together and hesitated just a moment before he spoke again. "She just wants to make sure Rainbow is safe, Mike. For what it's worth, I know you're not abusing her. Andrea wants to meet with you next week."

"Okay. Did you raise the issue of the cat? Did she have any ideas about how we should handle that?"

"She dismissed it as not important right now. She said we needed to give Rainbow a stable situation." Timmy paused a moment as if gathering his thoughts. "Mike, the truth is, I took a look at the family photo albums, and there aren't any pictures of me before the age of about three. I'm not going to be surprised if the investigator comes back and verifies your story. So I think we need to think about finding Tigger a new home."

Mike said nothing. The sudden pressure on his chest made speaking impossible. It suddenly occurred to him that, after all these years, he'd finally found his little brother. And Angie's death might prove to be the catalyst that brought them back together. He might find a family here in Timmy.

And that scared the crap out of him at the same time that he longed for it with all his heart. He'd left behind the small, vulnerable kid he'd once been. He'd slammed the door on him. He'd pushed his pain way down deep. He didn't want to drag it all back out again.

But reconnecting with Timmy would require it. If

Timmy took Rainbow, would Mike be able to walk away from both of them?

Damn.

"I'll see what I can do about the cat," Mike said. Focusing on the cat meant he didn't have to take this conversation to any kind of emotional place.

Except Timmy had other ideas. "So," his brother said on a long breath, "tell me about us as kids."

"You were adorable," Mike managed through his tight throat. "Daddy would take you to the grocery store and everyone would ooh and aah over you. Not me. I was the red-headed stepchild. Literally."

Timmy said nothing. He got the message. They sat there quietly for the next two minutes, and then his little brother got up and went back to the sandbox.

Thank God. It took Mike a good ten minutes to get his heart rate back to normal. He didn't want to drag out these memories, and he wouldn't.

He could hand Rainbow off to Timmy, and they could make some new memories. And he'd go back to Vegas and sign a deal with Dragon Casinos.

Timmy and Mike skirted the minefield of their childhood for the rest of the day, even when Timmy suggested dinner at a barbecue joint called the Red Hot Pig Place. The place was pretty busy, and they got a lot of stares from the other customers, no doubt wondering what two white guys were doing with a kid like Rainbow. Or maybe the people there were Timmy's congregants. It didn't matter.

They got stared at.

To say they all enjoyed dinner would be to exaggerate. Timmy and Mike chowed down on some really good barbecue. Rainbow tried one hush puppy and turned her nose up at the rest.

It was almost Rainbow's bedtime by the time they got back to the apartment. But she needed a bath, because she had sand everywhere. And, of course, she wanted to bring Tigger into the tub with her like a rubber ducky. Tigger wanted no part of that. So the day ended with another battle royale.

And then Mike screwed up and got soap in Rainbow's eye when he washed her hair. And when a lot of Rainbow's hair fell out when he rinsed, Mike kind of freaked. This was what came of feeding her nothing but pizza.

But that's exactly what he planned to do before putting her to bed. He got her dressed in her new Dora the Explorer PJs and let her watch crap on the Cartoon Network while he headed for the kitchen.

The kid needed someone competent to take care of her. After watching Timmy play with her today, Mike had concluded that his brother was as clueless about kids as Mike himself.

Rainbow needed a mother. Which meant Timmy needed a wife.

And Sabina Grey wasn't the right choice. The antiques dealer wanted no part of any kind of relationship with Timmy. And Timmy didn't seem all that interested in Sabina.

He would need to compile a list of the single women in town and check them out. He was standing in the kitchen nuking a slice of frozen pizza and thinking about how to approach this subject with Elsie when the doorbell rang.

Boy, Elsie was good. She must have ESP or something.

He strode to the door and opened it, prepared for an onslaught of church lady nosiness.

Oops, wrong busybody. The cute one with the amazing rack stood on his threshold looking like a wholesome take on a Vegas showgirl. Gone were the muddy jeans and smelly boots, traded in on a sundress that showed off her shoulders. And, wow, they had adorable freckles.

What had happened? Up until this moment, the only shoulders he'd seen on Dr. Charlene Polk had been cold ones.

"What?" he said, forcing himself to be abrupt. He knew a lot of babes with cute shoulders. He could resist.

"Um, well, uh, I brought a couple of things, you know, toys and books. For Rainbow."

He noticed the yellow shopping bag with the words "Flights of Fancy Bookstore" on its side. Okay, he'd figured it out. She had decided to employ subterfuge to check up on him. He wanted to tell her to take her books and toys and boobs and go bother someone else.

But then he figured Rainbow probably had never been given a book in her short life. At least not a new one bought just for her. So, for the kid's sake, he relented.

"Come on in. She's watching TV."

He backed away from the door. Dr. Polk hesitated for a moment on the threshold, eyeing his wet shirt. "What happened to you?"

"Bath time," he muttered. "Can I get you anything? I've got Cokes and beer in the fridge."

"That sounds about right," she muttered as she crossed the room and sat down next to the little girl.

The demon cat came over to investigate the moment Charlene sat down.

"Watch out, she scratches," he said.

Charlene gave him one of those female looks, like she knew what she was doing and he should just butt out. Which, he supposed, was fair since she was a vet. And besides, Tigger seemed to be bonding with her. Kind of the way she'd bonded with Elsie the other day.

Of course that had ended badly. But she'd been warned.

Mike headed back to the kitchen just as the microwave timer dinged.

He pulled the pizza out of the oven and fixed a tray for the kid, with the pizza and a glass of milk. He brought the tray to the threshold of the living room and got no farther.

Dr. Charlene Polk had switched off the television. Rainbow, Tigger, and Charlene were all snuggled up together, and the cute vet was reading from a bright yellow book with a goofy-looking blue cat on the cover. The story was all about a cat with a new pair of tennis shoes walking down the street singing a song. "*I love my white shoes. I love my white shoes. I love my white shoes.*" Dr. Polk sang the stupid, repetitive song and started to sway with her upper body. So naturally Mike got sidetracked watching the doctor's chest. He was so mesmerized that he almost missed the fact that Rainbow was moving to the song, too. Tigger was not.

In fact, Tigger seemed to be offended by the entire scenario. She left Charlene's lap and walked her majestic self back into the bedroom.

Mike, on the other hand, stood there enjoying the floor show as Charlene read all about Pete the Cat's adventures as he walked through berries and mud and water, changing the color of his shoes each time. When the story ended, Rainbow spoke for the first time in two weeks.

"Again."

Something clutched at his insides. He could hardly draw breath as Charlene read the book again. And again. And again.

Then it hit him like a ton of bricks. Dr. Polk worked with animals. She had a knack for reaching out to those who couldn't speak. He could almost see the way her touch healed Rainbow. Not just the words from the book, but the way she looked at the kid, the way she wrapped her arm around her.

Rainbow felt safe with Charlene.

Mike checked out Charlene's hands. No wedding or engagement rings. He hadn't seen any boyfriends hanging out at her place, not that he'd been looking. She gave off wholesome, single-girl vibes, but with a seriously hot body.

She'd be perfect for Timmy.

Charlene read *Pete the Cat* half a dozen times, enjoying the way Rainbow's head snuggled against her shoulder. And she loved the way Rainbow smelled—like freshly bathed little girl. As the child's head got heavier against her shoulder, warm, seductive feelings crept deep into her heart.

She should run away from this. It said more about the unresolved issues from her life than it did about Rainbow's problems, or Mike's skills as a child-care provider. From all she could see, Mike was doing the best he could to take care of a child who had lost her parents.

The apartment was cleaner by far than her own place. The living room looked freshly vacuumed, which was a huge improvement over the way Martha kept the place.

You couldn't step into Martha's house without picking up cat hair. But not now, with Mike in residence. And Rainbow was clean, too, and dressed in appropriate PJs.

Just then, Mike entered the living room with a tray bearing a piece of pizza and a glass of milk. "It's time to eat," he said. "Give Dr. Polk a chance to rest her voice." He said it kindly and brought the tray into the living room, where he placed it on the coffee table.

It wasn't the most well-balanced meal. And he'd served it in front of the television. But letting a kid eat pizza on a tray didn't seem like a crime. Parents all over the country let their kids eat pizza without any vegetables. And hadn't he told her that Rainbow only wanted pizza, and the little girl had been traumatized? So really, pizza seemed like a silly thing to hassle him about.

Rainbow picked up the TV remote and turned the set on before she fell on her pizza like a starving waif. The Cartoon Network flickered to life with a garishly painted animated show featuring a character named Uncle Grandpa who was kind of gross and inappropriate for a child Rainbow's age. Charlene wanted to suggest that Mike turn on the Disney Channel instead, but she had already overstepped her boundaries.

She needed to make a truce with her neighbor. She needed to recognize the truth. She'd come here because Rainbow drew her like a blooming wisteria attracts honey bees. And not really because of any other reason.

She pushed up from the sofa. "I should be going." She awkwardly pointed over her shoulder toward the front door.

"You sure you don't want a beer or something?"

"No. No, thanks." She headed for the door.

Mike followed her. "Thanks for the book, and for reading to Rainbow. She hasn't said one word in almost two weeks. You managed to break her silence. I'm grateful. Really. You can come read to her anytime."

Charlene turned around, putting the door behind her. She needed to back off. Rainbow would move on with Mike, or stay and become Pastor Tim's child. Charlene didn't factor in either scenario at all.

So she drew herself up and looked Mike in the eye. "You can read to her anytime. Have you ever tried?"

Red crept up his neck and merged with the fiery stubble on his cheeks. She had to stomp on the sudden urge to touch that stubble, to feel the warmth of his skin. She couldn't deny the truth. She found him almost irresistible.

"Busted," he said, pulling her back from her suddenly raging libido. "You're right, Dr. Polk. I haven't read to her. I don't even have any kids' books here. So I appreciate your thoughtfulness. And please, do not hesitate to make suggestions. I don't pretend to know a damn thing about kids. I'm a gambler, not a father figure. And I sure do wish folks would quit blaming me for who I am."

"I haven't done that, have I?" She said the words before she thought about them.

"No, actually you haven't. You've blamed me for being something that I'm not." He said this with the slightest tilt to his mouth.

He was right. She had thought the worst of him. "I guess that's fair. I'm sorry. I just don't understand how you could walk away from her." Except that she could imagine. Hadn't she walked away from a child once?

"I have no intention of walking away. I intend to find her the best possible family. And while we're clearing the air, you should know that I intend to put aside a portion of my winnings for her, so that she wants for nothing in the future. I used to send her mother money, but I figure Angie probably used it to buy drugs. With Rainbow, the money is going into a trust, and I'll make Timmy the trustee."

"Money can't buy love," she said.

"I actually know that, Dr. Polk. That's why I'm here. I can support her, but I can't give her what she needs. I need good-hearted people like you and Timmy to take care of loving her. I'm no damn good at that sort of thing."

Charlene opened her mouth to argue, but what could she say?

She couldn't quibble with his goals. They were noble in their own way. And you couldn't argue someone into love. Love had to be nurtured. You either felt it or you didn't. And if Mike didn't love Rainbow, then he had no business raising her or caring for her.

Charlene ought to go. Now. But she seemed to be stuck there, looking up into his blue, blue eyes. Something needy and terribly sad flickered in the depths of that deep, blue gaze. And it occurred to her that Rainbow might not be the only person in this apartment who needed love.

"So," Mike finally said into that awkward moment, "I think it would be terrific if you came by to read to her. She really likes you. I think you make her feel safe."

And just like that Charlene knew she'd allowed herself to be sucked into a situation that would, eventually, shatter her heart.

CHAPTER 8

On Sunday afternoon Charlene rushed up the steps to the classic portico of her parents' Greek revival home. She was a half-hour late to her daddy's birthday party, and she'd missed church entirely, all because one of George Nelson's milk cows had come down with mastitis.

She'd had to rush out to the farm early this morning, make her diagnosis, prescribe the antibiotics, inspect his milking equipment, and quarantine two additional cows.

No one could argue about her excuses today, but her parents would still find a way to say something ugly and hurtful to her. They didn't understand her passion for farm animals.

They wanted her to marry someone like John, the real estate lawyer who had actually proposed to her two years ago. But John wanted her to move to Atlanta, give up her practice, and be happy spending his money on decorating and redecorating his large monstrosity of a house.

She had tried to change John. She had failed. And when she refused his marriage proposal, Mother and Daddy had both had conniptions.

They didn't understand her. They never had.

"There you are, at last. We were starting to think you were planning to boycott," Mother said as Charlene made her way into the formal front parlor. Mother gave her an air-kiss. Heaven help her if she actually deigned to kiss Charlene on the cheek like a normal mother. Charlene smelled the wine on Mother's breath.

Daddy stood by the fireplace, bourbon in hand, talking to Uncle Rob. The brothers looked like a couple of bookends dressed in their dark gray business suits.

Aunt Millie, Uncle Rob's wife, played peek-a-boo down on the carpet with her grandson, Upton Lockheart, Cousin Rachel's seven-month-old. The dark-haired child drooled all over Mother's priceless Persian rug, but luckily Mother was riding her Riesling-high and didn't notice.

"I need to speak with you," Daddy said, turning away from Uncle Rob.

Uh-oh. Charlene knew that tone of voice. He crossed the carpet on his highly polished wing tips, effectively blocking her path to the bar, where Cousin Simon hung out with the other male cousins, Bubba and Drew. Molly and Rachel sat together on the couch cooing over Valerie, Simon's three-month-old daughter.

Charlene wished she could teleport herself over to the bar. Like Mother, she suddenly needed a little pick-me-up.

"Drew tells me that you've been all over town, trying to sign people up for this ridiculous auction," Daddy said. "I gather he's agreed, and I've been trying to get Rob and Millie to put their feet down on this issue. It's embarrassing to have one of my nephews participating in something like this. And I have to say, Charlene, that I'm disappointed in you for running around town trying to sign up unmarried men." His disappointment didn't surprise Charlene one bit. She had never, ever made him happy. Not once.

"Sorry, Daddy," she said in her best phony-contrite voice.

Unfortunately Daddy knew all her tricks. "Do not take that tone of voice with me, Charlene. I deserve respect."

She worked hard not to roll her eyes. "Yes, sir," she said, investing the honorific with as much irony as she could muster.

"You and Drew will not participate in any auction that involves selling human beings, is that clear?"

"Gee, Daddy, you make it sound like we've brought back slavery to the new South. It's just a fund-raiser. And since I'm a vet and a member of AARC's board, I'm doing more than participating. I'm *organizing*. As for Drew, he's already signed his papers and given me his promise, so I think that ship has sailed." She looked past her father to her cousin Drew, who grinned back at her. He raised his beer in her direction and gave her a wink and a beery salute.

He had really grown up and filled out the last couple of years. He bore the unmistakable brown eyes and dark hair of the Polk clan. Like Cousin Simon, he kept his hair a tad too long for convention. And he had chosen not to wear a suit.

Yeah, Drew looked like a Polk, but he was his mother's child, kind to a fault and slightly rebellious. Some lucky lady was going to buy him on June fourteenth, and he would probably woo her by singing sweet love songs to her. The boy had been busking his way through Europe for the last year and a half.

Daddy took a big gulp of his bourbon. The ice in his glass rattled. "The entire concept is tacky and... obscene."

"No, it isn't. Don't be dramatic."

"Charlene, honey, don't disrespect your father," Mother said.

Charlene ignored her mother. She always took Daddy's side. Not once had Mother ever come to Charlene's defense, even when she'd needed it most. "Daddy, nonprofits hold bachelor auctions all the time. It's a fun way to raise money for the animal shelter. It's not all that different from what Christ Church does at the Watermelon Festival when they sell kisses. I manned the kissing booth any number of times over the years, and you never objected. Not once."

Charlene pivoted slightly and cast her gaze to Cousin Simon at the bar. "Hey Simon, could you pour me a glass of what Mother's drinking, please?"

"Coming right up," Simon said.

She turned back toward Daddy. "I'm sorry you're unhappy about the fund-raiser, but I'm committed to helping AARC raise money for the shelter. The Allenberg shelter is pitiful."

"I am well aware of that. But Dennis Hayden has a perfectly rational plan for dealing with the animal shelter that will achieve economies of scale."

She folded her arms across her chest. "Economies of scale? Is that what you call it?"

"The county executive's plan will mean fewer burdens on the taxpayers."

"It also means more animals euthanized. And I'm not a fan of euthanizing animals. But we all know you have a different point of view, don't you?" She tried to bite back her anger. But old grudges seemed to be surfacing. No doubt the appearance of Rainbow Taggart had opened the door to old wounds. Charlene needed to take a deep breath and regain her self-control.

"There are too many stray animals," Daddy said. "And it's not right to make taxpayers bear the burden of bad decisions made by pet owners. And you, of all people, should recognize that, in this county, the only animals that matter are the large ones. Dash Randall's horses and George Nelson's milk cows. You—"

"If you don't want me to work on signing up bachelors then make a contribution to AARC. I'm thinking a couple of thousand dollars should do it. That's equal to the donation we get every year from Dash Randall."

"I will make no such contribution. AARC is misguided. We need to close the shelter. It's the only economically sound decision."

"I guess we'll just have to agree to disagree, okay? Now, if you don't mind, I'd like to go visit with Valerie."

"I do mind. You are not going to participate in a man auction. I will not have you making a laughingstock of our family by buying some man for obscene purposes. You've already shown a decided lack of propriety in your private life."

Finally they had reached the nub of the problem.

Daddy never failed to bring up Charlene's big mistake and subsequent love affairs. If they were arguing, it would always come down to Charlene's "lack of propriety," which was a big, fat euphemism for the fact that she'd gotten pregnant when she was nineteen.

And the boy she loved was not white.

When would Daddy forgive her for that sin? Shoot, when would she forgive herself? Not anytime soon, apparently.

She raised her chin and stared Daddy right in the eye. "We're auctioning off dinner with a single man. It's more wholesome than the kissing booth. So stay out of it, okay?"

"No, it's not okay. This has already generated a lot of malicious gossip, especially since it's the brainchild of Simon's assistant, who we all know is a pervert. You will not participate, is that clear?"

"I'm thirty-one years old. I make my own—"

Simon interrupted. "Uncle Ryan, I'm going to butt in. I take exception to you calling Angel a pervert."

Holy God, this had gotten really out of hand if Simon felt the need to butt in. But Angel Menendez was Simon's friend in addition to being his employee.

Dad's face began to turn red. "You should fire that man. I don't like the fact that he's Charlotte's main caregiver. I can point out sections of the Bible that—"

Simon held up his hand. "Don't quote the Bible. I've heard it before. I'm just saying that if you quit spouting scripture and look at what Angel does every day for Mother you might change your mind. Angel is a kind, good, talented person. Mother likes him. And you, Uncle Ryan, have your head up your butt."

Simon delivered his speech and Charlene's wine glass, then sauntered back across the room to where his wife and Cousin Rachel were sitting. Each of them looked utterly dumbfounded at what Simon had said.

"Daddy, let's drop it, okay?"

"You participate in this obscene fund-raiser, and I'll—"

"For heaven's sake, Ryan, please." Aunt Millie cut Daddy off before he said something ugly. Millie stood, scooping up the baby with her. She balanced Upton on her hip and stepped between Charlene and her father. "It's a birthday party, y'all. Let's not argue. And Ryan, don't make threats you don't mean."

Thank goodness Millie didn't mention the one time when Daddy *had* threatened to cut Charlene off. Charlene had believed that threat. She'd been all of nineteen, and she'd taken the coward's way out. She should have followed Cousin Simon's lead and walked away from her mother and father when they'd bullied her.

Simon had stayed away for eighteen years. But she lacked her cousin's courage. She couldn't imagine living anywhere except Last Chance. Although, to be truthful, she had sustained her rebellion against them for years and years. She almost enjoyed annoying them now. Which wasn't very mature.

Especially since she loved them, warts and all. She wanted them to love her back, without making that love conditional on her staying in line and doing as they bid.

"Happy birthday, Daddy," Charlene said in her most contrite voice, getting up on tiptoes and giving him a quick peck on the cheek. She pulled her peace offering out of her purse. "Here, I found you a terrific present."

She handed him the wrapped pen, which he immediately handed off to Mother. "Put this with the others," he commanded, and Mother did as she was told. He drained his bourbon, turned on his heel, and headed off to the bar for another one.

On Monday morning, Mike got Rainbow up at seven in the morning, fed her the obligatory cold pizza, and got her ready for her first day at summer camp.

He had learned that the kid had trouble making transitions from one thing to the next. And leaving the house was hard for her. Rainbow hated being separated from her cat.

So Mike had been telling her all weekend that summer camp started on Monday and that she couldn't bring Tigger. This morning he used another trick that had worked on Friday and Saturday. He'd found an old-fashioned egg timer in Miss Spalding's kitchen. He set it for ten minutes and told Rainbow that she had until the timer chimed to say good-bye to Tigger.

When the timer went off, she complained but she didn't throw a tantrum. So, when they ran into Dr. Polk on the landing, Rainbow behaved like an angel.

This time, Charlene gave Rainbow a big, wide smile, and the kid almost returned it. Charlene squatted down and asked Rainbow where she was heading so early in the morning. Rainbow surprised the crap out of Mike by saying the words. "Summer camp."

Mike's insides melted. This moment made everything crystal clear. Rainbow needed Charlene. Now, if he could just figure out a way to make Charlene fall in love with Timmy it would be perfect.

Charlene stood up and Mike's warm, melty feelings morphed into something else entirely. Today the curvy vet wore a pair of tight jeans and a little T-shirt and her big rubber boots. The boots were clean this morning.

For some reason he couldn't quite fathom, she looked hotter than a chili in that outfit. But these work clothes also conveyed a sense of quiet competence. She had a refreshingly pure and genuine aura about her. You didn't find women like this on the Vegas Strip.

"Good morning," he said in a friendly voice, resolving to undo the damage he'd done the last few days. She'd definitely poked him in his most vulnerable spot with her questions and her suspicions when they first met. But he needed to get over that. She had a big heart—the kind that could give Rainbow everything she needed.

"Morning," she said. An awkward silence stretched out for several seconds. He should retreat now, before he said something stupid.

"Okay, kiddo, we gotta go," he said as he gave Rainbow's shoulder a little squeeze. "Summer camp awaits."

"Have fun, sweetie," Charlene said.

Rainbow shrugged away Mike's hand and rushed to Charlene. The hug lasted mere seconds before the kid turned away and skipped down the rest of the stairs.

"Hey, kiddo, wait for me before you cross the parking

lot," Mike said as he followed after Rainbow. He looked over his shoulder for an instant. "Have a nice day," he said to Charlene. It was lame, but it wasn't hostile so he counted it as progress.

Fifteen minutes later, he and Rainbow arrived at the Methodist church only to find things on the chaotic side. There were kids everywhere, ranging in age from five to twelve, and all of them seemed to have arrived before Mike and Rainbow. The sheer number of campers immediately overwhelmed Rainbow. She leaned into him and clung against his side.

Mike figured Rainbow had never been in day care, and she was too young for kindergarten. So this situation had to be pretty scary, especially since she didn't know a single soul.

They were directed to one of the Sunday school classrooms filled with nine five-year-olds. The minute they walked into the room, Rainbow must have realized that Mike intended to leave her there, so the clinging intensified. She wrapped herself around Mike's legs and wouldn't let go.

That same strange melty feeling assaulted his gut. He pried her arms from around his legs and left her crying in her awful, silent way. He was a louse and a jerk and had no business taking care of a kid.

He might have rethought the whole summer camp thing right there except that the camp counselor, who looked like a teenager, told him that Rainbow would be fine. But leaving her there made him feel like crap. And even when he got back to the apartment and fired up his computer to get in some day trading, the look on Rainbow's face haunted him.

He struggled not to make comparisons between Rainbow and Angie. But he failed.

He had wanted to stay with Angie, too. But Richard, Mom's boyfriend of the moment, had been a mean son-ofabitch. Mike had to get out. He'd chosen to save himself, instead of his little sister.

He would have to live with that for the rest of his life.

He set up his laptop on the kitchen table and tried to get some work done. He had an email from Rachel Sanger, Rainbow's caseworker in Chicago. She let him know that a private investigator had given her a call. Apparently the guy was working for Timmy and checking out Mike and Rainbow's story. So that was a good thing. Timmy was coming around.

Ms. Sanger also told him that she was trying to solve the mystery of the telephone number on Tigger's name tag. Mike didn't care one way or another about Tigger's past. But Ms. Sanger was a cat lover and seemed all concerned that someone in Chicago was missing their pet.

He looked at the cat, who had made herself comfortable on the tabletop where he'd set up his computer. "You're a lucky cat," he said. She gave him a strange, half-lidded stare.

If he lived to be a hundred, Mike was never, ever going to be a cat person. Especially after the demon animal spent the day right beside him giving him the feline equivalent of the evil eye. The message was clear. Tigger didn't like him. Not one bit.

The U.S. markets closed at four p.m., and he decided to call it a day. It was time to get to work on his plan to match up Timmy and Charlene. And the first thing he needed was information.

And what better place to begin his research than the Kountry Kitchen café? In his experience, the waitresses at local cafés always had the straight skinny on everything. Besides, he could go for a cup of coffee and a slice of pie.

Fifteen minutes later, he found himself seated at the lunch counter, where Flo, the waitress, greeted him bearing a coffee urn and a crockery mug.

"Hey, there, Mike. You want coffee?" She gave him a big smile and batted her eyes. He and Flo had hit it off almost from the moment he had entered the café on Friday afternoon. Of course the Kountry Kitchen didn't serve pizza, so Rainbow went hungry that lunchtime. But Mike had enjoyed a pretty good barbecue sandwich. Not to mention the coffee and pie.

Mike had honed his waitress-flirting skills on the Vegas Strip. He put them to good use now. "Bring it on, Flo."

Flo giggled like a girl as she poured his coffee. "I declare, Mike, you're like a breath of fresh air."

"Thanks, but I think Last Chance has more fresh air than any other place I've ever been."

"You probably have that right. I'm sure our air is fresher than Vegas. But folks around here get into an awful rut. And you don't strike me as that kind. Besides, I always did have a weakness for ramblers and gamblers, if you know what I mean."

"Uh-huh, I know."

"So I heard Rainbow is at summer camp today."

He shook his head in wonder. "Now how did you know that?"

"Because Elsie Campbell and the gals from the Altar

Guild were in here this morning, and Pastor Tim and Rainbow have become their main topic of conversation. I heard she's going to counseling with Dr. Newsome, too."

"There isn't much you don't know, is there?"

"I'm not really a gossip, you know," she said in a near whisper. "It's just an occupational hazard that I end up hearing stuff. How's it going with Rainbow? She eating anything?"

"She eats pizza, and that's it. I've tried hamburgers, barbecue, chicken nuggets, and French fries. But all she'll eat is pizza. Things are getting better, though. Charlene Polk came by on Saturday night and read her a story. Rainbow spoke to Charlene that night. Just a word or two. And she said something this morning."

Flo leaned her hip into the counter. "Charlene is a sweetie."

He had Flo thinking exactly what he wanted her to think. And if he didn't say anything else, Flo would probably tell the world that Charlene had come over to his house on Saturday night. And that would get the church ladies going in entirely the wrong direction. But, oddly, this was exactly the opening he needed to begin his matchmaking campaign. "Flo," he said in his most earnest voice, "I need your advice."

Flo leaned a little closer, no doubt expecting him to admit that he had the hots for the shapely little vet, which was sort of true, but he planned to ignore that.

"What is it, honey?" Flo asked.

"I was thinking that Timmy is single and Charlene is single and, well…I feel as if the two of them would be perfect parents for Rainbow. The truth is Dr. Polk seems to have bonded with the kid, you know?"

"Really?" The surprised look on her face was priceless. But the hook was set.

"She has," Mike said in an earnest tone. "She even made Rainbow smile. I've been with the kid for days, and she hasn't smiled once for me. I'm no good at parenting, Flo. I think Charlene would be great at it."

"I'm sure Charlene will make a fine mother one day. But, honey, I hate to disappoint you. It will be a cold day in July when Charlene Polk and Reverend Tim Lake get together."

"Really? Why?"

"Because she's an Episcopalian and he's a Methodist."

It was as if Flo had pulled a fifth ace out of her sleeve. "Flo, aren't those two Christian denominations?"

"I guess, but the Methodists are a whole lot more Protestant than the Episcopalians are."

He frowned.

The waitress leaned a little closer. "Honey, in these parts people take their religion very seriously. It would be odd for the Methodist minister to marry an Episcopalian, although I imagine there would be fewer potential conflicts of interest if he were to court someone from another church. You see, it's usually considered bad form for a minister to actually date a member of his own church. Although I reckon Bill Ellis did that when he ran off with Hettie Marshall. But that was kind of different because those two never dated, you know. They just kind of danced around each other for a while."

Mike made no reply, because Flo had managed to confuse the crap out of him. Life in a small town was way more complex than he had first thought. Luckily, Flo didn't seem to care if she'd confused him. She carried on with her gossip.

"Of course, the Altar Guild members are in a real hot hurry to help your brother find a wife, but they are convinced that Sabina Grey is the woman for the job."

"I know. I've spoken with Elsie."

"Have you really?"

"Yes, I have. I've also spoken with Sabina, and I don't think that match is going to work. Besides, I need to think about Rainbow. And Rainbow really likes Charlene."

Flo gave him a long look. "I reckon it might work. But it would be mighty unusual." She paused for a moment as if gathering her breath. "If you really want to try to match up your brother with someone, you need to talk to Miriam Randall."

"Who's she?"

"The local matchmaker."

"You have a matchmaker? Isn't that a bit old-fashioned?"

"You see, Miriam isn't your regular kind of matchmaker. She's got some kind of supernatural gift or something. She can spot when two people belong together, like soulmates, you know?"

No, he didn't know, but that didn't matter. What mattered was what Flo believed. Perception was always reality; that's why he was so good at bluffing. "I never heard of such a thing," he said.

"It's true, every word. This town believes that whoever Miriam matches up stays matched forever. But it isn't always easy, you know, on account of the fact that she doesn't really match people; she just gives marital advice."

"Marital advice, what do you mean?"

Flo topped off Mike's coffee. "Miriam is sort of like a fortuneteller. I mean she'll tell folks what sort of person they should be looking for. Or sometimes she'll tell someone that their soulmate is coming on the nine-thirty bus from Atlanta. That's what she did with Clay and Jane."

"I see." But he didn't.

"So if you want to find out if Tim should be looking at Charlene, I suggest you pay Miriam a visit. She might be helpful. But you're going to have to do something about the denominational barrier. And then there's the fact that Charlene is sweet on Dr. Dave. And if she can persuade him to participate in the bachelor auction, she's probably going to buy him."

Uh-oh, that was a problem. Charlene had a boy-friend? "Uh, what's the bachelor auction you're talking about?"

"Oh that's a fund-raiser that the animal lovers in town are holding in a couple of weeks to benefit the Allenberg County Animal Shelter." She stepped back a pace. "And honey, I'm figuring it's only a matter of time before Angel or Wilma or Charlene ask you to donate an evening of your time."

"What?"

"You know, to be auctioned off for charity."

Before Mike could ask any further clarifying questions, a group of teens came through the front door, bringing a lot of noise and activity with them. Flo became a busy woman taking orders for milkshakes and cherry Cokes.

Mike had to leave the café to pick up Rainbow. So he didn't get another chance to question the waitress. It was okay, though. He had enough to begin his campaign. And the first step would be finding Miriam Randall.

• • •

During her lunch hour on Tuesday, Charlene stopped into the ladies' room and checked her hair and makeup. She looked fine. She stared at her face. Not exactly beauty queen material. She didn't have blonde hair. She didn't have blue eyes. She didn't have a skinny little body. She was tall and awkward. Not to mention the fact that button-up-the-front blouses always gapped across her chest.

Good thing the sweater she'd worn today didn't have buttons, just a relatively demure neckline. But still the sweater had drawn any number of glances from male pet owners. So much so that, after her ten o'clock appointment with Roy Burdett and his hound dog, she'd buttoned her white lab coat all the way to her neck.

But here she was unbuttoning it again and wondering if Dr. Dave would even notice.

It was now or never. Angel Menendez had called this morning thanking her for stiff-arming Cousin Drew into the bachelor auction. Then he reminded her that she was still on the hook for delivering a few more bachelors. So she figured she might as well get busy and ask Dr. Dave first.

She headed toward her boss's office and caught him at his desk reviewing financial statements. A bookkeeper came in twice a month to do the essentials, but Dave spent too much time on administrative stuff like this. Charlene and Cindy had told him a few times that he needed an office administrator, but he'd been resistant.

"Hi," she said as she arrived at his doorway.

He looked up with his brilliant blue eyes. His black hair fell over his forehead and every rational thought in

Charlene's head evaporated. How did he manage to make his hair do that little Superman curl? He was stunning. Gorgeous even.

He cleared his throat. "Is something up? How are George Nelson's cows?"

"Uh, they're recovering, and he's sanitized his milking equipment." She ventured a few more steps into his office and got as far as the side chair. She grabbed hold of the chair back, suddenly conscious of her sweaty palms. "I was wondering..."

"Yes."

"Well, I'm sure you know that AARC is planning this fund-raiser for June fourteenth and..."

A smile touched his perfect mouth. "Charlene, are you trying to ask me if I would agree to be auctioned off?"

Heat flamed up her cheeks. "Um, yeah, I guess." She paused for a horrible moment and then rushed ahead. "You see, it's for a good cause. You know that this plan of County Executive Hayden's is going to result in more animals being euthanized. And our bachelors are only committing to dinner with whoever buys them. And I know—"

He held up his hand, palm outward. "Stop. I'll do it."

"You will?"

"Only if you promise to buy me." He flashed his perfect dimple.

Good thing she was holding the chair back in a vise grip, because she experienced a dizzy moment and her knees almost gave out. "You want me to buy you? Really?" The words popped right out of her mouth before she could think about them. If she had taken a moment to actually think, those were not the words she would have said. She probably would have said something along the lines of "Of course I will. Where do you want to go to dinner?" But no, she didn't say that. She said the first stupid thing that crossed her mind.

Dave studied her for a moment, carefully avoiding any glances at her chest, and said, "I suppose you're right. That might be a bad idea."

"What's a bad idea? You being auctioned or me buying you and then..." There was no good place for this sentence to go, so she just shut up.

"Charlene, I'm happy to participate as one of the bachelors. But you're absolutely right. It would be a mistake for you to bid on me, since you're my employee and all. It would look odd, you know? Inappropriate. I didn't mean to suggest that at all. It's just that... well...I'm a little shy. But you should certainly not bid on me."

What the hell. Shy was not the word Charlene would have used. Dr. Dave was living the life of a freaking monk, probably because he was so scrupulously scrupled. Or maybe it was because he was a member of Calvary Baptist.

She needed to retreat before she did any more damage. "Thanks, Dave. The fund-raising committee will be thrilled to have you sign up. I'll email you the forms."

"You do that."

She stood there for a moment feasting her eyes on his beauty and mentally kicking herself for being such a dolt until he gave her the oddest look. Like he might be wondering if she'd lost her mind or something. Which she had. She turned and ran all the way to her office, where she closed the door and fired up her cell phone.

"I blew it," she semiwailed when Amanda answered her call.

"Blew what? Honey, are you all right?"

"I went into Dave's office and asked him to be one of the bachelors in the auction. And he said yes."

"That's good, I guess." Amanda didn't actually sound overjoyed by this news.

"You guess? Of course it's good."

"All right, it's good. So how did you blow it?"

"He said something about how he'd do it if I promised to buy him. And then I got all surprised. And he immediately backed off. And then he told me that he would participate but only if I promised *not* to bid on him. Since that would be unethical or something because he's my boss, you know? Damn, I'm such a dolt."

Amanda said nothing on the other end of the line for a long moment.

"Are you still there?"

"Yeah."

"How am I going to fix this?"

Another long silence stretched out before Amanda spoke again. "Charlene, honey, I have something I need to say. And I think you aren't going to like it. But I just want you to remember how you told me the truth that day last summer when I met Grant. You remember what you said?"

"No, not really."

"Well, you told me exactly what I needed to hear. So I'm going to return the favor. I'm not trying to be ugly, but it's high time you gave up this crush you have on Dr. Dave."

"But he's perfect, aside from the fact that he's my boss."

"Right. Charlene, he's too perfect, if you know what I mean."

"Too perfect? What's that supposed to mean?"

"It means he's gay. Deep-in-the-closet gay."

"No. How can that be? He belongs to Calvary Baptist."

"I know, it's strange. But I'd stake my life on it. I knew it the moment I met him."

"You're wrong, Amanda. You have to be." Although a little piece of her mind started making connections to the fact that Dave had never, ever ogled her boobs. Or any other part of her body. And even devout Baptists like Jimmy Carter had been known to lust in their hearts from time to time.

"I'm not wrong," Amanda said. "And I'm just a little bit worried that he might be one of those guys who try to deny it. You know, the guy who gets married even though he knows he's not straight. I wouldn't be a good friend if I didn't put my foot down and tell you what I thought. You need to give up on Dr. Dave and find someone else. And this auction may be just the thing you need. There will be a whole boatload of single men to choose from."

"But I don't want a boatload of single men. I want Dave."

"Yes, Charlene, I know. Everyone in town knows. But Dr. Dave is never going to want you back. And at the risk of making you angry, I need to say something else you need to hear. You have a knack for picking guys who aren't emotionally available. You seem to think you can fix them or something. It's time you found a guy without a boatload of baggage."

Amanda's words stunned Charlene so badly that she pulled the phone from her ear and pressed the off button. It was the first time, ever, that she'd hung up on her best friend.

CHAPTER 10

On Tuesday afternoon, after the markets closed, Mike went off in search of Miriam Randall. It didn't take him more than five minutes at Lovett's Hardware to discover the whereabouts of the mysterious matchmaker. The manager there, a big guy named Clay, was a font of information.

Mrs. Randall's house turned out to be a big, sprawling Victorian that was undergoing a major restoration. Its foundation sat on lolly columns, construction materials littered the lawn, and one side of the house was encased in a scaffold. A shirtless man perched up there, diligently scraping away dozens of layers of paint.

"Is this Miriam Randall's house?" Mike called up to him.

The man stopped scraping and stared down at Mike, his eyes shaded by a Houston Astros baseball cap. "Yep." He put down his scraper and descended. "I'm her nephew, Dash. You're that guy everyone in town is talking about, aren't you?"

"I have no clue about the gossip in town," Mike said, extending his hand. "I'm Mike Taggart. I understand your aunt is the town matchmaker."

Dash had an easy face to read. And right now the tiny smirk at the corners of his mouth made Mike wonder if he'd become the victim of a small-town prank. Dash cleared his throat. "Uh, you here for a professional consultation?"

Mike forced himself into his poker mode. "I am." His voice came out neutral.

"Really?" Dash's eyebrows rose. Clearly Mike's response had surprised the crap out of him.

"Is Mrs. Randall in?"

Dash tipped his hat back. "Yeah, she's in. I'll see if she's interested in visiting with anyone."

Just then a little old lady came through the front door, leaning on an aluminum cane. She had white hair piled up on her head in a couple of braids. She peered at them through a pair of rhinestone-studded glasses that looked as if they came right out of the 1950s. She wore baggy khakis and a purple T-shirt with a photo of a fluffy white cat on the front. "Dash, honey," she said with a scowl, "quit being ugly and invite the man up here. I've been expecting him."

"Well, I'll be," Dash said, shaking his head. "Guess it's your lucky day. You do know that once she matches you up, you're done for, right?"

Mike didn't respond to this rhetorical question. Instead, he strode across the weedy yard and up onto the porch. "I'm Mike Taggart," he said, extending his hand toward the little old lady.

Miriam gave him a surprisingly firm shake. Her hand

felt cool and dry. "I'm Miriam. Have a seat," she said, gesturing to one of the ladder-back porch rockers. "I do most of my consultations out here on the porch."

Thank goodness. After what Flo had told him, Mike had expected Miriam to lead him into a darkened room where she would consult her crystal ball. Not that he believed in any of that fortune-telling crap. But he knew one overriding truth: people were capable of believing anything, even stuff that was patently untrue or impossible. Emotions always trumped rationality. And a good gambler could use this to his benefit. If he played his cards right.

He took a seat in one of the rockers. "So you've been expecting me, huh?" he asked.

She sat down in a facing chair. She gave the appearance of being a sweet, harmless old lady. But that was a mask for something else. He got the feeling that this woman could con anyone.

"I have been," she said. "You might be surprised to know that I've been expecting you for quite some time."

"Then you know I'm here to see about finding a wife for my brother, Timmy. You'd know him as Reverend Lake, the Methodist minister. I was thinking that Charlene Polk would be perfect for him. But I'm at a loss as to how to get the two of them together."

Mrs. Randall turned away, casting her gaze toward the trees that screened the house from the sidewalk. She didn't say anything for a long, long time, and Mike wondered if she'd fallen asleep or something. Or maybe she had a wandering mind.

He was about to repeat his request when she turned back toward him and said, "So what makes you think Charlene Polk would be a good match for Pastor Tim?"

"I don't know, exactly. She seems like a nice person, and Tim needs a nice person." Had he ever said anything more lame? Probably not.

The old woman stared at him for another interminable moment, conveying the feeling that she could pierce even his emotional mask. He sure didn't ever want to face this woman across a poker table.

"Uh," he stammered, "and she's nice looking and has a great..." He didn't finish the sentence because telling the old woman that he admired Charlene's rack seemed way off topic.

"Yes, she most certainly does, doesn't she?" Mrs. Randall said, her dark black eyes sparking behind her trifocals.

"Yes, ma'am." He found himself nodding.

"Son, I'm sorry, but my matchmaking doesn't work exactly like you might think. I'm not like that character Barbra Streisand played in *Hello, Dolly!* I don't send people off on dates. And I'm sure not like those Internet places where people fill out personality questionnaires to find their compatible mates. I think love is more magical than that, don't you?"

"Uh, well..." He leaned back in his rocker and tried to relax. "I guess, um...to be honest, Mrs. Randall, I've never really thought all that much about it. I've never been in love."

"I'm not surprised," she said, staring off into space again.

"So, can you help me? It's real important that I find the right wife for Timmy because, whoever she is, she's going to become my niece's mother. You see, my sister was killed a few weeks ago, and I need to find a good home for my niece. I want her to grow up in a family with both a mom and a dad. You see, Charlene and Rainbow—that's my niece—have kind of bonded. I think she'd make a great mother."

"I'm sure Charlene would make a great mother. She's a big-hearted woman."

"That's good. I think every minister should have a big-hearted woman as a wife. Don't you?"

Mrs. Randall drummed her knobby-jointed fingers on the armrest of her rocking chair, while her brow wrinkled in thought. He took this as a positive sign.

"Son, are you an animal lover?"

"Uh, well, no, not especially. Does this have anything to do with Timmy and Charlene?"

She gave him a myopic kind of look and flashed her dentures. "That's a shame, really. Because the Allenberg Animal Rescue Council is hosting a man auction coming up on June fourteenth."

"I heard something about that from Flo. But what does this event have to do with Charlene and Timmy?"

"I'm just an old girl, you know, but I gather this auction is a newfangled fund-raising thing. AARC is asking single men to volunteer to be auctioned off. The proceeds of the auction go to funding AARC's efforts to keep our animal shelter going."

"So you think I should encourage Tim to be part of the auction? And then I could encourage Charlene to buy him?"

She shook her head. "I didn't say that. I'm just pointing out that a lot of interesting things could happen at an auction like that. The Lord works in mysterious ways, and I'd say that having a man auction in our town is a pretty significant event. It gives us an opportunity to help the Lord with his plans. You know?"

No, he didn't know. "The Lord has plans?"

"He most definitely does. And I can tell you right now that Pastor Lake is probably going to end up with someone in the medical profession."

"Really? That's great news."

She nodded. "It's always great news when young people find their soulmates. And here's the thing you need to keep in mind, son. That bachelor auction is like an intersection in the ebb and flow of the universe. It's like creating a point in time where we can help the Lord along by shoving things in the right direction. Sort of like a snowball rolling downhill. Not that I've ever seen any appreciable amount of snow, mind you."

"Right. The Lord," Mike said as if he agreed. In truth, his rational mind scoffed at the idea. Still, Mrs. Randall had given him enough advice to formulate a rational plan. Step one would be to get Tim to volunteer for this auction. Step two would be to convince Charlene to buy Tim.

With Mrs. Randall's endorsement of this plan, Mike had a shot at overcoming Tim and Charlene's natural resistance. Better yet, the Altar Guild would embrace this plan with both arms.

And hadn't Timmy said those women could move mountains?

"Thank you," he said with a little nod. "Your advice has been invaluable. What do I owe you for this consultation?"

She snorted a laugh. "Honey, my consultations are free. I'm only doing what the Lord wants me to do. It wouldn't be right to take money for it." Her dark eyes sparked with something. Was it amusement? He found her face impossible to read.

She leaned forward and patted his hand where it rested on the arm of his rocker. "You'll figure it out, son. You just need to remember that love is one of the safest bets you can make. Even when the odds appear to be a million to one."

Angel pulled his Jeep into the parking lot behind the Last Chance Knit & Stitch. The Purly Girls, the senior charity knitting group, met every Tuesday afternoon at the shop, and Simon's mother, Charlotte Wolfe, was an avid knitter. Angel's job required him to meet her at the shop and take her home afterward.

He usually got there on the early side in order to help Pat Canaday, the shop's owner, with the old ladies who were members of the Purly Girls. Since he loved to knit, he really enjoyed Purly Girl meetings.

He had just gotten out of his SUV when his phone rang. He checked the caller ID before he pushed the talk button. "Hi, Charlene."

"Hey," she said. Charlene's voice sounded shaky. Like maybe she had been crying.

"Qué pasa?"

"I spoke with Dave, and he's okay with being in the auction."

Oh, my God. Why had she done that? Poor Dr. Dave. "He agreed?" Angel asked.

Charlene was quiet for a long time before she spoke again. "Of course he did, but he doesn't want me to bid on him, though. He thinks it would be improper since he's my boss."

"I guess that makes sense." What could he say? Having Dave in the auction made no sense at all. That's why he'd tried to keep Dave's name off the bachelor's list.

"Angel," Charlene said in a small, tight voice, "I need to ask you a question. It's kind of personal."

Oh, boy. Here it came. "Okay."

"Is Dave...? I mean is he...?" Her voice faded out.

Finally. Thank God. He could be honest with his friend. "Yes, Charlene, he is gay. He does not want to admit it, I am afraid. And while I think he would be happier if he came out, we have to respect that he wishes not to. But, *chica,* I have been worried about asking him to be part of the auction. That is why he was not on my list."

Charlene said a curse word. "Why didn't I see it? My crush on him has been... well, it's just been pathetic." Her voice cracked, and Angel wished he did not have to help Pat Canaday with the Purly Girls. Otherwise he would have gone straight to the animal hospital and tried to help Charlene deal with this reality.

Guys like Dave who could sometimes fly below the gaydar could be hard on women. They could be equally hard on themselves. Dave was a devout Baptist. And the Baptists in town were the most adamant in their views about gay people.

"Look, *chica,* it will be all right. It is better to know the truth, yes? And you are a beautiful woman with a big heart. I'm sure there will be someone for you. Maybe another one of our bachelors."

"Yeah. Maybe." She sounded so sad—almost tragic, really. "I gotta go, Angel. But you can add Dave to the list. Maybe *you* should buy him."

• • •

Charlene cried herself to sleep on Tuesday night. And then she called in sick on Wednesday. Her emotions were too raw, and her eyes too puffy, for her to face Dave.

Maybe if she consumed enough chocolate and watched the entire Cary Grant marathon on Turner Classics she could get a grip and move on.

Amanda was right. Charlene *did* have a propensity for falling in love with men who were unavailable. Usually this meant they were emotionally wounded and unable to commit. But, for the first time, she'd actually picked a mature guy who was *physically* unavailable.

She fluffed her pillow and turned up the TV volume. She had watched three Cary Grant movies so far, and she had reached the part in *Affair to Remember* where Cary discovers that Deborah Kerr is crippled. Charlene had her box of tissues ready.

But the doorbell rang.

Dang. It had to be Amanda coming to haul her out of this well of self-pity. Amanda had left half a dozen voice-mail messages. But Charlene had not returned the calls. She didn't need her friend dissecting her pitiful life.

She could pretend not to be home. But Amanda wouldn't give up. Besides, Charlene's truck was in the parking lot, so it would be hard to do that.

She threw a terrycloth robe over her flannel PJs, pulled on her sock monkey slippers, and peeked through the peephole on her door. No one was there.

She moved to the side window, which gave a better view of her front doorstep. Something had been left on her stoop.

She hauled open the door to find a wicker basket lined

with an old towel and filled with three of the most adorable and waiflike kittens. They were typical farm cats,
with random gray and white spots. They looked to be
about six weeks old—at the point where they might (and
might not) be weaned.

She came out onto the stoop just as Mike and Rainbow
came up the path from the parking lot. As usual, he had a
pizza box in his hands. Rainbow looked a little more girl-
ish today in a purple T-shirt and a pair of jean shorts.

"Fetching outfit," Mike said as they reached the
landing.

Her face flared red hot right to the tip of her nose. "Uh,
well, I was . . ."

"Sleeping in?" he said. The afternoon sunshine
glowed in his red hair. He grinned.

His smile wasn't friendly, or neighborly. In a word, it
reeked of sex.

It knocked her sideways. He could ogle with the best
of the heterosexuals. Equally important, Mike was handsome enough to actually qualify as Prince Charming
material.

He also had more baggage than a Pullman porter. So in
summary, he looked precisely like the mistake she didn't
need to make at this particular moment. It occurred to her
that Mike could probably drive thoughts of Dave Underhill
right out of her head. And then, once she became addicted
to Mike, he would leave. She could see the scenario playing itself out in Technicolor.

She hastily wrapped her robe around herself and
cinched the tie-belt. Denying him any view of her chest
seemed prudent. Especially since her libido had suddenly
registered Mike's hotness.

Now that she'd hidden her boobs, she could rely on the fact that the rest of her wasn't all that red hot. Especially today, with her hair all tangled from being in bed, and her eyes kind of puffy from all the tears she'd recently shed. And then there were the sock monkey slippers and the matching PJs.

The whole package would turn Mike off.

But that flame in his eyes said otherwise.

Just then, the largest of the kitties climbed out of the basket and dropped, somewhat awkwardly, onto the stoop. The kitten let forth a tiny but nevertheless brave *meow*.

"Kitty," Rainbow said, clear as a bell. She rushed up the stairs and picked up the kitten and immediately rubbed his little, soft head against her cheek. Then she looked up at Charlene with an expression in her amber eyes that made Charlene melt.

She wanted to fold that little girl up into her arms, then take a comb to her hair. But she held back. Heartbreak lay in that direction, too.

"Looks like the stork delivered you several bundles of joy," Mike said.

She looked up at him. The corner of his mouth tilted upward and an up-to-no-good twinkle glinted in his eyes. What was he up to?

"Did you put these kittens here for me to find?"

His eyebrows rose. "Me? Why would I do that?"

"I don't know."

"I'll take them," Rainbow said as she sat down on the stoop. She put the kitten she'd been holding back into the basket and picked up another one. She seemed to be an expert in handling cats, as if she'd done it many times before. It was rare to see such gentleness in a child so young.

"Where'd you learn to pick up kitties?" Charlene asked.

"Miss Mary," she said, stroking the kitten she'd tucked into the corner of her arm.

Mike squatted down and looked Rainbow in the eye. "Who's Miss Mary?" he asked.

Rainbow looked away from him and made no reply. Instead she put the kitten back with its mates, and then attempted to pick up the basket.

"Whoa, there," Mike said, putting the pizza box down on the stoop and taking the basket from Rainbow's wobbly grasp. "These kitties belong to Dr. Polk."

And just like that, Charlene became the mother of three orphaned cats. In one fell swoop, she'd become a crazy cat lady. Clearly the Lord was sending her a sign.

"But I want them." Rainbow's brow lowered into a scowl, and Charlene knew she needed to defuse the situation.

"Rainbow, sweetie," she said, finally giving in to the urge to hug the child. "I know you want them, but you already have a cat. And I don't have one anymore. My cat, who was very old, died a few months ago. Someone must have known that I was looking for a kitten. They left these here so I wouldn't be lonesome. So I'd like to keep them. But you can come visit them anytime you want. And you can help me name them."

Rainbow's frown turned into a winning smile. "Like Miss Mary?" she said.

"Who is Miss Mary?" Mike asked again.

"She let me name Tigger." Rainbow pulled away from Charlene's hug. Her arms felt so empty.

Rainbow stood up and marched to the door of Mike's condo and folded her arms.

"What is she trying to tell us, I wonder?" Charlene said.

"I have no idea. But I'm suddenly wondering if Tigger belongs to this Miss Mary person."

"You have reason to believe the Tigger doesn't belong to Rainbow?"

"Yeah, Rainbow's caseworker in Chicago said the cat had a tag with a telephone number, but it didn't match up with Angie's cell phone."

"Whose number was it?"

"I don't know. It was no longer in service. But Rainbow's caseworker is trying to figure it out." He picked up the pizza box and turned toward Charlene. "Did you mean what you said about letting her come over to play with the kittens? I know she would enjoy that."

"I did."

"Thank you. I know she's not the cutest little girl on the face of the planet. She can be really difficult. But she's going to be okay. She's made a friend in summer camp. A little boy named Ethan. I gather they've been thick as thieves for the last couple of days. Lizzy Rhodes, one of the junior counselors, told me Ethan is kind of a motormouth."

"Ethan Wright?"

"I don't know his last name."

"I'll bet it's Amanda's little boy. And you're right, he is a motormouth. A perfect friend for Rainbow."

"Well, anyway, I'm starting to believe that things will work out for her. They have to. She's not a demon child."

"Of course she's not. Is that how you see her?"

He blushed to the tips of his ears. And his pale, red-headed skin made the blush incredibly obvious. How the heck did he manage to play poker with a face like that?

"No, I don't see her as a demon child. But she sometimes behaves like one." He took another step toward the door and stopped again.

"Thank you for coming over to read to her last Saturday. She really liked that. And don't be surprised when she knocks on your door in the next five minutes."

"I won't be."

CHAPTER
11

Mike came out of the kitchen bearing a paper plate with a slice of pizza only to discover the front door wide open and Rainbow nowhere in sight. He was processing this fact when Charlene shouted, "Rainbow, no!" Her voice came from right outside.

He raced through the front door just in time to see Rainbow dashing down the stairs in hot pursuit of Tigger, who seemed to be on a suicide mission that involved crossing the parking lot. Dr. Polk, still fetchingly dressed in her sock monkey PJs and slippers, raced after Rainbow.

Mike dropped the pizza and took the stairs two at a time. Luckily, Charlene caught the girl before she could venture into the parking lot. The cat, however, scampered across the blacktop and went to ground under a giant bush.

"Tigggeerrrrrrrrrrrr!" the girl wailed and tried to escape from Dr. Polk's firm grasp.

"Rainbow, you do not ever cross a street or a parking lot without holding a grownup's hand, is that clear?" Charlene said.

Rainbow seemed unimpressed by this scolding. Although Mike decided, now that Rainbow was no longer in jeopardy, that Charlene's approach to this situation had "mother" written all over it.

How could he not like a woman who loved kittens, and little girls, and wore sock monkey pajamas? Not to mention the fact that she was built like a brick outhouse and could probably get a high-paying gig as a Vegas showgirl if the whole veterinary thing didn't work out for her.

He came up behind them, allowing himself a moment to admire the vet's derriere. "So, what happened?"

"I'm afraid it's my fault," Charlene said, looking up at him, her big brown eyes awash in emotion, her cheeks flushed.

"I doubt that," he said.

"Rainbow came to the door with Tigger. I think she wanted to introduce her cat to the kittens, and I told her that it wouldn't be a good idea because Tigger has an active herpes infection, and we don't want the kitties exposed. I'm not sure Rainbow understood my concern, but I could have sworn that the cat did. No sooner had I tried to explain than the cat jumped off Rainbow's shoulders and took off. And Rainbow followed her. I'm so sorry, Mike. I was being careless, and I—"

"You have nothing to apologize for. It's no biggie."

Rainbow took that moment to look up at him with a frown. That frown said it all. It might not be a biggie for him. But it sure was a biggie for Rainbow.

Mike had obviously not inherited the animal lover gene. But that didn't mean he couldn't prove his manly worth by recovering the wayward cat. "You guys just hang tight. I'll get the cat."

He marched across the parking lot to the bush where the cat had taken refuge. He got down on his knees and peered through the thicket of branches.

Yup, Tigger was there, with her back up against the main branch of the shrub. Was it his imagination or was the cat trying to look friendly? Not that he was about to be suckered by a cat trying to look adorable. The cat had almost caused a major disaster. So he frowned at it. "Look, Tigger, I know you don't like me. And I'm not exactly fond of you. But for Rainbow's sake, we can't have you running across busy parking lots. I don't know what Rainbow would do without you..."

A strange knot lodged in his throat. And for an instant, all he could think about was the look in Angie's eyes the day he'd walked out of Mom's apartment.

A guilty tear leaked from his eye, and he backhanded it. Angie might have had a chance if he hadn't abandoned her. She might not have been in the path of the bullet that took her life. And she might not have used drugs to numb the pain of what she'd gone through as a kid. Someone should have protected Angie. But nobody had.

"You need help?" Charlene called.

He looked over his shoulder. The doc stood across the blacktop with her hand casually on Rainbow's shoulders, as if that were the most natural thing in the world.

He decided right there that he would move heaven and earth to make sure Charlene became Rainbow's mother.

He waved. "I've got it handled," he said.

He turned back to the cat. "Don't prove me wrong, cat. You know damn well that Rainbow needs you. So no games. Understand?"

He reached in to nab the cat by the scruff of her neck.

He halfway expected to earn himself another battle scar, but the cat seemed unusually docile. He had no problem hauling the wayward feline from under the bush. And for some goofy reason, he felt like a conquering hero when he walked across the blacktop with Tigger in his arms. Strangely, the cat had stopped hissing and clawing and had settled into his arms like a loving lap cat, which she wasn't.

Before he handed Tigger over to her owner, he squatted down and looked Rainbow right in the eye.

"Don't you ever leave the house without permission again. Is that clear? You could have gotten hurt, and I wouldn't have known where you were. I can't keep you safe if you don't tell me where you are all the time. And it's my job to keep you safe." By the end of the speech he seemed strangely out of breath.

And then Rainbow nearly undid him altogether when her bottom lip started trembling and she turned away from him and buried her head in Charlene's middle.

And the demon cat started to purr.

Charlene's heart wrenched in her chest. She didn't hesitate. She gave the child the hug she'd wanted to bestow from the first moment she'd clapped eyes on her.

Rainbow needed hugs. In the worst way.

And she wasn't alone.

Charlene gazed down at Mike. His poker face had shattered. His deep-set blue eyes shimmered with unshed guy tears—the kind a man would never confess to having.

Those tears seduced her.

Mike had told her right up front that he didn't know anything about love. But that had to be a big, fat lie.

Maybe he'd been hurt by love. Maybe she could heal what ailed him. Maybe he could be persuaded to commit, long term, to the child. And maybe she was a fool.

Mike stood up. He had the grace of an athlete, even if he was a poker player. The man-tears had disappeared, and he was safely tucked behind his mask again.

"Could I interest you guys in some pizza? It's probably cold, but at least it came from Pizza Hut instead of the frozen food section of your local grocery store." His voice seemed falsely bright.

Rainbow let Charlene go and looked up at her uncle. She reached out for the cat. Mike gently passed the feline off, and Tigger settled herself into Rainbow's arms.

They all walked toward the shared stairway, but Rainbow stopped and turned toward Mike. "Can we eat pizza with the kittens?"

"If you take Tigger home first. You remember what Dr. Polk said about how it's not a good idea for the kitties to spend too much time with a grown-up cat."

"Tigger wouldn't ever hurt kitties," Rainbow said, giving Charlene a long sober look. "Miss Mary would be mad if she did."

This was the second time Rainbow had mentioned someone by that name. "Have you figured out who this Miss Mary person is?" Charlene asked.

Mike shook his head. "The caseworker in Chicago is working on it."

"It sounds like Miss Mary was an important person in Rainbow's life."

"Yeah, I guess."

They headed up the stairs together, Charlene still wondering about the Miss Mary mystery. It wasn't until she reached the landing that she realized she had consented to play host to her handsome neighbor wearing her sock monkey PJs and matching slippers.

"Uh, can y'all give me a moment to change my clothes?"

Mike smirked. "Why? You look perfectly fine to me."

What could she say to that? Especially since Mike's gaze fixed on her face, not her chest. Their gazes almost collided, and a rush of hormones swept through her.

"I'd feel better if I put on some clothes." Wow, had she ever come up with a bigger understatement?

"Okay, we'll be over in five," he said, bounding up the left side of the stairway to his own door. He stopped and looked back. "But you don't have to get dressed up for me. I'm a pretty informal kind of guy."

Informal. Right. But be that as it may, Charlene hurried to her bedroom and found herself contemplating four pairs of jeans, none of which fit precisely right. There were the fat jeans, which were too big now that she had been working out semiregularly. And the skinny jeans, which were still too tight—by a long shot. Either way she was screwed.

So she threw up her hands and gave a mini primal scream. She refused to obsess over jeans. She refused to obsess over Mike Taggart.

So when Mike and Rainbow arrived, less than five minutes later, she answered the door wearing her baggy University of North Carolina sweatshirt and sweat pants, with her hair pulled back into a ponytail. She'd ditched the monkey slippers for a pair of athletic socks.

No one could accuse her of dressing to impress. Or seduce.

Rainbow brushed past her the moment the door opened, making a beeline for the basket of kittens, who were all awake and making lots of noise, as if they missed their mommy. The kittens looked on the tiny side. She hoped they'd been fully weaned.

"Have cold pizza, will travel," Mike said as he crossed her threshold bearing the Pizza Hut box. "Point me in the direction of the microwave, and I'll try to remedy the situation. Although I think Rainbow is so excited about the kittens that she's unlikely to eat even hot pizza."

Charlene led him to the kitchen, a tiny room that seemed to get smaller the moment Mike entered it. Two people trying to microwave pizza and get out the paper plates and napkins had to get kind of chummy. Charlene kept brushing past Mike, and every touch seemed to spark like static electricity.

Or maybe she had reached the desperate-spinster phase of her existence where she was guaranteed to have hot flashes merely because an unmarried man had entered her kitchen.

She needed to put distance between them—if not physically, at least mentally. "So," she said, "I realize pizza is easy for a bachelor to make, but you know it's loaded with carbohydrates and fat. It's okay for once in a while, but every day? Really?"

Yep, that did it. Mike turned toward her with an annoyed glance. "Okay, I give up." He plopped down into one of the ice-cream parlor chairs that she kept in the kitchen. He folded his arms. "You got something better to feed her?"

"Right now? All I've got in my pantry at the moment are some olives, pimentos, and canned okra. The refrigerator is kind of empty at the moment."

"But you have olives and pimentos? Really?"

How embarrassing. "I have a girlfriend who likes her martinis dirty."

"And the pimentos?"

"Left over from the last time I made pimento and cheese spread."

"What?"

"It's a southern thing."

"I see."

She rolled her eyes like an adorable teenager. "Okay, okay. You win. I eat out a lot."

"Pizza?"

"Sometimes. But I'm not trying to raise a child, either."

"Neither am I. I'm trying to find a family for a child. There's a huge difference."

"Right."

"And Rainbow won't eat anything other than pizza," he said.

"So you've said. What have you tried?"

"McDonald's. Burger King. Chick-fil-A. I also took her to the Pig Place, and she turned up her nose at their barbecue sandwich."

"Right. Have you tried vegetables?"

He gave her an assessing stare. "Yeah. We went to an Applebees, and I ordered her a grilled chicken sandwich with some string beans on the side. She didn't eat any of it."

"You know, she'd eat good food if you stopped filling her up with pizza. It's not a good idea to let her have her way on this."

"Is that so? And clearly you have experience in this?"

Her face went hot. "No. But you have to admit that pizza for every meal isn't healthy."

"Okay. I admit it. But here's the challenge. Do you think you can get her to eat something better?"

"I don't know."

"You have my permission to try." His gaze narrowed. "In fact, I'll bet you can't get her to eat anything other than pizza."

"You bet me?"

"Yeah. I do. And just to make it interesting, let's agree that, if you win, then you have to buy my brother at the upcoming auction."

"What? Pastor Tim hasn't even signed up, and no one is trying to get him to do that. It would be crazy to have a minister participate in the auction."

He chuckled. "If that's the case, then you're home free, right? But if I can get him to participate in the auction, and you lose this bet, you have to buy him and take him to dinner."

He had that I'm-up-to-no-good twinkle in his eye again. "Mike, are you trying to match me up with Tim Lake?"

His eyes widened into a "who, me?" expression that didn't fool her for one instant.

She folded her arms across her chest.

"Okay, it *has* occurred to me," he said in a light tone, "that you'd be a perfect mother for Rainbow." He held up his hand before she could explode with outrage. "And before you scream at me, I just want you to know that I spoke with Miriam Randall about this, and she seems to think that you and Tim might be good together. She told me point-blank that Tim would marry a doctor, and that we should use the bachelor auction to make that happen."

"You're joking."

He shook his head. "Nope."

"I can't buy Tim Lake. I'm not sure I like him all that much. And I've heard his sermons are kind of boring."

"I don't know if a man's sermons are a gauge of his suitability as a husband and father. But okay. You don't have to take the bet."

"Wait one second. What do *you* have to do if *I* win this bet?"

He snorted a laugh. "You think you can actually get Rainbow to eat vegetables?"

"Yeah. I think I can."

"Okay, which vegetable are we talking about here?"

"Name one."

"Broccoli. I hate broccoli."

"Okay, then, if I can get Rainbow to eat broccoli, then *you* have to enter the auction."

"Me?"

"Yeah, you. You're kind of cute, you know. And we're perilously short on bachelors. I'll bet there are lots of women who'd like to buy you for a few laughs."

"A few laughs? I would hope I'd fetch more than that."

"Ha, very funny. So have we got a deal?"

He chuckled. And his blue eyes lit up. When he laughed like that, his face changed. He was unbelievably handsome. And he reeked sex appeal. He would definitely go for more than a few laughs. He leaned forward, bracing his elbows on her tiny kitchen table. The little ice-cream shop chair seemed undersized for him.

"So, let me review what's on the table," he said. "I'm betting you that you can't get Rainbow to eat broccoli. And if I win, then you will purchase Timmy in the auction, assuming that Tim participates. And if you win by getting

Rainbow to eat broccoli, then I will participate in the auction and allow myself to be bought and sold."

"Yeah, that sounds right."

"So when is the broccoli-eating event going to take place?"

"How about Saturday. I'll make you and Rainbow a dinner you won't forget."

He held out his hand. "Okay, I take the bet."

CHAPTER 12

On Thursday morning before she headed out for her rounds with the local farmers, Charlene stopped by Mother's house to pick up the boxes of old toys and books that had been stashed in the attic. These boxes had been lovingly put away for the day when Charlene would have a baby of her own.

Faye Tippit, Mother's housekeeper, greeted Charlene at the side door. "Miss Charlene, you better be quiet. Your momma is having one of her headaches this morning."

Right. Mother's headaches were becoming a chronic condition, along with Mother's weakness for wine. Charlene needed to make an intervention. But how? Her parents never took her seriously.

"Thanks, Faye," she said, giving the woman a big hug. "I'm only here for a minute. I want to get some things out of the attic. I'll try to be as quiet as a mouse."

She failed. Or maybe Mother's headache hadn't incapacitated her that badly. Because the moment Charlene

reached the pull-down attic stairs, Mother emerged from
the master bedroom, still wearing her robe and pajamas.

"What do you think you're doing?" she asked.

"I'm just getting a couple of boxes of old stuff."

"What old stuff?"

"My books and toys."

Mother crossed her arms and gave Charlene one
of those looks that had always terrified her as a child.
"Charlene, I've been hearing things about you all over
town."

"What things?"

"Gossip about that awful bachelor auction. Gossip
about you and Reverend Lake. Gossip about how you've
taken a special interest in that dark little girl that everyone
claims is the preacher's niece."

That dark little girl. Boy, Mother could really work
those euphemisms.

"Rainbow is mixed race. And she doesn't have many
books or toys, and I have boxes of them stored up there.
Seems like a match made in heaven. Books for a girl who
doesn't have many."

"You're a fool," Mother said. "I've heard all about this
man who's living in Martha's apartment. He's a gambler,
Charlene. A low-class gambler. And probably a con man.
Tim Lake may be a Methodist, but he seems like a good,
upstanding, godly man. I can't imagine him being related
to people like that."

People like that. "What kind of people, Mother?
Blacks? Poor people?"

She sniffed. "Obviously the preacher is a white man."

"Yeah, I guess he is. But his niece isn't. And you know
what? I don't think Rainbow's race matters to either Mike

or Tim. They are both trying to do the best they can for her. And that's why I'm here."

"You're going to get hurt."

Charlene pulled down the attic stairs. Yeah, she might get hurt. But she needed to risk her heart this time. She started up the stairs.

"Why on earth are you doing this?" Mother shouted up the stairs.

"Because Rainbow needs me. And I'd be a terrible person if I didn't give that child what she needs right now."

"Oh, for goodness' sake," Mother grumbled.

Mother continued to fume as Charlene carried three boxes from the attic to her pickup. By the time Charlene folded the attic stairs, Mother had worked herself up into a full-fledged hissy fit.

She followed Charlene out into the driveway. "You will regret this. That girl is nothing but a mutt, born of low-class people. You have no business getting involved in that sordid situation."

"Mother, shut up." Charlene shoved the last box into the crew cab of her truck.

"You will not talk to me like that—"

"Yes, I will." She turned and faced her mother. "Don't you understand? Rainbow Taggart is my redemption."

"Redemption for what?"

"Oh, my God, Mother. How can you pretend that I didn't make a big mistake when I was nineteen?"

"I'm not pretending. You made a mistake. Your father and I fixed it."

"No! You didn't fix it. You made it worse. Don't you see?" She was in tears now.

"Honey, you've worked yourself up to—"

"Just stop talking, Mother. You and Daddy think you fixed everything, but you didn't. You can't wash away a mistake like that. It haunts you for the rest of your life."

"Really, Charlene, you're thirty-one years old. It's time to get over your childhood. Your father and I only did—"

"Shut *up*."

Mother's eyes widened.

"You can't argue me out of this. I've decided to be a fool over Rainbow Taggart. She needs me. And the truth is I need her. And if you can't say anything nice about that, then keep your mouth shut. Because talking about her race and telling me I'm a fool is just mean. You're a good Christian woman. Start acting like one."

The kittens were not fully weaned. As Charlene had suspected, they had been taken away from their mother too soon. Judging by their size, they were probably six weeks old—certainly old enough to eat solid food, but clearly they had not been exposed to solids until Charlene put down some kitten chow for them. The bigger boys immediately pounced on it. But the little girl kitten seemed lost without her momma.

Charlene had used a pet nurser to feed the kitten before she went to bed on Wednesday and again early Thursday morning before she went off to Mother's house and then on her rounds. The little girl seemed to be waiting for the milk when Charlene got back home in the afternoon, but Charlene was determined to wean her. Unfortunately, the kitten had other ideas and turned her nose up at the solid food. Charlene held off nursing her while she kept an eye out on the front walkway. If the kitten got hungry enough, she might try the solid food, and if not, then Rainbow would be in for a treat.

At about five o'clock, Mike and Rainbow finally showed up. Charlene opened her front door as they came up the stairs, her heart suddenly beating hard in her chest.

Charlene's altercation with Mother this morning had solidified her feelings for Rainbow. She had decided to fling open her heart.

But this breathless, flighty feeling had little to do with Rainbow. It was Mike that her gaze traveled to. Mike whose face she found herself studying.

Her suspicions about him had evaporated, replaced by a strong tug on her heart. He seemed genuinely determined to do the best by Rainbow. And suddenly he seemed like a completely different person.

"Hey," she said, "I was wondering if y'all would like to come over and help me feed the kittens. One of them needs to be fed with a bottle."

Rainbow's face lit up, but she didn't say anything. Charlene shifted her gaze to Mike. The corner of his mouth tipped up. The laugh lines at the corner of his eyes crinkled and something deep and warm flickered in his gaze. Every single one of her dormant girl parts awakened.

"Rainbow needs her dinner, too," Mike said. "Maybe after she eats something."

"I'm having ham sandwiches." Charlene looked down at Rainbow. "You want a sandwich?"

Rainbow didn't react, but Mike said, "Good luck with that."

"I'm willing to try. You want a sandwich, too?" she asked, and then mentally kicked herself. She had sort of envisioned Rainbow coming over without Mike. That would be safer all the way around. Much safer.

But having Mike come over sounded like a lot more fun.

"Sure," he said.

Charlene's insides went weightless, like that moment when a roller-coaster hits the first big dip.

"Come on in, then." She opened her door and ushered them across her threshold.

Rainbow scampered across the living room and fell down on her knees beside the basket of kittens. She started petting the littlest one with long strokes along her head, as if she'd been petting kittens her whole life.

"I wonder where she learned to do that?" Charlene said. "It's really unusual to find a five-year-old who knows how to handle kittens like that. And the animals trust her, which is also unusual. She must have been exposed to cats her whole life."

Mike shook his head. "I don't know. But it's a huge problem."

"A problem?" His warm, spicy scent tickled her hormones. What was that? Aftershave? Shampoo? She took a step away from him.

"Yeah, Timmy is deathly allergic to cats. He's stopped by the apartment a couple of times, and the minute he sets foot in that place, his eyes start watering." Mike's voice dropped into a whisper. "I need to find a home for Tigger."

"No. That would break Rainbow's heart."

"I hope it won't. I've stepped up my efforts to find the

cat's original owner. I'm hoping the cat can go all the way home, where it belongs."

"With Miss Mary?"

He shook his head. "I don't know, but it really does look as if the cat never belonged to Rainbow. And I can't see Angie having a cat. Tigger was well cared for, and I don't think Angie had the money for that. Anyway, I'm on it. If I can return Tigger to her rightful owner, that's a good thing, isn't it?"

"I guess it is. But it's also true that taking Tigger away from Rainbow after she's already lost so much will set her back. Besides, look at her—she loves animals."

"It can't be helped. Once Timmy accepts that I'm truly his brother and Rainbow is truly his niece, he will step up. She'll have to give up the cat, but she'll get a father. And really, trading a cat for a father is a good deal."

"Depends on the father."

Mike blinked, and his shoulders tensed a tiny bit. "Timmy will make a great father."

"Maybe. But right now, if you asked Rainbow, she'd choose the cat. If you want my opinion, Pastor Tim should sign up for allergy shots."

"I didn't ask for your opinion."

She couldn't miss the annoyance in his voice. Well, too bad. Today was her day for speaking her mind. "The girl needs her cat, Mike. Just look at her with the kittens."

He hesitated for a beat and then shifted the conversation. "Are you going to keep all three of them?"

"Keeping three is really no more work than one. Cats are easy."

"Yeah, but three? Really? What if you meet a guy who doesn't like cats? Or who's allergic like Tim? Besides, you don't look like the kind of woman who would have three cats."

"Really? And what kind of woman is that?"

His cheeks reddened. "I don't know. A crazy cat lady, I guess. You don't look at all like my idea of a crazy cat lady."

"Thanks."

"Don't mention it." His voice went all husky, and his eyelids lowered a bit, and a wave of sexual energy hit Charlene right in her belly.

Right. Ham sandwiches. "You want mustard or mayo on your sandwich?" she asked as she scurried into the kitchen.

"Both, please," he said to her retreating back.

She made the sandwiches. Mike devoured his along with a long-neck Bud. Rainbow turned her nose up at the food, just as Mike had predicted.

"You're in trouble, you know," he said as Charlene settled Rainbow on her couch, with a towel on her lap.

"How?"

"I'm going to win the bet on Saturday, and you're going to have to go to dinner with Timmy."

"Angel says Tim hasn't signed up for the auction."

"There's still time to persuade him." Mike seemed supremely confident, almost smug. She found it both annoying and attractive for some insane reason.

Rainbow took that moment to snuggle up next to her, and Charlene's heart wrenched in her chest.

She hated to admit it, but maybe Mike was on to something. Maybe she ought to make a play for Tim. He would probably meet with Amanda's approval. Mother would object to him being a Methodist. But Aunt Millie would be overjoyed. Tim's allergies were the only trouble spot.

What? No.

She pushed these idiotic thoughts right out of her mind. The best thing would be to focus on the here and now and not get way ahead of herself. She looked down at Rainbow. "So are you ready to feed the little one?"

Rainbow nodded solemnly, and Charlene took the kitten out of the basket and handed it to Rainbow. "Now put her on her back," Charlene directed.

Rainbow took the critter with a gentleness beyond her years. Charlene spent the next few minutes showing Rainbow how to use the pet nurser. The kitten was pretty hungry, and while Charlene really wanted the critter to learn how to eat solid food like her brothers, the angelic smile on Rainbow's face was worth spoiling the animal.

Rainbow held the kitten as if she were a baby doll, and soon she began to whisper baby talk to it. Obviously she'd heard someone soothe a baby or a kitten before.

This got a big reaction from Mike, who leaned forward, elbows on knees, listening to the little girl. Charlene gave him points for listening. The child didn't say anything new or startling. She just whispered nonsense to the kitten.

Any idiot could see how the kitten could be powerful therapy for this wounded child. And that made Rainbow's situation even more heartbreaking. Neither Tim nor Mike could have a cat. And clearly this child needed one.

Later, Charlene hauled out one of the books she'd rescued from the attic that morning—a collection of children's literature and poems. She snuggled up with Rainbow while Mike looked on, sipping his beer. Charlene read several of her favorites, like "The Gingham Dog and the Calico Cat" and "The Sugar-Plum Tree." But Rainbow seemed to like "Wynken, Blynken, and Nod," Eugene Field's beloved poem, best of all.

And that's how the three little kittens got their names. She named the big one with the spot of gray over one eye Winkin'. The other male, with the all-white face, she called Blinkin'. And Nod was the little female, who sat on Rainbow's lap after she nursed and literally nodded off so completely that she fell over.

When it came time for Rainbow to go to bed, Mike took her home. And Charlene found herself wishing that both of them could have stayed. She wanted to play house with them some more. Because for an instant, while she read to the child, the three of them almost felt like a family.

It didn't surprise her one bit when Rainbow came knocking at her door the next morning before summer camp to check on the kittens. And she came again, on Friday evening, to give Nod another feeding, but Charlene had decided that it was time to encourage Nod to eat solid food. So she let Rainbow help her work on that problem by putting a drop of milk and wet cat food on the little girl's finger and letting Nod lick it off. Eventually Charlene and Rainbow led the kitten to a bowl of food, and she ate like a grown-up.

Each time Rainbow visited, Mike called ahead to give Charlene fair warning, but he opted to stay home. She couldn't say that made her happy, but she understood why he stayed away. Her feelings about him had become convoluted and complicated. And maybe Mike had figured that out.

But what she felt for Rainbow was simple and pure. The child gave her joy. And the kittens gave them both a place to connect. God bless the soul who had put Winkin', Blinkin', and Nod on her doorstep.

CHAPTER 13

The private investigator called on Friday afternoon with the news that Tim had been expecting and dreading. Mike had told the truth.

The investigator elaborated on Mike's story. Tim and Mike's birth mother was still living, at least for the moment, in a nursing home in Chicago. Tim spoke with the nursing staff and learned that a lifetime of abusing alcohol had done its damage. Her name was Alice, and they didn't expect her to live much longer.

He sat at his desk, looking down at the sermon he'd been trying to write for Ascension Sunday. His words were completely uninspired. His mind was not on his job.

What would he do now that he knew the truth?

He wanted to pick up the phone and call Andrea. But she wasn't his therapist. This news wouldn't really change whatever she and Rainbow talked about in their sessions.

But it would change Tim's life forever. It already had.

He had a brother. He had a niece.

He should be overjoyed. But instead, it overwhelmed him. He hadn't expected to become a parent in this way—thrown into it without a life partner, without time to prepare.

He would need to spend more time with Rainbow and Mike. Up until now he'd been using his cat allergy to keep his distance. Even with the child down the hall at Bible camp, he hadn't really made much of an effort to visit.

He put his sermon aside and headed down the hall to the kindergarten class, where Liz Rhodes, one of the high school kids the church hired as counselors, was leading the children in a bunch of songs that also had hand motions.

The kids jumped around, making a joyful sound. Even Rainbow. She and Ethan Wright were in the back row. Ethan sang with a big, booming voice. Rainbow not so much, but she followed along with the other kids, making all the hand gestures.

A fissure opened in his heart. She was his kin. His family. God had brought her here because she needed him. She needed his love.

And that's where he failed. His tangled feelings for the child included concern, but not love. Not yet, at least. For the last week and a half, he'd been working hard to keep his distance. And now he had no reason to hold himself back, except that Rainbow Taggart scared him to death. He didn't want to be a parent. Not yet.

He joined in with the singing, surprising Liz. He probably looked like a fool, dancing there wearing his somber black collar and gray pants, surrounded by kids in bright-colored T-shirts and shorts.

But singing eased his heart. He could do this. He just needed to apply himself.

Ten minutes later, parents began to show up to collect their kids.

Mike was one of the first through the door, which surprised Tim. He had expected Mike to leave Rainbow until the last minute. More important, Rainbow seemed to know the moment Mike arrived. She turned and gave him a small, shy smile, and then ran across the classroom and right into him, giving him a big hug. Mike picked her up and balanced her on his hip, as if he'd been hauling children around for his entire life.

Something had changed. Mike didn't look like the harried and unhappy man he'd been a week ago. Rainbow had changed, too. Clearly the two of them were beginning to bond.

Tim suddenly realized he'd made a big mistake the first day Mike and Rainbow had darkened his door. He should have invited them into the parish house from the beginning. He shouldn't have stayed so aloof. He should have visited an allergist and found a solution to his cat allergy instead of using it as an excuse.

But he hadn't done any of those things. And when Mike left, as Tim knew he would, Rainbow would be heartbroken a second time.

He crossed the room. "Mike, do you have a moment?"

"Sure, what's up?"

"I'd like to talk with you in the office for a minute." Tim gave Rainbow's shoulder a friendly pat. "Can you stay here with Lizzy and Ethan for a moment, sweetie? I need to talk with Uncle Mike." Rainbow nodded solemnly, and Mike put her down. She scampered off to join Ethan, who was playing with Legos as he waited for his mom.

Tim ushered Mike back to his office. Instead of sitting behind his desk, he took a seat in the chair, leaving the couch for Mike.

"I've heard from my investigator," Tim said.

Mike's face went blank. His half-brother did that a lot, especially when confronted with something that required an emotional response. "That's good," Mike said.

"You've gotten pretty high praise from Rainbow's caseworker in Chicago."

Mike looked away, and his jaw tensed.

"Look, I think I made a mistake when you first showed up. I'd like you and Rainbow to move into the parish house with me. It will give me a chance to get to know Rainbow better. And I guess we should talk with Eugene Hanks about legal adoption."

Mike's gaze snapped back. "I'm not sure that's a good idea."

"What? You don't want me to legally adopt her?"

"No, I do, but I'm not sure moving her into the parish house is the right thing to do."

"What? Isn't that what you came here for?"

He nodded his head, and his brow furrowed. "Yeah, I did. But now it's gotten way more complicated."

"You're falling in love with her, aren't you?"

Mike startled. And for an instant, his poker face faltered. "Her?"

"Rainbow. You're getting attached to her, aren't you?"

"I guess. But I'm not going to take her back to Vegas with me. I'm clear on that. It's not my emotions I'm worried about, Timmy. The thing is, Rainbow has become infatuated with Charlene Polk."

"Charlene Polk?"

"She lives right next door. She has kittens, and I guess it's the vet thing or something, but she seems to have a real natural way with Rainbow. I'm not sure that taking Rainbow away from all that would be smart. In fact, if you wanted to do the right thing, you might think about asking Charlene out on a date. You could take Rainbow with you."

"Wait, wait, *wait*. Are you trying to match me up with Charlene Polk?"

"Yup. And if you wanted to help things along, you might think about signing up for the bachelor auction."

"You're not serious."

"I'm completely serious. I'm working on this problem pretty hard, Timmy. I've even consulted Miriam Randall, and, for what it's worth, she told me that you were fated to marry someone with a background in medicine. And then she went on to say that the bachelor auction was all part of the Lord's plan."

"The Lord's plan? Really?"

"That's what she said. So, if you're smart, you'll sign up for the bachelor auction. And then let me maneuver Charlene into buying you. I've almost got that one in the bag. Wherever Charlene goes, Rainbow will follow willingly. So, if you want my advice, you should start courting Charlene in a big way. She'll make Rainbow the perfect mother."

"Wow, you *have* been busy."

"I have a plan. I need to get back to Vegas fast. My agent has a sponsor almost lined up for me. It's a lot of money if they make an offer. So I haven't been sitting around on my backside. The only fly in the ointment right now is the kittens."

"Kittens? Plural?"

"Someone left a basket of kittens on Charlene's door-step, and I think she's planning to keep them. That's obvi-ously a problem. I know it's presumptuous of me, but I think you should schedule an appointment with an allergist and see what can be done about that cat allergy. I'm going to try to find homes for Winkin', Blinkin', and Nod. But Tigger is going to be a much bigger problem for Rainbow."

"Winkin', Blinkin', and Nod?"

"That's what Rainbow named the kittens. She's been going over to Charlene's place every morning and night to feed the littlest one with a bottle. And I'm not going to uproot her again until I check with Dr. Newsome."

Mike had rendered Tim speechless. If he didn't know better, he would say that Mike had become infatuated with Charlene Polk, but he didn't say so aloud. He had a feeling Mike didn't even realize it. But his notion of checking with Andrea made perfect sense.

So he decided not to push the parish house idea. If Mike wanted to give this transition a little more time and thought, Tim would not argue. After all, Tim had sug-gested this transition in the first place. And besides, Tim needed more time to figure out his feelings about this brother he had wanted all his life but had never known.

"Look, Mike, the fact is we're family. Maybe only because of biology, but that's important. I'd like to spend more time with you and Rainbow both. Preferably away from the cats. The thing is, when I was a child, I pestered my folks for a little brother. And they tried, but Mom had three miscarriages. Until you walked through that door, I thought the Lord had decided I was supposed to go through life an only child. So it's a blessing to discover I have a brother."

Mike's expression softened. It was almost as if he'd taken off a mask.

"So," Tim continued, "how about if you and Rainbow join me for some fun at the Edisto Country Club tomorrow?"

"The country club? Really?" Mike's voice took on an edge, and suddenly he retreated back into his shell.

Tim had to chuckle. "The Edisto Country Club isn't the kind of country club that has a golf course and exclusive membership policies, if that's what's worrying you."

"Okay, then what kind of country club is it?"

"It's a swimming hole on the Edisto River, where a number of townfolk have built summer homes. It's exclusive in the sense that you have to be a property owner to use the swimming hole—or a guest of a property owner. And in my case, Martha Spalding asked me to keep an eye on her river house for her while she's in Tampa. And before you go envisioning fancy log cabins and what-not, most of these homes started out as tin-roofed shacks. There have been some upgrades over the years, but they aren't very fancy at all."

"Okay, I suppose there isn't anything inherently wrong with a minister belonging to a country club." Mike didn't sound so sure.

"I don't actually belong. But I'm welcome there. All of the clergy in town are. Y'all will have fun. Pack a bathing suit for both of you. I'll bet Rainbow has never been swimming in a river."

"Uh, she's not the only one," Mike said. "And I'll bet Rainbow has never been swimming at all."

"Well, then, this is going to be a fun place for her to learn. And I volunteer to give her a swimming lesson."

By the time Saturday rolled around, Charlene had ceased to worry about the stakes of her bet with Mike. If she lost, she would have to buy Tim Lake at the auction. But that wasn't all that terrible. After all, Tim would one day be Rainbow's guardian. If Charlene wanted to keep the girl in her life, she would have to befriend Tim.

Losing the bet wouldn't be bad at all.

Except that she wanted to wean Rainbow off pizza just as much as she had wanted to wean Nod off the pet nurser. So she asked Faye Tippit, Mother's housekeeper, for cooking advice. If anyone had a recipe for disguising broccoli, Faye would.

She recommended a broccoli and cheese casserole made with jack cheese and a can of mushroom soup. Charlene could have left the meal at that, but she didn't.

After the lovely evening she'd spent with Rainbow and Mike on Thursday, she decided to go all out. So she made up a batch of fried chicken and some butter beans and rice to accompany the casserole.

She'd probably bitten off more than she could chew, because it took her way too long to get everything cooked. Not to mention the grease explosion in her kitchen.

So with all the cooking and cleaning up and setting the table and playing with the kittens, she had no time to dress before her guests arrived. She stood in front of her closet trying to decide if she should wear a sundress or try to pour herself into a pair of her skinny jeans. She was still standing there in her underwear when the doorbell rang.

"Just a minute," she hollered, and opted for her sundress, which exposed a lot of skin. But it had the advantage of being quick to put on.

She opened the door, and within one second, Mike's gaze dropped right down to her chest. His lips twitched, and heat spilled through her. The dress had been a mistake.

Neither Mike nor Rainbow had dressed up for the occasion. He wore standard-issue jeans and a golf shirt, while Rainbow arrived wearing jean shorts and a teal T-shirt. As always, her hair was out of control.

Rainbow gave her an adorable little-girl look as she held out a piece of paper.

"For me?" Charlene asked.

Rainbow nodded solemnly. Charlene took the paper, which turned out to be a piece of lined notebook paper with a gray pencil drawing of the basket and the kittens. "Oh, Rainbow, this is beautiful." Charlene looked up at Mike. "She's got talent."

"Yeah. Dr. Newsome says we should encourage her to draw. It's something she loves to do, and it's supposed to be good therapy."

The child turned her head, hiding her face against Mike's side. Charlene immediately noticed the way Mike put his big hand on the little girl's shoulder. Oh, yeah, this guy talked about walking out, but maybe he didn't really mean it.

She mentally kicked herself. All of Charlene's infatuations started this way. She'd pick one good thing about a guy and then blow it out of proportion.

And her fantasies always wanted to go in one direction. She'd revisited the quiet moments she'd spent with Mike and Rainbow on Thursday evening. She wanted to recapture them tonight. In truth, she wanted to have moments like that for the rest of her life.

She longed for a family.

But it wasn't going to happen with Mike. Mike wanted to return to Vegas for a poker tournament. He might have bonded with Rainbow, but that didn't make him a family man. Just the favorite uncle.

So she mentally backed off. She would make this evening about the bet, and nothing more. "Come on in, supper is ready."

Charlene's apartment mirrored Martha Spalding's place. But while the layout was similar, the decor could not have been more different. Charlene's condo was contemporary, with just enough clutter to give her home a lived-in feeling. It was comfortable, and tonight it was filled with the aroma of good home cooking.

Everything about Charlene's home was perfect. She would make a terrific minister's wife. He could see her entertaining the ladies of the Altar Guild in a place like this. Of course, when she married Timmy, she'd have to move into the parish house. He made a mental note to check the place out. But even if the parish house was horrible, he had confidence that Charlene could turn it into a home.

Everything seemed to be going according to plan.

And once Rainbow turned her nose up at whatever broccoli dish Charlene had made, Mike could put a check after phase one. Phase two would require Mike to get

Timmy to actually commit to participating in the auction, but he'd already planted those seeds. And phase three would be finding a solution to the cat situation.

His stomach rumbled. He'd burned a lot of calories today out at the Edisto Country Club swimming and building sand castles. He'd spent a golden day with Timmy. They had avoided all discussion of their parents and focused on Rainbow.

And now Mike realized that he might actually have a place to go on Thanksgiving and Christmas. Even if he gave up the role of father, he could still be an uncle.

"Was that a rumble I heard?" Charlene said as she gave him a frank and incredibly sexy smile. Damn.

His future sister-in-law ought to be matronly and maternal, not sexy. His future plans for Thanksgiving and Christmas might turn awkward if he didn't find some way to turn off his libido.

"Uh, yeah, you know how it goes when you're on a steady pizza diet. By the way, what is that delicious smell?"

She grinned. "Homemade fried chicken."

"Wow. Obviously you're not worried about saturated fat, huh?"

"Nope," she said with an exaggerated head shake, "I'm not. I'm here to win a bet. And as I recall, there was no rule about any ingredients besides the broccoli."

It suddenly occurred to him that he might actually lose this bet. What if Rainbow liked whatever Charlene cooked? Damn. Rainbow had probably never had a home-cooked meal. As a kid, Angie certainly never had. Her diet had been limited to the school breakfast and lunch program and whatever Mike had been able to scrounge in the evening, usually mac and cheese or ramen noodles.

Thinking about Angie immediately soured his stomach.

Charlene's smile faded into a wide-eyed, compassionate look. Was she a mind reader, too? "What is it?" she asked.

He went into poker mode. "Nothing. Just hungry." Although that was suddenly a big lie. The acid in his stomach had gone into overdrive.

His stomach almost throbbed by the time they sat down to dinner at Charlene's small dining table. Charlene had gone all in with good china and cloth napkins and candlelight. Not to mention the family-style food presentation with a big bowl of fried chicken, a basket of biscuits wrapped up in a checkered cloth, and two side dishes with serving spoons. One of those dishes looked like broccoli smothered in cheese.

He turned toward Rainbow. The candlelight gleamed in her amber eyes, which looked as if they might bug right out of her face as she gazed at the cornucopia of food on the table. Oh, boy, he had seriously miscalculated.

And then, just before Mike dug into the bowl of chicken, Rainbow pressed her little hands together and bowed her head, obviously waiting for someone to say grace. No doubt the counselors at summer camp were responsible for this behavior.

The village of Last Chance had begun the process of taming the wild child, hadn't it?

Charlene didn't miss a beat either, being the sweet, wholesome girl next door. She bowed her head and said, "Lord, make us truly grateful for what we're about to receive."

Rainbow chimed in with a big "amen."

Wow! Had he fallen into an episode of *Touched by an Angel* or something? The whole scene was perfect in every way, except that he didn't exactly fit here. And, besides, lust almost overwhelmed him every time he looked at Charlene wearing that little pink dress that exposed her shoulders. Charlene fixed Rainbow's plate with a chicken wing, a biscuit, some rice and beans, and a big helping of the broccoli and cheese dish. And the kid said "thank you." And then she picked up the chicken leg and took a ferocious bite.

"So you like chicken?" Charlene asked.

Rainbow nodded and spoke with her mouth full. "Miss Mary made chicken, too."

"Did she now," Mike said. "And you ate at her house?"

"Uh-huh. She was a good cook."

"So you lived nearby?"

"Uh-huh."

He leaned in Charlene's direction and whispered, "I'm still trying to solve the Miss Mary mystery. But so far, I've got more questions than answers."

Charlene nodded. Then she gave him a wicked, up-to-no-good smile. She turned toward Rainbow. "Honey, you should try the broccoli. It has lots of cheese in it, like pizza."

Rainbow eyed the vegetable. No way Rainbow would eat the broccoli. What kid liked broccoli? Mike didn't much like broccoli himself. He refrained from telling Rainbow that broccoli was yucky, though. He never cheated on a bet. Ever.

Rainbow leaned over her plate and gave the casserole a little sniff. And then she picked up her fork and tried a tiny little bit. And the moment that casserole hit the kid's tongue, her eyes practically popped from her head. "This is good," she said, and then proceeded to stuff her mouth so that she looked like a chipmunk as she chewed.

"What the hell did you put in that?" he asked.

"You should try it, Mikey. You might like it," Charlene said with a grin.

So he tried a taste and it was incredible. He looked up from his plate and met the triumphant gleam in her dark brown eyes. Damn, damn, damn. This was not going according to plan.

"You know," she said lightly, "it wasn't a fair bet, because no one can resist Faye's broccoli casserole. And, Mike, I'm going to hold you to your pledge. I've got the auction sign-up forms for you to take home with you."

It occurred to him right then that he wouldn't mind participating in the auction if Charlene bought him and then cooked him another dinner like this.

But he stomped on that thought the moment it crossed his mind. Charlene belonged with Timmy.

CHAPTER 14

I can't believe you're really going to go through with it," Charlene said as she watched Mike filling out the bachelor auction form.

"I never welsh on a bet. And besides, I figure it's a good deal. I now have your recipe for broccoli casserole."

She tried to stifle a smile and failed.

"Don't gloat, Charlene. It's considered rude."

"I'm sorry. I didn't mean to gloat. I'm amused by the idea of you cooking something that doesn't involve frozen food and a microwave. And besides, you have to admit that you're happy Rainbow gobbled up those vegetables. You can't fool me, Mike. I know you care about that little girl."

He finished filling out the form and looked up, his blue, blue eyes twinkling a little bit. "All right, you win. I *am* happy. I've been worried about her nutrition. Especially since her hair is falling out." The glint in his eye faded a bit.

"She's losing her hair?" she asked.

He nodded as he slid the paper across the table. "Every time I brush it."

"You brush her hair?"

"Uh, yeah, is there something wrong with that?"

"Oh, well, you should use a comb. And you should work from the ends in, not the scalp out. It's like the opposite of all the hair care you ever learned. And you shouldn't wash it every day."

"I *shouldn't* wash it every day?"

She leaned forward a little bit. "She's not a white girl. Her hair is different. It's really fine and dry. You should probably only wash it every week or maybe longer. And her scalp probably needs some jojoba or coconut oil if it's really dry."

He gaped at her. "How do you know this stuff?"

Her face flamed. She didn't want to tell Mike about Derrick. He might get the wrong idea.

She was trying to figure out a way to deflect this question when her pantry exploded.

The bifold doors unfolded, and a white mushroom cloud billowed out of the closet. A second later, the broom and mop tumbled out, bonking Mike on the head. He stood up quickly, trying to get away from the unexpected assault, only to step on something that went "*eeeeeeek.*"

He jumped back, losing his balance, and toppled right into the pantry, knocking the shelving askew. Cans of okra tipped over, a flour sack exploded, and a jar of olives and another of pimentos crashed to the floor, both of them shattering. And from out of this chaos came a tiger-striped blur that used her claws on Mike's thigh for leverage as she launched herself out of the pantry in hot pursuit of the something that was still going "eek eek" as it scampered across the kitchen floor.

A mouse. A big, well-fed mouse.

Charlene took off her loafer and ran after the mouse herself. She *hated* mice, which probably made her a failure as an animal doctor. But this gray critter scampering into her living room bore no resemblance to those cute, white lab mice. This mouse was the kind who pooped all over the place and attracted unwanted guests. Like disease and snakes.

She had no fear of snakes. But she didn't want any snakes finding their way into her pantry. Obviously she had gone too long without a cat, if the mice had moved in. Whoever had left the kittens had done her a huge favor in more ways than one.

She raced after the rodent, intent on mashing it flat with the heel of her shoe, but Tigger came out of nowhere and beat her to it. The cat pinned the unfortunate mouse with one swipe of her claws. She didn't kill the critter, of course. But she had complete control of it.

She picked the squirming mouse up in her mouth, carried it over to the kittens, and proceeded to show them how to play with it.

Tigger's presence inside her apartment surprised Charlene, but she completely approved of the lesson the cat was teaching the kittens. In her practice, Charlene cared for a great many barn cats, and Tigger clearly had the instincts of a mouser. And good mousers were a godsend.

Charlene found herself smiling at the life-and-death scene playing itself out in her living room. She'd have to take the mouse away in a minute, but not before the kittens got a little taste of what their life was supposed to be about.

Her satisfaction faded a moment later when she looked up to find Mike in the kitchen doorway, dusted in flour from his head to his toe and covered in something brown and sticky. Was that leftover molasses from the time she baked gingerbread for the Christmas bazaar?

The sight might have been humorous except that he was bleeding profusely from a cut in his scalp. As the blood dripped down his forehead and into his eye, he said, "I'm going to murder that cat."

Mike watched as the expression on Rainbow's face shattered.

"Noooooooooooo!" she wailed.

Rainbow's out-of-control emotions hit him like a punch to the gut. What had he been thinking to say such a thing? Of course he didn't want to kill the cat. Okay, he had thought about it for a nanosecond. Probably because his thigh smarted from Tigger's claws and his head pounded, thanks to the canned goods that had pummeled him.

"I didn't mean it literally," he said, as something trickled down the side of his face. He wiped at it, expecting to find more of the sticky stuff that was all over his pants and shoes.

But his hand came away bloody.

"Christ."

Rainbow stood up and raced across the living room and hit his abs like a mini linebacker. She almost knocked him sideways as she wrapped her arms around his waist. She buried her head right into the middle of his gut, getting molasses and flour and probably blood all over one of her new outfits.

He suddenly didn't know where to put his hands, so they ended up on her shoulders. His meaningless death threat against Tigger hadn't upset Rainbow, but the blood on his face probably had. She'd seen her mother shot in the head.

"I'm okay," he said, because it seemed to be the right thing to say. And because, well, she was hugging him so hard that it almost broke his heart.

"Don't move." Charlene put out her hands. "Let me get the first-aid kit."

She disappeared down the hall for a moment and came back with an industrial-strength first-aid box. She seemed to be prepared for anything. Not to mention the fact that he'd been kind of impressed by the murderous look in her eye when she'd taken off after the mouse wearing only one shoe.

She was one heck of a woman: kind, loving, a good cook, a veritable encyclopedia when it came to the care and maintenance of African-American hair, and she had a murderous, but fun, side to her. Timmy was one lucky man.

Mike gave Rainbow a little shoulder squeeze. "I'm okay, Rainbow. I fell into the shelves, and one of them hit me."

She looked up at him. No tears in her eyes, but a world of hurt and fear down in their depths. He squatted down to be on her level. The child immediately threw her arms around his neck and hung on.

"Come on, kiddo, it's okay. I tripped over a mouse. How silly is that?"

She said nothing, and she wouldn't let go. So he squatted there holding the kid. His nose buried in her nappy hair. His heart breaking. How much crap had she seen in her short life? Too much.

He pressed a kiss into the top of her head, closed his eyes, and went all in. He'd get her a mother and father she could depend on. He'd keep her safe.

"Come on, Rainbow, it's okay," Charlene said, as she touched the girl's thin arms.

Rainbow relaxed and stepped away from him. He had no name for this ache in the pit of his stomach. It wasn't the usual heartburn. And it sure wasn't guilt.

Charlene squeezed Rainbow's shoulder. "Mike's all right, angel. I'll take care of the cut on his head. He just got between Tigger and her mouse, and I have a feeling Tigger is a determined mouse catcher, isn't she?"

Rainbow nodded solemnly. "And rats, too, sometimes," she said in a small voice. "Mama hates rats."

Mike and Charlene's gazes met over the top of Rainbow's head. This was the first time Rainbow had spoken of her mother since the shooting.

"I'm sure your mama hated rats," Charlene said without missing a beat. "I hate them, too. And I think it's terrific that Tigger is already teaching the kitties about mice. Although I'm trying to figure out how she got in here."

Rainbow looked down at her toes. "She came to the door, and I let her in."

"But how did she get out of your apartment?"

"Oh, crap," Mike muttered. "I bet she got out through the kitchen window. I left it open this morning when I burned the toast. I forgot to close it before we went to the river."

"You went to the river?" Charlene asked, sounding surprised.

"Yeah, we did. Tim invited us out there. Rainbow is a

little scared of the water, but Timmy had her doing a dog paddle. And she loved the sand at the swimming beach."

"If y'all like swimming," Charlene said, "I'll give you the key to our house down at the country club. You can use it anytime you like."

"That would be nice. Rainbow had a great time down there today."

Charlene looked up at him and went into doctor mode. "All right, big guy, back up and let me see that scalp wound." She put her hand in the middle of his chest and gave him the gentlest of pushes. He backed up, but for an instant, he didn't want to. Her touch ignited a fire under his skin. It blindsided him with its ferocity.

He'd already cataloged Charlene Polk as being show-girl sexy. She had a great figure and a little wiggle in her walk. But when she touched him, all that sex appeal became tangible, and hot. Very hot. So hot that it carried his libido to a place that he didn't want it to go. It was just *wrong* for him to lust after the woman he'd chosen to be Rainbow's new mother. Wrong on so many levels.

But he found himself checking out her silky skin, and drinking in her buttery scent, and getting lost in those big brown eyes. She pushed him back, over the sticky slime on the floor, and into one of her kitchen chairs. Rainbow climbed up into the other one and watched solemnly as Charlene opened her first-aid kit, tore open some gauze, and started cleaning the wound on his head.

Her touch was gentle and deeply disturbing. He itched to snake his hands around her cute, curvy hips. He wanted to pull her into his lap. He couldn't stop thinking about how nice it would be to give her a molasses-laden kiss. In fact, it would be even better if he could convince her to lick it off his lips and his face and his neck.

Oh, yeah.

Damn. He needed to purge his mind of these thoughts and concentrate on the mission that had brought him to this one-horse town in the first place.

He'd found Rainbow a perfect mother and father. Now he just needed to get them together.

CHAPTER 15

Mike knew he ought to take Rainbow to church on Sunday, but the idea of sitting in a pew listening to Timmy sermonize gave him the heebie-jeebies. There would be plenty of time for Rainbow to attend Sunday school and church once Mike headed back to Nevada.

Instead he took Charlene up on her open invitation to use her family's river house. And since Rainbow had had such a great time at the river on Saturday, going back on Sunday morning seemed like a reasonable plan.

The Polk family's river house was a far cry from the one belonging to Martha Spalding. It looked like something from out of *Better Homes and Gardens*. The kitchen had state-of-the-art appliances, the bathroom sported granite tile, and the bedroom where Rainbow and Mike changed into their bathing suits had a brass bed that looked like a real antique.

Charlene Polk came from money, which surprised Mike because she seemed so down-to-earth, especially when she wore her stinky rubber boots.

Mike left his car in the driveway, and the two of them walked down the sloping banks to the man-made beach, where the homeowners had carved out a spot along the bank and dumped a bunch of sand to make a shallow wading area.

They had the beach to themselves, and Rainbow got busy building a sand castle while Mike settled into one of the wooden benches and snapped open his Sunday edition of the *Orangeburg Times Democrat.*

He couldn't keep his mind on the news. Instead, he worried about his plan to get Charlene and Timmy together, which had suffered a setback last night, when he'd lost his bet with Charlene. Not to mention the fact that Timmy didn't seem all that interested in courting Charlene, even if he had clearly changed his mind about Rainbow.

And that troubled Mike in ways he didn't wish to examine too closely. A week ago, he would have been overjoyed by Timmy's change of heart, but now he wanted more. He wanted Rainbow to have Charlene in her life.

And really, Timmy needed Charlene in his life, too. The woman was beautiful. And kind. And smart. And... His thoughts began to wander back to the moment when she was doctoring the cut on his forehead.

Hot. Very, very hot.

Just then, a piping voice said, "Hey, Rainbow. Whatcha building?"

He looked up to find Ethan Wright, Rainbow's camp friend, standing beside Rainbow admiring her sand castle. Ethan was dressed in swim trunks and had a big sand bucket and a bright yellow plastic trowel. He fell to his knees. "You wanna build some roads and a moat around the castle? I brought my cars." He dumped half a dozen or more Matchbox cars out of his bucket.

Rainbow didn't say a word, but she nodded. Something eased in Mike's chest. This place was healing her. She was beginning to connect with people.

A minute later, Ethan's mother sat down on the bench beside him. She was pretty in a small-town, wholesome way, wearing a demure one-piece bathing suit and a white, see-through cover-up. "So," she said, "you're Pastor Tim's brother."

He looked over his paper. "I'm Mike. And you're Ethan's mother and Charlene's best friend, but I can't remember your first name."

Her eyebrow arched, conveying her surprise. "I'm Amanda. And how do you know that I'm Charlene's best friend?"

"She's my next-door neighbor. And she's very neighborly. And I want to know, are you the friend who likes dirty martinis?"

Amanda snorted a laugh. "I guess I'm guilty. So, how neighborly has she been?" Amanda's gaze turned sly. It occurred to him that Charlene's best friend might become an important ally in resurrecting his plans for Timmy and the girl next door.

"Just the usual stuff. She's been kind to Rainbow. She's given her several books, and she lets Rainbow come over to play with her new kittens. And all in all, I would say that Charlene has been good for Rainbow. So has Ethan, by the way. He's a pretty talkative kid."

That got a big smile. "Yes, he is. Gets it from his great-grandfather who was a radio broadcaster for years and years. So I take it Rainbow liked *Pete the Cat?*"

"You know about the book?"

"I helped Charlene pick it out. She wanted to give Rainbow a present, and she wasn't sure what would be good. I recommended the book because Ethan loves it."

"Rainbow loves it, too. It might be the first book anyone has ever given her. Last night I heard her singing that silly song before she fell asleep. Hearing Rainbow sing, even if it's in the privacy of her own room, is a pretty big thing. So I guess I need to thank you."

"Oh, no, I just facilitated things. Charlene is the one you should thank. I'll tell you a little secret. I think she's got a crush on Rainbow."

It was Mike's turn to smile, so he turned up the wattage. He needed Amanda as an ally. "You're right. Charlene seems to have really bonded with Rainbow. It seemed to happen so easily, and I'm wondering why."

"It's really complicated."

They lapsed into silence while Mike processed this information. He wanted to ask a dozen follow-up questions, but he held back. He didn't want to seem as if he were interrogating her or something.

He looked up and discovered Rainbow talking to Ethan, while the little boy listened with rapt attention. Rainbow appeared to be whispering, sharing secrets with her friend. He couldn't hear the kid's words but that didn't matter. She had a friend, and that seemed like a miracle.

Mike didn't believe in miracles. Heck, he didn't even believe in luck. Life was random, like the roll of the dice. But he nevertheless found himself ready to believe that running into Amanda and Ethan could be turned into a piece of extraordinary luck.

He turned toward Amanda. "I'm about to ask you a

personal question that you might not want to answer. And if you don't, that's okay. But I was wondering, is Charlene interested in marriage?"

Amanda startled. "That *is* a personal question. Why? Are you interested? I'm not sure you're her type." She studied him again. She seemed to be judging him with that look.

"No," he said, shaking his head. "I'm not the marrying kind. And you probably already know that I'm here for only one purpose—to find Rainbow the perfect family. It's occurred to me that, since Rainbow really likes Charlene and you just said Charlene has a crush on Rainbow, it follows that your friend would make a great mother for her."

"She probably would."

Amanda's gaze intensified until it seared his insides. But he continued laying his cards out for her to see. "So if Charlene would make a perfect mother, and Timmy is Rainbow's uncle, ready and willing to permanently adopt her, then the perfect thing would be to figure out a way to get Timmy to..." He made a gesture with his hands.

Amanda threw back her head and laughed. "Mike, let me tell you something. You aren't the only one in this town who's tried to match Charlene up with Tim. Charlene's aunt Millie has been nudging her in that direction for some time.

"Of course she would have to give up being an Episcopalian. And that's hard in this town, where you kind of come up knowing who you belong to. And besides, the Methodists move their ministers around every ten years or so. I don't think Charlene wants to live like a vagabond. And of course, Charlene's mother would have a hissy fit. But even if Charlene found the gumption to tell her mother where to go, the fact that they belong to different churches also means they don't have many occasions to, you know, meet and mingle."

"Precisely my point. We need to help them meet and mingle."

"How? And by the way, Charlene would skin me alive if I tried any matchmaking tricks."

He folded his arms across his chest. "Really? What would you say if I told you that Miriam Randall suggested that Charlene and Timmy were a match made in heaven? What if I told you she even said that the solution to this problem was to have Timmy volunteer for the AARC bachelor auction and to find some way of encouraging Charlene to buy him?"

Amanda's eyes widened. "Miriam Randall suggested this? When did that happen?"

"I went to see her last week, on Tuesday, I think. I told her I was looking for a wife for Timmy. I suggested Charlene might be perfect for him."

"You did? Really? And Miriam thought this was a good idea?"

"I did and she did."

"Well, I'll be...Really?"

"Yes."

"Okay. That changes everything. I mean if Miriam thinks they belong together, then it will happen. I'm not even sure we need to do anything."

Uh-oh, he hadn't seen that curve coming. "But I thought Miriam helped people see the truth."

"Sometimes. And sometimes people get it all wrong, like they did with Jenny Carpenter and Reverend Lake."

"What?"

She waved her hand in dismissal. "Everyone thought Miriam wanted Pastor Tim to marry the woman who owns the Jonquil House. But they were wrong. I'm just saying that sometimes people misinterpret what Miriam says."

"She was explicit with me. She told me that a little nudge from us would set the *Lord's plan* into action. She also said that Timmy was destined to marry someone with a medical background."

"The Lord's plan?"

"That's what Miriam said. She suggested that the bachelor auction represented a confluence of forces or some such thing. I'm a bit skeptical of that part, but she believed it."

"Okay, I get that. I mean, there will be all those single men and all those single women."

"Yeah, that, too," he said.

"But even if you could get Pastor Tim to enter the auction, how are you going to convince her to buy him?"

"I don't know. That's why I'm talking to you."

"You want me to convince her?"

"You're her best friend. If not you, then who?"

"Yeah, but that doesn't mean she's going to take my advice. She rarely does when it comes to men."

"Oh, that's too bad. Of course you could force the issue. You could buy Timmy for her. You know, like setting her up on a blind date or something."

"No. I told you, I don't play matchmaker for my friends. Ever."

"Oh, that's too bad. But maybe you could break that rule, you know, just this once. I'm telling you, Miriam made it sound like getting them together for dinner might be all it would take for true love to bloom. And if we're wrong about that, and no fires are ignited, then we haven't really lost anything, have we? You know the old saying about nothing ventured, nothing gained."

"You *are* a gambler, aren't you?"

"I never said I wasn't."

"But, wait, I just thought of another problem. Pastor Tim is arguably the best-looking bachelor in town." She paused a moment. "Who isn't gay," she added as an afterthought. "Every single woman is going to want to bid on him."

"Money is not a problem. I would be happy to underwrite the entire plan."

"It's kind of tempting, actually. And Charlene is already kind of angry with me."

"She is? About what?"

"I gave her some relationship advice that she resented…" Amanda's voice trailed off for a moment before she took a deep breath and continued. "You know, Mike, Charlene needs an intervention in her life. But I'm having a hard time seeing her with your brother. I'm really sorry."

"But he would make a terrific husband for someone. And he's going to become Rainbow's father."

Amanda gave Mike a measuring look. "No. I can't help you."

"Would you at least think about it?" He gave her the most earnest look he could muster.

"Okay. But I think you're barking up the wrong tree."

He hadn't closed the deal but he'd planted the seed. He needed to back off a little. She'd refuse if he pressed.

"Fair enough," he said. "But the auction is next Saturday, less than a week away. And I still need to figure out a way to get Timmy to volunteer."

"Oh, I'm happy to help you there. I'll talk to Wilma Riley. She's been everywhere signing guys up for this."

"I have no idea who that is," he said.

"You don't need to. But just so you know, Wilma is the biggest animal lover in town, and she's a vocal member of Tim's congregation. Wilma will guilt him into it. Let me see what I can do."

"So you'll help me?"

"I'll help you get Tim into the auction. But I think you're cracked if you think Charlene and Tim are a match made in heaven."

"Even if Miriam Randall has guaranteed it?"

"Mike, if Miriam's right and Charlene and Tim are a match, they will find each other."

Ethan came scurrying up to his mother. "Mom, you won't believe it. Rainbow's cat caught a mouse, and she ripped off its head, and there was blood and gore everywhere. Isn't that cool?"

Amanda blanched. "Did she tell you that?"

"Yeah. She said her cat was teaching the kittens how to kill mice."

Amanda took her child by the shoulders. "Ethan, I'm sure she was merely—"

"No," Mike interrupted. "Tigger is quite a mouse killer."

"Is that why you have a Band-Aid on your head? Did you really trip over a mouse?" the boy asked.

"Yeah," Mike had to admit. And once he answered that question, Ethan was all over him for the rest of the gory mouse story.

• • •

Mike took a long swim against the Edisto's current while Amanda watched the kids. Then he gave both Ethan and Rainbow swimming lessons. Ethan took to the water like a baby seal. Rainbow, not so much.

But they both made progress.

Amanda left around noon, and Mike rounded up Rainbow for lunch, too. They packed up the new sand toys and headed back to the Polk family's river house, where he'd stashed a pizza in the freezer.

He had just topped the hill when a tan police car came crunching down the gravel access road. The cruiser passed them and then rolled to a stop ahead, blocking their way to Charlene's house.

An African-American officer wearing the uniform of the Last Chance police department emerged. The guy gave the words "poker face" a whole new meaning. He wore mirrored glasses and a Stetson that shaded his face. He gave nothing away.

He strode toward them, invading Mike's space. He put his hands on his hips, the threat clear. Rainbow freaked out. She leaned into Mike, throwing her arm around his waist. She was trembling.

"You Michael C. Taggart?" the cop asked.

"I am."

"You'll need to come with me."

"On what grounds?"

"Trespassing. Breaking and entering. I don't want to cuff you, sir. If you come without a fight, we can get the child into emergency protective custody without causing a scene. I've already notified the county."

"What are you talking about?"

"Did you not break into the house up yonder?" He pointed toward Charlene's house. Mike noticed a second car in the drive right behind his—a big-ass, black Town Car that he didn't recognize.

"Uh, look, there's some mistake. Charlene Polk gave me the keys to the house and told me that I could use it whenever I wanted. You can call her and check it out. And for the record I don't want Rainbow to go into emergency protective custody. She's already had enough of that. Just call Reverend Lake."

The cop let go of a sigh. "Look, Reverend Lake is busy. It's Sunday. And Miz Frances says you broke into her house. She wants us to have you arrested, and when that happens to a single parent, we call the county and put the kids into protective custody."

"I didn't break into her house. I had permission."

"Not from Miz Frances you didn't. And when a property owner out here tells us that someone has broken into their house, then it's my job to bring that person in." He paused for a moment, his face utterly impassive. "So, you coming? Or do I have to put cuffs on you and scare the little girl? You've got three seconds to decide."

Rainbow might not say much, but she could hear just fine. The moment the cop said the word "cuffs," she took off up the hill running like there was no tomorrow.

Had she learned this tactic from Angie? Mike's sister had been arrested a number of times, which meant this wasn't the first bust Rainbow had witnessed.

All this flashed through Mike's head in an instant, along with an overwhelming need to protect Rainbow no matter what. So he didn't think about the situation, he ran after the kid. And that's how he ended up being tackled by the cop and cuffed without ceremony. The moment he was incapacitated, he swiveled his head searching for Rainbow, who was still screaming her head off.

Someone—a woman he didn't recognize—had captured Rainbow. The kid was struggling to get away, kicking at the woman, who was screaming right back at her. But the words coming out of the adult's mouth were mean and bigoted.

The cop hurried up the hill to take charge of Rainbow, who was still struggling, although her screams were starting to subside. "Miz Frances, there's no need to be ugly, now. And I surely do hope you are right about this," the cop said.

Miz Frances glowered at the cop. "It's not your job to question me. I'm Ryan Polk's wife, and that man did not have my permission to use this house. I hope you charge him with resisting arrest." She turned her nose up in the air and headed back inside. Wow. Was that woman Charlene's mother?

Mike muttered a low curse. Maybe Charlene wasn't such a good mate for Tim, after all. Not if Rainbow's future granny was a bigot. He hoped the kid hadn't understood some of the nasty things the woman had said. Wow, it was incredible to see that kind of bigotry on display. And with an African-American officer on the scene.

The cop picked Rainbow up and threw her over his shoulder—a move that was pretty much standard practice when Rainbow was behaving this way. Mike didn't blame him for doing that. It wasn't unkind. It was merely expedient.

But then Rainbow did the unthinkable. She bit the cop hard, right on his ass.

It was wrong to take any satisfaction from the kid's violent behavior. Rainbow needed to learn how to control herself. But he couldn't help it. A small part of him—the street kid he'd once been—admired Rainbow's grit.

CHAPTER 16

Tim's cell phone rang just as he walked through the front door of the parish house after Sunday services. It was Andrea. His heart lifted. "Hey, Andrea."

"Tim. I'm sorry to call you on a Sunday like this. I know this is your busy day, but there's an emergency."

"What?"

"Your brother has been arrested. And the officer in charge took emergency custody of Rainbow, which is allowed under South Carolina law. Unless we get Mike to specify in writing that you should take charge of Rainbow, she's going to go into foster care. So you need to get down to the municipal building right away."

Tim's heart started hammering in his chest. Mike was arrested? He couldn't believe it. And hearing this news made him wonder if he'd been too gullible. "How do you know this?"

"I get called in on these cases to make an assessment as to whether the child has been abused. Rainbow is with me right at the moment. I have to tell you that the policeman started out insisting that Rainbow be sent to juvenile detention. Which is ridiculous for a child her age. But she apparently bit the officer."

"She bit him?"

"Yes, she bit him on the backside." Andrea sounded as if she were trying not to be amused.

"You know," Tim said, "violence like that is not amusing."

"No, it's not. But in this case, if you ask me, the officer had it coming. In my judgment, he could have handled things a little differently. In any case, Mike has been arrested, so you need to get down here."

"Arrested? For what?"

"I gather he broke into a house down at the country club. I don't know all the details, only that he's being held at the county municipal building."

"Why would he break into a house down at the country club? He just needed to ask for keys to Martha's house."

"He didn't break into Martha's house, Tim. He broke into Frances Polk's house, and Frances is pressing charges."

"Frances Polk?"

"Tim, I know you're new in town, but Frances is married to Ryan Polk, who runs the First National Bank. When Frances has a hissy fit, everyone in the government pays attention, right down to the Last Chance police department. So Mike's in big trouble. You need to get down here before someone does something stupid and throws Rainbow into a foster home. I'm trying to get the sheriff's department to let me talk to Mike. He needs to specify in writing that you are Rainbow's temporary guardian. But I need you here to take custody of her."

"But I'm not—"

"I know you don't think you're ready. But you are. You're a good person, Timothy Lake. You may be still trying to process the fact that you have an extended family, but please ask yourself: Would you rather they put Rainbow in a home with complete strangers or let her stay with you? Didn't you say last week that you regretted the fact that you didn't offer Mike and Rainbow a place in the parish house?"

Tim's heart came right up into his throat, and his body flushed. He couldn't breathe. He started to reach for his rescue inhaler.

"Tim, are you still there?"

"Yes, I'm here. What on earth was Mike thinking, breaking into Frances Polk's house?"

"I have no idea. But that's beside the point."

Was it? Mike had been raised without religion, without a moral code, without a father figure. The fact that he got himself into trouble shouldn't be so shocking. And yet it was.

"All right," Tim said through his suddenly tight throat. "I'll be there just as soon as I can."

Charlene's phone rang as she was finishing up at George Nelson's farm. She didn't recognize the caller ID, but it was a local area code.

An emergency, probably. She pressed the talk button. "Dr. Polk."

"Hey, Doc, it's Sheriff Rhodes. I've got a little situation down here at the county building and I thought maybe you could help."

"Uh, Sheriff, if you have an animal situation, you should call animal control."

"It's not an animal situation. I need to ask you a question. Did you give Michael C. Taggart permission to use your family's river house?"

"Yes. I gave him the keys yesterday."

The sheriff, who was normally a cool and collected guy, used a swear word.

"Uh-oh. Sheriff, please don't tell me someone hassled him out there."

"I'm afraid it's worse. Your momma called the Last Chance Police Department when she found a strange car in the drive and clothes in one of the bedrooms. I guess she went a little nuts when she realized it was Mr. Taggart and his little girl."

"Nuts?"

"Well, ma'am, Meryl, the dispatcher on duty, said your momma pitched a fit. Meryl didn't know what to do with her so she patched her in with Royal Sherman, the new deputy chief in Last Chance. And I reckon he decided this represented his big opportunity to show the folks that they could count on him. Unfortunately, Royal doesn't really know how things work in a small town. I'm afraid he treated the situation like we were in downtown Atlanta or something. I'm afraid he arrested Mr. Taggart for trespassing and resisting arrest."

"Oh, my goodness, where was Rainbow when this happened?"

"Right there. She's with Dr. Newsome right now, and I gather some attempt is being made to name Reverend Lake as a temporary custodian. I'm on my way down there, and I hope to have this straightened out. It would be helpful if you could get your momma to call me and let me know this was one big misunderstanding."

"Isn't my word good enough, Sheriff?"

"I reckon. But you know how she can be."

"My mother can go to hell. You can't hold Mike. He had permission from me to use the house. I gave him my key. I can't believe this."

Fury coursed through every atom in her body. Mother hadn't wanted Charlene to keep Derrick's baby. And now she wanted to make Rainbow pay just because Charlene had grown attached to her.

Mother's cruelty was breathtaking.

Sheriff Rhodes sighed audibly. "Look, Charlene, I'm on my way down to the office. I'll get this straightened out. But for everyone's sake, it would be helpful if your momma would apologize."

"She won't."

"That's too bad."

"You need to let Mike go. Now."

She didn't wait for Sheriff Rhodes's response. She hung up on him and stood in George Nelson's barn taking deep breaths as she calmed herself.

She knew exactly why Stone Rhodes wanted Mother's apology. He had to stand for election every four years, so it only made sense that he didn't want to get crosswise with one of the wealthiest and most politically connected families in Allenberg. But even so, the sheriff had no case against Mike. And he knew it.

Charlene left the farm and drove straight to the river. Mike's car was still in the drive, but Mother's sedan was nowhere in sight. So Charlene drove to her parents' house in town.

She purposely wore her boots and neglected to wipe her feet as she hurried into the family room, where she found Daddy watching a baseball game and Mother sitting beside him drinking a glass of wine.

They looked as if nothing untoward had occurred in their lives this Sunday afternoon.

She strode across the room and turned off the television.

"Charlene Ellen Polk, you know better than to—"

"Shut up, Mother." She put both fists on her hips.

"You need to pick up the phone and call Sheriff Rhodes. He's waiting on you. You need to tell him that Mike Taggart had permission to use the river house. And, so help me, if you take after Sheriff Rhodes for doing the right thing, I will be so disappointed in you."

"I will do no such thing. Mike Taggart and that half-breed child didn't have *my* permission to use the house. And do not ever come into this house and order me around, is that clear?" Mother said, elevating her chin.

"Mother, that house belongs to the Polk family. That means that we all share it. You, me, Aunt Charlotte, and Uncle Rob. I have a key, and I gave it to Mike and told him to make himself at home. So he had permission. You should have checked with other members of the family before calling the police. You could have asked him. And if you wanted, you could have asked him politely to leave. You didn't have to get him arrested. Do you have any idea how this must have affected Rainbow?"

"I know precisely how it affected her. I was there. I saw it all. She turned into a demon child. You should have seen the way she bit Deputy Chief Sherman. Why would we want a person like that to use our river house?"

"I'm sure the policeman scared Rainbow. She probably felt as if the cop were taking away the only solid thing in her life. You should have seen the way she reacted last night when Mike injured his head. She depends on him. I think she's come to love him. Honestly, Mother, I would have screamed and kicked and bit, too."

"You most certainly would not have done any such thing. We raised you better than that. And besides, that man isn't worth much. He's white trash. He's a gambler." This comment came from her father.

"He's a day trader, Daddy, and I think there's little difference between what your bank does and what he does. So you can get off your high horse."

"You will not raise your voice to me, young lady." By his suddenly red cheeks, Daddy looked as if he might work himself into a fit. But this time, Charlene didn't give a rat's behind.

"Mother, you will call Sheriff Rhodes right now."

"I will not."

"All right then, don't expect me to ever darken your door again."

She turned and walked away.

"Charlene, you come back here."

She turned around. "No, I'm never coming back here. I'm tired of your bigotry. I'm tired of your hypocrisy. I'm tired of the constant guilt I feel for all the things you talked me into doing. I'm tired of both of you telling me I'm a fine upstanding person in the community when I know I'm not. You're mean and cruel, and I hate you both."

She broke down in tears as she hurried back to her truck. She had just behaved like an out-of-control teenager. She didn't hate her parents. If she hated them, it would be easy to walk away from them. But this wasn't easy. Her parents were ripping her apart.

She climbed back into the truck and headed toward the Allenberg County Center and the county lock-up. On the way, she gave a call to Aunt Millie, who could be counted upon to restore peace in the Polk family whenever the yelling started.

"Hey, darlin', I've been expecting your call," Aunt Millie said as she came on the line.

"You have?"

"Yes, ma'am. I heard what happened to Mike from Ruby Rhodes, who heard it from the sheriff. Ruby called about half an hour ago, and I hope you don't mind, but I gave Thelma Hanks a call and Eugene is already on his way down to the municipal building. Frances is wrong on this. There is no way I'm going to stand by and let her prejudice cost that man custody of his niece. I'm so glad to hear that you intend to go down there and tell everyone what really happened."

"Aunt Millie, I love you. Thank you so much."

"I love you too, darlin'. You get that boy out of jail. Let me take care of Frances."

They put him in an orange jumpsuit and held him in an empty holding cell with a stainless-steel toilet in the corner. He had not been interrogated. He had not been given a chance to make a phone call. They *had* read him his rights and fingerprinted him. He had demanded a lawyer, but so far no one had shown up at the jailhouse door.

He had also begged and pleaded with the arresting officer to call Charlene, but the guy had no interest in listening, especially after Rainbow had bitten his ass.

Mike didn't know where they had taken Rainbow.

He only knew that the arresting officer called for backup because Rainbow had been so out of control.

He worried that they might take her away from him. He worried that they might put her in some awful juvenile detention center, although rationally he had to assume that they didn't have juvenile detention for five-year-olds.

But rationality had flown out the window, replaced by a frantic, over-the-top fury that made him shake.

A man should not have his kid taken away like that.

So he screamed to let out the rage. And got little reaction for the first thirty minutes of his rant, until the door to the outer office opened. A big guy wearing a tan uniform with the words Allenberg County Sheriff's Department on the sleeve patch came striding down the hall.

Mike wanted to pop this guy in the mouth, and he pretty much told him so in a stream of profanity-laced verbal abuse. The guy stood there impassively.

Talk about poker faces. After Mike had pretty much used up his lexicon of filthy words, the man's mouth twitched. "Feel better now?" he asked.

Mike still wanted to pop him one.

"You could have saved your breath, Mr. Taggart," the guy said, "because I'm here to apologize." He pulled a big key ring from his belt and unlocked the cell door.

"You're letting me go?"

"I've heard from Charlene Polk. And, for the record, it was not my department that arrested you. It was the Last Chance police department, and Chief Easley is very embarrassed. Royal Sherman is new on the force, and I think he doesn't quite get our laid-back method of policing. I'm sorry you were detained at all."

"Was Deputy Chief Sherman the guy who scared the crap out of my niece?"

The big cop nodded. "I figure he's gotten what he deserves. Everyone's amused by the bite on his butt. And I think this incident has taught him something important about community."

"Where is my niece now?"

"Come with me."

The sheriff turned on his heel and headed down the hall. Mike followed him through the same squad room where he'd been booked and fingerprinted and then out into the main lobby of the county government building, where Timmy and Dr. Newsome waited with Rainbow.

Someone had gotten the kid some clothes, because the last time he'd seen her she'd been wearing her Strawberry Shortcake bathing suit. Now she wore a pair of pink shorts and a frilly little top—the kind of clothes Rainbow hated. But in Mike's opinion, she looked like heaven itself.

"Hey, kiddo," he said.

Rainbow dropped the doctor's hand and ran toward him. He fell to his knees and she came right into his arms.

He buried his nose into the corner of her neck, hiding the tears that suddenly sprang to his eyes. There weren't that many, but they might as well have been a deluge, because they swept away the walls he'd built around his heart. He'd been piling up those bricks and stones for years and years, from the moment Colin Lake had walked out of his life to the time Mike had walked out of Angie's life. Those walls were protection against the pain of rejection and abuse, against the sure knowledge that love was unreliable. Love hurt.

But he couldn't fool himself any longer. He loved

Rainbow. He didn't exactly know when it had started, but he loved her with every fiber of his being. The last two hours had been an agony for him. He squeezed her tight and renewed his vow to make sure nothing ever scared her again.

Then he picked her up and she straddled his hip, her arms still around his neck in a death grip. "Uh, I guess I need to thank you guys for being here for her," Mike said.

Andrea gave him a wide-eyed look. "Not just for her, Mike, but for you, too."

He shifted his gaze to Timmy and had another emotional shock. Tears glittered in his eyes. "Mike, for goodness' sake, the next time you want to go swimming, call me. I've got the keys to Martha's house."

"It's Sunday, and I assumed—"

"Don't ever assume I don't have time for y'all. I know I may have conveyed that impression the last few days. But the truth is the truth. You're family. And I had a good time yesterday, and I would have loved to join you this afternoon to give Rainbow a second swimming lesson." Timmy crossed the distance and gave both of them a quick hug.

You're family. Holy crap, Tim had accepted the truth. But to him family meant way more than a label. And that blew Mike's mind. He'd never known a real family. Up until right this minute, his family had only ever given him deep, deep pain.

It didn't have to be that way, did it?

But before he could fully process that thought, Charlene came striding through the front doors, followed by a middle-aged man with a bad comb-over and equally unfashionable shorts and polo shirt.

"Mike, don't sign anything," she said. "This here is

Eugene Hanks, and he's one of the best family lawyers in Allenberg County. He will—"

"It's okay, Charlene," the sheriff said. "Mike is free to go, and Rainbow is still in his custody, as you can clearly see. Hey, Eugene."

"I thought you needed Mother to call you and—"

"Nope. My momma set me straight, and y'all know how Ruby can be. So, I reckon I'll have to take my chances next election. I hope y'all remember this when voting day comes around."

Eugene Hanks nodded. "You got my vote, Stone. And since I don't appear to be needed, I think I'll get on home and get back to trimming the boxwoods and finishing off the rest of Thelma's honey-do list." The lawyer made a quick about-face and headed back out the doors.

"I hope y'all have a much better day from here forward," the sheriff said. "Now I need to get going, because I've got my own honey-do list waiting back home." The sheriff strolled back through the door to the squad room.

"You called a lawyer?" Mike said, once the lawyer and the lawman had departed.

"Of course I did. I'm so sorry. My mother is..." Charlene's voice cracked, and she wiped a tear from her eye. "I'm so sorry," she repeated, her chin quivering.

Mike longed to cross the space between them and give her a big hug. The kind of hug that lasted for more than a few seconds. But he restrained himself. He'd come way too close to kissing her last night, and this moment seemed far too emotional to get too close to her.

Besides, hugging Charlene would send the wrong message to his brother.

Mike still believed that Timmy and Charlene and

Rainbow belonged together. His libido needed to get down with that program and accept the fact that he was destined to be the uncle in this family.

"No one's blaming you, Charlene," Dr. Newsome said. She didn't have any problem bestowing hugs, because she laid one on Charlene and then handed her a wad of tissues that she magically pulled out of her purse.

Therapists must go through a ton of tissues.

Charlene wiped her eyes and blew her nose. "Uh, Mike, if you want, I can take you back to the river so you can pick up your car and other stuff. Mother tossed everything into the trash, but I rescued it."

"Sort of like you rescued me?" The words popped out of his mouth. Maybe they would substitute for the hug he really, really wanted to give her.

"A rescue mission should not have been necessary, Mike. I'm so embarrassed and…" her voice wobbled again, and Mike really needed to do something to stop her pain.

"It's okay. I kind of like being rescued." The words left his mouth before he fully evaluated them. But they seemed so right. And so true. A whole group of people had come together to rescue him. Dr. Newsome, Timmy, Rainbow. And Charlene, who'd brought a lawyer with her. Bless her heart, as Elsie would say.

But Charlene continued to cry. And right then, Mike recognized the price for smashing the walls around his emotions.

Charlene's tears nearly broke his heart.

CHAPTER 17

Dr. Newsome had a talent for heading off awkward moments. The moment Charlene started bawling, she dug for more tissues and suggested that it might be good if everyone got together for a late lunch at Pizza Hut, Rainbow's favorite eatery.

There were no two ways about her suggestion. It was mandatory.

And before long, the doctor had managed to create a space where everyone could decompress. The lunch turned into a debriefing as much as a family get-together.

For Mike, the family connection seemed to overwhelm all the other emotions he'd experienced. If he'd been told two hours ago that he'd end up here with friends and family who deeply cared about him, he would never have believed it.

He'd never had anyone who watched his back. If anything, the back-watching had always fallen to him. He'd certainly watched Timmy's and Angie's backs when Mom got nasty. But he'd failed them somehow. So it came as a big surprise that anyone would be willing to come to his rescue when the crap started flying.

But they had. And that changed him in ways he couldn't yet fathom.

After lunch, Dr. Newsome suggested that it might be best if Rainbow didn't return to the country club to collect Mike's car. So Timmy drove Rainbow home, since he had a booster seat in his car. And Charlene agreed to take Mike to the river house to collect his car and clothes.

She apologized about six times in the first ten minutes of the drive. Clearly she needed to forgive herself. Mike understood that emotion. He sure hadn't forgiven himself for what happened to Angie, and he bore a lot more responsibility for that than Charlene did for what had happened today.

He turned toward her. She gripped the pickup's steering wheel so hard that her knuckles had turned white. "Stop apologizing," he said. "What happened today was *not* your fault. Let's just get that straight, okay?"

She kept her gaze fixed on the two-lane road. "It *was* my fault. All my fault. At the least, I should have told Mother and Daddy that I was letting you use the house. But, really, knowing Mother and Daddy, I should have had my head examined for even giving you the key. They are bigots, Mike, and I'm so ashamed."

He'd seen the bigotry on display this afternoon. He still couldn't quite understand how a person like Frances Polk could have raised a woman like Charlene. It didn't compute, somehow.

"Look, just because your mom sent that cop after us doesn't make you responsible. Her views are hers and hers alone."

"You don't understand, Mike. You're not from around here. There are a lot of people like her." Her voice sounded fragile but she remained dry-eyed.

"So far, I've gotten the impression that Last Chance is just about the best place I could dream up for a kid like Rainbow. I mean people seem to care about her, and there are a lot of folks who don't seem to notice her race. White people like Lizzy Rhodes and Maryanne Carpenter at the Bible camp seem to care deeply about her and all the other kids. And Elsie Campbell and Flo Johnson, who are black, care about her, too. Then there is you."

"Me?"

"Yeah, you. You bring her books. You let her play with your kittens. You got her to eat broccoli and fried chicken. You've connected with her in some way I can't understand. She talks to you, Charlene. The only other person she talks to is her friend Ethan. So explain to me how this isn't some kind of wonderful place for a kid who is mixed race."

A tear leaked from the corner of her eye. "I think it might be better if I backed off a little."

"Damnit, Charlene. Stop. You don't want to back off any more than I want you to. You're good for Rainbow. And, the truth is, Amanda told me just this morning that she thinks Rainbow is good for you. So what's this all about?"

"Amanda said that? When did you talk to her?"

"This morning before I was arrested. She and Ethan were at the river, and we got to talking."

"For goodness' sake, Amanda needs to mind her own business. Just leave it alone." She bit her lip to stop it from quivering.

"No. I won't."

"You don't need to know everything about me." She turned the wheel hard, and the truck hit the gravel of the country club's private road a little on the fast side. She obviously wanted to get him out of her truck as quickly as possible.

She pulled up beside the Hyundai. "Here you go. I've got your clothes in the back." She threw the truck into park and didn't even turn off the engine.

He decided not to get out of the cab.

It took her a moment to figure out his strategy. She strode around the truck, got out, and opened the passenger's side door. "It's the end of the line, Mike."

"No, Charlene, it's not. Let me lay my cards out on the table. You and Rainbow have something special going on, so if you think for one minute I'm going to let you walk out on her, you're crazy. You once accused me of wanting to abandon her. So I'm turning the tables on you."

"Mike, you don't understand."

"Then explain it to me. I've been honest with you. I've told you that it would please me to no end if I could find a way for you and Timmy to be permanently part of Rainbow's life. So I gotta know what the hell is going on with you."

She turned away and started walking down toward the water. He shut off the engine, hopped out of the cab, and followed her.

"Don't walk away from me, damnit."

Charlene didn't listen. He followed her all the way down to the river and then up a weedy path to a pier that jutted out into the river's brown water. There were plenty of people swimming downriver, but up here it was deserted. She walked right out onto the pier and leaned her elbows into the railing.

Mike followed. He handed her the keys to her truck. "I turned off the engine. I figured we might be here a while."

"You're a pain in the backside."

He managed a small laugh. "Yup, me and Rainbow both."

She sucked in a deep breath. Mike expected her to let forth with a torrent of words, but she remained silent. He held his ground. It was peaceful here with the river gurgling as it flowed past.

She stayed quiet for so long that, when she finally spoke, it almost surprised him.

"You think I'm such a good person, but you're wrong. You think I'd make such a great mother. But you're mistaken."

"Okay, why?" He turned toward her, leaning his hip into the railing.

"My freshman year at UNC, I fell in love with this guy, and I stupidly got pregnant. We loved each other, or so I thought. So we decided to get married, and we came home to tell my folks. As you might expect, they weren't very happy. But you might be surprised by the reason. Their biggest problem with the situation was that Derrick was African American. If I'd come home with a white guy from a Charleston family, Mother and Daddy would have probably thrown me the wedding of the century."

She stopped speaking for a moment. Mike could see her struggling for control.

"Anyway," she said in a fragile voice, "instead of paying for a wedding, Daddy took out his checkbook and offered to pay for Derrick's college lock, stock, and barrel.

The only catch was that Derrick had to agree never to see me again."

"And he took that deal?"

She nodded.

"Jeez."

"That's how I discovered Derrick had a larcenous soul. He betrayed me like Judas."

"What about the baby?"

She looked away for a moment, pain in her dark eyes. "Well, that's where Mother went to work. She felt I was too young to become a single mother. And then she managed to convince me that a child like mine would have a hard time finding adoptive parents."

"Let me get this straight. They fixed it so the guy who had agreed to marry you walked away, and then they started in on you about how it would be awful to be a single mother?"

She nodded but wouldn't meet his gaze. "You wanted the truth. Here it is. I got rid of the baby. I had an abortion. I told myself it was the right thing to do. That I couldn't give that child anything positive. But I was so wrong. And I'm never ever going to be able to forgive myself for what I did. Don't you see? I've been thinking that I could change the past by helping Rainbow now. But it's not true. If I get involved, Mother is going to go out of her way to be mean like she was today."

Her voice broke, and she finished the last words on a sob.

Mike pulled her into his arms. She came willingly and gripped the fabric of the county-issued jumpsuit as she wept against his chest.

"It's okay, doll, just let it all hang out. *I* forgive you."

• • •

I forgive you.

Mike's words sneaked past her defenses. Or maybe she let them pass because his fierce embrace made her feel safe. No one had ever given her a place to cry her heart out. Not like this. Not John, or Phillip, or Erik.

She'd never told any of them her secret because she was afraid they would walk away if they knew. It turned out they walked away anyway.

But not Mike. He'd followed her. He'd waited her out. And now his touch was magic. He had some serious Prince Charming attributes. He seemed intent on slaying all her inner monsters.

"You're fine," he said softly. "You're not a bad person, Charlene."

Why did he, of all people, have the power to forgive her? She had no answer for that. But the harder she cried the sturdier his chest seemed, until she had emptied herself of tears. Now she had to raise her head and look him in the eye.

She was searching for her courage when he said, "So, I guess we're even now. You rescued me, and I've forgiven you."

"It doesn't change anything," she said in a last-gasp effort to hang on to her guilt.

"Of course it does," he insisted.

"No." She eased back, finally. "The truth is, I should stay away from Rainbow because Mother will make her life horrible."

He brushed the last few tears from her cheeks. His touch was warm and kind. Her body suddenly noticed that they were kind of mashed up against each other. Yeah, he was sturdy all right. And hard-muscled, and male. He smelled good, too.

"I think it would be stupid for you to stay away from Rainbow."

"How can you say that after what happened today?"

"Charlene, your mother is one person. But five or six other people came to Rainbow's rescue today. Dr. Newsome, Timmy, the sheriff, the lawyer. And you. You came running to her defense like a mama lion. And I think if the situation had lasted any longer, Elsie Campbell would have delivered a coconut cake to the jail."

"Don't laugh at her. She'll probably have a cake waiting for you at home."

"My point exactly. Don't you see?"

"Don't I see what?"

"Boy, you really are having trouble seeing the forest. Dollface, there are some incredibly caring people in your town. When Timmy takes custody of Rainbow, there isn't a thing your mother is going to be able to do to hurt Rainbow. If she does, she's going to look small and petty. Timmy's got an army of church ladies protecting him. It's kind of impressive, actually. And I'll bet every single one of them is filled to the brim with Christian forgiveness."

Charlene didn't say a word. This truth had never occurred to her before. Of course she'd prayed for forgiveness. The Lord was supposed to forgive. But maybe she'd been looking in the wrong place. Maybe she shouldn't have kept this secret locked up for so long.

Maybe with a little help, she could forgive herself.

Mike tucked a strand of dark hair behind her ear. "Amanda told me Rainbow was your redemption. I think it's true."

Maybe Rainbow was his redemption, too. She didn't say that out loud. But the thought blossomed inside her as they stood, arms entwined, while a silent and powerful connection sprang up between them. So when Mike dipped his head and pressed his mouth to hers, she was waiting for his kiss. She opened her mouth for him and discovered magic of the healing kind. What was it about him? He seemed to be able to chase the bad things out of her head and replace them with something fine and good. And it struck her, as he deepened the kiss, that he'd been doing the same thing for Rainbow. In his own bumbling way, he'd been chasing away all the kid fears, all the monsters, and replacing them with something solid and dependable.

She let herself fall into the kiss, her body catching fire in ways that it hadn't in so long. He backed her up against the railing, pressing his body against hers as he ran his hands down the curve of her back and then over to her hip and up to her breast. It felt so good. So right.

She was about to suggest that they take this up to the river house for more privacy when he suddenly groaned and then backed up three spaces.

They stood there staring at each other, eyes wide, breathing hard, aroused.

"I can't do this," he said.

All her self-doubts came crashing down on her once again. "But—"

"Look, Charlene, I want you to think seriously about buying Timmy at the upcoming auction. You guys would be perfect together. You'd be the perfect parents for Rainbow, and believe me, Timmy's Altar Guild can handle your mother. I want the best for you and Rainbow, and the best means for you and Timmy to hook up and adopt Rainbow as your own. I'm going back to Vegas, and that's no place for a kid. I love Rainbow, and I'm smart enough to know that I'm not the guy she needs as a father."

And with that statement, Mike turned away from her and marched up the hill to his car.

A keen sense of guilt had turned Mike's stomach sour by the time he walked into Martha Spalding's condo. Timmy's weeping eyes and red nose didn't make him feel any better. He found Timmy hanging out in the kitchen with a box of tissues while Rainbow sprawled on the couch watching cartoons with her cat.

"Took you a little longer than I expected," Timmy said, then sneezed.

"Man, I'm sorry. I stopped to get gas." It was such a lame excuse. And really, aside from the kiss, he shouldn't feel all that guilty about letting Charlene cry on his shoulder. But he sure didn't want to tell Timmy what he'd been up to. Timmy might get the wrong idea. And Mike still wanted to find some way to get Timmy and Charlene together.

But clearly, he had a big cat problem.

Timmy blew his nose. "Mike, I've been praying on this for a few days and I've had several long conversations with Andrea, and I've finally come to the conclusion that it's time for us to get the adoption process rolling. Andrea seems to think that the sooner we get Rainbow into a permanent situation, the better it will be for her. And I know you want to get back to your life in Vegas."

Mike shouldn't have been surprised. Not after what had happened today. They'd all come together as a family, and Timmy was ready to jump into parenthood.

But Charlene wasn't.

And even though Charlene hadn't been a part of his initial plan, Mike's plan had changed. He wanted Rainbow to have Charlene as a mom, and he couldn't leave that to chance.

He needed time.

Which he really didn't have. Paul, his agent, still wanted him to get his butt back to Vegas so he could schmooze the Dragon Casino people. A week ago, he probably would have signed Rainbow over to Timmy and booked the next flight out.

But not now. Making sure Rainbow had the right mother trumped everything. And after what Charlene had told him, Mike had no doubts about her as mother material. *That* was a match made in heaven.

But how to convince Timmy of that?

"So," Timmy said, "I'll give Eugene Hanks a call tomorrow. You met him today, briefly."

"The guy with the comb-over and madras shorts?"

"One and the same."

Damn. If this guy was willing to drop his hedge trimming on a moment's notice, he probably didn't have a terribly full calendar.

"Okay, we can get that ball rolling, but we need to have a plan about the cat."

Timmy frowned. "A plan? What kind of plan? The cat can't come to the parish house."

"I know, that's why we need a plan." Mike was extemporizing.

"I thought we had agreed that you needed to find the cat a home."

"Or maybe you could sign up for allergy shots."

"Allergy shots don't work. I've tried them," Timmy said, and then promptly sneezed.

"You have, really?"

He nodded and sneezed again. He blew his nose and then said, "The cat has to go. I thought you were trying to find a home for it."

Right. "Turns out I haven't done anything about that."

"Why not?"

"Because Rainbow is pretty attached to the cat. So..."

"Mike, if you can't find a home for it, then the cat needs to go to the shelter."

"No, we can't do that."

"Why not? It's just a cat."

"Haven't you heard about the animal shelter? I mean it's in a bad way. That's why they're having the auction."

"Okay, maybe Charlene will take the cat." Timmy sneezed again.

"No. Charlene already has three cats." Which was a problem in and of itself. Mike needed to deal with Tigger and Winkin', Blinkin', and Nod. He needed time. So he brought out the big guns. Timmy always deferred to Andrea on matters pertaining to Rainbow, so he invoked the therapist's name. "Andrea thinks Tigger is important to Rainbow's recovery." That was true. Mike and Andrea had discussed Rainbow's dependence on the cat at great length.

Obviously Timmy had not, because he said, "Oh?" as if he'd never heard of Rainbow's dependence on the cat.

"So I think we need to give Rainbow a few days to get used to this idea. It's like what I do when it's time to go to camp. I put on a timer."

"A timer? What are you talking about?"

"Rainbow has trouble separating from the cat. So every time we go out, I set the kitchen timer and give her ten minutes to snuggle, and when the timer goes off, she's usually ready to make the transition to something new. It works. I'm telling you, I've avoided a lot of tantrums this way. So we kind of need to set a timer on the cat."

"Okay. What did you have in mind?"

"Let's say a week." That would get him past the auction. He really needed to step up his game and get Timmy to volunteer and Charlene to buy him.

"Okay, that seems reasonable."

"Good, so I'll call the lawyer, okay?" Mike said.

"If you like."

Good. Now Mike was in charge of the scheduling, and he could make sure the meeting took place later rather than sooner.

Timmy stood up. "Okay, I guess we're set then."

"Yup, all set." Mike gave Timmy his best poker-player smile.

CHAPTER
18

Tim sat in his office Monday morning staring out his window at the church's side lawn, which had been overtaken by a group of Bible campers. The children were stretched out on the grass with their eyes closed. No doubt the counselors were having the children commune with nature.

Right now Tim was communing with his own nature. Now that he'd made up his mind he wanted to move forward. The delay bothered him.

So he called Andrea, and to his astonishment, she'd endorsed Mike's cat plan. She even praised Mike for being so creative. She also warned that it might not be so easy to separate Rainbow from her cat.

She suggested that it might take more than a week.

"He won't stay longer than that," Tim said.

"He might surprise you."

"He's a gambler. He loves money too much. There's a passage in Ecclesiastes that says it best. *Whoever loves money never has money enough.*"

"You think he loves money?" Andrea asked.

"Of course."

"Hmmm. Could have fooled me. I got the impression that he loved Rainbow."

That stopped Tim right in his tracks. "Then why is he giving her up?"

"That's an excellent question, Tim. Maybe you can help him figure that one out."

After she laid that bombshell on him, she had the temerity to tell him that her next patient had arrived. She hung up, leaving him alone to ponder her question all on his own.

He was brooding about it when Wilma Riley came striding into his office. She dropped into the chair facing his desk. "Pastor Tim," she said in her gravelly voice, "it has come to my attention that you have not volunteered for the Allenberg Animal Rescue Committee's gala fundraiser next Saturday. I'm here to sign you up."

Oh, boy, he needed this like a hole in the head. "Are you talking about the bachelor auction?"

"I am." She reached into her oversized purse and pulled out some papers. "Here are the entry forms."

"I'm not participating in a bachelor auction."

"Why the hell not?"

He scowled at her. "Really, Wilma, we're in a church."

"Oh, sorry. Why the heck not?"

"Because it's..." He didn't really have a word for it.

"Oh, come on, Pastor Tim, don't tell me you're embarrassed?"

"No, that wasn't the word I was looking for. I just don't think it's appropriate for a clergyman to participate in something like that."

"Something that's raising money for animal welfare? I've noticed you don't have any pets. Are you antipet or something?"

Guilt had his face growing hot. Hadn't Mike gotten all over him last night when he'd suggested that Rainbow's cat should be taken to the shelter?

"No, I'm just allergic. Violently allergic to cats. Which reminds me, I need your help finding a home for Rainbow's cat. I don't want her to end up in the shelter."

"You're going to take the cat away from the child?"

Oh, boy, everyone had an opinion, and it seemed that they all agreed with Andrea. It was the first time that he and Andrea hadn't seen eye to eye on something. But then, she didn't understand how it felt to be that allergic. "I have no other choice. I can't be in the same room with a cat. They make my eyes weep, and I sneeze, and sometimes they trigger an asthma attack. So I need a plan for the cat, Wilma. Not a lecture."

"Oh, you poor thing. I'll talk to Angel and see if he has any ideas. But your allergies notwithstanding, we still need you to step up and help. You've heard about what the county is planning to do to our shelter?"

He shook his head, which was a big mistake because Wilma launched into a tirade about Dennis Hayden and all the little kittens and puppies that were being euthanized. And then she leaned in. "Pastor Tim, can I be frank?"

He nodded. He'd never known Wilma to be anything other than ruthlessly frank.

"I think participating would be good for your image," Wilma said.

"My image?"

"Yes. I'm afraid you are widely regarded as something of a bore."

"A bore?"

She cocked her head and gave him her "give no quarter" look. "I'm afraid so. You're putting people to sleep with your sermons, and you aren't ever going to find a wife if you don't spruce yourself up some. You're a good-looking guy, but kind of dull."

"I'm happy being dull."

"No, you're not. In fact, you've become much sexier now that Mike Taggart has arrived. I've heard all about how you rushed down to the county building to protect the little girl yesterday. That's very seductive stuff, you know, especially since you aren't really a pet person. Everyone thinks you're going to make a terrific father for Rainbow."

He had no idea what Wilma was trying to say, but his patience had officially been tried. "I'm not going to participate in the auction, and I don't see why there's any connection to Mike and Rainbow and this event."

Wilma heaved a big sigh. "Look, Tim, I hate to tell you this, but it's all over town that Miriam Randall said that something magical is supposed to happen to you at the auction."

"Magical?"

"Okay, maybe I should say matrimonial. So you can't sit this one out. You've got to go and meet your soulmate, especially since you're about to become a daddy. I'm not much of a believer in marriage, but I do think that every child should be brought up in a home with a momma and a daddy. So you need to go find Rainbow a momma. And that's especially true if you're planning to take away her cat."

Finding a mother for Rainbow would be a good thing, but he doubted that he'd manage that at a bachelor auction. He was about to tell Wilma this when his phone rang. He opted to answer the phone rather than continue his argument.

Big mistake. "Pastor Tim?" The voice on the other end of the line was unmistakable.

"Elsie. What can I do for you?"

"You can sign up for the bachelor auction," she said.

"Did you plan this with Wilma?" he asked.

"No, has she called you about this?"

"She's right here in my office."

"Really? I guess that's because she's an animal lover. But look here, Pastor Tim, Miriam Randall says you're going to find your soulmate at the auction. So you need to be a part of it."

Tim cast his gaze out the window toward the campers lying in the grass. He wished mightily that he could escape out there like those kids. But no, he was stuck here in his office where every busybody in his congregation would be stopping by to urge his participation in the AARC fund-raiser.

He didn't believe in what the folks in Last Chance said about Miriam Randall. But that didn't make one iota of difference. If the female members of his congregation believed that the Lord wanted him to participate in this auction, then he'd better darn well do it.

"You tell the Altar Guild I'm in," he said on a long breath.

"Oh, good. I knew you'd see the light."

But later, as he was filling out the form, he began to second-guess himself. What if some hussy with loose morals purchased him? How would he ever live it down?

He bowed his head and prayed like he had never prayed before. Maybe the ladies of the Guild were right and the Lord had a plan for him. Otherwise this had disaster written all over it.

On Tuesday afternoon, Angel was having a latte at the Garden of Eatin' when Elsie Campbell marched into the place and sat down at his table. "We have a problem," she said.

Angel had many problems at that moment, most of them involving Dr. David Underhill and whether he should buy him at the auction scheduled for Saturday night, but he doubted that Elsie's problem corresponded to his.

"What is it?" he asked as he took a sip of his drink.

"Pastor Tim hates cats."

"I am sorry for him. But what do you want me to do about it?"

"Don't tell me that you haven't heard the news."

"What news? I have been preoccupied with caterers and florists."

"Miriam says that Pastor Tim and Charlene Polk are destined to find love at the auction. But someone left three kittens on Charlene's front steps. And you know how allergic Pastor Tim is to cats."

Angel almost choked on his coffee. "Miriam says Pastor Tim and Charlene Polk are soulmates?"

Elsie nodded, joy in her eyes. "Yessir, that's what I've heard. So we need to get busy and find homes for all those cats. Although I don't think the little girl wants to give up her cat, bless her heart. But she'll be getting a mommy and daddy, and that's better, don't you think? And I'm ready to murder the person who put those kittens on Charlene's front steps. Their timing could not have been worse."

Angel put his cup down. "Oh, boy," he muttered.

Elsie frowned at him. "What's wrong?"

"Elsie, I am afraid that I am the one who delivered those kittens."

"You?"

"Me. I thought they would be good for Charlene. Her cat died a little while ago, and she has been having trouble moving on. She needed a little kick in the behind." He also thought they might distract her from the pain of realizing that Dr. Dave was gay. But telling Elsie that would be like tweeting the news to the entire population of South Carolina.

Elsie gave him a look that could kill. "I guess I can understand your motives, Angel, but Charlene needs Pastor Tim and Rainbow more than she needs three kittens. And I say this as an animal lover. Where did you get them?"

"Daniel Jessup found them in the barn on the old Carpenter place. Their mother had abandoned them, or met her fate under the wheels of someone's car. Anyway, he called me when he found them."

"We'll just have to find other arrangements for them."

"Elsie, have you talked to Charlene about this? I think she loves those kittens."

"That may be, but they're standing in the way of her happiness, and since you're the one who left them on her doorstep, you're the one who needs to set things right. Every Methodist in town will thank you for it." She stood up and folded her arms across her chest. "And while you're at it, we need a home for the girl's cat, too. This is really important, Angel, and I don't know who else to talk to about it, seeing as our animal shelter is not exactly up to snuff."

"I will do what I can," he said.

Elsie left the Garden of Eatin' in a hurry. Angel took the time to finish his latte. Then he headed down to the Knit & Stitch, where the Purly Girls would soon be gathering for their weekly Tuesday charity knitting meeting.

Most of the girls had already arrived by the time he strolled into the shop. Charlotte Polk, Luanne Howe, and several other ladies had come over on the Senior Center bus. And as he had hoped, Miriam Randall and her niece Savannah were both there as well.

Pat Canaday, the shop's owner, was busy pouring sweet tea and handing out red velvet cupcakes when he arrived. Once the refreshments were disbursed, Angel made himself useful by helping the old ladies cast on their latest project—hats for the Hatbox Foundation, an organization that gives handmade hats to cancer patients undergoing chemotherapy.

"So," he said, once everyone had settled into their knitting, "the Methodists are all excited about the news that Pastor Tim is about to fall in love."

"Who told you that?" Miriam said.

"It is all over town that *you* said it was going to happen at the auction on Saturday," Angel said.

Miriam stared at him through her rhinestone trifocals. Savannah gave him an equally sober look. Oh, boy. Once again the church women of Last Chance had, perhaps, misinterpreted something Miriam had said. "This is not so?" he asked.

"I don't remember saying anything about Pastor Tim or the auction."

"No?" He cast a glance at Savannah, who had turned toward her aunt with a little frown. Miriam looked particularly frail today, her gaze a little cloudy. It made Angel sad to see the dementia setting in. She was not the woman she had been a year ago, when Angel had first come to town.

"Aunt Mim, I do think you spoke with Pastor Tim's brother. Dash said he came by the house a week ago or so," Savannah said.

"I don't think so. Dash must be mistaken."

Savannah let out a big breath. She leaned in toward Angel and whispered. "I think she *did* speak with Mr. Taggart. But I don't have any idea what she might have told him."

"What is she supposed to have said?" Pat asked.

"Elsie Campbell seems to think Pastor Tim is going to fall head over heels in love with Charlene Polk at the auction on Saturday," Angel said.

"What?" This from Charlotte. "There is no way my niece is marrying a Methodist minister. My father would spin in his grave. My family has been Episcopalians since we were Anglicans." This made no sense if you did not already know that Charlotte was a proud member of the DAR.

"Charlotte, I am not sure it would be a good match for other reasons. Pastor Tim is allergic to cats, and Charlene has three of them," Angel said.

"Oh, that's not good," Miriam said, shaking her head.

"What? She's marrying cats?" Luanne said. "That's unusual, isn't it?" Luanne was more senile than the rest of the girls.

"No, Luanne, she's marrying a Methodist, and that's practically unheard of," Charlotte said.

"You know," Angel said to no one in particular, "I am starting to wish I had never come up with this idea of a bachelor auction. It is all getting very complicated."

"Of course it is," Savannah said.

"What is that supposed to mean?"

"It means your soulmate is closer than you think. You just have to force the issue a little bit."

"Savannah, hon, are you taking over the family business?" Pat asked.

Savannah blushed. "The truth is I sometimes get feelings about things. And Aunt Mim tells me that I should listen to them. And about the auction, Angel, I'm starting to think that it would be a mistake for you to sit on the sidelines this Saturday."

"So do you have any feelings about Charlene?" Charlotte asked. "And please tell me they don't involve any Methodists." Thank God Charlotte asked this question before the girls realized that Savannah had just suggested that one of the bachelors was gay.

Savannah gave Charlotte a hard stare. "I don't have any feelings about Charlene one way or the other. But I do believe that Pastor Tim may be about to fall in love. And I get the sense that she's involved in medicine. So maybe that's where everyone came up with Charlene."

"So you think I should help Charlene find homes for her cats?" Angel asked.

Savannah shook her head. "I don't really know the answer to that. All I know is that this auction of yours has created opportunities for things to happen. We just need to nudge them along. That's especially true in your case, Angel. I feel very strongly about that."

Pat, who was one of the few nonsenile women in the

room, turned and gave Savannah a speculative glance. "Okay, this has me wondering. Which bachelor?"

Savannah held Pat's gaze. "That's entirely up to Angel, Pat."

Wednesday afternoon, Charlene had finished her last patient visit for the day and had settled at her desk to catch up on emails when Cindy buzzed on the intercom. "You better brace yourself."

"What?"

"Your aunt and mother are on their way back. I tried to stop them but—"

A moment later Mother burst into the office. She was dressed to kill in a Lilly Pulitzer dress that Charlene hadn't seen before. But then Mother had more Lilly Pulitzer dresses than the entire Palm Beach junior league. "Charlene, we need to talk. Miriam Randall is senile, and I will not have you dating a Methodist," she said.

"Now, Frances, don't get all excited." Aunt Millie followed Mother into the room. Unlike Mother, Millie was wearing a pair of plain khaki pants and a green striped blouse that she'd probably purchased online from L.L. Bean.

Charlene clamped down on her fury. Mother had not yet apologized for what she had done yesterday, and now she was passing judgment on Tim Lake as if she had one word to say about how Charlene lived her life.

She flashed back to those moments at the river yesterday when Mike had held her and told her he forgave her. There had been such deep kindness in his eyes right before he kissed her. As if he'd seen the very worst of her and still could find something worthy.

If she told Mother that she had fallen for a gambler, she'd be even more outraged. Unless she brought home someone exactly like Daddy—some lawyer or banker with a Charleston background—Mother would be equally outraged.

There was no pleasing her. Ever.

She suddenly appreciated Cousin Simon's decades-long rebellion against Aunt Charlotte.

"Mother, I'm not speaking with you, remember?" she said.

Mother stopped in her tracks and gave Charlene an odd look. But it didn't last long. She shook it off and said, "Don't be ridiculous. You spoke in anger yesterday. I didn't for one moment take anything you said personally."

"You didn't?" Man, that was disappointing. Mother seemed to be living her life inside some kind of shell composed of copious quantities of wine and self-delusion.

"No, I didn't. Now, we need to talk about Tim Lake. Miriam Randall says that he's your soulmate. Millie just heard that Reverend Lake has officially signed up for this bachelor auction. And everyone says the two of you are going to find love there."

"Pastor Tim signed up for the auction? I'm amazed."

"You can be amazed if you like," Mother said. "But it's a big problem. Your grandfather would spin in his grave if you became a Methodist, much less married one. And besides, everyone in this town knows that Miriam Randall is going senile. So I don't care what she may have said about you and that new minister. The fact is, we both know you don't care one fig for that man. It's that little black girl that's got you all twisted up inside. You marrying that man because of that girl would be a huge mistake."

All of yesterday's emotions came roaring back, along with Mike's words out at the river. For once, Charlene fought her way through the guilt and saw the truth. Nobody cared about Rainbow's racial background except Mother. The Methodist Altar Guild was actively trying to create a family for this little girl. And in Charlene's opinion, they were doing the Lord's work.

Charlene laced her fingers together and stared down at them, trying to control her rage. She'd let it loose yesterday, and it hadn't done any good. It hadn't changed Mother. She would never change.

Charlene had to change herself. She had to walk away, and she had to protect Rainbow from the ugliness that Mother insisted on spewing. But Mother had one thing right. Charlene didn't care one fig about Tim Lake. On the other hand, Mike didn't look like a paragon of husband material either.

Between the two of them, Tim would be the better bet. And besides, he was the one with Miriam Randall's endorsement. And she'd be a fool not to pay attention to that.

She looked up from her hands, right into her mother's censorious gaze. "Mother, I adore Rainbow Taggart. I want to be her mother more than anything I can think of. And since Miriam Randall thinks Tim Lake and I would be great together, I'd be a fool not to give it a try. So I've made up my mind. I'm going to buy Tim Lake at the auction this Saturday."

"No!" Mother gasped.

"All Riiiiight!" Millie said as she clapped her hands.

Mother glowered at her sister-in-law. "Millie, really. You've always been foolish and silly, but this time you've overstepped your bounds."

Millie gave Mother the stink eye. "Frances, go suck an egg."

Mother's mouth fell open, but Aunt Millie ignored her. Instead she turned toward Charlene, her face bright with her signature smile. "Now, honey, we need to schedule you for an appointment with Ruby and make you gorgeous for Saturday. I think you are a pretty girl, but as Ruby is always saying, it doesn't hurt to give nature a little boost from time to time."

Mike joined ranks with the Methodist Altar Guild, and boy, those ladies could move mountains. They got Timmy to sign up for the bachelor auction. They spread the word about Miriam's matrimonial forecast. And they were all on the lookout for permanent homes for the cats in Charlene and Rainbow's lives. So events seemed to be moving in the right direction.

By Saturday, everything would be settled.

And while he let the church ladies do their thing, he settled into a routine with Rainbow. He took the kid to day camp in the morning, then he picked her up in the afternoon, sometimes to take her to see Dr. Newsome and sometimes to bring her home.

He let her have an hour at Charlene's house playing with the kittens, but he stayed away so as not to confuse things. Then he made dinner—Rainbow had expanded her list of acceptable food choices to include macaroni and cheese, and she even tolerated broccoli if he cut it up finely and buried it in the noodles.

He bathed her, but he'd quit washing her hair every day. Instead, he had sought help from Amy at the Rexall drugstore, who directed him to a big section filled with special hair care products. And then he learned to braid Rainbow's hair by following the detailed instructions in a YouTube video designed specifically for white people caring for African-American kids.

Then he read to her, usually the book about Pete the cat.

And once they got through all that, he set the kitchen timer and gave her a final ten minutes with Tigger before bedtime. After that, she had to sleep on her own.

It made him feel terrible every night when he put Rainbow to bed and then closed the cat up in the large walk-in closet that served as his office. The kid cried. The cat meowed. And the first night, Rainbow had gotten up in the middle of the night and hauled the cat back into bed with her.

So Mike put a latch on the door, way up high, out of Rainbow's reach. That seemed to keep the cat and the kid where he wanted them. It wasn't the best situation in the world. But what could he do? In a few days, Rainbow would have to go live with Tim. She couldn't take Tigger with her. So he figured this was a case of tough love.

Besides, if his plans panned out, Rainbow would lose the cat, but gain a mother. And that seemed like a pretty good deal.

But on Wednesday, his routine got all fouled up because Timmy took Rainbow to dinner and off to see the new Disney animated feature up in Orangeburg. Everyone had agreed that it was important for Tim to do this on his own.

So Mike ended up sitting at his kitchen table with the

cat looking daggers at him, the two of them brooding over Rainbow's absence.

He used the time to check in with Paul Kozlowski and see where things stood with Dragon Casinos. Paul didn't have anything new to report, but his agent sure did give him a lecture about taking his sport seriously. Time was running out on him. He would have to get back to Vegas next week or lose his agent, in addition to losing a possible sponsor.

He'd bet everything on this bachelor auction. And if he lost, he would lose big.

He stewed on this while he sipped a beer and watched the parking lot. He pretended that he wasn't waiting for Charlene to come home from her rounds. But his mood lifted the moment she pulled her truck into her reserved spot and hopped down from the cab. She wore the same sundress she'd had on the night of the mouse disaster, with her hair down. The summer sun gave it fiery highlights and she looked adorably fresh and absolutely luscious. Lust seized him low and tight across his gut. He needed to keep his distance from that woman. Rainbow's future depended upon it.

But instead of following that advice, Mike pushed up from the table and headed for the front door. Talking to her for a moment on the front steps would be innocent enough. Besides, he needed to encourage her to buy his brother next Saturday.

He caught her on the landing. "Hi," he said, and then the words dried up in his suddenly parched throat.

"Hey," she said, taking the steps to her front door.

"Um, I just wanted you to know that Rainbow isn't going to darken your door tonight. She's off with Timmy."

"Oh? Well, that's a good thing, isn't it?"

"Yeah. I guess." He paused for a minute. "About Sunday, when I—" Damn. Why exactly had he come out here to talk to her? Not to discuss the kiss, surely.

"Look, kissing you was a big mistake, okay? I was emotionally distraught. And you were being sweet. So let's just put it right out of our minds and pretend it didn't happen."

"Okay." Of course forgetting the kiss would be impossible. Especially since he wanted nothing more than to kiss her again. But that would screw everything up, so he stood there stupidly, as wordless as Rainbow.

"Uh, look, Mike," she said, obviously not having the same problem with her brain or her mouth as he was. "I want to thank you for everything you said to me out at the river on Sunday. And I realize that I need to move on. I'm seriously considering this idea of me and Tim together."

"What?" Confusion stirred his brain, throwing everything into chaos.

"Don't act like you don't know what's going on. I know how you've encouraged the Altar Guild, talked to Miriam Randall, and convinced Tim to sign up for the auction. I'm just saying that I guess I appreciate it. And I've decided I'm going to buy him."

"Really?" Holy crap, all phases of his master plan had clicked into place, and just in time for him to still make the big tournament and maybe even land the deal with Dragon Casinos, too. He should be dancing in the streets.

Instead his chest hurt as if someone had taken a laser and cut out his heart.

"Yes, really. I imagine you're pleased," she said.

Right, he should be more than pleased. He should be ecstatic. Instead, he blurted, "You know you're going to have to give up your cats, don't you?" Why had these particular words popped out of his mouth? He struggled to breathe, as if maybe he might be having an asthma attack.

She rolled her eyes and tapped her cheek with her finger. "Hmmm, let me think about that for a moment. I could keep my cats and become a crazy spinster cat lady, or I could take a chance that Miriam Randall knows what she's talking about and find my soulmate." Her phony frown turned right into a brilliant smile. "Don't stand there looking flabbergasted. You've done a good thing. I adore my kitties, but I *would* give them up for love. Real love. The kind of love Miriam always finds for people. So I'm good with it."

He slapped his poker face on. "I'm glad to hear it. Really glad. Rainbow loves you."

"I love her back."

"Great. I need to get back to my computer. The overseas markets are opening." It was a lie. He needed to get away from her before he admitted that he hated the idea of her giving away Winkin', Blinkin', and Nod. Just as he hated the idea of taking Tigger away from Rainbow. But hey, maybe it would work out. Rainbow would get Charlene and Charlene would get Rainbow. And Timmy would get both of them.

And he'd get a sponsorship.

Everyone would get what they needed or wanted. A complete win-win-win-win scenario.

Except for the cats.

And for some strange reason that bothered him.

On Thursday afternoon, Angel Menendez dropped by Charlene's office unannounced and without his little dog, Muffin. Cindy sent him back to Charlene's office. He strode in, wearing his usual faded jeans and T-shirt, and slumped into one of her office chairs. "We need to talk," he said.

"What is it? Are we still short of bachelors for Saturday?"

"No, we have more bachelors than we know what to do with. You and Wilma have done a great job. I never thought Reverend Lake would participate." He gave Charlene a meaningful and direct stare.

"You can save your breath. I've already made up my mind. I'm buying him."

"*Chica,* I have spent the last day and a half trying to decide if I should talk to you about this or not. And I have concluded that I would not be a good friend if I did not let you know a few things."

Her chest constricted. "Angel, if you're about to tell me that Pastor Tim is gay, I think I will go off and join a nunnery."

"No, I am not here to tell you that."

"Good, then whatever it is you have to say about him, keep it to yourself. The truth is I'm tired of chasing after guys who have tons of emotional baggage. I've got enough baggage of my own. So I'm going to follow Amanda's advice and go after someone who is actually *available,* physically and emotionally."

"You think Pastor Tim is emotionally available? Really?"

Charlene didn't know the answer to this question. But in contrast to Mike, he definitely looked more mature. Tim was so mature he verged on boring. But really, boring would be better than having her heart mashed again.

And Tim came with a big fringe benefit—Rainbow. "I think Timmy is a good catch." She folded her hands on the desk in front of her.

Angel got up and started pacing the room.

"What's the matter?"

He sat back down. "Look, Charlene, I do not want to spoil your plans, but I spoke with Miriam Randall yesterday, and she cannot remember ever saying anything about you and Tim Lake. And I am only here telling you this because I would hate to see you throw yourself at a man who is going to make you give up your cats."

"You're kidding, right?"

"No, I am not kidding."

"You'd rather I become a crazy cat lady than a married woman with a family?"

"No, of course not. But I have a hard time seeing you with a guy who is allergic to cats."

"Well, love is blind, and we can always get a hypoallergenic cat, like a Sphynx."

"A Sphynx?"

"It's a hairless breed."

"You'd get a fancy cat when there are so many in the shelter?" He seemed truly upset with her now.

"Angel, I'm just saying that marrying Tim Lake would not necessarily require me to give up cats."

"Just the ones you have right now."

"I'm not choosing cats over Tim or Rainbow," she said, trying to ease the tension in her neck. Angel was literally becoming a pain.

"Do you love him?" Angel asked.

She hesitated a moment. She should have told him a lie, but lying to Angel was impossible. "No, I don't," she said on a long breath. "Not yet, anyway. But Miriam says I will, someday."

"Assuming Miriam said anything at all. Tell me, *chica,* do you even like him?"

He certainly had her there, didn't he? She stared at him until he blinked. "Damnit all, Angel, I'm trying to be mature. I'm trying to follow Amanda's advice."

"Amanda told you to go after Tim?"

"No. She told me to quit going after guys who need fixing. You know the kind. Guys like Dr. Dave and—" She bit off the rest of the sentence before she said what was really on her mind.

"Like who?"

She looked down and pretended to rearrange the papers on her desk.

"Like who, Charlene?"

"Damnit, it's none of your business. Why are you here?"

He braced his elbows on his knees, and this time he sank his head onto his hands. He was a picture of misery. "Angel? What's the matter?"

"I did not come here to upset you. Really. I just thought you should know that Miriam does not remember saying one thing about you and Tim. But I did talk to Savannah, and she said that Tim will soon find his soulmate, and she will be someone involved in medicine. So maybe that is you."

"Veterinary science is not exactly medicine."

He looked up. "Maybe she was using an expansive definition."

"Yeah, but you came in here mainly to tell me to rethink, didn't you? You came in here determined to burst my bubble."

He shook his head. "No, that actually was not my *main* reason." He paused for a moment, the tension building. "My main reason for coming was to ask your advice about something."

"You need *my* advice? On what?"

"Dr. Dave."

She tried hard not to let her mouth drop open.

"I know," Angel said with a fluent hand gesture. "It is crazy for me to be asking you for advice about Dave. But you know him better than almost anyone."

"Okay, what do you need to know?"

"Would it be wrong if I bought him on Saturday?"

"Angel, I don't have any problems with same-sex relationships. But I'm not sure that Dave is ready to come out. I'm not even sure he knows he's gay. God knows, I was fooled."

"He knows. The thing is, Savannah said something yesterday at the meeting of the Purly Girls about how I should go for it on Saturday. And Pat Canaday heard what she said and started speculating about which bachelor might be gay. And if Pat is speculating, that means every knitter in Last Chance is speculating, too." He paused for a moment, frowning. "Let me amend that, every knitter who isn't nearly deaf and over the age of eighty-five. So maybe I should tell him that, huh?"

"Crap. I don't know. Maybe. Or maybe you should ask some woman to buy him for you."

"Who would do that?"

A wicked look crossed her face. "Maybe you could get Wilma to do it."

He sat there for a moment as he thought it through. "Oh, my God, Charlene, you are a genius."

"I doubt it." After all, she planned to buy a man she didn't like much because of a forecast that probably hadn't happened. She leaned back in her chair feeling exactly like a desperate spinster.

Angel gave her a probing stare. "*Chica,* if you do not love the preacher, why are you planning to buy him?"

"Because the guy I really like is not emotionally available. And I really don't want to break my heart again."

"So you are going to settle for someone you do not really like?"

"I get to be with Rainbow if I do."

"Ah, I see. And this other person? It would not, by any chance, be the older brother of Tim Lake?"

She sighed. "I'm pathetic. I know. And if I thought for one minute that Mike Taggart might choose to settle down here in Last Chance, I'd be all over him. But he's never going to stay. He's a gambler, and he wants to get back to that life. And I can't change him. If I try, I'm going to break my heart. So I'm going to settle for second best. And you know, I won't be the first woman who ever did that."

CHAPTER
20

The Cut 'n Curl beauty shop was busy. The usual Saturday regulars were there—Aunt Millie, Thelma Hanks, and Lessie Anderson—when Charlene arrived for her "makeover." Miriam Randall was absent, thank goodness.

Charlene didn't want the old lady to take back her matrimonial forecast. She wanted to believe in it. She wanted to pretend that the stuff Savannah Randall had told Angel applied to her, too. After all, veterinary science could be called medicine.

So Charlene had embraced the whole idea of finding love at the bachelor auction. And now that Saturday had arrived, she couldn't wait for the fairy-tale moment to happen. She was going for the whole Cinderella thing in a big way, even if she didn't have a fairy godmother helping her out. Last evening, she'd run up to Orangeburg and bought herself one killer of a party dress for this evening's soiree.

Now she needed the hairdo and makeup to pull it all

together. She stared at Ruby, the proprietor of the Cut 'n Curl, in the mirror at her beauty station. "I want big, glamorous hair, Ruby."

Ruby arched an eyebrow. "Really?"

"What? You don't think I should go for big?"

"Uh, well, I guess it depends. You are trying to land a preacher, right?"

Charlene nodded. "But I also need a hairdo that will complement the new dress I bought. It's black and sequined. And it's got a mermaid silhouette that shows off my figure. Oh, and it has a terrific sweetheart neckline that should get Tim's attention."

In truth, she looked like a million dollars in that dress. It fit as if someone had tailored it for her. And to sweeten the deal, it had been marked down 50 percent, proving that the Lord *did* have a plan, and Belk's was part of it.

"Um, sweetie," Aunt Millie said, "are you sure Pastor Tim will like a dress like that? I've heard from some of my Methodist friends that he's a bit...*uptight.*" She leaned in and whispered the last word in a furtive voice. No one in the shop was a Methodist, but you never knew when one of them might pop in.

"I heard the same thing," Thelma said. She sat in one of the dryer chairs, her roots plastered with dye, and her hair standing on end as if she'd seen a ghost or something. "I was talking to Elsie Campbell the other day, and she was saying that his sermons are deadly dull."

"I'm sure it's only because he's unmarried," Lessie said. Jane Rhodes, Ruby's daughter-in-law, bent over Lessie's hands, working on the old lady's manicure. "He's probably a virgin, you know," Lessie added.

That shut everyone up for a moment. "You really think

so?" Charlene found herself saying right out loud as her stomach twisted itself into a knot.

"He's a devout minister," Thelma said. "I bet he's never even been to third base with a girl." And then she grinned. "I think the Methodists are going to be so happy when you and Pastor Tim are married. I'm sure you'll loosen him up a little."

Crap. Did the Methodist ladies expect her to *fix* him? No, she had sworn off that. She expected to find a soulmate—someone she loved, flaws and all.

Charlene stared at her reflection in the mirror, catching Ruby's arch look. It had never even occurred to her that she might be about to fall in love with a man who was that inexperienced. Wow, that didn't sound like all that much fun, did it?

"So," Ruby said, "I think we need to put the hair up in something classic, like a chignon. I'm not sure an uptight, thirty-something, virgin minister could handle you in a dress with a plunging neckline and big hair, too."

The Cut 'n Curl's door opened, and Amanda strode in looking like a woman on a mission. "I've been trying to call you for days and days, and you've been avoiding me. We need to talk."

Oh, boy. Why were her friends lining up against her plan? It was such a perfect plan. It would get her a sober and *dull* husband and a kid, all in one fell swoop.

"I don't want to talk," Charlene said.

"Of course you don't, or you would have answered my calls. But I wouldn't be a very good friend unless I made you talk. I saw your truck parked out back and figured you were here. And I'm not leaving until I speak my mind."

"Amanda, I'm getting my hair done. My mind's made up."

"This is all about Dr. Dave, isn't it? You've been sulking ever since I told you he was gay. And I feel so responsible for what happened. Honey, you don't have to go throw yourself at Tim Lake just because the man of your dreams isn't interested in girls."

"Dr. Dave is gay?" Aunt Millie said. The other women in the room didn't look all that surprised. But Millie's bubble certainly had been burst.

Amanda turned toward Millie. "Aunt Mil, I hate to tell you this, but everyone knows he's gay, except maybe you and your niece."

"Oh. My. God! Amanda! You've just outed him," Charlene said.

"Well, it's about time he climbed out of the closet."

"That's your opinion. But it's his life and his choice." Charlene turned and gave the rest of the ladies in the shop a stern look. "Y'all, just remember. What happens in the Cut 'n Curl stays in the Cut 'n Curl."

She got nothing but blank stares from the women, who were probably the biggest gossips in town. "I mean it," Charlene said. "There's a reason Dave hasn't wanted to come out, and it would hurt him if y'all started gossiping about him. So please don't do that."

They all closed their mouths and nodded, but Charlene had no faith that any of them would keep this quiet. Aunt Millie would be the first one blabbing all over town.

Charlene turned in her chair and put her face in her hands. Her life had gotten way too complicated the last few days.

"Charlene," Amanda said, "I don't give a rat's behind about David Underhill. But I do care about you. And I think the idea of you throwing yourself at a Methodist minister you don't love is just, well, I hate to say it, but it's dumb."

"Of course I don't love him. Not yet. All that's supposed to happen tonight at the party."

"Oh, good lord." Amanda sank down into one of the dryer chairs. "Honey, you're doing this because Mike Taggart talked you into it, aren't you?"

"No." She didn't sound all that convincing.

"Yes, you are. I've spoken with Mike. His heart's in the right place, and I believe he truly thinks you'd make a terrific mother for Rainbow. And you would. But you can't throw yourself at Pastor Tim because you're infatuated with the child. And using the rumor about Miriam Randall's prediction is just wrong. If you and Tim were truly soulmates, you'd know it. Believe me. The minute I saw Grant I knew it.

"I think Mike started this rumor about Miriam's prediction. He's a gambler, honey, and he knows how to play games with people. You want to know how crazy that man is? He almost had me convinced that *I* should buy Pastor Tim for *you,* just in case he couldn't get you to buy the man for yourself."

"He tried to get you to buy him for me?"

"He did. And honey, I had a conversation with Angel on Wednesday. He told me Miriam had no recollection of ever saying one word about you and Tim. I know Angel told you this. So you're just being ornery and bull-headed. And I wouldn't be any kind of friend if I didn't stop you from doing something destructive."

Charlene raised her head and looked at Ruby's reflection in the mirror. Kindness and sympathy filled the hairdresser's eyes, as if she understood how confusing things were. "Miz Ruby, you give me big, showgirl hair, you hear? I want to walk into that fund-raiser tonight looking like a sex kitten."

"Charlene, honey, you don't mean to buy..." Amanda's voice faded out when Charlene glared at her in the mirror.

"I don't know who I'm going to buy. But you better believe I'm going to buy someone, and I suddenly don't care if he's emotionally available. If Miriam Randall has no forecast for me, and I'm destined to become a spinster cat lady, then I'm going to go for one last outrageous fling."

21

On Saturday evening, Mike left a long list of instructions for Liz Rhodes, the teenager he'd hired to babysit Rainbow. He felt sort of stupid doing that, since Liz seemed really competent, and besides, she already knew Rainbow from Bible camp. But he couldn't help himself.

It only took fifteen minutes to drive to the VFW hall in Allenberg where the bachelor auction would be taking place. But the moment he parked the Hyundai, he had to stifle the urge to call Liz and check in. He had to remind himself that Liz was also the sheriff's oldest daughter. So if anything happened, she'd know how to get help fast.

He needed to relax. But relaxation had eluded him the last few days. He hadn't been sleeping well. Rainbow and Tigger were both rebelling against his plan for helping Rainbow "get over" her affection for her cat.

Clearly he needed to rethink. Mike certainly had never "gotten over" his affection for Angie. And he had doubts that he'd ever get over his growing affection and concern for Rainbow. And he sure was having a lot of trouble "getting over" his feelings for Charlene, which were admittedly a little on the X-rated side but still very affectionate. Avoiding his curvaceous next-door neighbor wasn't helping.

And neither were the cold showers.

He wondered if he'd still need cold showers when he got back to Vegas. He wondered if he'd be stifling the urge to call Timmy every five minutes to see if he was doing a good job with the kid. He wondered how on earth he could keep his mind on poker when he'd be worrying about Rainbow.

He heaved a huge sigh and headed toward the front doors of the VFW lodge, a windowless brick building with a big parking lot situated on Main Street in Allenberg. He pushed through the doors and into a small anteroom where tables had been set up for attendees to register for the opportunity to bid on a bachelor.

In addition to the tables, several big posters had been set up around the foyer with photographs of sad-looking dogs and cats peering through cage bars. Guilt assailed him. In a matter of days, Tigger would probably become one of these cast-off animals. He didn't exactly love Tigger, but the idea of sending the cat to death row in some animal shelter made him feel like the lowest scum of the earth.

A tall woman bearing a clipboard and an impatient expression came over to him. She was almost his height and wore an iridescent, light blue formal dress that matched her eye shadow. "You are late," she said.

"I'm sorry I was—"

"I'm Wilma Riley. I'm in charge of the bachelors. And

I know all about you, Mike, and the way you and Elsie have been manipulating things."

After this speech, Mike wondered what "in charge" meant. By the evil-looking smile on her lips, he had a feeling Wilma's notion of being in charge would probably irritate him.

"Uh, you know, Wilma, I'm thinking I ought to come with a disclaimer."

She snorted a laugh. "Honey, every man should come with one of those. But to ease your mind, I think our MC is planning to introduce you as a rambler and a gambler, which should tell the ladies all they need to know."

"Uh, thanks, I think. But kidding aside, I'm not going to be here for much longer. Maybe only a few days."

"Well, that's typical." She looked down at her clipboard and rearranged some of the papers. "Now, come on back with me. We're behind schedule, and I need to rehearse you boys."

"Rehearse us? In what?" His stomach churned with acid.

"Walking the runway, of course."

She bustled away, and he followed her into the main hall, which had been decorated with crepe paper streamers in various shades of blue. A runway had been set up perpendicular to the raised stage at the far end of the room. Table rounds, each with white tablecloths and blue flower arrangements, filled the space around the raised platform. Each folding chair sported a white fabric cover and a dark blue bow.

For all the streamers and flowers and big bows, the place still looked like a VFW hall, with gray linoleum floors and dark paneled walls sporting photos of heroes in uniform and unit citations. The veterans had also spared no expense when it came to the bar. It occupied the front corner of the room, and it looked exceptionally well-stocked. "Uh, Wilma, wait up. I need a beer."

She took him by the arm. "Not until after rehearsal." She led him down to the front of the room where the rest of the victims, including his brother, had convened. Timmy stuck out like a sore thumb. He'd bypassed the tuxedo and had come with his Roman collar firmly in place. And oddly, given that his backward collar looked kind of tight, Timmy managed to look way more comfortable than most of the other guys in their monkey suits.

"All right, y'all, now that everyone is here." Wilma gave Mike a little unfriendly glare. "I need to go over what we expect of you. We'll be having a silent auction for a number of items on the tables around the room. That will take place during the cocktail hour. We want y'all to meet and mingle with the crowd. Especially the single ladies wearing purple bead bracelets. The ladies with the bracelets have paid the fee to participate in the bachelor auction.

"Precisely at eight p.m., we'll begin the auction. Grant Trumbull, our local radio personality, will be our master of ceremonies."

She pointed to a guy standing at the bar hoisting a beer and wearing a white dinner jacket.

"Now, when the auction starts," Wilma rambled on, "each of you will be called by name. You're to come out from behind that curtain." She pointed to the navy blue curtain on the stage. "And then strut your stuff down the runway and back. Drew, you'll be the first one out, and when you're done, you go stand on top of the masking tape

X on the stage floor. The rest of y'all will take a position next to the man who preceded you onto the stage. When the introductions are done, y'all will exit to the left and go backstage. Then each of you will be called out one by one for the auction."

"You mean slaughter," Mike said under his breath.

This earned him another glare from Wilma.

"Uh, I have a question," Timmy said.

"What is it, Pastor Tim?"

"What exactly do you mean by *strut our stuff?*"

"Don't you worry, no one expects you to do any strutting. Just come out and walk to the end of the runway and wave and smile. You'll get a chance to rehearse it all." She cast her glance over the bachelors wearing tuxes. "I expect Pastor Tim to be the model of restraint. As for the rest of y'all, just remember to keep it clean."

Mike cast his gaze over the dozen or so bachelors. They ranged in age from their twenties to their seventies. And they all looked nervous. Especially the guy wearing a white dinner jacket with black lapels. His tux didn't look rented. Which begged the question, who kept a white dinner jacket in his wardrobe?

Easy answer: James Bond or a seriously gay guy. And this guy looked so nervous he had broken out in a sweat.

Mike stuck out his hand. "Hello, I'm Mike. I don't think we've met."

White dinner jacket guy nodded. "I've heard a lot about you. My receptionist is a Methodist, and Charlene is my associate. I'm Dave Underhill. Creature Comforts Animal Hospital is my veterinary practice."

So that explained how a gay guy got roped into a man auction. "So, did Charlene win a bet with you, too?"

"A bet?"

"Yeah. I'm only here because Charlene bet me that she could get Rainbow to eat broccoli. I was a fool to take that bet."

"No, she didn't bet me. But I kind of had to agree to do this, you know? Being the vet and all." The guy looked like he needed a stiff drink.

They all looked like they needed to have their attitudes adjusted.

"Wilma, sweetie," Mike said, taking charge of the situation. "I know we're just a bunch of dumb dudes, but I think we can handle the runway walk without practicing." He turned toward the rest of the bachelors. "What do you say, guys? I think we should adjourn this meeting to the bar."

To a man, the bachelors nodded their heads, even Timmy, who didn't drink. It was all over for Wilma, as a black-and-white herd of bachelors stampeded to the bar.

Twenty minutes later, with a beer in hand and a group of guys to bond with, Mike felt much better. Almost in control of himself. Until Charlene Polk walked into the room wearing the sexiest damn dress he'd ever seen in his life.

Holy God, it looked as if someone had spray-painted that thing on her. It displayed every one of her curves. And that didn't even count the fact that the neckline showed a ridiculous amount of cleavage. He drank it all in and then he checked out her hair.

He was done. Charlene looked hot while simultaneously sending out a good-girl vibe. Oh, yeah. How the hell had she known about his terminal weakness for smart, curvaceous, sweet women who knew how to dress trashy?

He sure hoped Timmy appreciated what he'd done for him.

Because, damn, Charlene looked like she'd come to the party intending to have a really good time.

Elsie Campbell took one look at Charlene's dress and big hairdo and blushed so hard that her dark skin turned rosy. "Gee, Charlene, that's quite a dress you're wearing."

Charlene didn't let Elsie's reaction daunt her. She was man-hunting tonight. And if Tim Lake and his Altar Guild didn't like her dress, then they could just lump it.

The Altar Guild chairwoman also frowned at the mantini in Charlene's hand—her second of the evening. The drink was a delicious concoction of bourbon and vermouth with a dash of chocolate bitters. She'd watched Hugh deBracy make them, and they were a masterpiece. They also made her lips tingle.

"I'm glad you like the dress," Charlene said, ignoring Elsie's clear disapproval. She hadn't married Tim yet. "I found it on sale at Belk's. I thought it made my boobs look great."

Elsie almost choked on her club soda and lime. "I reckon it does, hon. But you might think about not having another one of those drinks."

Charlene didn't respond. Instead she let her gaze wander over the crowd, and like a compass finding true north, she zoomed in on Mike Taggart. Good lord. He'd been born to wear a tuxedo.

Not only did he look comfy in formal wear, he also seemed to be a master at working the room. A veritable *herd* of women wearing purple bead bracelets had surrounded him. Where had these gals come from?

Not Last Chance, clearly. They all wore over-the-top dresses, some even more outrageous than Charlene's. The formal department at Belk's had probably made a killing this week. And if Charlene were keeping score, which she most definitely was not, the majority of the women had gravitated to Mike. Although Dr. Dave ran a close second.

Tim, wearing his sober Roman collar and drinking water, not so much. Only Andrea Newsome seemed interested in Tim. Charlene was kind of surprised to see the therapist wearing a purple bracelet. And now that Charlene gave it some thought, Andrea definitely had a medical background.

Drat. The competition had become ridiculous.

In fact, the single women had come out in droves. AARC would make a boatload of money on this event. But all these out-of-towners put a real crimp in Charlene's man-buying plans.

It might cost her plenty to buy the guy of her dreams. And his brother appeared to have actually found his soulmate. Which was kind of heartbreaking, because, if Tim hooked up with Andrea, then Rainbow would be set for life.

Andrea was thoughtful, kind, sweet, smart, and a child *therapist,* for heaven's sake.

She turned her gaze back to Mike. He seemed intent on flirting with every woman in sight. Except her.

Which kind of reminded her of that time in eighth grade when Brad Muller asked her to the harvest dance, and then turned around and danced with every other girl in attendance. Boy, she had been picking losers for a long, long time, hadn't she?

She drained her glass, causing Elsie's eyes to nearly

pop right out of her head. "Excuse me for a minute," Charlene said. She put her empty glass down on a tray that one of the servers was carrying, then she elbowed her way through the gaggle of women surrounding Mike.

"Hey," she said when she'd finally wormed her way to the front of the pack.

He looked down at her, and his pupils dilated the moment he glanced at the sweetheart neckline of her dress. That little crack in his otherwise neutral expression unleashed a tsunami of hormones. Her insides got all molten, and her knees almost gave way.

The feeling went way past hot flashes, right into killer chemistry. Either that or the mantinis were aphrodisiacs.

"Is it true that you made up the whole thing about Miriam Randall and me marrying your brother?"

He blinked. "No, I didn't make that up."

Disappointment nipped at her insides. "So she told you I was destined to marry Tim?"

"Charlene, I wouldn't lie about a thing like that." His face grew solemn, and for an instant, something flickered in the depths of his eyes. What was it? Pain? Heartache? Emotional baggage? Or was he just lying through his teeth? She couldn't tell. And wasn't that always the case?

She couldn't help herself. She yearned to lift him out of his sadness. Stupid fool that she was.

She might have leaned into him, or kissed him on the cheek, or said something sultry, but a buxom blonde wearing a strapless dress that was even more revealing than her own planted an elbow in her ribs and beat her to the punch.

Predictably, Mike looked down at her boobs, too. Which only proved that he was 100 percent heterosexual male. And not at all the kind who committed.

"Hey, Sugar, you're cute," Blondie said as she simultaneously grabbed him by the arm and took a salacious lick off the salted rim of her margarita glass. "Come on over here and meet my friend Tammy."

She pulled him away toward a red-headed woman with even bigger hair than Charlene's over-the-top do.

A sickening wave of jealousy percolated through Charlene. She took it as a warning. She needed to avoid Mike come hell or high water. She wasn't the kind of girl who could really carry off a one-night fling. In theory it sounded great, but in practice not so much.

She headed back to the bar. Drinking looked like a much better option than having her heart mashed flat.

Angel had every reason to be happy tonight.

The number of women who had bought tickets to the fund-raiser assured that AARC would more than break even. The silent auction had been well-supported by the merchants in Allenberg and Last Chance. Hugh deBracy's mantinis had the crowd floating on a happy buzz. Everything was going well.

But Angel's worries about Dave overshadowed everything. Five people had cornered him this evening with whispered questions about the vet. Somehow the gossip had started, and he could not help but feel that it was his fault.

Anyone who had heard what Savannah said last Tuesday at the Knit & Stitch could have figured it out. Dave should have worn the standard-issue tux like everyone else. That white dinner jacket was obvious, in addition to making him look handsome.

Angel stood at the corner of the bar, sipping a mantini

as he watched the man of his dreams. Dave was not comfortable with the crowd of women around him. He kept taking out his handkerchief and mopping his forehead. It only took a couple of moments before most women figured it out. One by one they came into the room, checked out the bachelors, and then gravitated toward Dave. And after a two- or three-minute conversation, they abandoned him for Mike Taggart.

Without question, Mike would bring the highest price tonight. The women loved him. Including Charlene, who had just thrown herself at him only to be usurped by a chubby blonde.

Angel worried about Charlene, too. She had already consumed two mantinis, and while the drinks were not very strong, Charlene was also not much of a drinker. Charlene finally turned away from Mike and headed back to the bar.

She came to stand next to him and ordered another drink. Then she turned with a sigh. "So, did you get Wilma to buy Dave for you?"

Angel shook his head and took a sip of his drink. "She would not do it for me. She quoted Betty Friedan."

"Oh, boy. Which quote?"

"The one about how it is easier to live through someone else than to become complete yourself. Basically she told me that, if I wanted to bid on Dave, I would have to do it myself. Then she suggested I read this poem by Longfellow about the courtship of Priscilla Mullins and Miles Standish."

Charlene snorted. "As in speak for yourself, John?"

He nodded and cast his glance toward Dave. "He's having a miserable time."

Charlene said nothing. And Angel let go of a long sigh that probably would classify as mournful. And if there was one thing Angel hated, it was gay men who got all mournful over relationships.

Maybe he should muscle the girls aside and make a heartfelt declaration of his admiration.

He was giving this idea serious consideration when Molly Wolfe, his employer's wife, came striding up with a frown on her face. "Angel, I just heard the strangest thing from Aunt Millie."

"Oh, boy," Charlene muttered.

"What?" Angel turned just as Hugh deBracy handed Charlene her mantini. Charlene took a big gulp. "I'm afraid Amanda opened her big mouth at the Cut 'n Curl this afternoon and let the cat out of the bag."

"What cat?"

"So it's true?" Molly's eyes rounded in surprise. "Oh, my God. I had no idea." She paused a moment. "Oh, Charlene, that's terrible. You had a big crush…" Her voice faded out.

So Molly and Millie hadn't figured it out either. Charlene felt better about her gaydar. "Yeah, I did," she said, taking another big sip of her drink. "I had a big, honking crush on a gay guy. Pathetic."

Molly put her arm around Charlene. "I'm so sorry. Life can throw some real curves sometimes, can't it? But, hey, things are looking up. From what I hear, you're going to find your soulmate tonight." She frowned. "Which kind of begs the question as to why you're over here at the bar and Pastor Tim is across the room with Andrea Newsome."

"Yup, that is the question of the century," Charlene said, taking another sip of the mantini.

"Honey, how many of those drinks have you had?"

She shrugged. "Lost count. You know, it's a shame I'm Drew's cousin, because he's one of the cutest guys here."

"I think we should get you some coffee," Molly said.

"No. No coffee for me. I intend to have a rip-roaring good time. And I'm not going to let either one of you spoil my fun. I think I'll go flirt with Ross Gardiner. He might be practically engaged to Lucy, but he's kind of hunky." She pushed off the bar and sailed across the room, martini in hand.

"I better go warn Simon that he's going to need to drive her home." Molly headed off in another direction, leaving Angel still standing at the bar trying to figure out what he should do. Dave had been outed by the gossips of Last Chance. By next week, all the people who had only suspected that he was gay would know for certain.

He could warn him. Or he could try to show him that being out was a whole lot better than trying to hide the person you really are. He pushed away from the bar and headed off to the foyer, where volunteers were selling purple bracelets.

He plunked down twenty-five bucks and bought one for himself.

CHAPTER 22

Tim felt exposed as he walked down the runway. He fervently wished he'd rehearsed this, but he kind of doubted that even a rehearsal would have prepared him for the flock of single women who had descended upon this event.

They had come from miles and miles away, and their presence here said something kind of sad about the state of love in South Carolina. Young people had to rely on bars and events like this.

His palms sweated, and his heart thumped. He plastered a stupid smile on his face and walked stiffly to the end of the walkway, while Grant Trumbull smoothly announced his name, date of birth, occupation, and a short summary of his life. Grant made him sound like some kind of paragon.

But Tim knew better. He squinted into the lights, looking for a familiar face, but the lights blinded him. He prayed that one of those predatory females wouldn't win this bid. He couldn't imagine having dinner with some of the women who had turned up for this event.

He took his place next to Drew Polk and stood there as the rest of the bachelors *strutted their stuff* up and down the runway. Allen Canaday didn't actually strut. He danced his way up and back, making some truly suggestive hip motions. The women hooted and hollered, but Tim noticed it was mostly the out-of-towners.

The rest of the bachelors walked and waved, except for Mike, who sort of sauntered and had to gently discourage several women from actually crawling up onto the stage with him. His ease with this event must have something to do with his living in Vegas.

After the introductions, everyone assembled backstage, peering from the wings as Drew Polk was auctioned off. The bidders had pink, heart-shaped bidding paddles, and Grant Trumbull turned out to have impressive skill at managing the bids.

The bidding for Drew started at fifty dollars and was pretty brisk for about a minute and a half. A young lady Tim didn't recognize won Drew for the price of $130.

Tim's turn next.

He pulled his inhaler out of his pocket and took a hit. It seemed to ease the pressure in his chest as he walked onto the stage. Still, his collar was strangling him, and he wondered how on earth he'd let Wilma Riley talk him into doing this.

"And now, ladies, we come to the catch of the night," Grant said in his mellifluous radio voice. "Tim Lake is a Methodist minister with a deep and abiding love for animals and the Lord. You can't go wrong with this guy, especially if you're looking for something long-term. The opening bid for this gent is set at fifty dollars. Do I hear fifty?"

He was such a hypocrite. He didn't have a deep and abiding love for animals. In fact, he mostly disliked them. Intensely.

The blinding light gave him a headache, and his chest squeezed so tight that he worried about having a full-fledged asthma attack. Long minutes seemed to go by; time hung suspended. And then someone in the audience put up a pink paddle and said, "I bid five hundred dollars."

Tim couldn't see her and didn't recognize the voice. He guessed that Charlene had saved him. He'd heard all the gossip about Miriam Randall and her prediction. Bless her. He didn't think he loved her, but at least she'd saved him from the clutches of those out-of-town floozies who had overtaken the event.

"Wow," Grant said. "Obviously Pastor Tim has a female admirer. Or maybe just a really committed animal lover. Do I hear five hundred and ten?"

No one upped the bid. Grant struck his wooden gavel. "Sold to number six ninety-eight, who I believe is the beautiful and wickedly smart Dr. Andrea Newsome."

Andrea? Andrea had bought him?

He stumbled on his way off the stage. Thank God, Mike was there to catch him before he landed on his face. They had a moment where they stood eye to eye as Grant Trumbull announced Allen Canaday's name.

"Andrea bought you?" Mike asked, frowning.

"I guess."

"Not Charlene?"

"No. I guess Charlene didn't have a spare five hundred lying around. Andrea's bid was preemptive."

"Damn," Mike said, releasing his grasp on Tim's shoulders.

Suddenly Tim had had enough of his newfound brother. "Look, Mike, I know you think Charlene and I are some kind of match made in heaven, but if you really want to know the truth, I'm glad Andrea bought me. I've wanted to ask her out to dinner for a while now. The fact is, I'm attracted to Andrea. Not Charlene. So, while I understand that you are looking out for Rainbow's interests, and I realize that Rainbow has connected with Dr. Polk, the fact is, the only woman I'm interested in courting right at the moment is Andrea. And I think she'd make a lovely mother for Rainbow. She understands children, and she's been extraordinarily helpful to me during this transition in my life."

If his words had upset Mike, he didn't show it on his face. Mike simply nodded. "I guess you have a point there. Andrea knows something about kids, doesn't she? We've been *paying* her for her expertise."

"Yes, we have. But she's gone above and beyond. Especially the day you were arrested."

Mike nodded as the audience erupted in a whole bunch of hoots and hollers. Tim turned to look over his shoulder as Allen Canaday took off his jacket and tossed it to the crowd. The bidding was going fast and furious.

"I'm so grateful I didn't have to go through that," Tim said as he turned back. "But I have a feeling it's going to be ugly when you get out there. You're liable to get torn to bits by those women."

Mike nodded. "Yeah, and I doubt that there's an Andrea Newsome out there ready to rescue me either. This is what happens when you make a sucker bet."

"Good luck."

"Thanks, I'm probably going to need it."

• • •

Charlene sat in the section reserved for bidders, clutching her auction paddle. She'd been assigned number 513, and so far she hadn't had any opportunity to use it. She'd been all ready to raise her paddle for Tim Lake, but Andrea Newsome beat her to it with a bid so large that Charlene couldn't afford to counter. Oddly, she wasn't all that disappointed. Clearly Miriam's forecast had been for someone other than her.

Story of Charlene's life.

"I'm sorry," Angel said as he leaned toward her. Angel had bought himself a purple bracelet and was carrying a paddle with the number 639. "I know you were trying to talk yourself into Pastor Tim, but it was not meant to be. Tonight, *chica,* you and I are going to throw caution to the wind and do what our hearts tell us is right."

Uh-huh, she'd believe that when she saw it.

Allen Canaday came out on stage and started taking off his clothes—a state of affairs that didn't surprise Charlene in the least. She might be man-hunting tonight but Allen was too young for her.

She picked up her drink and sipped. She'd lost track of how many mantinis she'd consumed. Her lips were definitely numb and her buzz had almost turned into dizziness.

"You do not believe me, *chica.*"

"Angel, are you really going to out Dave right here in front of everyone?"

He nodded soberly, which made her giggle, because Angel wasn't exactly sober. He'd probably consumed as many mantinis as she had. And that was a sizable number, even if she couldn't exactly remember the specific number.

"Okay. I can't wait for this." She giggled again.

They watched and sipped their drinks as six more bachelors were auctioned off for remarkably large sums. Charlene passed on all of them because they were either too young or too old. And then they called Dr. Dave's name.

And the dreamboat came strolling onto the stage looking perfectly perfect, as he always did. The white dinner jacket was the right touch. He looked classic and classy and drop-dead gorgeous. His black hair fell over his forehead, and he struck a pose that made him look exactly like a *GQ* model.

A number of women sighed in unison. Charlene expected the bidding to start quickly and escalate sharply.

But evidently, the out-of-towners had better gaydar than Charlene, because when Grant Trumbull said, "The bidding for Dr. Dave starts at fifty dollars," the hall got utterly silent.

Awkwardly silent.

It remained silent even when she gave Angel a sharp jolt to the ribs.

Dave stood there looking gorgeous and more than a little nervous. He cast his gaze over the crowd, and it locked with Charlene's. He was dying out there. She needed to do something.

She leaned over and whispered furiously. "It's time to throw caution to the wind and follow your heart."

But Angel shook his head. "I can't do it. He would hate me if I bid on him."

So Charlene raised her paddle. "I bid one hundred dollars," she said.

A little, grateful smile softened Dave's mouth.

"Thank you, Charlene," Grant Trumbull said in his smooth voice. "Any other bids on our good-looking vet?"

There were no other bids. The rest of the man-hunters were smart enough to know a bad deal when they saw one.

Grant banged his gavel, and that was it. Charlene had bought Dr. Dave. And the rules of the auction were clear. You could only buy one bachelor. So she was done for the evening.

"I better go pay my bill," she said. "You can find me at the bar later."

"Charlene, don't you think—"

"No, Angel, I'm not thinking right now. Thinking would be bad all the way around. Drinking, on the other hand, sounds like a good plan. And, by the way, I will gladly give you Dr. Dave. I have no use for him other than the fact that he's my boss."

She got up and wound her way out to the foyer where she whipped out her credit card and paid for her date with Dave.

Meanwhile, in the main room, the crowd had gotten really rowdy. Probably because Mike had sauntered out onstage. A little part of her wanted to see what became of him. But before she could return to the room, Dr. Dave intercepted her.

"Uh, Charlene, I'm really glad you were here."

She stared up at him and shook her head. "You and I need to have a chat." She grabbed him by the arm and hauled him outside into a beautiful, balmy June evening.

The sun sat right on the horizon painting everything in a soft, dreamy, romantic shade of purple. Too bad she'd left the party with a gay guy.

She looked up into his face. "Dave, I'm not going to go to dinner with you."

"No?"

"No. I'm giving you to Angel."

His mouth kind of twitched, and he looked like he was fixing to argue with her. So she held up her hand, palm out.

"Don't. You belong with Angel. And really, Angel should have bid on you himself, but he's kind of sensitive about outing you. But here's the thing: Amanda came into the Cut 'n Curl today and told Ruby Rhodes, Lessie Anderson, Thelma Hanks, and my aunt Millie that you are gay. So staying in the closet is going to be tough." She hauled in a big breath, which did nothing to control her dizziness. "Oh, and I understand that Savannah Randall, who is apparently just as good at matchmaking as her aunt, has given her blessing to you and Angel. So you'd be a fool not to go out to dinner with Angel, because chances are he's your soulmate."

Her voice kind of wavered when she got to the word "soulmate." Everyone seemed to be hooking up for life tonight. Except her. She seemed to be headed for a future as a crazy cat lady. She wasn't even going to get to buy Mike Taggart and have her way with him. Not that having her way with Mike Taggart was such a great idea, really, but it sounded better than becoming a crazy cat lady.

"I need another drink," she said abruptly. She returned to the VFW hall, leaving Dr. Dave out in the twilight, looking like a model at a photo shoot.

Mike's auction had ended by the time she returned. She hoped he'd been bought by some fat woman with bad breath and saggy boobage. A bunch of not-very-mature thoughts like that ran through her mind as she crossed the room toward the bar.

Angel had already beaten her to it and, bless him, he'd ordered her another mantini. She sidled up to him. "You need to march right outside and talk to Dave before he gets in his car and escapes."

"What?"

"I told him you were his soulmate. But I'm not sure he bought it. I may have shocked him by speaking so frankly about his sexual orientation. You need to rescue him, Angel."

"But—"

"No buts. Amanda has already done the damage by speaking openly about this at the Cut 'n Curl. You need to go pick up the pieces. I'll hold down the fort here and make sure everything is cleaned up. It's not as if I'll have a handsome bachelor on my arm or anything."

"*Chica*, you are the best."

He left his mantini on the bar as he hurried toward the exit. Charlene had no compunction about picking it up and downing it in a couple of big swallows. Then she picked up her own and wandered out into the foyer to make sure the volunteers collecting the auction money didn't need any help.

Not that she was sober enough to count money. But hanging out at the bar watching the last few auctions would depress her.

The redhead named Tammy had bought him for the whopping sum of $400. Less than Timmy had fetched, which amused Mike, for some reason.

He ought not to be amused at all. Andrea had purchased Tim. Tim had no interest in Charlene. And Charlene had purchased the gay guy.

So much for his well-laid plans.

He hadn't taken more than two steps into the main hall when Tammy came barreling toward him, boobs and hair bouncing. She was attractive, with a curvy body and a seductive southern accent that sounded slightly put on. She definitely had dressed on the trashy side.

But she didn't spark any fires.

"Mike," she squealed. "I'm so excited." She jumped up and down a couple of times and clapped her hands. The jumping truly impressed him, especially since she wore three-inch stiletto heels.

"So I was thinking," she said in her bubbly voice, "would you be willing to come up to Columbia next week? There's a cute little restaurant I'd love to take you to. And if you like you can stay the night."

"Uh, well, Tammy, I'm afraid I can't do either of those things. I have to be back at a reasonable hour, and Columbia has to be at least an hour's drive, maybe more."

She frowned. "Why do you have to get back early?"

"I've got a little girl." Of course he wouldn't have Rainbow for much longer, and that thought opened up a deep wound inside his chest. Giving Rainbow to Timmy would be hard.

Tammy's eyes got big and round. "You have kids? They listed you as a gambler in the program."

"I *am* a gambler. A professional poker player. But I'm still responsible for a kid. She's my niece. And I can't leave her with a babysitter so I can go up to Columbia for a dinner date. I think we should plan on dinner someplace closer. They have good barbecue at the Red Hot Pig Place in Scotia."

"Scotia? Oh, my God, I thought you were a bad boy out for some fun."

Mike didn't exactly know how to respond to that. He might have come from the wrong side of the tracks. And he might be a professional gambler. And he'd had his share of meaningless flings with mutually consenting females. But he didn't like being called a bad boy.

He'd never liked that label, even though it had been applied to him for his entire life. And to have someone be disappointed in him because he chose to behave like a responsible adult was both ironic and deeply annoying.

"Tammy, I'm happy to have dinner with you at a mutually agreed-upon location. That's what it says in the rules. I can't go to Columbia for dinner. And you should know that I'm only living here on a temporary basis. So if you want to have dinner someplace close by, we better schedule it now."

"I can't believe this. I just bought you for four hundred dollars."

"No, you made a tax-deductible contribution to the Allenberg Animal Rescue Council. And in return, you get a dinner with me at a mutually agreed-upon location."

She frowned. She pouted. And then she turned and stalked away. A minute later, she was shouting out in the foyer that she wanted her money back.

Mike strode out there, only to discover Tammy screaming at Charlene. His neighbor stood behind the table where volunteers were collecting the money from the auction winners. Charlene didn't argue with the woman. She calmly sipped her mantini while Tammy lost the southern belle vibe she'd had going for her.

When Tammy ran out of breath, Charlene gave her the stink eye and said, "You mean you don't want to have dinner with Mike? What? Are you nuts?"

Warmth bloomed in Mike's chest. Charlene was so beautiful. And so sweet. And intoxicated.

He made a snap decision and dug in his pocket for his money clip. He pulled off four crisp hundred-dollar bills and walked right up to Tammy and draped his arm across her shoulders. "Tammy, it's been nice knowing you, but clearly there has been a misunderstanding. So here's your money back. I hope you have a nice life." He leaned in and kissed her cheek.

"But—"

"I think it would be best if you left. You've made something of a scene," he said.

Tammy looked around at the annoyed faces of the volunteers and must have realized that retreat was probably the best move she could make. It didn't take her more than half a minute to find the outside door.

Mike turned to Charlene. "I'm sorry. I didn't mean to tick her off like that. She wanted me to go up to Columbia for dinner and suggested it would be terrific if I turned it into a sleepover. And I told her I couldn't do that because I had a kid. I don't think she was a kid-friendly kind of person."

Charlene blinked drunkenly at him, but said not a word.

"How many of those have you had?" he asked, nodding toward the martini glass in her hand.

She finished her drink in one big gulp then said, "I have no clue. But I need another one."

She headed toward the door to the main room in a wobbly walk that had nothing to do with high heels, because Charlene seemed to have lost her shoes.

"Uh, dollface, where did you leave your shoes?" he asked.

She looked down and wiggled her toes, the expression on her face a little surprised. "I have no clue. I must have left them at the bar."

Before she could take another step, Mike grabbed her gently by the upper arm and took the empty martini glass from her fingers. She smelled like bourbon and chocolate, as she gave him an unsteady look. "Are you going to buy me another one?"

"No. I'm going to cut you off and take you home."

She pulled away. "No, you can't, because Angel has gone off to be with his soulmate, and I have to stay here and help the volunteers clean up."

"And would this soulmate be the white dinner jacket guy?"

She nodded and stumbled a little. "Yup. I did my matchmaking duties. Now I can go home and become a crazy cat lady. Isn't that great? And by the way, I'm mad at you."

"What did I do now?"

"You lied about Miriam."

"I didn't lie. She led me to believe that you and Tim belonged together."

"That's so not true. He left with Andrea right after she bought him. I think they're having an assi...assig. You know, a secret get-together. Which is probably a good thing because Tim is a virgin."

"Timmy's a virgin?"

"Uh-huh. That's what Lessie Anderson says."

He didn't ask her who the hell Lessie Anderson was. It didn't matter. She was toasted, and kind of adorably so. Her big hair was still big. Her boobs were still fabulous. And her big chocolate eyes spoke of a vulnerability that he found irresistible.

He took her by the arm, and she surprised him by kind of leaning up against him. "Mmmmm, that's nice," she said, taking a deep breath.

"What?"

"You. You smell good. She sagged against him, and he put his arm around her. Predictably, his libido woke up. A damn nuisance. He didn't take advantage of drunken females. He'd seen too many guys do that to his mom.

"Okay, doll, where'd you put your purse?"

"I don't remember."

Great. He turned toward the volunteers at the table. Wilma sat there giving him the evil eye. "Wilma, I know you don't like me very much, but I need a favor."

Wilma gave him a frank stare. "Don't take it personally, honey. I'm not a big fan of most men."

"Don't worry, I don't. But as you can see, Charlene is wasted. And I need to get home to the babysitter. And since she lives next door, I'm going to take her with me. That is, I'm going to deliver her home. To *her* home. But she's lost her shoes and her purse. I need the purse because I don't have a key to her apartment."

Wilma frowned. "You aren't really trying to convince me that you're a Boy Scout, are you?"

"Could you find her purse?"

She pushed up from the table. "I'll take a turn around the room."

Charlene continued to lean against him, not fully

conscious. He waited five minutes before Wilma returned. "I don't see it, Mike. But you better take her home. And I promise I won't tell a soul she went home with you, and without her key."

"Thanks."

"Yeah, well, maybe you are a Boy Scout."

"Don't worry. I'm going to take care of her. I promise. And when you guys clean up the place, I'm sure she'd be so grateful if you'd keep an eye out for her shoes and purse."

"Sure thing." Wilma got up and came over toward them. She got in Charlene's face. "Honey, are you sure you want this oaf to take you home?"

"Definitely. It beats going home alone." Her words were just a tiny bit slurred.

"Maybe I should go find Simon and Molly, huh? I'm sure your cousin—"

"I'm fine. Mike is okay. Aren't you?" She gave him a drunken grin.

Wilma shook her head. "They never learn," she muttered, then gave Mike a hard stare. "If you take advantage of her, I will be so—"

"Shut up, Wilma. If Mike wants to take advantage of me, that's his business. But he might as well know that I came here looking for a good time."

"And you've apparently had it." Wilma threw up her hands and shook her head but returned to her place at the table, just as the last bachelor auction winner showed up to make her payment.

"All right," Mike said, "it's time to go. And since you are shoeless, I'm going to do the gallant thing." And with that he picked her up and carried her out the front door.

CHAPTER
23

Tim walked Andrea out to her car, trying to think of something smart or funny to say. Instead he came up with, "I didn't know you were an animal lover. I still can't believe you spent five hundred dollars on me."

He expected Andrea to open her car door, but instead she turned toward him and leaned back against the car. "Why? Don't you think you're worth it?"

His heart sped up. "You have a good point. The worth of one soul can't be measured in dollars and cents."

"Exactly," she replied. "So, really, a five-hundred-dollar donation to the local animal shelter is tiny. It merely depends on how you look at it."

"If you want to know how I look at it, I feel as if you rescued me."

The only light in the parking lot came from a distant streetlight, so he couldn't read her face, but he thought she might be smiling just a little bit.

"Tim," she said on a long breath, "did I rescue you from Charlene or merely from embarrassment?"

Did he imagine it? Loneliness rang in her voice. He leaned in, bracing his hands on either side of her. "Neither. You've made it easy for me to ask you out on a date."

Her breath caught, and Tim stopped hesitating. He moved in and kissed her. He halfway expected to earn himself a slap, but she yielded to him, opening her mouth, inviting him in.

He lost himself in the kiss for a long time, until her hands flattened against his chest. She gently pushed him back.

He disengaged. Her breathing seemed as rapid as his own. Was she dizzy? He was. Something had sparked the moment their lips met. Something wondrous and amazing and intoxicating.

"Tim, we need to think about this," she said. "Which is more than I did this evening. I'm afraid I acted rashly. In the heat of the moment. I just knew I had to bid on you. I couldn't stand the idea of Charlene winning you. I like Charlene a lot, but I don't think you and she belong together."

"I don't either. So don't beat yourself up over it. I'm sorry you spent so much. You probably could have had dinner with me for free."

She huffed out a breath. "It's not as easy as that."

"Why?"

"Because there's a conflict of interest. You're about to become Rainbow's guardian. And that means I can't have any kind of relationship with you. Although I have decided I want one. You have no idea how I look forward to Rainbow's visits when I know you're bringing her. But you see, that's wrong."

"How is it wrong?"

"It just is, and you know it. Wouldn't there be a problem if you dated a member of your own congregation?"

He nodded. "We're expressly warned about that. I guess I'm glad you're not a Methodist."

"I'm not anything. Which is another problem." She paused for a moment. "Tim, I worry that moving Rainbow to another therapist might set her back. But I think I have no choice now. And I probably have to have a conversation with the sanctioning board about this situation."

"You think that's necessary?"

"Yes, especially after that kiss. I've crossed a line. But there's more we need to think about very carefully."

"What?"

"I don't think I'd make a very good minister's wife. As I said, I'm not much of a believer."

"I see." His voice telegraphed his disappointment.

"And there's one final thing."

"Okay, since you're making a list."

"I'm not sure I'm cut out to be anyone's mother."

"But that's nonsense. You're a child therapist."

"Right. I'm a therapist, not a mother. The two things are not the same. They might be mutually exclusive. I've never really wanted to have children of my own. I've always been satisfied helping other people's kids."

He pushed back from the car, gut-punched. Over the last couple of weeks, he'd come to believe that Andrea was the woman he'd been searching for. Kissing her had confirmed it. In those moments, it was as if God had sent a blessing.

But this? He didn't know if he could handle this.

"It's a lot to think about, I know. I should never have made that bid. I'm sorry. I built up your hopes and then hit you with all my uncertainties."

"No, it's okay. Clearly we need to pray on this."

"You can pray. I'll think. Why am I so attracted to you? I just don't see how we can possibly find happiness."

He was tempted to tell her that Miriam or Savannah Randall had predicted his love would have a medical background. But he doubted that Andrea believed the nonsense his Altar Guild had been spreading through town. So he backed away a few steps, giving her space to leave. "Drive safely," he said.

She opened the car door and slipped into the driver's seat. "Take care, Tim."

Angel got to the parking lot just in time to see Dave's SUV turn onto Main Street. He stood there in the middle of the road cursing.

He should go back into the VFW hall and help the volunteers. Dave had no interest in coming out.

But Savannah's instructions had been clear. He needed to go for it. He needed to throw caution to the wind. And he sure had not done that during the auction, had he?

He strode to his Jeep, climbed in, and took off after Dave. It did not take him long to catch up. The vet drove like a little old woman, following the posted speed limits, and Angel drove like a crazy man.

He followed Dave all the way back to Last Chance, down Palmetto Avenue to Calhoun Street. Dave owned an old Victorian house right on the corner of Calhoun and Oak. Dave pulled his Ford Escape into the drive. Angel followed him.

Dave had not been paying attention to his rearview, apparently. Because he seemed surprised that he had been followed. He got out of his SUV with a frown on his face and stood by his open door looking handsome and perturbed.

Angel killed the Jeep's engine and climbed out.

"What the hell are you doing here?" Dave slammed the door of his Ford.

"Uh, look, Dave, I know your secret."

"What secret?"

Oh, boy. Dave was determined to play this charade. Disappointment and concern warred inside Angel's chest. "I want you to know that I am happy to help you if you are ready to come out," Angel said.

If looks could kill, Angel would be dead. "Why do you and Charlene think I'm gay? She told me she bought you for me. No thanks."

"Dave, there is something you should know."

"I'm going inside now." Dave turned toward the stairs leading to the back door.

Angel shouted at Dave's retreating back. "I am sorry. I really am. And I am here if you need a friend."

Dave stopped. His hands balled into fists. "I don't need your friendship." He turned around, his face so pale it almost looked gray.

"Look, Dave, this will be okay. Believe me. I have been openly gay since I got here, and aside from Molly's father and Simon's uncles, I rarely have problems. There are a few church ladies with backward views, but mostly I am accepted."

"I. Am. Not. Gay." Dave shouted the words. "Now get lost, okay?" His voice broke, and it took all of Angel's forbearance not to try to comfort him. A man should not have to pretend so hard. But, clearly, Dave was not ready to hear what Angel had to say.

"All right. I am going. But, Dave, you need to think about this. It is so much easier to be the person you were meant to be than to have to pretend and live behind a mask. It is not wrong to be who you are."

"Just leave," Dave said, then he turned and hurried up the steps of his house, slamming the door behind him.

A wave of intense nausea awakened Charlene. She sat up in bed, her stomach roiling and her brain playing wicked tricks on her. Her last, vague memory was of Mike carrying her out to his car.

She must have passed out somewhere between the VFW hall and home, and this must be Martha Spalding's apartment, a mirror image of her own. The bathroom that should be on the left was on the right. Someone had left the light on for her.

She made a dash for it, just in time to heave up the contents of her stomach, which mostly consisted of the cherry garnishes from all those mantinis she'd lost count of. How humiliating, especially since she'd lost her dress somewhere and now wore only her undies. Which were clean, thank goodness. Mother had always impressed upon her the importance of never leaving home without clean undies.

And in her case, the underwear was black and lacy and definitely not the kind she wore when she went tramping around in cow manure.

She was still kneeling before the porcelain throne, suffering through the worst case of dry heaves ever, when someone entered the room, pulled her hair back from her face, and applied a cool washcloth to her forehead.

Mike.

He had really gentle hands. And he didn't say a word.

He just waited until she was done barfing her guts out before he asked, "Better?"

She didn't reply, because the sound of his voice hit her eardrums and then rattled all of the brain cells she'd tried to pickle.

Bless him, he seemed to know this, because he swooped her up from her kneeling position and carried her back into his bed, which was actually Martha Spalding's bed. And instead of climbing into it with her, he tucked her in like a child and then handed her a glass of water and two Tylenol capsules.

She took the pills like a good girl.

"Get some sleep," he said. "I'm right out in the living room on the couch, if you need me."

She sank into the bed, still dizzy and disgusted with herself. She should probably get up and go home. But she didn't know where her purse or her clothes were and she didn't have the energy to go looking for them. Besides, her head had started to pound. So she sank back down under the covers and waited for the Tylenol to kick in. It must have done something, because she drifted back to sleep.

Sometime later, Rainbow climbed into bed with her. The little girl said not one word. But she snuggled up to Charlene's back. The child seemed to be crying again. In that silent way of hers.

Charlene rolled over and took Rainbow into her arms. It might be the last time she had a chance to hug her. In a few days, Tim Lake would take custody of her. And after that gargantuan bid, it appeared clear that Andrea Newsome and Tim Lake were an item. It was written in the stars, according to Miriam and Savannah Randall. Rainbow would never become her daughter. Ever.

Rainbow sniffled, and Charlene immediately swallowed down her own emotions. "What's the matter?" Charlene whispered.

"I miss Tigger." The child wiped a tear from her cheek.

Charlene was suddenly alarmed. Had something happened to the cat? "Where is she?"

"She has to sleep in the office. Mike says she can't sleep with me anymore." Rainbow buried her head on Charlene's shoulder, the picture of misery.

Charlene had a mind to get up and find the cat, but she couldn't interfere. She understood all too well. Mike had to get Rainbow ready to move in with Tim, who was allergic. Tigger wouldn't be going with Rainbow when she moved into the Methodist parish house.

She wished it could be different, but in the long run Rainbow needed a father. And Tim Lake seemed like a good guy. She snuggled Rainbow against her breast. "Honey, it's all going to be okay. You're safe here. No one is ever going to hurt you again. Now you go on back to sleep, you hear?"

And the two of them drifted off to sleep together.

Mike's cell phone alarm jolted him awake at seventhirty—a truly ungodly hour considering what had happened the night before.

But it was Sunday morning and Mike needed to rouse Rainbow and get her ready for Elsie Campbell, who had volunteered to take her to her first day of Sunday school. Afterward she would be spending the afternoon with Tim. The kid needed to get used to this routine. She'd be going to Sunday school from here on out.

Which was the way it should be, since Tim was going to adopt her.

But the whole setup made Mike a little grumpy, probably because he hadn't slept well last night. He'd checked Charlene every hour on the dot until two a.m., when she finally lost her cookies. After that, he figured she was probably okay, and he let himself doze off.

He pushed up from the couch, padded into the kitchen, and fired up the coffeemaker. He left it brewing as he headed for Rainbow's room. Full-out panic hit the minute he saw the open door. He rushed into the room. Rainbow's bed was empty and cold to the touch.

He immediately headed to the office, figuring she'd probably gone in there to visit with Tigger. But the door was still latched. He opened it anyway, only to find the demon cat. She meowed loudly, reminding him that she expected to be fed.

That left the master bedroom. He carefully opened the door and found Rainbow curled up in Charlene's arms. They were nestled like spoons under the comforter.

He stood in the doorway, his feet riveted to the carpet as wave after wave of emotion tumbled through him. His own mother would have yelled at him if he had ever presumed to climb into bed with her, especially after she'd been drinking. Not that he'd ever even thought of doing something like that. He'd learned how to tough it out as a kid when bad stuff happened. And the bad stuff happened all the time, especially when Mom was drunk.

No, Mike had never crawled into bed with anyone seeking safety. Or comfort. Or assurance.

Or love.

And God help him, he wanted to crawl into that bed right now. But he couldn't do that.

So he took a deep, deep breath and pushed that lonely,

abandoned kid back where he belonged—behind the steel doors of his defenses. He crossed the carpet and gently tapped Rainbow on the shoulder. "It's time to get up," he whispered.

She blinked and stared up at him, consciousness lighting her amber eyes. She shook her head and snuggled deeper against Charlene.

This was bad. Tim expected her at Sunday school, and she needed to get with that program. It was Mike's job to get her up, dressed, fed, and out the door to her new life. He didn't want tantrums. Her new life would be terrific.

"Time to get up, kiddo." He threw aside the covers on Rainbow's side of the bed and attempted to get her out of Charlene's embrace. That turned out to be harder than he expected, because his adorable next-door neighbor had a death grip on the kid, in addition to looking sexy as hell in that black bra, with all that wild hair haloing her face.

She also still looked a little green around the gills, but it was a cute shade of green. Charlene was cute all over. She was a cute drunk. She was cute wearing manure-covered boots. She was cute lying there half naked with her mascara smudged, cuddled up to Rainbow.

"Charlene," he said softly, "it's time for Rainbow to go to church. You need to let her go."

Her forehead furrowed with an adorable frown. She shook her head and mumbled something about not ever letting her go.

Rainbow took that moment to give him a wickedly wise smile, as if she fully understood his predicament. He gave Charlene a gentle poke in the shoulder, and her eyes fluttered a little and opened into slits. She winced at the light. He'd seen that look on his mother's face. Her hangover was going to be a doozy.

"Uh, hey, what time is it?" she asked.

"Early yet. But you need to let Rainbow go. I have to get her ready for Sunday school."

That did the trick. Charlene released her hold on the kid. "Oh, God," Charlene groaned, "I have to get up. There will be so much gossip if I miss church."

She tried to rise, but Mike gently pushed her back into bed. "Dollface, you're not going to church. For one thing, we don't have the key to your apartment because we didn't know where you left your purse. So all you have to wear is that killer dress from last night. Not exactly go-to-church attire. I'm sure God will understand. And besides, you aren't going to avoid the gossip. You've already crossed that bridge."

She gave him a slightly bloodshot stare. "Why do you say that?"

"Because I carried you from the VFW hall barefoot and semicomatose." He gave her what he hoped was a reassuring smile.

"Oh, God." She slunk down in the bed and pulled the comforter over her head.

"Come on, Rainbow, you have to go to Sunday School."

"Don't wanna."

Charlene peeked from under the covers. "Honey, you do have to go," she said.

"I do?"

"Uh-huh. All the kids go to Sunday school."

"Does Ethan?"

"Yes. He goes to a different Sunday school than yours. But he goes."

"Oh." Rainbow's shoulders slumped. "I wish I could go to Ethan's Sunday school."

"Sunday school is fun. You'll meet lots of other kids there. And then you'll get to spend the rest of the day with Uncle Tim," Mike said.

Rainbow's reaction to that news was less than enthusiastic. But he had to hand it to Charlene. She caressed Rainbow's face and gave her a motherly look. "You need to get up, honey. And do what Mike tells you. Okay?"

"If you say so." She scooted out of the bed, and Mike took her by the hand.

He turned toward Charlene before he headed out of the room. "Don't even think about getting out of bed. You can't go anywhere without a house key. So sit tight. I'll be back with water and more Tylenol."

CHAPTER
24

Charlene huddled under the covers, embarrassed and hung over. How could she have allowed herself to get so drunk last night that she lost her purse and needed to be carried from the VFW hall?

She should be ashamed of herself. She hadn't gotten that drunk since she'd been a freshman at UNC. She should have stuck to club soda.

And probably let Ruby put her hair up in something conservative like a chignon.

Now what?

She slipped from between the sheets and made a quick foray into Mike's dresser drawers, which proved interesting and intimate. His T-shirts were all white and neatly folded. He had nothing but black dress socks and white athletic socks. He was either color blind or boring.

But she knew otherwise. Somewhere he had a stash of AX jeans and Ralph Lauren polo shirts. That's pretty much all he wore.

Except for the tux last night, which was exactly like all the other tuxes the guys had rented from Allenberg Formal Wear. But, Lord have mercy, he filled out that tux like nobody's business. And then he'd behaved like a chivalrous knight, carrying her from the hall. He could have taken advantage of her. But instead he'd held her hair back while she puked in his toilet.

The memory made her face flame hot at the same time that her girl parts got kind of excited. Sort of pitiful all the way around.

She grabbed one of his T-shirts and a pair of sweats with a drawstring and hurried into the bathroom, where she borrowed his toothbrush. He used Colgate toothpaste, just like she did.

She turned on the hot water in his shower and hopped in. Maybe she could wash away last night's mistakes, but she seriously doubted it.

Sobriety had returned with a vengeance.

Rainbow looked adorable and ready for church. She'd washed her face, even behind the ears. She'd eaten a bowl of Cheerios, which constituted a minor miracle. She'd sat still for a whole ten minutes while Mike plaited her hair and secured each braid with a pretty yellow barrette that matched the yellow of the dress that Charlene had given her on Tuesday.

He felt insanely proud of her when Elsie knocked on the door to pick her up. The chairwoman of the Altar Guild took one look at her and beamed.

"Look at you, child, don't you look like a little cream puff today."

Cream puff? Elsie loved to bake, so he'd give her a

pass on that one. Rainbow looked adorable, but nothing like a cream puff.

"I declare, Mike, you've done wonders with this child. I'm sure Pastor Tim appreciates it all."

The comment irked him in so many ways.

He hadn't done wonders. The miracle worker had to be Charlene.

And Rainbow herself. Timmy would probably give Rainbow no credit for this achievement. When, in fact, the little girl had achieved a lot in a short time. She had gotten up when she didn't really want to. She'd behaved and followed instructions. She had even said one or two words.

Timmy would probably give all the credit for this transformation to Dr. Newsome. Timmy never stopped talking about the therapist. And after his brother's confession last night, Mike understood why.

So Andrea, not Charlene, would become Rainbow's mother.

He didn't like that idea, even though Andrea Newsome seemed to be a competent doctor and a wise therapist. She had kept a professional distance from Rainbow. Charlene had not. He flashed on the picture Rainbow and Charlene had made this morning, cuddled together in his bed.

It felt as if someone had put a tourniquet around his heart and had started to tighten it. He didn't want Andrea to become Rainbow's mother.

He squatted down and took Rainbow by the shoulders. "You'll be good in Sunday school? For me?"

The little girl said nothing. She merely threw her arms around his neck and gave him a quick hug. And whispered, "Will Tigger be here when I get back?"

He blew out a breath. The band around his chest ratcheted up a notch. Of course Rainbow could see what was happening. She was a bright kid. She understood that when she went to live with her uncle Tim, Tigger couldn't come with her. "She'll be here," he said. But, of course, he intended to drop the cat off at the shelter tomorrow.

The uncertain look on Rainbow's face shattered him. He connected with it in so many ways. Would she ever forgive him for taking Tigger away? Would she feel abandoned?

He gave her a quick kiss on the cheek. "Be good, kiddo."

He stood up, only to find Elsie giving him a sharp-eyed stare. Elsie's gaze took in his pajamas and then moved beyond to sweep the living room. The church lady was clearly seeking out evidence of hanky-panky. No doubt she'd heard that he'd taken Charlene home from the fund-raiser last night. He wasn't about to give Elsie any time to interrogate him, so he looked at his watch.

"Gee, it's getting late. You don't want Rainbow to be tardy for her first day at Sunday school, do you?"

She gave him thirty more seconds of the evil eye and then took Rainbow by the hand. "C'mon, sweetie, you're going to love Sunday school."

Mike stood in the doorway watching as Rainbow and Elsie headed down the stairs. It took a lot for him to close the door. As she walked away, it was almost as if a big hollow place opened up in his chest.

Damn, he needed to get his emotions under control. Coffee might help. He headed off to the kitchen, where Tigger immediately assaulted him, wrapping herself around his ankles.

Feeding time. The cat showed him nothing but disdain except early in the morning right before he put down food. He opened a pouch of cat food for her and then poured a cup of coffee for himself.

He leaned against the counter watching the parking lot, which seemed surprisingly busy this morning. Folks around here really took their Sundays seriously, didn't they?

He gradually became aware of the water running in the master bathroom. Charlene was taking a shower. An image of her naked and wet flashed through his head. A part of him—not his rational brain—wanted to go help her get clean. He could wash her back...or something.

He leaned against the countertop staring at nothing out the window, while he tried to sort out his feelings. Lust for the girl next door ranked pretty high on the list. Followed by the gut-wrenching tightness in his chest every time he thought about Rainbow being raised by Andrea Newsome.

He hated the idea.

But what the hell could he do about it? Let himself get sucked into a love affair with Charlene? Stay and raise Rainbow himself? Marry Charlene and become a day trader and a daddy?

No. No. No. No.

The lonely little kid at his core raised his battered head. Mike paid attention to that boy.

That boy had taught him to be independent. That boy had built walls. That boy lived behind a poker face. That boy walked out on Angie and saved Mike's life because Richard probably would have killed him sooner or later.

That boy knew when to walk away. And right now that

kid was screaming that the stakes in this game had gotten way, way too high.

Charlene stood in the kitchen doorway, her hair wet, her stomach empty, and her heart suddenly racing. Mike leaned against the counter, his head hung low. He seemed to be struggling to draw breath.

She crossed the room and put her hand on the middle of his back. His T-shirt was soft, the body beneath it hard and warm.

He straightened and let out a big breath. "Sorry."

"What's wrong?"

"Killer heartburn," he said, then immediately changed the subject. He moved toward the coffeemaker, shaking off her touch. "You want some coffee?"

He turned and gave her a quick glance. That's all it took.

Her heart wrenched, and she responded the way she always did when confronted with unspoken pain. She encountered it often, usually in the eyes of animals. But it was there, beyond that mild-mannered expression he tried to wear. He was hurting. She reached up to stroke his cheek. Her fingers encountered his warm skin and rough stubble. That touch flipped her switch. Electricity flowed inside her.

He closed his eyes and took a deep breath as her fingers moved over his face to his ear and up into his bright red hair.

"Don't," he whispered, but he made no attempt to move away. He reminded her of an abused animal that growls when all he wants is a little kindness. She cupped the nape of his neck and pulled him down as she rose up on tiptoes.

She gave him a soft, gentle kiss. Nothing deep or sexy, just a little kiss, intended to comfort. But it didn't stay that way. Mike grabbed her by the cheeks and pulled her up into the kiss like a man starving for love. His tongue stroked hers. His right hand dropped to her hip, and he yanked her forward and into his chest.

Her knees almost buckled. But she didn't fall, because Mike had her. His hand found the small of her back as he sagged against the counter. They leaned together, thigh to thigh, chest to chest. The kiss turned utterly carnal. His hand wandered up over her spine to her breast. He palmed it. Her nipples came alive. He groaned.

And her whole body throbbed.

She broke the kiss and looked up into his face. His eyes had dilated with desire. His breath sounded ragged. His skin flushed red.

"I want you," he said in a hoarse voice. "I want to strip you naked and do it right here in the kitchen."

His words ignited a bad-girl fire that pretty much torched her reservations about him. "Okay."

His gaze widened. "I'm not a reliable bet," he said.

She laughed. "You think I don't know that?"

"Oh."

She could almost feel him having second thoughts. And she had no intention of allowing that. She'd have the rest of her life to regret this choice. Or not.

Which would she regret more? Letting her reservations about him put the kibosh on this? Or spending the rest of her life wondering if maybe she should have bet on Mike Taggart?

Heartbreak was her middle name. "I'm a gambler," she whispered. "And sometimes the long shots pay off."

"Not usually," he said.

"Maybe not. But I'm the eternal optimist."

Call him crazy. Call him desperate. Call him immature. Whatever. But when Charlene started to move her hips against him, he put his brain in neutral and let his body take over. He lost himself in Charlene's deep, sweet, amazing kisses. She tasted so fine. Like nothing he'd ever tasted before. She had curves in all the right places, and her touch made his skin catch fire.

And maybe something else began to stir inside him, but he was too drunk on lust to identify it. Besides, he was preoccupied by her breasts, which were as amazing to touch as they were to look at. And she smelled really good, too.

He needed more skin. Right now. So he pulled the T-shirt over her head and spent one smoldering moment feasting his eyes on her breasts. And then he feasted his mouth on them.

Damn. He'd wanted to touch her boobs from the first time he'd seen her in one of her tight sweaters. But they weren't her only charms. Her butt was nice and round and soft. And she was making these really great noises that were an utter turn-on.

He wanted to bury himself in her.

Now.

"Uh, you want to do it here? I'm ready."

"Yeah, I noticed," she said with a laugh as she touched him through his pajamas. He couldn't breathe for a while as she kept it up. She had magical hands.

"Uh, look, we need to decide. Here or in the bedroom?"

She glanced at the kitchen window with its direct view to the busy parking lot. "I think bedroom."

"I'm glad someone's thinking." He hoisted her up into his arms.

She let go of a little squeak of alarm.

"Don't worry, dollface, I didn't drop you last night, and I won't do it now."

She rested her head on his shoulder. "You carried me like this last night?"

"You don't remember? You lost your shoes. I couldn't let you walk on the gravel."

"Sadly, no. And I'm kind of ticked off about it. Cinderella moments like that don't happen all that often, you know."

Somewhere in his brain an alarm went off. "Listen, doll, I'm not Prince Charming. Please don't confuse me with that guy."

"I know," she said as she twirled the hair at the base of his neck, sending shivers down his spine. "And I'm not really Cinderella."

He turned and looked into her face as they arrived at the bedroom door. God almighty, this woman had a face any fool could read.

She would fall for him.

"I'm going to break your heart," he said.

"I know."

He hadn't expected that. "You do?"

Her eyes went dark and mysterious. "Stop thinking, Mike. Just take me to your bed, okay?"

The words were like magic. He carried her across the bedroom floor, put her down on her feet, stripped off her clothes, and had his way with her.

CHAPTER 25

She awakened inside the circle of Mike's arms, skin to skin. The summer sun turned the window blinds golden. The light seemed so fresh, so new. As if she was seeing that precise color for the first time in her life.

Mike Taggart had breathed new life into her. She'd been so alone for the last few years, so stuck in her routine that she'd forgotten how it felt to wake up cradled in someone's arms. She looked around the room, and everything seemed different.

But these feelings couldn't be trusted. This after-sex giddiness had overtaken her before, and unfortunately her silly brain had mistaken it for love. It would be better to label it lunacy. That way she could avoid making the mistakes she'd made in the past.

Mike would be gone in a few days. And this euphoria was really more like a river at flood stage. It would tear through her life uprooting stuff for a while. It would be exciting and dangerous. But eventually her life would settle back between the riverbanks. She'd go back to her routine.

But right now, she would stay for the pleasure of it because Mike sure did know how to give and take pleasure. She closed her eyes and snuggled into him, listening to his even breathing.

She was thinking about waking him up for another round when his phone rang.

She turned and studied him as he groped for the phone. Sleep lines creased his face. His hair stuck out in all directions. He looked as if he'd been had—a few times. Which made her feel hot all over. He checked the caller ID, and then he glanced up at her.

His poker face was back.

He threw his legs over the side of the bed and pressed the talk button at the same time. He stood up and walked into the bathroom. Clearly the call was private. But being the niece of a first-class southern busybody, Charlene got out of bed and listened at the door.

Only every other word was intelligible, but she got the gist of the conversation. The call had come from someone in Vegas—someone involved with the World Series of Poker.

She let go of a sigh and headed back to the bed, where she found the T-shirt and sweatpants she'd borrowed from him. She put them on and then sat there for a long moment.

Tigger jumped up on the bed and meowed loudly. Without thinking, she stroked the cat's head, between her ears. Tigger closed her eyes and pressed up into the caress.

"I know," she said to the cat. "He's going back to Vegas. Sooner rather than later." A knot formed in her throat.

The cat climbed into her lap and curled up, purring loudly. "Are you worried, too? Tim Lake can't take you. And Mike's going to leave you behind."

The cat meowed as if she were actually carrying on a conversation. "Poor Tigger. What's to become of you? And me?"

She contemplated this rhetorical question while simultaneously wondering why the conversation in the bathroom was taking so long. Did Mike have someone waiting for him back in Vegas?

Oh, boy, that was a poisonous thought. It didn't matter if he did. She didn't want to fall in love with Mike. She knew that would be a fatal mistake.

The doorbell rang just as reality blasted through her.

"It's gotten busy in here all of a sudden," she said to Tigger. She picked up the cat and placed her on the carpet. Then she padded out to the front door and looked through the peephole.

Wilma Riley stood on Mike's stoop wearing a lavender, one-of-a-kind, go-to-church dress that she'd probably designed herself. Charlene decided it would be a good thing to hide from Wilma, but then Wilma hollered loud enough for everyone in the Edisto Pines Apartments to hear.

"Don't pretend you're not in there in Mike's apartment, Charlene. I know good and well that you are. I saw Mike carry you off last night, and since I have your keys, I'm thinking you probably want to talk to me."

Charlene jerked open the door. Wilma stood there with a disgusted look on her face as she took in the oversized T-shirt, baggy sweats, and messy hair.

Wilma rolled her eyes heavenward. "When will they

learn?" She shook her head. "I've got your purse and your keys and your wallet and your shoes. I looked all over for your common sense but couldn't find it." She held up the items.

Charlene blushed. "Sorry, Wilma."

"Don't apologize to me. I'm happy to help."

They stood there for an awkward moment. "You know, hon, he's not the staying kind," Wilma said in a much kinder tone of voice.

"I know."

"Okay, just so you're clear on that."

"I am."

"All right, guess I'll leave. And if you decide you need someone for a pity party in which we verbally emasculate the entire male species, you know where to find me."

"Thanks, Wilma, I appreciate it."

"It's nothing. But next time, hon, you might want to go easy on the mantinis."

And with that, Wilma turned and headed down the stairs.

Charlene closed the door just as Mike, wearing his PJ bottoms, came out of the bedroom. "Sorry about that. It was business."

"I figured." She held up her purse and evening shoes. "My keys have been returned. So I'm thinking maybe it might be better all the way around if I just scooted home now."

He frowned. "You don't have to go."

"I know. And truly, I had a great time this morning. But we both know this was just a little fun between the sheets. And I don't think I should be here when Rainbow gets back."

• • •

Charlene slipped out the front door before Mike could react. And when the door slammed in his face, he had a moment of self-doubt.

She left him? *She* left *him?*

Wow.

His pride wanted him to go right over to her place and drag her back. He briefly envisioned something like throwing her over his shoulder the way he did with Rainbow when she misbehaved.

But the other part of him—the careful part—was happy to let her go. She had called it correctly. The events of the morning had been triggered by lust.

But still, he couldn't believe that Charlene, adorable girl-next-door, was completely unfazed by buddy sex. Somehow that didn't fit his notions of her.

Still, she'd made it easy for him to walk away.

And given the news he'd just gotten, letting her go would be wise all the way around.

Dragon Casinos had finally offered a short-term sponsorship deal. They wanted Mike to wear their logo during the upcoming World Series of Poker, and they were willing to pay him a bundle to do it. And if he made it into the top ten money winners, they promised him a long-term contract.

Paul had been justifiably proud and happy about the work he'd put into schmoozing these guys, especially since Mike had been out of pocket for the last couple of weeks. The Taiwanese owners of Dragon Casinos were giving him twenty-four hours to accept the deal. And if he accepted, he needed to be back in Vegas by Thursday, at the latest, to meet with the principals and sign the contract.

He'd be a fool not to take this deal.

But for some stupid reason, he'd told Paul he needed a little time to think about it. Paul's reaction had been priceless. He'd spent five minutes yelling at Mike and accusing him of getting all mushy over a kid.

Paul had it halfway right. Mike *had* gotten mushy over Rainbow. But if it were just Rainbow, he'd be okay leaving her with Timmy. No, Rainbow didn't have him second-guessing his life. But Rainbow and Charlene *together* sure did.

Angel sat in the back booth at the Kountry Kitchen nursing a cup of coffee, a hangover, and a broken heart.

He should not have chased after Dave last night. Savannah might have told him to go for it, but he should have known better. A man like Dave, who was not ready to come out or even accept himself, could not be bullied or chased or seduced into it. Chasing him like some crazy person was not the right approach.

Angel looked down at the worn Formica tabletop, tracing the geometric designs with his fingertip while he counted up all the stupid mistakes he had made last night.

Starting with drinking too many mantinis. Not to mention driving after consuming that much alcohol. He had behaved in a shameless, dangerous manner. He was ashamed of himself.

He vowed that no matter how bad the situation got at the animal shelter, he was never, ever going to suggest a bachelor auction again. AARC had raised a lot of money last night, but people had behaved badly. He was not alone, but that did not make him feel any better.

"I thought I might find you here."

Angel looked up in astonishment. Dave Underhill stood beside the booth with his fingers jammed into the pockets of his jeans. His dark hair curled over his forehead. He was so handsome.

"I should apol—"

"No." Dave sat down in the facing booth. "I should apologize for yelling at you."

"You want some coffee, handsome?" Flo called from the counter.

Dave looked up and gave her one of his to-die-for smiles. "Uh, no thanks."

"So where's Charlene taking you to dinner?" Flo asked.

"Don't know yet. I guess it's up to her."

Flo winked and hurried off to refill empty cups at the other end of the dining room.

"You think Charlene bought me some time?" Dave asked.

Angel laughed. "I just heard from one of the volunteers that Mike Taggart carried Charlene off last night. Obviously Flo hasn't yet heard that bit of gossip. But I am thinking that, when the good church ladies are finished with Sunday services, they will get busy and soon everyone will be wondering why Charlene bought you but went home with Mike."

Dave shook his head. "I'm not ready for this."

"I know that."

"No, you don't understand," Dave said with some urgency. "I've known I was different since I was like thirteen. I don't want to be different. So I've tried to live a straight life. I'm still trying."

"That doesn't work, you know. And in the meantime you are not doing any of the women you date any favors."

"I haven't dated any women recently. The truth is I'm not attracted to them."

"Of course you're not."

"Look, Angel, maybe this is easy for you. But it's not for me. I am attracted to men but I don't want to be. I don't want to live my life as a gay man."

"Sometimes you do not get a choice."

"Maybe so. But I do have a choice about coming out. I can't imagine anything that would hurt my parents and sisters more. They are all pretty religious. I'll lose them if I come out, and I love them. My family is more important to me than anything. I can't do that to them."

"So you torture yourself instead? That makes no sense. I am sure your family loves you. Give them a chance to show it. I think they deserve the chance to love you for the way you truly are. I'm not guaranteeing that they will not walk away. Sometimes that happens. But more often, you discover that your family has always known. That they have been waiting for you to be honest."

"Daddy is not like that. He's a deacon in the church back home. This will destroy him."

Anger boiled through Angel. Why did it have to be so hard? Dave was not the only person who had stayed in the closet because he was afraid of losing his family. Angel had heard this story so many times. And sometimes it was true. Sometimes parents disowned their children because they couldn't accept the truth.

He pulled in a deep breath before he spoke again. Dave didn't need his anger. He needed so much more than that. Angel leaned in. "Dave, I want to tell you something important. A while ago, Miriam Randall told me that my soulmate would be a veterinarian. And shortly after she said this, I broke up with my boyfriend and moved here. And then you came to town. I believe in Miriam Randall. And she says that me finding love with a vet is part of what she calls 'the Lord's plan.' So you should take that as a sign. You need love to live a full life. So if your biological family can't love you for what you are, maybe you need to make a new family of people who can."

Anger and a killer hangover were two things that didn't go well together. If he stayed he might say something that would hurt Dave. Dave had to work this out for himself. So Angel stood up and threw a couple of dollars on the table for his coffee.

"Think it over. And when you are ready to be loved for the person you truly are, call me. I will be there for you."

"So tomorrow, after camp, we'll be packing up your things and moving you to the parish house," Mike said, using every skill he'd ever learned as a poker player to keep his voice and his face calm and neutral. It wasn't easy.

Rainbow's big amber eyes were dry. And in some weird way the fact that she wasn't crying made this explanation of what was about to happen all the more difficult.

And damned if her big solemn eyes didn't remind him of Angie.

Of course the situation was entirely different. He wasn't a scared, hurt kid anymore. He was a grown man, with the chance of a lifetime waiting for him in Vegas. And while he might have wanted to find a way so that Rainbow could keep her cat, the tragedy of losing Tigger paled in comparison to what she would be getting. Tim and Andrea would make sure she grew up right. And Mike would make sure she never wanted for anything her heart desired.

Except for Tigger. "I don't want to move into the parish house," Rainbow said. And the frown on her face suggested that a tantrum might be only moments away.

"It's called a *parish* house. That's what they call the place where ministers live. And you are going to live in the parish house because Pastor Tim is going to become your dad."

Rainbow continued to stare daggers at him. And damned if the cat didn't join in. The animal was sitting on Rainbow's lap, and they were all on Martha Spalding's ugly green velour couch.

The cat's half-lidded, slightly creepy stare seemed to suggest that Tigger understood perfectly where she was going tomorrow morning—and it wasn't the parish house. It was actually a place where she was likely to perish. And at the hands of humankind.

A wave of guilt percolated up through him. He'd tried so hard to find the cat a home. But there wasn't a soul who wanted or needed another cat. The only person he hadn't asked was the girl next door. And things being what they were, he was not about to initiate any kind of conversation with Charlene. Charlene was best left in the past.

"Okay, it's time for bed," he said, because he didn't know what else to say. He couldn't fix this situation. Rainbow would just have to live through tomorrow. She'd forgive him one day. He was giving her a good life.

Rainbow hugged Tigger to her chest.

"You know the rules," he said, his heart breaking for her. "Tigger sleeps in the office." Every part of him wanted to let Rainbow take the cat into her bedroom one last time. But that would only make the parting much more difficult tomorrow morning.

Rainbow bent over her cat and whispered something into the animal's ear. Maybe it was good-bye, because she put Tigger on the floor and headed off to her bedroom.

Mike didn't know what to make of that behavior. Had she come to realize that tantrums didn't work? Or had he utterly broken her spirit?

Two hours later, he was still worrying about that question while Sports Center played on the television. His ringing telephone pulled him from his dark thoughts. It was nearly ten o'clock. Who could be calling at this hour?

He checked the number, hoping it might be Charlene, but it wasn't. The call came from Chicago, but he didn't recognize the number.

He pushed the connect button. "Mike Taggart."

"Oh, Mr. Taggart, I'm sorry to call so late. My name is Norah Blake, and I think you have my aunt's cat."

"What?"

A warm laugh came over the line. "I'm sorry. I'm sure you're confused. Ms. Sanger from the Chicago Department of Social Services contacted me just a minute ago. Do you know her?"

"Uh, yeah, she's Rainbow's caseworker."

"Rainbow. I can hardly believe it. How is she? She must be five or six now."

"You know Rainbow?"

"I do. She's one of my aunt's strays."

"What?" Mike put his beer down on the table and used the remote to reduce the sound on the television.

"Mr. Taggart," the woman said, "my aunt was once a registered nurse before she suffered a back injury that put her on disability. She made it her business to look after people. She took in strays. Sometimes they were cats, but most of the time they were neighborhood kids whose parents didn't give them what they needed. Rainbow was someone she looked after. She was pretty much Rainbow's babysitter and caregiver from the time that baby came home from the hospital until Angie broke up with Deon and moved away. I guess Rainbow was about four years old or something like that."

"Uh, Ms. Blake, did people call your aunt Miss Mary?"

"Yes, they did. She was always Miss Mary at church. And the kids in the neighborhood always called her that. Why?"

"I think Rainbow remembers her."

"I'm so glad to hear that. Actually it's kind of amazing. She was such a little girl when they moved away."

"So I'm still confused," Mike said. "Why did Ms. Sanger get in touch with you?"

"Oh, she figured out that Rainbow's cat is my aunt Mary's kitty, Tigger. I'm not sure how she figured it out. Something about the rabies tag on Tigger's collar. And then she found the nursing home, and someone there gave her my number."

"Well, thanks for calling. I've been wondering about Miss Mary. It's been quite a mystery, and Rainbow's explanations have been vague."

"Uh, Mr. Taggart, it's more of a mystery than you think. Ms. Sanger said I needed to call you and tell you the story. You see, a few months ago, my aunt was attacked in her home. She suffered a blow to the head, and was in a coma for a while. She passed about a month ago. Anyway, when we found her, the apartment was locked, but her cat was gone. As you can imagine, we searched high and low for Tigger, but we never found her."

"Why didn't you check with Rainbow's mother? Or with some of the neighborhood kids?"

"We did check with the neighborhood kids. And the neighborhood watch, and eventually her attacker was identified as one of those stray kids she used to take in. He's a troubled boy with a drug problem. Apparently he came to Mary's apartment looking for money and she argued with him. He gave her a shove, and she fell because her back is not right. She hit her head and fractured her skull. And then I gather Tigger scratched him. He told police he got so angry with the cat that he threw her out the window. It's a four-story drop to the sidewalk. So, naturally, we thought Tigger had died, even though we never found her body."

"But you said Rainbow lived next door. Why didn't you—"

"No, you don't understand. This was about four months ago. Rainbow hasn't lived in my aunt's neighborhood for at least a year."

"How far away did Rainbow move? Angie was living on the South Side when she was murdered."

"Mr. Taggart, that's why I'm calling. When Ms. Sanger told me where Rainbow was living, I couldn't believe it. My aunt lived north of the city in a middle-class neighborhood that's a good fifteen miles from where Rainbow and Angie moved. I can't explain how the cat got from one place to another. I can't even understand how the cat knew where Rainbow had gone. But it's a miracle." Norah Blake's voice wobbled a little bit.

Mike didn't really believe in miracles. There had to be some rational explanation. "Maybe Rainbow came back to the old neighborhood for a visit and found Tigger," Mike said, but the moment the words came out of his mouth a shiver worked its way up his spine.

"I suppose that's the only rational explanation. Maybe you can ask her. But the thing is, getting that call today from Ms. Sanger was like a gift, you know?"

"Uh, Ms. Blake," Mike said, "would you be interested in having the cat back?"

The woman on the other end of the line let go of an audible sigh. "I can't ask for the cat back. Ms. Sanger told me how much Rainbow loves Tigger, and clearly the cat loves Rainbow back."

"No, you don't understand. Rainbow is about to be adopted by her uncle, and he's allergic. I need to find a home for Tigger. If you want her back, she's yours."

"You mean it? Really?" There was a note of relief in Norah Blake's voice. "I'd be happy to pay for the airfare to have her flown back here. I checked with the airlines, and you can do that, you know. I got your email address from Ms. Sanger. I'll make the arrangements for Tigger, if someone can deliver her to the airport in Columbia."

"That's not a problem. I'll be heading up there in a day or two."

"Good. We can finalize the details by email. Mr. Taggart, you have no idea how glad we are that Tigger is still with us. She's a wonderful cat, as I'm sure you've already learned."

"Yes, she is," he said. The lie came easily to his lips.

CHAPTER 26

At five-thirty on Monday morning, Charlene got tired of revisiting the mistakes she'd made on Sunday morning and finally gave up trying to sleep. She wandered into her kitchen to start a pot of coffee. A faint glimmer of purple lit up the eastern sky. It would be dawn soon.

The moment she got out of bed, Winkin', Blinkin', and Nod came tumbling into the kitchen after her, looking for their morning handout. She opened a pouch of cat food and divided it into three bowls. She fed Winkin' and Blinkin' separately from Nod because the boys were bullies, and Nod had only just learned the joys of solid food.

Charlene had just poured her first cup of the day when she heard Mike's voice coming from the front landing. "Rainbow, what do you think you're doing?" he shouted.

She looked through the kitchen window just in time to see Mike grab Rainbow by the arm and give her a little yank backward. Tigger, who was riding on the little girl's shoulders, took that moment to make her escape.

She jumped and took off down the steps toward the parking lot.

"Let me go," Rainbow cried. "I hate you. I hate you. I hate you. I hate you. I hate you." The child turned on Mike and started punching him in the chest.

Adrenaline rushed through Charlene. And in the next moment, she found herself on the front stoop not entirely certain how she'd arrived there.

Mike and Rainbow occupied the landing, and Mike had Rainbow's shoulders in a viselike grip that looked so tight it had to be bruising the child. Rainbow had stopped punching him, but now she seemed to be determined to get away from him.

Charlene stopped thinking. She needed to help them both right now. She needed to stop their pain.

"What happened?" she said in her calmest voice, the one she reserved for panicked animals.

Neither of them responded.

She touched Mike's shoulder. "You're holding her too tight, Mike. What happened?"

Mike blinked and looked over his shoulder. Something changed in his gaze. "She tried to run away." He relaxed his hold on the child a tiny fraction.

Rainbow took that moment to twist out of Mike's grasp. She raced down the stairs, a backpack bouncing on her back.

"No!" Mike and Charlene spoke as one. Mike took off after her, and Charlene followed in her bedroom slippers.

Rainbow ran as if her life depended on it. Mike was right on her heels, but the little girl dashed off the curb between two parked cars and then darted out into the lane right into the path of Ned Payton's Malibu.

"Stop!" Charlene screamed at both Ned and Rainbow, but neither of them heard. She watched in horror as the Chevrolet's front bumper connected with Rainbow's leg and knocked her to the ground with a sickening thump. Ned wasn't going very fast, and he stopped almost immediately.

Rainbow wailed the moment she hit the ground. The pain in that scream knifed right through Charlene.

What had she done? Her interference had ended in disaster.

She stood frozen on the sidewalk, unable to move forward.

She should have kept her distance. She had no part in Rainbow's life. What made her think she could give Mike advice? What made her think she belonged in this family?

She held her breath as Mike fell to his knees, cradling the little girl's head.

By this time, Ned had gotten out of his car and had called the EMTs. Ned was upset. He kept saying "I didn't see her," over and over again, in a shaky voice.

Lights winked on. Neighbors came out of their apartments.

"Tigggerrrrrrrrr!" Rainbow screamed. Over and over again.

Mike looked up, lines she'd never seen chiseled into his face. "Charlene, the cat ran away. We need to find it. Fast. Can you help?"

"Of course. Oh, Mike, I'm so sorry I shouldn't—"

"Just find the damn cat. I can't stand to hear her calling for it that way."

She wanted to rush to his side, because he looked so scared and alone crouched there beside the child.

She held back. She'd created this disaster.

"Charlene?"

"Uh, yeah. I saw her head down the stairs, but where did she go after that?"

"I don't know." He pointed vaguely toward the commons. "That way, I think. This is all my fault, Charlene. I told Rainbow that Tigger was going to her new home today."

"You found her a home?"

He looked up at Charlene, his face gray in the morning light. "I planned to take the cat to the shelter. But then I got a call last night from Chicago. Charlene, I know who Miss Mary is. Tigger belonged to her. And the cat is going back to Miss Mary's niece in a couple of days. The cat never belonged to Rainbow."

A frisson of anger boiled through Charlene. "You told Rainbow the cat was going to the shelter?"

"I had to tell her the truth."

"For goodness' sake, all you had to do was ask me. I would have taken the cat gladly. Rainbow could visit her anytime she wanted."

For a moment, their gazes caught and clashed. Oh, heaven help her, she was such a fool. Didn't the guy understand how many people in this town stood ready to help him, if he just made the right decision?

Apparently not. And like as not, Mike Taggart, loner and gambler, would never learn that lesson.

An hour and a half after the accident, Timmy came striding into the waiting room of the orthopedic wing of the Orangeburg Medical Center. "How could you have let this happen?" he said in a censorious voice.

"I didn't expect Rainbow to try to run away with the cat," Mike replied. He'd been sitting in the waiting room for half an hour, since the orthopedist on call had arrived, and they'd moved Rainbow from the emergency room to prep her for surgery.

"You're not serious. I thought you planned to take the cat to the shelter," Timmy said.

"I did. This morning. But I made the mistake of telling Rainbow what I was planning and why. And then I got a weird call last night. Apparently the cat never really belonged to Rainbow. The niece of the cat's owner called me, and we made arrangements to send Tigger back to Chicago."

"You told Rainbow you were taking the cat to the shelter?" The incredulity in Timmy's voice hit its mark. He was the second person this morning to give him crap for his decision to be honest.

"I thought being honest was the right thing to do. Don't you believe in honesty?"

"Yeah, but maybe not like that. Andrea told me once that parents lie to their kids all the time."

"Okay, I'm an idiot. I just thought that she needed to know what was going to happen so she could prepare. And after the call I got last night, I'm starting to think I've completely underestimated her attachment to the cat and vice versa."

Except he hadn't. For the last week, he'd known precisely how cruel it would be to take away Rainbow's cat. But he'd forged ahead with that plan, sure that the trade-off would be worth it. Rainbow would get Charlene as a mother and Timmy as a father. And the cat seemed like a small sacrifice.

But now, with Charlene clearly not in the picture, losing her cat seemed like a pretty raw deal for Rainbow. The kid had been right to beat on him and tell him how much she hated him. He'd been ready to destroy Rainbow's best friend.

"Is she going to be okay?" Timmy asked in a softer voice. It occurred to Mike that this question should have been asked first.

"She's got a broken leg that requires something called an open reduction. The orthopedist just arrived, and she's gone into surgery. She's going to need a plate and some screws to hold the lower leg bones in place. But her injury isn't life-threatening."

Timmy strode across the room and threw himself into one of the standard-issue chairs. "Thank God. But it means more hurdles for her." Timmy's voice still had that accusatory tone.

Mike didn't dispute his brother's words or the tone. He deserved all the censure Timmy wanted to throw in his direction. He had failed to keep Rainbow safe.

Cat or no cat, she would be better off with Timmy and Andrea. The two of them looked like a set of model parents. And maybe Mrs. Blake from Chicago would understand about letting Tigger stay with Charlene. Then Timmy could arrange visitation for Rainbow.

So it was time to leave. Time to pull the plug on this distraction.

"Look, Timmy, I got a call yesterday from a casino that wants to sponsor me. The initial signing bonus is a substantial sum, and I plan to put it in a trust for Rainbow. If I do well in the upcoming tournament, I'll be getting a pretty steady paycheck. And it's my hope that, by the time

Rainbow graduates from high school, I will have saved a big pot of money that she can use for college or whatever it is she wants to do in life. I'll need you to manage that trust. But I think supporting her financially is about the best I can offer her."

"You're leaving? Now?" Timmy's voice sounded hard and angry.

"I need to get back by Thursday at the latest." He looked up at his brother, and noted the disgust on Timmy's face. Well, so be it. Mike wasn't any kind of angel. And he was nobody's idea of the perfect father or spouse. It would be better all the way around if he cleared out as quickly as possible.

"If money is so important to you, then you should go." The soft-spoken minister had clearly lost his patience.

"It's not about the money."

"Isn't it?"

"You think it's a bad thing for me to set up a trust for Rainbow?"

Timmy shook his head and let go of a big breath. "No. But I think it's despicable of you to run out on Rainbow for a big sponsorship deal when she's hurt and needs you."

"She needs me like she needs a hole in the head. I'm no good for her, Timmy. And you got it right when you came in here a moment ago. She wouldn't be hurt if anyone but me had been looking after her. I'm no good at this."

Mike stood up and headed for the door. "We have an appointment with Eugene Hanks this afternoon. You stay here, and I'll keep the appointment. I'll see about getting you a medical power of attorney. Send me text updates on her condition, okay?"

"What am I supposed to tell Rainbow when she gets out of surgery?"

Mike stopped and stared at his brother. "Just tell her you love her, for chrissake."

His brother's eyes widened, no doubt because Mike had taken the Lord's name in vain. Well, tough.

He walked out of the waiting room without looking back. He'd learned not to do that the day he'd walked out on Angie. Walking out on Timmy was just as hard, even though his brother was pissed off at him right at the moment. He hadn't even fully processed the idea of walking away from Rainbow. Or Charlene. But that was going to be even harder.

CHAPTER 27

Charlene left a message on the answering machine at work, letting Dave and Cindy know about the crisis. Then she dressed in the clothes she usually wore for farm rounds and headed out the front door on foot, with a baggie of cat treats in her pocket.

She walked a mile and a half down Julia Street, poking under bushes and in alleyways and up people's drives. She'd almost reached Palmetto Avenue when her cell phone rang. She checked the ID, hoping it might be Mike with some word about Rainbow.

Disappointment. It was Elsie Campbell, but then Elsie probably had all the latest on Rainbow's condition, so she pressed the talk button.

"Hey," she said.

"Oh, honey, the minute I heard about little Rainbow I got in touch with everyone and we've got a rotating prayer vigil going at the hospital in Orangeburg. Sabina went up there right away, and thank God the news is good. I gather Rainbow broke her leg and needs surgery but it could have been so much worse. So, anyway, I know you're not a member of the Altar Guild but I thought maybe you might want to sign up for the vigil and all. We're trying to make sure Pastor Tim isn't alone in this time of need. We've got a slot this afternoon at two."

"Isn't Mike with him?"

"I don't think so." The disappointment in Elsie's voice came through loud and clear. "I had such high hopes for him, you know? He seems like such a good man, and he's done such a fabulous job with Rainbow. So I was shocked when Sabina Grey told me that he'd left the hospital. Pastor Tim told Sabina that Mike has some kind of big poker deal. And since Rainbow is going to be okay, and Pastor Tim has all but agreed to become her daddy, there's no real reason for him to stay."

Charlene gritted her teeth. Why did this hurt so bad? It wasn't as if she hadn't expected it. After all, the guy admitted that he planned to take Rainbow's cat to the animal shelter. And he was planning to leave Rainbow because of a big payday. He was exactly like all the other guys who'd traipsed through her bedroom.

They all chose money instead of her.

"Elsie," she said on a long sigh, "I'm out here looking for Rainbow's cat. I don't think I can commit to a specific time at the hospital." In truth, she planned to stay away from the hospital. If she had to bet, she'd say that Andrea Newsome would eventually become Rainbow's momma. And for Rainbow's sake, Charlene needed to back off.

"Honey, this could be your chance to bond with Pastor Tim. You know that, don't you?"

Oh, boy, Elsie and the rest of the ladies were sweet but so misguided. "Uh, yeah, but I don't think Tim and

I are a match made in heaven, Elsie. And besides..." Her voice choked, and she couldn't go on. The truth was hard to take.

"Hon, what's up?"

"Nothing. I just need to find Rainbow's cat, okay?"

"Honey, are you out there searching all by your lonesome?"

"Yeah. The cat ran away just before the accident. Rainbow was running to catch her. Tigger couldn't have gotten that far, but I can't find her. She's probably hiding or something. Poor thing."

"I'll see if I can get you some help on that, okay?"

"Thanks."

"All right, hon. You take care."

"Uh, Elsie—"

"What?"

"Ah, could you call if you hear any news about the child?"

There was a long pause. "Honey, don't you think you should be down at the hospital?"

"Elsie, come on. I'm not marrying Tim. But I'd appreciate it if you could pass along any information your Altar Guild ladies get."

Another long pause. "All right, Charlene."

"Thanks."

She disconnected, and two minutes later, Angel pulled his Jeep to the curb and got out.

He looked exhausted, the skin beneath his eyes dark with fatigue. "Wow, you look like something the cat dragged in. Did you and Dave get any sleep on Saturday and Sunday?"

"Not much. We did a lot of talking."

"Talking?"

"It's complicated," he said. "But I'm not here to talk about me and Dave. Dave called this morning and told me about what happened to Rainbow. I'm here to take you to the hospital, which is where you belong right now."

"You know, I'm tired of everyone in this town thinking they know what I should be doing. As it turns out, Rainbow got hurt chasing her cat. The cat is missing, and Mike asked me to find it. He said it was important for Rainbow. And I agree with that. And there are dozens of church ladies holding vigil at the hospital. But no one is actually trying to find Tigger. So I think, all in all, I should stick with this job and keep my distance."

"*Chica,* that is silly. You care about her . . . and Mike."

"I do," she whispered. "I care about them too much. Don't you see? I think it would be better if I stayed away. I'm not marrying Tim. And I don't think Mike sees me as his soulmate. Bed buddy would be a better description."

"Oh, my God. You slept with him?"

She nodded. "Don't worry. I was sober."

"And . . . ?"

"And he's got talent between the sheets. But right afterward, he got a call from someone in Vegas with a big sponsorship deal. He's going back. He's exactly like Derrick and John and Phillip and Erik."

"Oh, I am sorry."

"It's okay. I just need to find Tigger." Her voice shook.

Angel didn't say anything, but his big brown eyes filled with compassion.

"I'm fine. Are you fine?"

He shook his head. "No, I'm confused. Ready to start a

protest against the small-minded members of the Baptist church. But mostly fine."

Her eyes started tearing up. "Damnit," she swore as she wiped the tears from her cheeks. "How many times am I going to make the same mistake?"

"I—"

"No, don't answer that." She put up her hand. "I am done making that mistake. Because, look at me, I'm the one looking for the cat. Do you think four cats are too many for an unmarried woman in her early thirties?"

Angel had the good grace not to answer that question either.

Rainbow reminded Tim of a sleeping angel. The docs had sedated her so she was pain free at the moment. He looked up from his prayers. She would survive relatively unscathed except for a scar on her leg.

He had not left her side since she'd come out of recovery.

The clock on the wall had just clicked over to two in the afternoon. The next Altar Guild volunteer should be arriving shortly. They had come as a tag team to sit with him, get him drinks and sandwiches from the cafeteria, and pray. Their prayers were simple and direct and powerful. His own prayers were far more complicated. He didn't think his Altar Guild would fully understand his doubts.

Especially now that the clock read two. Back in Last Chance, Mike would be about to meet with Eugene and start the process of making him Rainbow's guardian.

The door opened. He looked up, expecting Elsie or Wilma, but instead Andrea Newsome strolled in.

After the words they'd shared on Saturday night, he hadn't expected to see her here. But the moment she arrived, the tension in his neck and shoulders eased. He'd had visitors all day, and finally someone had come who had the power to give him comfort, or at least listen without prejudice to his honest thoughts.

"Hey," she said in a soft voice. "I've been fighting with my better judgment all day, and I'm pleased to say that my judgment lost."

"So this isn't a professional visit?"

Was it guilt that made her cheeks get pink? She shook her head. "Well, I justified it as a professional visit. Rainbow is still one of my patients, at least for the time being. But, Tim, I think we need to make a change. I've spent a lot of time thinking about last Saturday, and the truth is I want to pursue a relationship with you."

It wasn't exactly a breathless declaration of love, but it felt like one.

"I'd like to do the same thing," he said as he stood up and moved to her side. He took her into his arms. She came willingly, her hair brushing against his chin, her scent enveloping him. He drank it in. Her soft, feminine body fit perfectly against his. A spark of desire ignited inside him.

He gave her a long, deep kiss, which she returned in kind. He knew, right then, that the Lord had sent him something precious and wonderful. If Miriam Randall had predicted this, then she truly had a link with the Lord and his plans.

The kiss didn't last nearly long enough. But they stood in a hospital room, and one of his parishioners was likely to turn up at any moment. Restraint was called for. And

Andrea seemed to understand that. She understood so much.

She turned, still in his arms, and gazed down at the sleeping child. "So how did this happen?"

"She was running after her cat." He almost choked on the words. "Andrea, why would God send me a child who loved a cat that much? Is this His idea of a joke or a test?"

She looked up at him, a gentle smile on her face. "I can't answer that. You know my views on God."

"You don't believe in Him."

"Oh, I think I do. But my God is not so deeply involved in our daily travails. I think he thought up the universe and walked away, just to see what we'd do with it."

"That's a depressing way of looking at things."

She cupped his face in her hand, setting off little waves of internal longing. "I think it's a realistic way of thinking. Bad things happen to people who don't deserve it. And irony abounds, Tim. You know that."

"When I heard about the accident, I lost it. I don't even understand why I got so upset. But I came in here with my emotions out of control."

"I'm not surprised."

"I took my feelings out on Mike. I think I made a terrible mistake."

Andrea's eyebrow arched. "Why do you say that?"

He tucked a wayward strand of hair behind her ear. "I came in here ready to blame Mike for what happened, but the longer I pray, the better I see the truth.

"Rainbow would never have been trying to run away if I had been willing to find some accommodation for her cat. But I took such a firm, unwavering stance. I showed that child no pity. No compassion. No love."

"I think you sell yourself short. You said yourself that you came here today emotionally undone. Why do you think you felt that way?"

"I just told you."

"No, Tim, you told me you came running here out of control. You probably didn't even know about the cat. But you were already upset. Why do you think that happened?"

He stood blinking down at her as the clock on the wall ticked down seconds. He mentally pushed his guilt aside and tried to recapture that moment this morning when Mike had called him.

His throat constricted. Mike had been out of control, too.

Tim closed his eyes and took a deep breath. "I was afraid she might die, and I don't want to lose her. I don't want to lose Mike either," he whispered.

"Of course not. They're your family." She gave him a big hug and stroked his back for a moment.

"But Andrea, there's something else."

She eased back. "I know."

"You know?"

She nodded. "But you need to say it out loud. You need to give yourself that space and be honest."

He nodded, emotions churning inside him. "I know I'm expected to take care of Rainbow. And I'm sure I will find a lot of joy in it. I've come to love her, and last Saturday down at the river I had a blast swimming with her. But I don't feel *called* to be her father, Andrea. I don't expect you to quite understand this. But the more I pray on this, the deeper I feel about it. I've put this in Christ's hands, and He keeps giving me an answer that I'm having trouble accepting."

"So you think maybe your Lord has another plan, huh?"

He managed a chuckle. "That's funny coming from a nonbeliever like you."

"I have been told I've got a good bedside manner." She grinned.

He tried to smile. He couldn't quite manage it.

"Just say it out loud, Tim. I'm not going to judge you for your feelings. They are just feelings."

"I don't want to be her father. I don't think I'm right for her." He blurted the words, and they sounded so horrible being spoken out loud. "I care about her. I even love her. But I just don't feel ready to take care of her. I wish..."

"What?"

"I wish Mike had never come here and dumped this on me." He took several big breaths. "I'm a terrible person." He let her go and strode to the single window in the room. He leaned against the windowsill and looked out at a darkening sky. A summer thunderstorm was headed this way.

"Tim, you just punted. You fell back on guilt, which is a common thing that we all do. But you have to push those guilty feelings aside and go hunting for the truth. You don't really wish that Mike had never turned up. You just admitted to me that you're afraid they might leave you. And you don't want them to go. Isn't that true?"

He nodded.

"So your heart's desire is for Rainbow and Mike to stay in Allenberg County?"

"Yes." He turned from the window. "Yes, yes. I want them to stay. But I don't..." His voice trailed off.

"Say it out loud."

"I don't think I should be Rainbow's guardian." He said the words in a rush. Just saying them seemed so terribly selfish. But saying them aloud was such a relief.

"I don't think you should be Rainbow's guardian either," she said.

"Is that your professional judgment?"

"That's a slight problem, because I'm not certain that I've maintained my professional distance. But I strongly feel that Rainbow belongs with Mike, not you. And it has nothing to do with the cat. It's become clear to me that Rainbow has strongly bonded with Mike. She trusts him. He's provided stability that she desperately needs. She communicates through art, and most of her drawings are of him."

"So what should I do?" Tim asked. "Mike's bailed. He's got some kind of deal in Vegas that he's running off to. I guess money is more important to him than the child."

"Do you really believe that's true?"

He turned his back on the window and looked deep into Andrea's eyes. Did he believe it?

He thought about the pain in Mike's voice this morning. He thought about the look on Mike's face that day Frances Polk had gotten him arrested. He thought about the way Rainbow looked yesterday in church.

"No," he whispered the word. "No. I think he's scared."

"I think so, too."

"What should I do?"

"I think you need to change Mike's mind. He's got so many options. He doesn't have to give up his career to be a dad. He doesn't have to move to Vegas to be a gambler. He needs to see that he's got a safety net here. He's not used to having one. You know?"

Rainbow stirred and cried out the way any hurt child might. Tim rushed to her bedside and stroked her head. "Hey, Rainbow. You're okay."

Tears filled her eyes. The same silent tears she'd been crying on and off for weeks.

"Uncle Mike?" It was a plea and a demand and a need.

Tim took her hand and whispered to her. "I'll get him for you, sweetheart. Just hang in there. I'll get him for you, I promise."

He looked up at the clock. It was two-thirty already. The appointment with Eugene was for two.

God help him, he might be too late.

CHAPTER
28

Eugene Hanks's office occupied a suite of rooms above the florist shop in a century-old brick building at the corner of Palmetto Avenue and Chancellor Street. The lawyer's offices smelled heavily of roses. And the old-fashioned furniture suggested the antebellum South.

The receptionist ushered Mike into a conference room with a mahogany table and formal chairs that had to be Chippendale originals. The tabletop was so shiny and pristine Mike was afraid of leaving fingerprints.

He sat alone for about five minutes before Eugene strolled into the conference room wearing a gray worsted suit and red power tie—a definite improvement in his appearance over last Sunday's madras shorts. He greeted Mike warmly then sat in a facing chair. He unfolded a pair of metal reading glasses, popped them on the end of his nose, and opened a manila file folder that had been labeled with the name Taggart on the tab.

The lawyer read silently for a moment. Then he looked up at Mike, over the rims of his glasses. "My wife called me this morning. She told me about Rainbow's accident. I'm surprised you kept this appointment."

Mike's sour stomach churned. "Rainbow is going to be fine, but she has some medical issues, and I need to return to Vegas. I left a message with your secretary this morning. I need a medical power of attorney right away. I thought we could handle the permanent custody issues by email and snail mail. You said on the phone that transferring custody from me to Tim is relatively straightforward, since we're both Rainbow's uncles."

The lawyer nodded. "I got your message. I've drawn up the medical power of attorney." He pulled a single sheet of paper from the file and slid it across the table. "Do you have a pen?" he asked.

Mike had thrown on a pair of jeans and a golf shirt this morning right after the ambulance had taken Rainbow off to the hospital. He had been doing well to remember his wallet and driver's license.

"No."

Eugene nodded, reached into his suit jacket, and pulled out one of those big black pens that looked like an old fountain pen. He unscrewed the top, and it turned out to actually *be* a fountain pen.

"I'm an old-fashioned guy." He handed Mike the pen, but the look in his blue eyes seemed hard and unforgiving. Was Eugene judging him?

Mike suddenly had this deep desire to explain himself. But he pressed his lips together. He had no words that could actually describe his emotions at that moment. He didn't even know what he was feeling.

He'd killed the last few hours aimlessly driving around trying to control his heartburn and get his act together.

He was no closer to understanding himself now than he had been in that angry moment when he stalked out of the hospital.

He took the pen and started to read the document. Before he got very far, Eugene spoke again. "I hear the Methodist Altar Guild has started a prayer vigil for Rainbow."

Mike looked up. "A prayer vigil?"

Eugene nodded. "That's the way it always is in this town. Someone gets hurt or sick and you can count on the ladies organizing prayer teams. Someone dies, the ladies make casseroles and pray some more. Someone needs help and the prayers are said at the same time helping hands are extended."

Eugene chuckled and leaned back in his chair. "Yessir, we take our prayer seriously down here. We're kind of old-fashioned that way. In fact, us old-timers still socialize face to face at the country club, although I understand the Episcopal Ladies Auxiliary now has a Facebook page. I'm not sure that's progress, if you want to know the truth."

He finished talking and glanced down at the paper as if to say Mike needed to get on with it.

So Mike resumed his reading. He had made it to the second paragraph when Eugene interrupted again. "So my wife told me you're about to sign some big deal with a casino."

"Your wife?" Mike didn't think he'd ever met Eugene's wife.

The lawyer chuckled again. "Don't worry, son, you can't keep anything quiet in this town. I guess someone from the Altar Guild heard it from Reverend Lake and passed it on to Ruby or Lillian or Lessie or someone. Or maybe Millie Polk heard it from Charlene. Either way, the news jumped from the Methodists to the Episcopalians. I'm sure the Baptists know now, too." He looked at the paper lying between them.

Mike said nothing. He went back to reading the document. It designated Tim as the responsible party for making all medical decisions affecting Rainbow. It would take effect as soon as Mike signed it and Eugene witnessed it.

"So how much did they offer you?" Eugene asked as Mike poised the pen above the signature line.

He looked up. "What?"

"How much money did they offer you? It must have been a lot, huh?"

Mike was about to tell Eugene to mind his own business when the guy leaned forward, looking over the top of his glasses.

"I'm just curious," Eugene said. "I know it's not really my business. But you see, Thelma and I don't have children. Not that we didn't try, mind you. But I wonder what I would do in your situation."

"I'm not walking away from Rainbow because of the money. Just get that straight. And you can tell the gossips in town that, too."

"No? Oh, I'm sorry. Everyone in town seems to think that's the reason. I'm glad to hear it, because I knew in my heart you weren't that kind of guy."

"What kind of guy?"

"The kind who puts money above love. You do love Rainbow, don't you?"

"Of course I do." The words came so easy. He loved that kid. He didn't exactly know how it had happened, but he would sacrifice anything for her. And signing this paper was the proof of that.

He put the pen on the paper. Ink flowed out of the pen's nib as the paper absorbed it, but he didn't sign his name. He sat there breathing hard.

"You know, Mike," Eugene said, "I've had a lot of experience dealing with families in crisis. And folks almost always come in here thinking the world is black and white. And I've always felt like it's my job to make them see the colors."

Mike lifted the pen off the page. "Colors?"

Eugene nodded. "Yep. Colors. In addition to the shades of gray." He leaned back again and took off his glasses. He made a great show of folding them before he spoke again. "So, just out of curiosity. If you love Rainbow, why are you in such a hurry to leave her?"

"Because this is a better place than Vegas."

The lawyer nodded. "I agree. But you don't have to live in Vegas, do you?"

Before he tried to explain, Eugene pressed on. "Oh, I understand that you'd have to take business trips to play poker in Vegas and Atlantic City and maybe even overseas. But it seems to me that you've got yourself a built-in support network right here in town. I mean there must be at least a dozen members of the Altar Guild willing to help you. And I'm sure Reverend Lake wouldn't mind sharing custody or babysitting when you have to travel. And it's clear Charlene Polk would help you if you ever got into a jam. I only say that because she gave you the key to her parents' river house. I won't mention anything about how you carried her home the other night when she'd had too much to drink. That was very chivalrous of you, by the way."

Mike put the pen down on the table. "Eugene, all of that might be true. But the thing is, I'm no good for Rainbow. It's my fault she got hurt today. And I'm sort of responsible for what happened to her mother. She doesn't need someone like me."

Eugene nodded. "All right, I do understand that. But what if Rainbow disagrees with you?"

"What?"

"Just asking. What if Rainbow loves you and thinks she needs you? Are you ready to walk out on that? I think that's the essential question." He pushed up from the table. "Take your time. I'll be down the hall in my office when you're ready to have the document witnessed."

Eugene turned and strolled out of the conference room.

Mike stared at the paper in front of him. All his past experiences screamed at him to pick up the damn pen and sign.

And just like that, he was the eighteen-year-old-boy who had reached his limit. The boy who had known what Richard was doing to Angie. The boy who couldn't get Mom to stop it. The boy who tried to take the big man on and got his ass kicked. He knew why Angie dressed her daughter like a boy and went out of her way to make her look unattractive. He knew why she had fallen to drugs to numb the pain.

And he would always be partially responsible for that. He should sign this paper and get the hell out of here.

But he couldn't do it. He came face-to-face with the kid he'd been. The kid trying to solve a problem that was beyond his abilities. He should have had loving parents, like Colin Lake, who had protected his son. And barring that, there should have been someone like Eugene Hanks or an Altar Guild, or a village of people—like so many of the people he'd met these last few weeks in Last Chance.

But this situation was different, wasn't it? That's what Eugene Hanks and his country lawyer manner was trying to tell him.

No one here in Last Chance wanted to hurt him. Most of the people here, with the possible exception of Charlene's mother, wanted to help. They had meddled in his life. And now they were praying for Rainbow and him.

Why?

These people believed he deserved their prayers.

That thought blew him away even though he wasn't much of a believer. It didn't matter if he believed—just knowing that believers were willing to put their faith on the line for him was sort of a miracle.

And then he suddenly remembered something the senile Miriam Randall had told him weeks ago. Words she'd tossed out as if they didn't mean anything. And yet from the mouth of a crazy old lady had come wisdom.

Love wasn't a long shot. Here in Last Chance, South Carolina, it was one of the safest bets he could make.

CHAPTER
29

Charlene finished up the sandwich Angel had insisted she eat. It was almost three in the afternoon. She was demoralized, hoarse, and footsore. And to make matters worse, the sky above Last Chance was darkening with big, black clouds. The rumble of thunder vibrated the front windows of the Kountry Kitchen.

"I've got to go," she said, pushing up from the table. "I need to find that cat."

"In the rain?" Angel asked.

"If need be."

"I think you should put up some lost cat posters or something. But before that you should go to the hospital."

"We've already been through that. Tigger is the best medicine I could give Rainbow. I want to be able to tell her the cat is safe and sound. Now, I have to go."

She threw a ten-dollar bill on the table and headed out the door.

Angel didn't follow her. Either he'd given up trying to tell her what she should do with her life or he'd decided not to get wet. He was probably waiting for the deluge. Knowing Angel, once the skies opened up, he'd come find her in his Jeep.

She looked up at the sky. Big, gray thunderheads were amassing overhead, and the humidity had reached critical mass.

She should turn around and go back. But she was a fool. She'd already been up and down Julia Street five times—as far west as the old abandoned Smith house and east all the way to Allenberg Pike. For all she knew, the cat might be trying to get back to Chicago.

Sometimes animals did that kind of thing.

But she didn't want to admit failure. So she blew out a sigh and headed south on Palmetto Avenue toward Julia Street one more time. She got as far as Chancellor Street before the raindrops started to fall.

Lightning flashed while she waited for the light. The thunder came quickly, and the rain increased. No time for turning back now. Traffic was light, and she dashed across Palmetto against the light. She ducked under the florist shop's awning just as the skies opened up in earnest.

She was about to call Angel and let him know she planned to take refuge down the block at Dot's Spot when she heard the *meow*.

She looked up through the dark, gray rain just in time to see a drowned-looking cat on the other side of Palmetto Avenue. She squinted at the poor, drenched animal.

Its ears were flat to its head, and its coat was almost saturated. But the curl at the end of the cat's tail was unmistakable. It was Tigger.

"Stay right there," Charlene said, putting out her hand in an utterly useless gesture. She left the shelter of the awning. Rain beat down on her and soaked her T-shirt in a matter of seconds. She glanced at the light. It was about to change again, going green for the traffic on Palmetto. But the road that had been deserted a moment ago now seemed crowded with traffic.

A truck was heading north, and a car with its right turn indicator flashing waited at the stop light on Chancellor Street. "Stay put, Tigger," she pleaded.

She took two steps out into the street and thought about running across the road before the light changed.

But the truck was coming on fast. And then Tigger jumped out into the traffic on Palmetto Avenue just as the light changed. The driver of the truck slammed on his brakes. It fishtailed and slid sideways over the slick pavement. The pickup crossed the centerline and careened headlong toward Charlene.

She lost sight of the cat and stood there a moment, paralyzed by the oncoming vehicle as time seemed to slow down. And then her instinct for survival kicked in. She hopped back onto the curb, just as the truck slammed into the car making a right turn on the red light.

"No," she wailed, her voice drowned out by the thunder overhead and the groan of bending metal.

Tigger was gone. Tigger was gone. What the hell was she going to do?

Tears filled her eyes, and she forced herself to take a step back into the road. The Mazda sedan had been totaled, but the driver seemed to be okay. The truck seemed remarkably unscathed, probably because it was a big, honking Dodge Ram.

She took another step out into the street. The Mazda was leaking fuel or oil or something.

"Tigger?" she called.

And then, miraculously, she heard the meow.

She took several more steps out into the street, calling the cat's name, sure that the animal had been seriously hurt. But she found the cat, wet and trembling, hunkered down under the back end of the Dodge.

"Come on, girl, come to me," she said as she got down on her knees. There wasn't any blood. The cat didn't seem hurt, but it was hard to tell because thick clouds had turned the afternoon dark. The rain continued to fall as she tried to coax the cat from under the truck. Tigger was soaked right through to the skin.

"Is that your cat?" The Mazda's driver had gotten out of her car and managed to find an umbrella. Charlene didn't recognize the woman, but the look on her face said everything. She shook her finger in Charlene's face. "Someone should take that cat away from you. Look at what your carelessness has caused." The woman turned toward the truck driver, who turned out to be Roy Burdett. "Would have served her right if you'd just run the cat over."

Roy ignored the woman and hunkered down beside Charlene. "Is that the cat that belongs to the little girl who got run over this morning?" he asked.

It was always a little amazing how everyone in town seemed to know the latest news, especially if it involved someone getting hurt. "Yeah. I've been looking for her all day. Bless you for putting on the brakes."

Roy got down on his belly and scooped the cat up in his big hands. "Here you go, Dr. Polk." He put the cat in Charlene's arms and then continued. "And mind yourself when you get up. It looks like the car I hit is leaking some oil."

"Thanks, Roy." Charlene snuggled Tigger against her soaking wet chest. The animal was shaking like a leaf. But it didn't look as if she'd been injured. She was panicky and wanted to get down, out of Charlene's arms. But there was no way in hell she was letting that cat go. She stood up, trying vainly to protect it from the rain.

"What the hell are you doing?"

Mike. What was he doing here? She turned around, and there he stood on the sidewalk right by the door to Eugene Hanks's law firm. Well, that explained his presence here. He'd come to sign Rainbow over to Reverend Lake.

The thought soured Charlene's stomach. "I'm finding the cat. Isn't that what you asked me to do this morning?"

"Yeah," he said, taking a step forward, his voice sounding strange and tight, "but I didn't intend for you to go rushing out into the middle of traffic and putting your life at risk. Damnit all, Charlene, that cat is a nuisance and a demon. You could have gotten hit. Shit, you almost did get hit. Don't you have any brains?"

Charlene took one step forward, intent on giving Mike Taggart a piece of her mind. He had some nerve getting mad at her for trying to save Tigger's life. Obviously he wasn't the man for her if he didn't understand how important the cat was.

"You listen up, mister—"

She didn't get any further with her tirade because she must have planted her foot square onto the oil Roy had just warned her about. Her feet slipped right out from underneath her, and she fell backward, hard onto the blacktop.

She saw stars for a moment. And pain exploded in the back of her head. Somehow she managed to keep her hold on Tigger. She closed her eyes against the rain. The world began to spin, making her stomach roil.

"Don't move." She knew that voice. Mike stepped into view and tried to take the animal, but she wouldn't let go.

"Tigger isn't a demon cat."

"Come on, Charlene. I didn't mean what I said about the cat. It's just that…" His voice broke and he stopped talking, and somewhere in Charlene's rattled brains she knew that his tone of voice meant something important. But she was kind of having trouble making sense of the world right at that moment.

Sirens blared. She looked up at Mike and saw the tears running down his face. Or maybe it was just the rain. "I was just coming out of Eugene's office. I saw it all happen. The cat is not that important, Charlene," he said.

"I needed to save her. Rainbow needs her."

"Rainbow needs you more."

"That's nice, Mike. But I'm not going to marry Tim. Can we get that clear?"

He caressed her cheek. That was very nice. She wished he would do more of that. "Of course you're not," he said. "You're going to marry me. So you better stay with me. I don't think I could bear being left again."

Whoa, the head injury must be pretty damn serious. Did he just propose? No, not possible.

She tried to get up but the pain exploded in her head.

"Don't. Wait until the EMTs get here."

"Okay. But I'm wet."

Someone threw a blanket over her. And she didn't have the heart to tell them that it did nothing for the water that was flowing like a river under her back. Not to mention that the pavement was kind of hard.

"I think I may be concussed. Did you just ask me to marry you?"

Mike smiled. "Uh, yeah, I think I did."

"You *think* you did? Boy, that's the story of my life. I wait thirty years for someone to pop the question, and he's not even sure he asked."

"I'm sure." Charlene was just settling herself in for a little romance when the EMTs arrived. They pulled Mike away, forcing him to take Tigger with him. And the next thing she knew, Ross Gardiner was there asking her a bunch of questions and shining a light in her eyes.

And then Mother and Daddy showed up, and before long, there was a whole crowd right there in the middle of Palmetto Avenue standing under the only stoplight in town.

The ER waiting room was crowded with a boatload of people from Last Chance, most of whom Mike didn't even know. Mike had gone home to change into dry clothes and to drop off and feed the cat. And in that short time, Charlene's family had gotten the jump on him.

Her mother was at her bedside while the doctors conferred. Since Mike wasn't family, no one in charge would let him get close. And her father, a tall man who looked exactly like her, had already told him in no uncertain terms that he disapproved of Mike on every level possible.

Mike was thinking about giving the guy a piece of his mind when Timmy came striding across the room. "Mike. Where have you been? I've been trying to call you for the last three hours. You need to get upstairs to Rainbow's room."

Oh. God. "Is she okay?"

"She's fine, but she's awake and she keeps asking for you. Look, Mike, I just heard about Charlene. Is she going to be okay?"

He nodded. "They think so. She's got a nasty bump on her head, but I gather they did an MRI or something and she didn't fracture her skull. She's concussed, and they're trying to decide if she should stay the night. I swear, Timmy, that cat almost took out the two people I care most about in this world. You think it was some kind of crazy payback or something?"

"The two people you care about most in the world?" Timmy asked.

"Uh, yeah. Sorry, Timmy, I think you come in third."

"Mike, I'm glad you care about Charlene and Rainbow, because I have something important to say. Something you might not want to hear." He paused for a moment. "I refuse to be Rainbow's guardian."

Mike blinked.

"It's not that I don't care about her. I love her. But she belongs with you, and I'm not going to let you cop out. But I'll be here to help you in any way you need."

And hadn't Timmy been there from the beginning, making him stay, making him take responsibility, allowing his flock of church ladies to get all up in Mike's business? Like a village.

"Uh, Timmy, I kept my appointment with Eugene Hanks."

"I intend to rip up that medical power of attorney."

"No need. Because I didn't sign it."

"You didn't?"

He shook his head. "I can't leave Rainbow like I left Angie. Even if I do know that she's in great hands. I just can't. I love her. But the thing is, I still want to enter the World Series of Poker, so I'm going to have to figure out some babysitting arrangements."

Tim chuckled. "If you want my advice, I'd take that up with Charlene."

"I intend to. If I can ever get past her parents."

"Don't worry. Charlene is way beyond listening to them. Just give it time, Mike. In the meantime, Rainbow needs you."

In the past, Mike might have argued. But Timmy was right. Mike had plenty of time.

He'd already called Paul and told him to nix the Dragon Casinos deal. Mike still planned to enter the main event at the World Series of Poker, but he'd do it without a sponsor. If he played well, the Dragon Casinos people might still be interested. Or not. He didn't care. He could play poker for the thrill of it, and maybe turn day trading into the day-to-day job. He'd been doing pretty well in the markets these last two weeks.

But he wasn't worried about any of that right now. Right now he was sticking around for Rainbow and for Charlene.

They decided Charlene could go home, so long as her parents kept an eye on her. Head injuries could be tricky, but they were pretty sure she'd been lucky.

In truth, she had a raging headache, but she wasn't sure if it was because of her stupid fall or the hours she'd spent listening to Mother rant on about this and that.

It was almost dark when they wheeled her out of the emergency treatment center and to the curb where Daddy had pulled up his big Cadillac.

It was now or never.

Charlene stood up. Every muscle screamed in pain. Falling flat on one's back created bruises in all kinds of places. And with a head injury they were reluctant to prescribe pain meds. Which was just as well, because she had a conversation she needed to continue with Mike Taggart. It was a tossup whether the conversation would turn into a fight or something else. She prayed that her mind hadn't played tricks on her. She distinctly remembered him saying something about marriage.

"Mother, Daddy, thanks for staying with me. But I've got to go upstairs now."

"What?" They spoke in unison.

"I don't want to make a scene. So we're going to be adult about this, okay? I'm going back into the hospital to visit with Rainbow. I should have been there all day with the rest of the Methodist women praying for her speedy recovery. If I hadn't been so stubborn about staying away today, perhaps I wouldn't have gotten hurt. But it wouldn't be the first time that my stubbornness got me hurt. Only this time, being stubborn almost cost me everything, and I'm not talking about the car accident either. I'm talking about losing Rainbow and Mike. I love them, and I was an idiot to run away from what I feel."

She turned and walked, slowly and painfully, back into the hospital. She expected her parents to follow her, but maybe they'd finally gotten the message.

Because they let her go.

She limped her way to the information desk and then up to Rainbow's room. She pushed through the door.

Mike sat in the bed with the child. Rainbow, sporting a big cast on her leg, leaned her head up against his side as he read to her from a picture book. And when he got to the right place in the story he started to sing in a slightly off-tune baritone, *"I love my white shoes, I love my white shoes."*

Rainbow turned the page for him.

Charlene let go of a completely sappy sigh because she couldn't help but feel as if she'd come home. To her family. The one she'd always pictured in her mind.

"Hey," she said.

Mike looked up, a big smile lighting his face. And in the next instant, he was across the room, holding her gently as if she might break.

Which, actually, was kind of true. She probably should have waited until tomorrow for this. But she'd been waiting for so long.

He eased back and caressed her cheek. "I'm sorry I yelled at you. I feel so guilty. But I was upset. I thought that truck was going to hit you. I thought I was going to lose you, just when I had come to realize how much I want you in my life."

"Just so long as we get one thing clear: Tigger is not a demon cat."

"Whatever you say," he said with a half smile.

"I don't imagine Rainbow and I are ever going to turn you into a cat person, are we?"

"You could try." He hesitated for a moment, the smile sobering. "Look, doll, I'm not good at love. I haven't had a lot of practice at it. But a wise woman told me that I should always bet on it. She said it was a sure winner. So here I am."

"A wise woman?"

"I never lied to you about the fact that I spoke with

Miriam Randall," he said softly. "I was trying to get her to bless this stupid idea I had about you and Timmy. And thinking back over that conversation, I guess I heard only the stuff I wanted to hear. But here's the thing. At the end of that conversation, she told me to bet on love, even if the odds seemed a million to one. She told me I couldn't lose."

"Did she?"

"Yeah. She was talking about you. I had already decided that you were perfect. And now that I think about my conversation with her, I spent a lot of time telling her how terrific I think you are."

Her face heated. "Terrific, huh?"

"Yeah. Charlene, I love you. Nothing brought that home like standing there this afternoon watching that truck barreling toward you. And I just know that you and me and Rainbow are a match made in heaven. Miriam Randall is a miracle worker."

Charlene couldn't believe it. All these years and Miriam had actually sent her the soulmate she had been looking for. And she'd done it in a sneaky, underhanded way.

But then, come to think about it, Miriam was sort of like that. She always made her matches work for it, didn't she?

"I've been waiting my whole life for someone like you. I love you, Mike. I think I fell in love with you that day you rescued the cat from under the bush," she said as she sank her head against his chest.

"You've been waiting for a guy like me? Screwed up and confused?"

She laughed. "No. I've had lots of guys like that. I'm talking about a guy who put his whole life on hold for a little girl. A guy who put up with a demon cat, just because the little girl needed it. A guy who learned how to braid hair. And who has learned the *Pete the Cat* song." She looked up at him. "Amanda told me to go find a guy like that. And finally, I've found him. And in the most unlikely of places, right next door."

"Are you guys going to get married?" Rainbow said.

They both turned. "Yes," they said in unison.

"So that means I don't have to move into the perish house?"

They nodded, and neither one of them corrected her pronunciation.

"I can keep Tigger?"

"Yes, you can," said Mike.

"And Winkin', Blinkin', and Nod, too?"

"Uh-huh," said Charlene.

"And I can still be friends with Ethan?"

"You'll both start kindergarten together next fall."

Rainbow smiled, and for the first time ever, she looked like a little girl who might one day live up to her name.

Molly Canaday is a tomboy with a passion for cars—and little time for romance.

But Simon Wolfe is about to race in and change her priorities.

Please turn this page for an excerpt from

Last Chance Knit & Stitch

Molly hadn't planned to attend tonight's meeting of the Last Chance Book Club. She didn't have anything nice to say about their book selection this time. Besides, she had planned to work on the Shelby.

But the bank had screwed up that option. And when she got home from work, she found her lazy, no-account brother sleeping on the couch, dirty dishes in the sink, and laundry overflowing the hamper in the bathroom.

She probably should have gone grocery shopping or tackled the laundry, but that would have ticked her off worse than she already was. So she took a shower, made herself a grilled cheese sandwich with the last remaining piece of American cheese, and headed out for her meeting.

Thank goodness Savannah White was on refreshment detail this week. She arrived with the most amazingly delicious apple strudel.

Molly found herself standing around the refreshment table with several club members including Jenny Carpenter, Arlene Whitaker, and Rocky deBracy, the wife of the English baron whose textile machinery plant was single-handedly creating an economic renaissance in Last Chance.

"Honey," Rocky said to Savannah as more members of the club trickled through the library doors, "you have to enter this strudel in the pie contest at this year's Watermelon Festival."

Savannah gave Jenny a little smile, as if she knew that Jenny's string of pie-baking victories was about to come to an ignominious end. "Oh, I don't know," she said sweetly. "It's not my recipe. It's my granny's. And I think she already won a few blue ribbons at the festival."

Jenny maintained her composure. And why not? Jenny's pies were as amazing as Savannah's strudel. Molly was impressed by the baking prowess of both of them. When it was Molly's time to bring refreshments, she always stopped at the doughnut shop.

Jane Rhodes waddled in carrying her knitting bag and looking like an over-inflated hot-air balloon. "Hey, honey," Arlene said, draping an arm around her niece-by-marriage, "when are you going to have that baby?"

"I don't know. I'm already three days past my due date, and I'm tired of people looking at me slant-wise and asking me why I'm still here. Like I'm going to disappear once baby Faith is born." She ran her hand over her baby bump.

"So you've settled on a name?" Rocky asked. The baby in question was going to be Rocky's niece.

Jane nodded. "Yeah. But I'm starting to think that she's holding out until I finish this sweater." She reached into her bag and pulled out a pink baby sweater that was missing one arm. Jane had been working on this sweater for weeks and weeks.

She gave Molly a pleading look. "I'm desperate. How do I pick up the stitches around the armhole again? You walked me through it on the first arm, but then I forgot how to do it. And I was going to go ask your mother, but I saw the notice on the door. Where is your mom?"

"That's one of those unanswerable questions," Molly said. "Apparently she's gone to see the world. And she didn't think she needed to take Coach with her."

"Well, good for her," Arlene said. "Don't get me wrong, Moll. I love your daddy. He's a great football coach and all, but he's been ignoring your momma for some time."

Molly didn't respond to this. Because the more she thought about the situation, the more she realized there was blame on both sides. Coach had ignored Momma, but it wasn't right for Momma to take off without a word and leave everything on Molly's shoulders. She clamped her mouth shut and took Jane's knitting into her hands.

She immediately relaxed. What was it about knitting that always calmed her down? She felt the same way when she was working on a car. Whenever her hands got busy, her brain slowed down, and she could live in the moment.

She was deep into a knitting lesson when Nita Wills, the town librarian, called the group together. Hettie Marshall Ellis had arrived. Hettie was the CEO of Country Pride Chicken, the second largest employer in Allenberg County. She had also recently eloped with Reverend William Ellis, the pastor of Christ Episcopal.

No one in town, much less the book club, knew how to deal with this new reality. Hettie was often regarded as the Queen Bee of Last Chance, but that seemed like a very unlikely role for a minister's wife.

When everyone had settled down, Nita kicked off the book discussion. "I have a number of questions about our selection this time, but before I start, does anyone have a question of their own?"

"Yeah," Molly said. "Why on earth did we pick this book?"

A titter of laughter met this comment, but Nita wasn't smiling. "I take it you didn't like the book."

"Nita, the book is over a thousand pages. I got to page two hundred and threw the paperback against the wall. Honestly, this was the most depressing thing I've read since *The Road*. Why do we read these books?"

"She's got a point," Arlene said. "I mean, I'm all for capitalism and freedom and all that, but honestly the author goes on and on about it. And she seems to think that anyone who gives to charity is either misguided or downright evil."

Lola May snorted. "Arlene, didn't you know that the best way to help poor folks is to let rich folks get richer?"

"Well, that is the morality that Ayn Rand espouses in this book," Nita said.

"Well, it ain't very moral," Lola May countered.

Cathy Niles let go of a long, mournful sigh. "Can we read something light and fun next time? I really liked it when we read *Pride and Prejudice*. I'd like to read a love story that doesn't involve the characters having long-winded conversations about original sin, morality, and free love. I don't know about y'all but I don't find any of that even remotely romantic."

"That's the point," Nita said. "We're reading to—"

"Nita, the book is just BS, and frankly someone should have edited it. It was boring," Savannah said.

Everyone looked in Savannah's direction. The use of even abbreviated profanity was frowned upon, especially with a minister's wife in attendance.

Savannah faced them all with cool aplomb. "I'm sorry, y'all, but the ideas in this book are just mean. For instance, if folks followed Ayn Rand's philosophy, The Kismet would have been torn down and replaced with a new, shiny, soulless multiplex. Instead, Dash helped Angel Development put money into the old theater, even though we all know it's probably never going to show a profit. But having a theater will build up our community. And that's important. Sometimes the community is just as important as the individual. And sometimes an individual needs help."

"Hear, hear," Molly said. "If it weren't for Ira Wolfe and his generosity, I wouldn't be anywhere near getting my own business off the ground. Of course, I can't say the same about his no-account son, or Ira's brother-in-law. Did y'all hear about how the bank closed the dealership?"

Everyone nodded except Savannah. She just stared at Molly, kind of the same way she'd stared yesterday at the Purly Girls meeting.

"Savannah, I know I don't have grease on my face this time. What is it?"

Savannah blinked. "Oh, nothing. I was just thinking." Savannah turned toward Nita. "We should stop reading dystopian fiction. It's depressing everyone, especially since things are improving here in Last Chance. I know we talked about reading *Hunger Games* next, but I really don't want to spend time with kids who are forced to kill each other for the amusement of the state."

"Me neither," said Cathy. "And you know what? It's kind of disturbing that every other book you pick up these days at the bookstore has a vampire or a werewolf or kids run amok. Doesn't anyone read the sweet books anymore? You know, like *Little Women*?"

"*Little Women*?" Hettie finally spoke. "My goodness, I haven't read that since I was twelve. I did love that book."

"I've never read it at all," Arlene said. "But I did see the movie. I loved Christian Bale, but I could never understand why Winona Ryder threw him over for Gabriel Byrne."

While Arlene was speaking, Savannah stared across the table at Molly. Her gaze was intensely probing. Just before Molly was about to check to see if she'd spilled cheese on her T-shirt, Savannah turned toward Nita. "You know, I think we should read *Little Women*."

"Could we talk about this book first, before we select the next one?" Nita said.

"No," Hettie said, looking around the table. "Is there anyone here who finished this book?"

Jenny Carpenter was the only one who raised her hand. But that hardly counted because Jenny had no life beyond teaching algebra at the high school. And, truth to tell, Jenny had been kind of depressed since Reverend Ellis had run off with Hettie. So of course she'd had time to read a book with a thousand pages.

Hettie stared at Nita. "I rest my case. Who wants to read something sweet like *Little Women* next time?"

All the hands went up. Of course, more than half the ladies of the book club were members of Christ Episcopal. So if their minister's wife, who also happened to be the second largest employer in town, suggested a book, it was a lead-pipe cinch that everyone would agree to read it.

• • •

"Hold up a minute, Molly," Savannah called. Molly was heading toward her canary yellow Charger, parked in the lot behind the library.

She turned as Savannah hurried up to her. "What?"

"Uh…" Savannah stood there for a moment looking awkward.

"What the heck is it? Do I have BO or something?"

Savannah shook her head. "No, it's just that I have something I need to tell you."

"About what?"

Savannah danced from foot to foot and continued to look awkward. When she spoke, her words came out like a racing freight train. "It's a message from Aunt Miriam."

Wariness scrambled over Molly's backbone. "From Miriam?" she asked. Crap, she didn't need another surprise today.

Savannah's aunt was practically legendary. She was one part fortune-teller, one part busybody, and she'd made it her life's work to find soulmates for every blessed single person in Last Chance. She'd been implicated in several recent weddings. Miriam also had a hand in matching Savannah up with Dash Randall. Molly glanced at the big, fat diamond on Savannah's hand. The wedding of the decade was planned for the first week of June.

Molly wanted nothing to do with one of Miriam Randall's predictions. She didn't believe in that crap, which put her in the minority. If Miriam made a forecast, the church ladies of Last Chance—and that was a majority of the female population—would be working overtime to get her hitched up to someone.

Yuck.

"Don't look so astonished and petrified." Savannah was actually wringing her hands, which seemed like a bad omen.

"What is it? Are you about to tell me that I should be looking for a man just like my father? I'm not sure that's what I want. I mean, look at where it left Momma."

Savannah frowned. "Uh, well, I'm not sure. He might be like your father. I mean, well, most men like football, don't they?"

"Yeah, I guess. What exactly did Miriam tell you?"

"She told me you should be looking for someone who has known you for a long time. Since you were little."

The forecast was a little underwhelming. And also annoying.

"Great. So every past member of the Davis High School football team is a possible match."

"Uh, well..." Savannah's voice faded out.

"Or are you trying to tell me that I belong with Les? Because if that's what you're saying, you can just forget it. Les is my friend. We are not romantically involved. In fact, he's on a date right now with Tammy Nelson."

"Tammy? With the teeth and boobs?"

"Yeah. I'm thinking the boobs are the main attraction. Les is a pretty simple and straightforward kind of guy."

"Uh, well, I don't know," Savannah said in a rush, like she was suddenly trying to get away from Molly.

"Do me a favor. Tell your aunt not to repeat this crap, okay? I've already got problems out the wazoo. I do not need a bunch of busybodies trying to turn me into a bride. I am not bride material."

Fall in Love with Forever Romance

LAST CHANCE FAMILY
by Hope Ramsay

Mike Taggart may be a high roller in Las Vegas, but is he ready to take a gamble on love in Last Chance? Fans of Debbie Macomber, Robyn Carr, and Sherryl Woods will love this sassy and heartwarming story from *USA Today* bestselling author Hope Ramsay.

SUGAR'S TWICE AS SWEET
by Marina Adair

Fans of Jill Shalvis, Rachel Gibson, and Carly Phillips will enjoy this sexy and sweet romance about a woman who's renovating her beloved grandmother's house—even though she doesn't know a nut from a bolt—and the bad boy who can't resist helping her... even as she steals his heart!

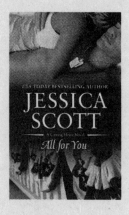

Fall in Love with Forever Romance

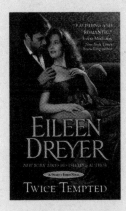

TWICE TEMPTED
by Eileen Dreyer

As two sisters each discover love, *New York Times* bestselling author Eileen Dreyer delivers twice the fun in her newest of the Drake's Rakes Regency series, which will appeal to fans of Mary Balogh and Eloisa James.

A BRIDE FOR
THE SEASON
by Jennifer Delamere

Can a wallflower and a rake find happily ever after in each other's arms? Jennifer Delamere's Love's Grace trilogy comes to a stunning conclusion.

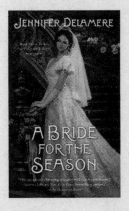

Find out more about Forever Romance!

Visit us at
www.hachettebookgroup.com/publishing_forever.aspx

Find us on Facebook
http://www.facebook.com/ForeverRomance

Follow us on Twitter
http://twitter.com/ForeverRomance

NEW AND UPCOMING TITLES

Each month we feature our new titles
and reader favorites.

CONTESTS AND GIVEAWAYS

We give away galleys, autographed copies,
and all kinds of exclusive items.

AUTHOR INFO

You'll find bios, articles, and links to personal websites
for all your favorite authors—and so much more.

GET SOCIAL

Connect with your favorite authors, editors, and
other Forever fans, and share what's important to you.

THE BUZZ

Sign up for our monthly romance newsletter,
and be the first to read all about it.